PRELUDE TO A PROPHECY
SORCERER'S DOOR – BOOK 1

by

Steve Graziani

Printed in the United States of America

First Printing, 2015

ISBN: 978-0-9961375-0-8

Grazarts Publishing
1839 Blake Ave, Loft 12
Los Angeles, CA, 90039

www.grazartspubishing.com

Cover Art by Steve Graziani

Dedicated to
Virginia & Joseph M Graziani

Prologue

Time often fades ancient Prophecies. This is even true on the Sphere, a planet where it should not be so.

Long ago, five species were placed on the Sphere and separated by virtually impenetrable walls. Left hidden in each of the five lands was the Sorcerer's Door, a spell not bound by these walls. Also left behind, a Prophecy that someday two round-ears would come from the stars and topple the walls. The Prophecy did not tell if this would be a good thing or a bad thing.

But, as with old Prophecies, most people forgot... but not all.

Chapter One

Peter Capwell's dirt bike roars loudly as he whips the curves out of the two-lane mountain road. It's just what Peter needs this morning. The wind washing past his head eases the slight hangover he has from a night of partying at the cave.

But wind can only wash away so much.

Before reaching the valley, Peter sideslips the bike to a stop on a turnout overlooking Goldendale, Oregon. Goldendale -population 1267 - is one of those tiny towns buried in the hills where if anyone passes wind most everybody knows.

It's yet another place Peter doesn't feel he belongs.

Peter sits with a leg crossed over the bike staring at the postage stamp size town, wondering how he and his kid brother, Devon, ended up there. Actually he knows very well how they landed there. The social workers ran out of homes to place two teens who wanted to stay together.

Since their parents died in a car accident ten years ago, they had bounced around more than a few foster homes. With no direct family to take them in, they got dumped into the system. Peter would have bailed long ago except for a promise he made to his kid brother to stick by his side no matter what.

Peter also knows why they were bounced around so much... he tends to have a little trouble with authority figures.

But Goldendale! Ugh!

Peter has the classic look of a seventeen-year old rebel without a cause - blue jeans, white tee shirt and leather jacket. The look would be a cliché if he was trying for it, but in Peter's case he honestly doesn't care what others think. He's come to see everywhere and everyone as just temporary - except for his brother.

Up till about six months ago they were always placed in homes in or around the Portland area. For some reason their social worker figured they might fare better in the boonies. For Peter, the jury is still out.

At least they're still together.

Peter glances down at his watch not relishing that it's time to head into town and make sure Devon gets to school. He knows Devon is sitting on a fence slightly out of sight of this foster family's house, just waiting till he shows up.

This bewilders Peter since Devon loves school. Before kick starting the bike, he chuckles over how they could not be more opposite.

His musing is cut off by the loud rumble of a dump truck passing behind him, no doubt on its way to the local gravel quarry. The quarry is the largest industry - loosely using the term - in town. One third of the residents work there or depend on it. 'The boonies' rushes back through Peter's mind.

He kick starts the bike.

As Peter motors through the outskirts of town, Deputy Tom Clancy drives past him going the opposite direction. Clancy glares at Peter in passing with his usual dislike. With little hope of his own life improving, Deputy Clancy has an unpleasant attitude towards anyone whose life hasn't gone to hell already. He also drinks more than his fair share.

About half way down the block Peter hears Clancy's patrol car spin a U-turn. Peter thinks, 'Now what's Deputy Crocked want?' This is the nickname many of the kids have given Clancy... most, though, not to his face.

Peter attempts to ignore Deputy Clancy and he hears the chirp of the patrol car closing behind him. In a split second Peter makes one of those decisions that he often regrets making in a split second. He turns his head back towards Clancy and with a smile offers an impolite finger gesture. He guns his bike forward.

Peter figures that if he's going to get in trouble for something he didn't do, he might as well have some fun getting caught for it. There's not a whole lot else to do in Goldendale.

It's not exactly a high-speed chase... otherwise the two of them would miss town in a few blinks. The main part of town is only nine by seven blocks. Peter sees it more as a maze game. He figures Clancy doesn't see it as a game at all... the guy has no sense of humor.

Though Peter has only been in Goldendale six months, he already knows the sparse layout fairly well. As he rides down Main Street with the deputy a block behind him, Peter whips a hard right into an alleyway just past Swenson's Bakery.

Apparently he doesn't know the town that well. The alley is long and, worst of all, it's a box canyon. Along one side, a short ramp leads up to a four-foot high dock and load-in door. Along the other are trashcans and a number of closed doors. At the back is a two-story brick wall. Yep, no exit!

Peter stops his bike near the wall. He waits.

Deputy Clancy skids to a quarter-turn stop at the mouth of the alley. Peter can see the smile broaden on Clancy's face through the windshield. Clancy eases the patrol car into the alley, driving forward to the loading dock where there's not enough room on either side for an escape.

Peter watches patiently as Deputy Clancy squeezes out the driver's side, nightstick in hand. He figures Clancy is about forty-five, or a worn out forty, with a waning hairline.

The man's not large as a whole, just beer belly fat. It's clear his sweat-stained uniform shirt has only had a brief encounter with an iron and not recently.

There's no pretense of friendliness to the smile on his face. Clancy is parked so close to the wall he has to back up and close the door to move forward.

"Not so smart now, are you, kid?" Clancy oozes.

With the Deputy's last word, Peter guns the bike forward up the load-in ramp onto the landing and takes air over the back of Clancy's patrol car. He hits a perfect landing and kicks over a trashcan before roaring out of the alley.

Peter speeds away, suspecting that taunting the often hung-over town deputy is probably not the best idea... but it sure perks up his day.

Deputy Tom Clancy loses his smile.

Clancy struggles to get his out-of-shape body back into the car as quickly as can. He slams the car into reverse and peels backwards. All of a sudden there's a horrendous screeching sound from behind.

He climbs out to discover a trashcan wedged under the rear bumper. Clancy gives the car a good kick before trying to un-wedge the can. It doesn't cooperate. He gives the car another kick.

He turns back to the street where Peter is disappearing and yells, "I'm going to get my hands on you and that cave trash you hang with!"

As he wrestles with the can again, there's a cracking sound over the police radio and a coarse female voice comes out,

"Tom, the chief wants you out on Route Nine. There's a jack-knifed lumber truck. Over."

Clancy goes to the driver's side and reaches in to grab the mic.

He keys it and says in a rather impatient tone, "Dale, I'm in the middle of something right now. Over."

The response is just as sharp. "I heard. You're hassling one of those kids again. Doc phoned in about your big high-speed chase. The chief still wants you out on Route Nine. Over."

"I know this kid broke into Jake's Hardware. I'll get out to Nine soon as I... "

A deep male voice over the radio cuts him off, "Jake tied one on last night. Sara got pissed and broke her old man's window. Now, get your ass out onto Route Nine like I said. Over and out!"

Clancy figures he can try to give Dale a hard time, though she rarely takes it, but Chief Bailey is another matter. He bites his lip and tosses the mic back into the car. Clancy gives the car another good kick, pretending it was everything he hated... which in his case was pretty much everything.

Peter pulls up near the front of a lower-middle class house on the outskirts of Goldendale. Devon Capwell, his fourteen-year old brother, sits on a split-rail fence by the road, slightly out of view of the house... just where Peter expected to find him.

Devon is swinging his backpack back and forth, pretending not to notice. There's a fresh boyishness to Devon that Peter, even at seventeen, has long lost. He's actually a normal-looking young teen with floppy hair and dimples... no rebel look. Devon even has a travel chess set sticking out of his pack and a skateboard leaning against the fence.

Peter shuts down the bike and lifts one leg up to sit sidesaddle. He stares at Devon who's still trying not to pay him any attention.

Peter glances at the folded chess set sticking out of the pack, something Devon always has with him. Devon's a different sort, more introspective, while Peter is more about action. Over all the years, Peter can't remember ever beating his kid brother at that damn silly game.

Peter breaks the silence, "So, if I didn't come along you were gonna sit on that fence all day and not go to school?"

Devon does a quarter-turn away in a silent pout.

Peter lets out a sigh, "OK, what's the beef?"

Still looking away, "You didn't come home last night."

"It got late. I decided to hang at the cave with the guys. What's the big deal?"

Devon blurts out, "She tried to get me to call her 'Mom'."

Peter laughs, which only causes Devon to bristle. He realizes that what might not be a big thing to him affects Devon differently. Time to play big brother...

"Look, Dev, we've been through a few of these homes. Kathy and Bob aren't that bad. At least they're keeping us together."

The thought that it could be any other way hits Devon like a thunderbolt.

"They can't separate us, can they?"

"No, nobody's gonna separate us... trust me. Another year or so and we'll get our own place," Peter says with as much conviction as he can put into it.

That's good enough for Devon. He's not very good at holding a pout, real or put on. A smile washes over his face and he glances at his watch.

"We're going to be late."

Peter's pleased by the upswing.

"Not if you jump on back of the bike and we fly like the wind." As a preemptive strike, knowing Devon's not going to take it well, he adds, "I'm just dropping you. Old man Russell's got work at the shop for me."

As Devon gets on the bike, "Why can't I go with you? We'll make twice as much. No one will care."

"Not true. I do. School's not me, but you're good at it."

"Wish I wasn't," says Devon, pouty again.

"No, you don't. You like being good at it, especially science. Remember we're blood, a team... brains and brawn. Now, you're gonna go be brainy."

Peter revs the bike and they peel out. Devon grabs on tight. The spokes of the bike's spinning front tire creates a silver circle as it speeds away.

Chapter Two

A light green spinning globe is filled with a fisheye reflection of colors rushing by – blues spotted with patches of purple and golden yellows. The globe is a three-inch flying Orb. It stops spinning, freezes in mid-air and shoots off in another direction.

The Orb swooshes about in an environment filled with rolling hills of deep blue grass speckled with bright purple trees, an occasional red or yellow one, and a soft bluish-lavender sky. In the distance there are rock formations, but even they appear soft in this lush alien landscape.

This is the Land of Spirin, one of five lands that make up the Sphere... a world far from Goldendale, Oregon.

The Orb comes swooshing back. Shan Dee, the tomboyish sixteen-year old makings of a beautiful young woman, flies in on a hoverboard and redirects the little Orb with a swipe of her hand. It rockets away.

Shan zooms along three feet above a blanket of blue grass, her hoverboard cutting a wake as she goes. She has flowing red hair, green eyes and a distinctive curl to the bottom of her earlobes.

She's dressed in loose fitting, gently flowing pants and a blouse of lime green. The fabric accents her bright hair. On Earth the fabric might get lost in the hills, but here in Spirin it pops out against all the blue.

Far off, her fourteen-year old brother, Ramie Dee, soars along on another hoverboard. He has the same family traits of red hair, green eyes and bottom-curled ears, but he managed to hoard all the freckles.

As he approaches, it's clear from all the blue grass stains on his clothes that he didn't inherit all the grace of his sister.

They're playing a game of Orb, which is somewhat like Jai Alai on speed. The major differences are that it's played out-doors and the kids, both being sorcerers, don't need wicker gloves.

Each kid has their own colored Orb. Shan's is green and Ramie's yellow. The object of the game is to return both Orbs into the other player's zone... a task easier said than done since both players are rocketing all over hill and dale on their hover-boards.

It's not about hitting your opponent - it's about causing them to miss a return. In Ramie's case, he loves to throw Shan off balance and see her tumble in the grass... something he rarely manages to do. Ramie is reckless while Shan brings a confident, poised daring to her game.

Zipping by, Ramie yells, "Try this!"

He whips Shan's Orb around, returning it and, at the same time, fires his towards her. Shan easily returns the low one and does a barrel roll to send the other rocketing back.

Ramie is caught off guard reaching for the second one, tum-bling off his board into the thick blue grass. It's a place he of-ten finds himself when playing Shan.

She swoops up to him as he pulls grass out of his hair. "Your mouth's bigger than your play. Had enough yet?"

Ramie gets up, puffs out his small chest, re-conjures his board and pleads, "Just a little longer... To the log?"

"OK, but stay clear of..." she starts to warn.

"I know, I know!"

Ramie knows all too well how his older sister constantly tries to keep him out of trouble. Somehow he manages to get into it anyway.

It's not that Ramie intends to find trouble... he just has an overwhelming curiosity for things he probably shouldn't have. He can't help it if trouble seems to attach itself to things that are fascinating and fun.

She glares, "I mean it."

He waves her off with a nod and a mischievous smile.

They swoop along, zigzagging over the rolling hills, leaving temporary creases in the grass. It's late afternoon and the sky is darkening lavender. Two of the Sphere's three moons lightly sit on the horizon.

They sweep over the crest of a hill to see the Graveyard of Spells looming atop the next one. Even from afar the Grave-yard casts an ominous aura over its peaceful surroundings.

A high, ornate black metal fence encloses the Graveyard. Within the enclosure is a knee-high layer of eerie green mist that doesn't seep out. It's as if it knows it belongs there.

Rising from the blanket of green are dozens of tall red rock columns, each topped with a glow. Although making a sharp contrast to the lush and alien countryside that surrounds it, even in its darker tone there's a magical feel to the Graveyard of Spells.

Down the hill from the Graveyard is a fallen log, shaded by a bright purple tree. Shan attempts to sway the game towards the log, but Ramie moves their play up closer to the Graveyard's fence, as if he's captivated by another place he shouldn't go.

"You're pushing it," yells Shan.

He vigorously shakes his head 'no'. He releases his Orb to-wards her. It's a wide miss that boomerangs back and flies directly over the fence. It immediately loses its glow and plummets down into the green mist.

Ramie tells himself it was an accident but he knows it was an intriguing accident.

If it weren't against Spirinese nature to be violent, Shan would be tempted to fling her Orb at his head... but unfortunately it is.

Ramie floats up to the front gate of the Graveyard and settles. His board disappears. Shan mumbles indistinctly under her breath as she flies up to join him.

Ramie is not sure what raises the hairs on the back of his neck more at the moment, the ominous Graveyard or his sister. He backs away from her a couple steps and holds his breath lest she zap him with a spell.

She settles for, "I told you so".

Ramie lets out the breath.

He glances back at the Graveyard, then pleadingly at her, "I've already lost one".

Not swayed, she calmly holds up two fingers.

He intensifies his pleading face. No effect. Ramie figures if he plays things up long enough she will relent.

"Maybe I can conjure it out."

Shan rolls her eyes.

He turns to the Graveyard, raises a hand and concentrates. Ramie's hand begins to glow the same yellow as his orb. Nothing. He ramps up his focus until he's red in the face. Still nothing.

Shan shakes her head.

"Rockhead, it's called the Graveyard of Spells for a reason - spells don't work in there."

"No one ever goes in?"

"The Masters, I suppose."

Renewing his hope, "Then I won't turn into stone?"

"Of course you won't... because, you're not going!"

Ramie glances back and forth between the Graveyard and Shan, ramping up his begging arsenal with puppy dog eyes.

"If I lose another one I'll be grounded for moons... restricted to our loft... all of the time."

He knows this will get to her if nothing else does. The two of them share a spacious loft at home. The thought of Ramie, who's usually out getting in trouble, being under foot all the time, would be far too much for her to handle.

He adds, "A couple dashes... I'll have it and be right back out."

His strategy gets to her.

After a silence and with the sternest face she can muster, "Ten dashes, no more!"

Ramie turns to the Graveyard's entrance arch and stops. He's having second thoughts about his victory. Shan raises one finger to him.

"OK... I'm going."

He nervously inches his way into the green mist. After a few yards, he pats his body to make sure he's not melting and then turns around toward Shan.

"See, still all here."

Shan waves him forward with an irritated glare.

As Ramie creeps through the forest of stone columns, a breeze whistles past. It stirs the mist about his legs. The best Ramie can remember, there was no breeze outside the Graveyard. He thinks again that this is perhaps not one of his greatest ideas.

Ramie continues forward with more cautious steps. The mist is so dense he can't see the ground - that is, if it was still there to be seen. Somehow it seems softer than normal. He reaches down and tries to brush the mist away but wherever he does it fills in too quickly.

He turns in a slow circle and mumbles to himself, "I'm never going to find it".

As if the mist around his legs understands his frustration, it forms into narrow fingers that begin to worm their way up around him.

For some reason Ramie doesn't feel threatened. He has no sudden urge to struggle. He just stands still and watches. The fingers continue up his body.

They're soft and cause no pain. It's almost like they are probing him as they continue to snake upwards. One creeping finger makes its way to Ramie's ear and gently taps at the bottom curl causing his lobe to swing.

"Stop it... that tickles."

He tries to swat at the finger. The misty finger pulls back and curls around directly in front of his face. Ramie stares at it, not quite sure what to do next. It stares right back with as much curiosity.

Living in a land of sorcery, Ramie has seen many beguiling things even at his young age, but a sorcerer conjured up most of those things. There's no sorcerer here to make the mist behave so. Ramie reminds himself he has never been in the Graveyard of Spells before.

The point of the misty finger, floating a few inches before his eyes, forms into a globe about the size of Ramie's lost Orb. Ramie smiles. The misty globe and fingers evaporate back into the groundcover.

"So, you know where my Orb is?"

In answer the thick layer of mist in front of Ramie parts, revealing the ground and his missing globe a few yards away. Ramie glances around... half hoping to see the sorcerer who controls the strange mist and half not wanting to because he may have made a new friend in this most unusual of places.

Finally he nods, "Thanks... green stuff".

Growing more irritated by the moment, Shan paces back and forth outside the entrance gate of the Graveyard of Spells. She takes a deep breath and starts to enter but a sudden low wall of mist springs up between the arches. Not to be deterred she tries to walk through the mist barrier but it's no longer porous vapor.

The five-foot high wall is now a malleable but solid obstruction. Shan presses at it and it presses back. She looks over the top into the Graveyard, her expression now filled with concern for her missing brother.

Ramie smiles at his quick victory. He steps forward and reaches for the Orb. It starts rolling away from him. He steps closer. The Orb rolls farther away, the mist splitting a path for it as it goes.

"Now we're playing games, are we?"

Ramie follows the rolling Orb... slowly, then faster. The Orb matches each change in his pace. Frustrated, Ramie stops. The Orb rolls a few inches back towards him, as if to entice him into playing more.

Ramie crosses his arms and turns away. A finger of the green mist forms and slaps at his leg. After a pause, Ramie turns to give his new friend a second chance. The Orb moves again, but this time directly up against a rock pillar. It stops.

Ramie stares at it, pretending not to care. The Orb begins repeatedly tapping like Morse code against the column, as if trying to convince Ramie it's through running.

Ramie reminds himself that his Orb has never had a life of its own and the mist is obviously controlling it. Who's controlling the mist he doesn't know.

He's never been able to hold a stern face or attitude for long. At last he steps forward and reaches down for the little dull Orb. Just as he touches it, the column it rests against begins to hum with energy. Ramie jerks back.

This is more puzzling than the rolling Orb. Not being big on caution he reaches in and touches the column. Handholds in the stone begin to glow and the hum grows louder. He looks up towards a red glow atop the tall column. It gets brighter.

Ramie is sure that everything is speaking to him - whether it's wise to listen, he's not so sure. That's never stopped him before. He hesitates a moment more, shakes his head 'no'... and starts to climb.

Passing a chiseled plaque that reads 'Sorcerer's Door'... he glances at it briefly. He sets aside the thought that the spell may conjure some sort of door lest the spell's name dissuade him from his plans to get into trouble.

Hand over hand Ramie climbs the pillar towards the ever-brightening red glow atop. He glances down, thinking that any moment Shan will come storming in after him. If he's going to mess up, he had better do it quickly.

Reaching the pinnacle of the column he finds a perfectly round glowing cloud - floating within the cloud, a golden pendant on a delicate chain with a jewel in its center.

The housing appears to be more of a resting place than a prison to Ramie. It may be his imagination but the pendant doesn't seem to want to remain contained. As usual, Ramie interprets his imagination in the direction he wants to go.

The urgent reality of time rushes back into his mind and Ramie reaches into the porous globe. The golden chain of the pendant flows to wrap around Ramie's wrist. He sees this as it choosing him... again, a matter of agreeable interpretation.

He pulls his hand out, looks at his treasure a brief second and stuffs the pendant in his pack. He starts climbing back down before Shan comes to get him.

Shan stands with her arms crossed glaring at the barrier. She knows the wise decision would be to go home for help, but she was the one that let the brat go into the Graveyard in the first place.

She could easily clear a mere five-foot barrier on her hoverboard but she's well aware that spells don't work in there. Who knows what would happen in mid-air.

Then she thinks she could dive over the wall, no spells needed. As if the mist could hear her thoughts, the barrier raises another two feet. Shan stamps the ground in frustration.

Not to be deterred by dumb mist, Shan starts to climb the supports of the entrance arch. After all, how high can the mist go? Just as she scales to the top of the solid mist, Ramie emerges from the foggy groundcover inside the Graveyard. He quickly waves his Orb over his head.

The barrier confronting Shan dissolves back into vapor and seeps into the ground. She jumps down and stands just outside the gate staring at Ramie. He waves the Orb again, trying to distract her attention from his eyes.

Her sisterly nature slips out, "I was..." She catches herself, "Never mind. What happened in there?"

"Nothing!" Ramie exclaims.

Exasperated, she says, "Mom tugged twice while you were playing around in there."

'Tugs' are like sorcerer's phone calls and Ramie ignores them routinely... and gets in trouble for doing so routinely. He pays little attention to the remark as he squeezes his pack tight and rushes past Shan.

Intently, on his way, "I thought you were in a hurry."

For a few seconds, Shan would love to turn him into a Grim-ick, something not pleasant to be on Spirin. Instead she play-fully slaps his head as he passes, grateful that he's OK.

Chapter Three

Lord Kildemar stands on a turret atop his fortress and glares out over the bleak landscape of his domain, the Land of Goreipor. Goreipor is made up of slate-like black rock, jagged cliffs and steep canyons. The blackness of the land almost glistens.

It's an extreme contrast to its neighboring Eastern Land of Spirin. But, their radical difference goes unrecognized since the inhabitants of neither land have the ability to see beyond the walls that encompass and separate them.

Lord Kildemar is as jagged as the rocks below. Scars acquired in his rise to power cover his sixty-two year old face. A five-fingered steel claw has long ago replaced his left hand. He peers down on the troop encampment just outside the fortress walls. All seems calm - except to the watchful eye.

Far below, Lord Kildemar's two sons, Taligarr and Janick, wander among the troops. Taligarr, the older of the two, has begun his collection of scars... the most prominent is one that slashes from the bridge of his nose down across the left side of his face.

He received that a year ago when his father quashed the last cell of resistance led by a warlord in the northern province of Goreipor. He is very proud of his one scar.

Janick, at a young twenty-four, has yet to earn his share of battle scars. This could mean that he's less experienced than his older brother... or he's smarter.

The two young men bull-nose their way through the encampment with the arrogance of the entitled. Men step aside more out of fear of the boys' father than of them. Men give nodded salutes to not show disrespect... there's a vast difference between not showing disrespect and showing respect.

The encampment of soldiers is loud and, for the most part, in various stages of drunkenness. Near one of the many campfires, two soldiers pull knives and break into open blows. If dressed as usual in their black leathers, this would be a minor threat to either, but both are bare-chested.

They circle, jabbing small knicks into each other with their blades. The encircling crowd of soldiers eggs them on with yells. It would be hard for either man to end the fight even if they wanted to. Whenever one backs up into the circle, he's shoved back into the center. Blood fuels the crowd's entertainment.

The larger of the two soldiers scores a deep cut on his opponent. Just then Taligarr and Janick break through the outer ring of onlookers. All, including the combatants, freeze at their appearance.

Taligarr yells out, "Four pieces on the big one."

"I'll double that," Janick chimes in.

The fever of the crowd boots back up once they know there will be no repercussions.

Janick adds, "And the loser dies!"

The action doesn't stop at this... but a pronounced spasm of discomfort ripples through the whole crowd.

Through a slight gap in the circle, Captain Pirus can be seen leaning against a war wagon. He watches the ruckus with a look of neutrality... neither of judgment nor enjoyment, just the deadpan face of a hardened soldier. That is, until the sons of Lord Kildemar join in.

He shakes his head with a slight measure of disgust. The captain has the air of a line officer, visible in both his bearing and the crimson stripes on his black leather uniform. His dress is not pompous like Taligarr and Janick's, but it's clearly the uniform of some rank.

Pirus moves forward towards the ongoing fight. Soldiers he passes back away and become silent. It's clear from their looks that it's more out of respect than fear.

Without hesitation he steps directly between the two fighting soldiers. The wounded one is happy to stand down but the larger soldier's adrenaline is still surging. He charges again.

With an economy of movement, Captain Pirus grabs his arm and flips him to the ground. With the soldier on his face and an arm stretched up behind his back, Pirus easily takes the knife from his grasp.

Janick, having had his entertainment interrupted, storms towards Pirus, "How dare you... "

Holding up a single finger of caution, Captain Pirus cuts him off. Before Janick can figure out how to respond to such impudence, his older brother takes his arm and pulls him back.

"Captain Pirus, you're far from being a commander. Are you sure you want to challenge our decisions?" says Taligarr in an oily tone.

Pirus doesn't appear impressed by the young lords.

"I am a captain in your father's army and I doubt he would tolerate losing one of his soldiers over a childish whim."

Pirus knows he's playing with fire, but that's sometimes what soldiers have to do. It's more important that he retain the respect of his troops than the favor of these two children.

Taligarr glares at Pirus with contempt as he simply nods. Janick starts to get his hackles back up.

Never taking his eyes off Pirus, Taligarr slaps Janick on the shoulder, "We're late for court, brother." As they back away, he adds, "Perhaps another day, Captain Pirus."

Pirus nods with a slight smile. He knows to never take eyes off an enemy till they are out of range. Once the two are gone he shakes his head at the childishness and helps the thrown soldier up. The others milling around silently nod their approval of the Captain's small victory.

Pirus recognizes the value of having the trust of his troops. He also knows troop morale is low and soldiers without a task become dangerously restless.

Lord Kildemar has watched all the activity below from his turret. Too high to make out what was actually being said, he still knows what has taken place.

His army is stagnating... they need a war. If they don't long for a war, he does. The problem is he has no one left in the land of Goreipor to fight.

A cold-faced woman whose beauty has been worn away steps out of the darkness behind Lord Kildemar. Witch Racinda moves cautiously up behind the dark lord's left shoulder. Nervously she fingers the nub of what once was a curl to the bottom of her right ear.

Lord Kildemar senses her presence but ignores it. His witch too often speaks in terms of feelings and he prefers talk of action... something he can understand.

Without warning, Witch Racinda grabs her stomach as if something very unpleasant stirred inside her. She looks off to the East - where distantly lies the land of Spirin – and tries to get some sense of what might have taken place there.

The Lord vaguely notices, "What troubles you now, witch?"

Racinda straightens up and turns her gaze away from the East, "Nothing, my lord".

She's learned to temper her thoughts around her harsh master... especially when they are still yet abstract. The look in her eyes says that something has stirred beyond those walls separating the kingdoms... something recalled from ancient memories that she's almost managed to forget.

Chapter Four

As Shan and Ramie float toward the Dees' home, Ramie makes a point of keeping some separation between them. Shan finds this very suspicious because he's usually a pest when they fly together. She tries to close the gap but he widens it. Shan knows something's up... she just doesn't know what.

The Dees' home comes into sight nestled in its own little valley. The two-story house is whimsical even from afar, shaped like a steep pyramid built from a rainbow of brightly colored flagstones.

Atop the pyramid, resting on its uppermost tip is a widespread, four-sided umbrella roof. It extends out like the petals of a flower, providing shade in the heat and keeping the structure dry in foul weather.

Looking at it, one would think a gust of wind could send the whole house drifting like the seed head of a dandelion. Bright red and purple trees flank the structure and a garden borders the front porch. All is enclosed by a rail fence.

The two kids settle to the ground and their boards disappear. Shan and Ramie enter the house to find their parents, Kalish and Atta Dee, playing one of their favorite games, 'Floating Twos'. It's a game played in mid-air with floating cards. No one in Spirin would find it unusual that cards float since to some degree everyone in Spirin is a sorcerer.

Kalish Dee is a hulk of a man with a surprisingly kind face for his bear-like frame. He's pretty much the same on the inside... a bit of gruffness encasing a warm heart.

Atta Dee is 'mother' incarnate, with a rosy round face and eyes that look like they hold the answer to all personal problems - or can at least make them more tolerable. As in many families the softer-spoken member often pulls the strings. Atta tamed Kalish the bear many years ago.

The Dees' home has that warmth coming from a family that decorates the walls with small knick-knacks collected by proud and caring generations. A glowing fire bathes the living room. You can almost see the smell of fresh home-cooked cookies.

The home is not filled with ostentatious displays of sorcery since there is no one to impress with them. Granted, fish swimming in the water of a painting over the fireplace might be unusual on another world but not here in Spirin.

Atta sees Ramie and cheerfully says, "I made your favorite."

Ramie, too preoccupied with thoughts of his new treasure, bounds up the stairs without responding.

Kalish growls, "Young man, did you hear your mother?"

Ramie freezes on the stairs. He knows that tone and turns.

"Sorry, I was... I was in a hurry to get to my studies."

Shan rolls her eyes at this absurdity.

"You're never in such a hurry that you can't be polite."

Atta pats Kalish's hand, as if to say studying is a little strange for Ramie but it's better to take rare gifts when they come. Kalish waves Ramie on and sits back down at the table.

With a glance up at the boy heading into his room, he says, "Maybe he is settling down a bit."

"You have to be kidding... him, study?" Shan carps.

Atta tries to soothe her, "Shan, give your brother the benefit of the doubt. He's growing up."

"Into what?" mutters Shan.

Her mother gives her one of her 'tsk-tsk' looks. Shan brushes it off, knowing she's right about the brat.

Glancing around at the living room, she says, "Where's Gran-D?"

With a note of irritation, Atta answers, "Down at the pub, as usual."

Gran-D, Atta's father, is the one member of the family whom she has not managed to tame.

Shan knows she should probably confide in someone about the Graveyard. She's actually happy Gran-D is not there since she doesn't know what to say about what happened there. She senses something strange is afoot with Ramie and somehow it has to do with that place.

Ramie sits on his bed studying the large pendant from the Graveyard. There's a red jewel in the center, encircled by two rings of etched characters. Each ring has eight symbols, none of which are familiar to Ramie.

Even though he has no idea what he's looking at, it fascinates him. He knows he shouldn't have it and, perhaps, that's the reason it fascinates him so.

He shares a spacious second-story loft with Shan. A simple draw curtain divides the deceptively large space. When the candles are out, the whole loft is magically bathed by the night sky through the roof.

Hearing the sound of footsteps on the stairs, Ramie assumes it's Shan coming to give him a hard time. He quickly stashes the pendant behind his pillow and grabs a book. Donning his most nonchalant face, he opens the book.

It's upside down. That much of studying registers with him and he flips it around as the door opens. Shan comes in, knives

for eyes darting right at Ramie. He looks up with a totally innocent expression.

With a glimpse of his book, she lets out a little chuckle, "I'm
surprised the book's not upside down."

Knowing he's hiding something, Shan walks towards him,
leaning side to side. Ramie pretends not to be shaken by her ac-
cusing stare. She keeps inching towards him.

He's sure there's a tattooed image of a pendant glowing on
his forehead growing brighter with every inch she moves forward. Shan's always been too good at breaking him down.

Finally he blurts out, "What?"

She shrugs with a slight smile and continues grilling him with
her eyes.

To deflect her third degree, Ramie thrusts his hand out,
pointing a finger across the loft, "That's your side of the room.
Let me light your candles for you."

A sudden look of panic rushes over Shan. Before she can
protest, he flips tiny fireballs from his fingertips towards the
candleholder. They fly right by it, hitting a blouse draped over
her dresser.

The blouse bursts into flames.

Shan runs to the blouse and does her best to smother the
fire, but not before it has taken its toll on the poor blouse.
Once the flames are out, she snaps around to see Ramie's
sheepish, apologetic grin.

He's quick to say, "Sorry... Want me to try again?"

As a clear answer, Shan lifts the ruined blouse, and then
throws it on the dresser and storms out.

Ramie has once again embarrassed himself with a spell that
went haywire... but then again, it worked. A triumphant look
comes over his face.

After a couple seconds to make sure Shan is gone, he takes the pendant from under his pillow. With one last look, he stuffs it in his pack and puts the pack under the bed. He's determined to do the right thing and return it to the Graveyard where it belongs... and to do so before Shan figures out what he's done. Maybe tomorrow.

It's mid-morning at the Dees'. Atta's father, Gran-D, sits in the living room nursing a mild hangover. He's a kindly looking old man with medium-long white hair, a well-trimmed beard and a forever-mischievous smile.

Atta walks in from the kitchen, plopping a cup of coffee undaintily next to him with no comment other than unsympathetic body language.

He gives her a shrug and a broader mischievous smile. She's not swayed by his antics. Atta turns with a 'huh' and tromps back to the kitchen.

Clutching his pack, Ramie bounds down the stairs. He pays no attention to Gran-D as he barges through the entry and out the front door, almost knocking over Shan as she enters.

"Watch it, Rockhead!" she yells.

Ramie is in too much of a hurry to hear her. She shakes her head and comes inside. Seeing Gran-D, Shan pauses a moment, unsure if she should breach the subject of yesterday.

Finally she approaches him, "Where's the Rockhead going in such a rush?"

Gran-D looks up as if pondering the question, "Trouble's all that gets him moving that fast. What's on your mind, girl?"

Gran-D has a knack for getting past dancing around.

Shan attempts to sound casual, "Nothing. He didn't mention the Graveyard, did he?"

Scratching his chin, "May I ask, why would he?"

Shan shifts back and forth in place, the dance of discomfort.

"It's nothing. We just happened to be... it's nothing." Trying to change the subject, "Was I that much trouble at his age?"

"You mean, all that long ago?" he slyly says. "We all have our own kind of trouble. Don't you remember yours?"

Shan sighs, "Do you ever give a straight answer about anything? Is everything a riddle?"

"Not often... and yes. You like that from me because it makes you think," he says with a glint in his eye.

Exasperated, she turns to leave knowing he is absolutely right about why she loves him so much. She likes that he brings curiosity to almost everything.

As she's leaving, Gran-D says, "You better get to the Graveyard before Ramie finds more of his kind of trouble."

The sun's shining on the kids' favorite log as Ramie sits there swinging his pack back and forth in his hands. He occasionally glances up the hill at the Graveyard of Spells. He's struggling with irritating thoughts that resemble responsibility.

In his mind, everything is a potential adventure. He doesn't like to waste time clouding it with pesky little worries about consequences. Dwelling on such things causes his head to hurt.

He'd rather think about how glorious a morning it is... how the sun makes his spot on the log oh so comfortable... anything but what he came there to do. When he looks back up at the Graveyard he knows it's going to be cold in there and the green mist is probably going to give him a hard time.

What's the rush? He figures he might as well take another little look at the pendant. After all, he's not going to do anything with it. One more look and then he'll put it back where it belongs.

Sufficiently convincing himself of his good intentions, Ramie pulls out the pendant. The two rings of symbols that circle the red jewel seem to call to him. As long as he only plays around with one of them what could happen... probably nothing.

He gently presses his thumbs on the inner ring of symbols. It turns with ease. When he takes his thumbs off, the center jewel begins to glow and changes from red to blue.

"Interesting," Ramie says to himself.

No real harm done. He wonders what the outer ring does. As long as he doesn't touch both at the same time nothing much could happen. Ramie is an expert at talking his way into trouble in innocently small increments. That way if something does happen it's a total surprise to him... and most assuredly not his fault.

He twists the outer ring of symbols. When he stops, the two symbols aligned at the top and the center jewel glow a bright white. A beam of light bursts from the diamond's center and forms a large rotating vertical plane of light in front of Ramie. It's like a swirling pool of whiteness.

Ramie falls backwards off the log. He pulls himself up and peeks over at the swirling plane.

The diameter of the light pool begins to decrease. As it does, it gets brighter. It reduces all the way down to a blindingly bright white dot... and suddenly winks out!

After some hesitation, Ramie stands up from behind the log and brushes the grass from his hair.

Shaking his head in puzzlement, "That's it? No wonder it's in the Graveyard."

Disappointed, Ramie comes around the log to where the circle once was. Nothing. Then he notices an ever so slight distortion in the air.

He reaches out and softly brushes at the distortion. He's startled to feel something like an invisible curtain made of heavier
air. Ramie yanks his hand away and steps back a bit to think for
a moment.

Thinking doesn't stop his insatiable curiosity. He steps towards the space again. Once again he reaches out and brushes
at the empty air, this time more aggressively.

A slit of bright light opens and a hollow echo escapes. He
pulls his hand away. The light and the sound disappear.

Ramie backs up and sits down on the log, never taking his
eyes away from the direction of the invisible curtain. He looks
back towards home, then up towards the Graveyard of Spells
and back to the curtain that he cannot see.

As too many times before, he feels this mystery is calling
him. Ramie knows that somewhere beyond that light, something exciting awaits. Maybe it will be the first time anyone
from Spirin gets to see beyond the border walls.

Now he remembers it's called Sorcerer's Door... maybe the
Door's just waiting for him. It briefly rushes through his mind
that maybe someone has used the Door before, and that's why
the spell was outlawed... but it's only a brief flash of a thought.

For the official record he shakes his head 'no'. This is just a
personal ritual... he knows very well he will give in to the imagi-
nary voices in his head that scream adventure.

Ramie stands up, puts the pendant around his neck and proclaims, "Jazmar!"

He walks up, spreads the invisible curtain, and plunges into
the slit of light... and through the Sorcerer's Door.

The Grand Hall of the fortress of Goreipor is filled with upper echelon military and courtesans wagering on a fight be-

tween two Goreiporian warriors. Such entertainment appeals to more than the common rank and file soldiers.

A dead silence washes over the hall as Lord Kildemar enters. The fight stops as well. It's clear that this court revels only at his permission. Lord Kildemar waves for the fight to continue. In a heartbeat the frenzy of the match roars on.

Goreiporians in general - including the women - have much of the same leather hardness of the Dark Lord. It would be difficult to choose the weakest foe in the room, regardless of sex.

Like the hardness of those in the room, the walls of the Grand Hall are a testament to war. They display alien-looking weapons of all sorts. This appears to be a world of swords and spears unless more advanced weaponry is kept out of sight. Proudly displayed as well are tattered flags of conquered enemies.

Lord Kildemar walks up to his two sons, "Which of those oafs are you betting on?"

Janick answers enthusiastically, "Taligarr thinks the small one is faster. I'm betting on the strength of the larger one."

Taligarr shakes his head as if he knows what is coming.

Lord Kildemar slaps Janick on the side of the head, "Never bet against family!"

Janick recovers, but looks confused.

Kildemar adds, "Stack the fight in your favor and then always bet together."

To Lord Kildemar even a casual match is no place for chance or fairness. Everything is a lesson to be learned as a prelude to war.

Witch Racinda comes scurrying up to Lord Kildemar and whispers something in the Lord's ear. She is one of the few in

Goreipor that can approach him on her own... but even she's cautious about doing so unless the matter is urgent.

He pushes her aside and yells, "All, save my sons, out!"

Kildemar's slightest word is equal to his utmost command. The hall clears quickly.

Once the massive doors slam shut he turns to Witch Racinda, "Say that again."

"That ancient spell has been used."

"Where?" he demands.

"It comes from somewhere beyond the Eastern wall, where exactly I know not... but I feel it in the stars."

Witch Racinda backs up a bit, more than aware that the Lord does not take bad news well... especially of a 'feeling' nature.

He snaps, "You know the spell's name all too well, though you have not powers to use it. The Sorcerer's Door... isn't it?"

She nods 'yes' with caution, "But it has never been used off our world..." Then, more quietly, "Even on our planet, only twice."

Lord Kildemar turns and strides with resolve towards a recess in the hall's wall. A dusty tapestry covers the alcove. His sons dutifully follow. When he reaches the alcove he turns to Taligarr and Janick.

"Maybe my father was not as much a fool as I always took him to be. Keep that in mind when you're not in my company."

He yanks down the tapestry, revealing behind it a massive pedestal. Sitting on the pedestal is an even more massive black crystal ball suspended in a clear force field.

The black crystal resembles the rock formations that make up Goreipor... except for the crystal's perfect roundness. There's a purplish glint coming from deep within the crystal as if it were alive. Its appearance suggests the stench of death.

"You've never told us what that is, Father", says Janick.

Taligarr elbows Janick... not in time.

The Lord glares at his youngest son, "I have told you to never reveal your weapons till needed... haven't I?"

Taligarr shakes his head, knowing his younger brother often opens his mouth before thinking of his father's reaction.

Having gotten his point across, Lord Kildemar says, "It's the answer to outside interference."

He turns to Witch Racinda.

"My father's fathers said this could be attached to that spell if it ever went off our world. Knowing my family, I presume it is meant to destroy whatever place the spell goes."

Witch Racinda studies the ancient crystal, having no true idea of what it is... and even less of whether it will work.

All she knows is that the black crystal was formed in the fortress long before any of them were born. She has heard it rumored to be the creation of a wizard who long ago served Lord Kildemar's great-grandfather.

She knows not. Aside from her own ill fate, no wizards, sorcerers or witches have ever made their home in the Land of Goreipor. Can this old black crystal truly be a defense against an equally ancient Prophecy?

Kildemar tires of her silent musing, "If you value your life, attach this crystal to the spell before it can cause damage to my world. To whatever world this spell goes — and all that it touches - I want destroyed! Do this now!"

Knowing this is no idle request, Racinda leans in close to the force field encasing the crystal. Looking up she sees how it rests beneath some sort of launching tube... a hollow chimney extending high up through the fortress.

With a general idea of what's needed, she backs away... as do Lord Kildemar and his sons.

Holding her hands straight out, she concentrates.

The force field around the crystal slowly begins to glow red. As the glow grows brighter, all four back away even farther.

Racinda has a passing thought that it might very well blow up in their faces... a thought that does not disturb her.

Glowing bright red and now humming shrilly, the globe and its crystal abruptly shoot up the chimney... and out of the fortress.

Standing on a fortress battlement, Captain Pirus turns to see a bright red object rocket out of the top of the fortress and far off into the stars.

Chapter Five

It's night in the hills above Goldendale. Peter sits on a boulder outside a cave's entrance sipping on a beer and staring up at the stars. Rock music drifts out of the cave not far away.

Peter is not in a party mood. His mind is lost in daydreams of being somewhere else... of being someone else. At least he's got Devon. A thought quickly followed by, 'I have Devon to take care of.' Everything has a double edge.

Jerry, one of Peter's hang-with friends, comes out of the cave with two bottles of beer in one hand and a joint in the other. He saunters over and plops down on the rock next to Peter and hands him one of the bottles.

"What's up? You missed a rad food fight today at school."

Peter, still a little distant, "Had to work."

"Thought you loved working on bikes," says Jerry.

Still looking into the stars, Peter responds, "Funny how needing to zaps that. I'd just like to get the kid and me outta here."

Peter doesn't have high expectations for his life... maybe being a reasonably good mechanic like his dad, that's about it. But he holds onto higher expectations for Devon - that is, if they ever get away.

Jerry interrupts his thoughts, "Where you gonna go, man?"

"I don't know. Anywhere, as long as it's a million miles from here."

Jerry holds out the joint, "This will take you there."

Peter sets down his beer and gets up.

"Nah, gotta get home to the kid before he has another fake family fit."

He starts towards his bike.

"Start bringing him up with you."

Peter turns with a friendly laugh, "I'm keeping him away from the likes of you and our other no account friends."

Jerry laughs, gives Peter a wave and heads back into the cave for more partying. There's not a lot else to do around a small town filled with non-ambitious people.

Just as Peter straddles his bike and readies to kick-start it, a beam of light shoots down from the heavens towards the ground. Where the beam ends is not clear but he figures it must be touching down a couple miles away... somewhere around Gypsy Meadow.

At first the long beam stays bright all the way from the stars to the ground. Within a few seconds, it fades to a ghost of a beam... yet just ghostly enough to see against the night sky. Astounded, Peter glances back at the cave to see if anyone else saw it... no one's there.

He kick starts the bike. With a loud rev he peels down the dirt path towards the road to chase the mysterious beam.

Redlining the bike, Peter zips along the mountain road with an eye fixed on the beam faintly wavering against the night sky.

He has no idea what he's chasing but it's at least a change from the normal night. Maybe he's still caught in daydreams of being somewhere else, but the beam is real... at least he thinks so.

A cloud of dust from the crystal's blast off still floats heavily in the air of the Grand Hall. Lord Kildemar and his sons had gone off to another part of the hall to discuss something private, but now they are back.

Witch Racinda stares at the gaping hole where the crystal departed, not wanting to turn and face Lord Kildemar until she must. She can feel the knives of his stare.

Finally the Dark Lord snaps, "Will it work?"

She takes a breath and turns.

"It is attached to the spell. If it works, I cannot say... I did not create it. I have only done as you command."

"But you know well of the spell!"

With more sadness than fear, she responds, "Only of an ancient memory... like my life."

She wishes the Dark Lord will know to stop pushing. If not, so be it... life is not as precious as it once was.

Her skills being still useful to him, Kildemar brings his tone down, "Keep your senses open. Let me know of any change."

Letting out a guttural grumble, he storms towards the hall's doors with his sons in tow.

He yells back, "I share my world with no one!"

Turning away from the door, the old woman calmly anticipates Kildemar acting on his repeated threats. She still serves him enough to realize she must cling to life for some reason... perhaps time will reveal to her why she tolerates his abuse instead of simply letting go.

Peter whips around a bend in the road to find himself at the edge of Gypsy Meadow. The beam touches down right there as he guessed.

The meadow is a large open field surrounded by dense forest. The open ground is speckled with knee-high patches of wildflowers. The moonlit field almost seems to cradle the strange dart from the sky.

He sideslips his bike to a stop on a turnout. Still faintly defined, the beam stands well out in the meadow, close to the tree line. Even from a distance he can see a vague light where it touches the ground like the spot of a large, but weak flashlight.

Sitting on the bike staring out at the seemingly impossible event, it dawns on Peter that things are getting a little Twilight Zone about all this. The thought of leaving only barely crosses his mind. He dismounts and starts walking into the meadow.

As he walks forward he glances all around at the shadows darting about in the nearby trees. They are just the play of moonlight and breeze. Despite knowing what they are, their illusory movement makes Peter a little jumpy.

When he reaches the spot where the beam touches down, the circle that he thought would be brighter is merely a vague four-foot round lightness in the dirt. Its apparent size was the optical illusion created by seeing it horizontally from his bike.

Same with the beam — from afar it stood out against the darkness. But now, right upon it, it's little more than a distortion in the air.

Peter reaches out and swipes at the air, a sudden slash of bright light appears along with a hollow echo. He recoils and the light is gone.

He steps away a few feet trying to get his head around it. He looks all about, knowing that there has to be some logic to this. He sees none.

Peter inches towards it again.

A sudden sound of loud cracking limbs comes from the woods off to Peter's right. Still pumping adrenaline from chasing the beam, Peter drops to the ground.

He peers with all his might at the shifting shadows along the tree line and tries to isolate the noise. Nothing.

More branches break deep among the trees. Whatever it is, it's getting closer. He reminds himself he doesn't believe in monsters... but he stays on the ground.

The commotion in the woods gets louder, closer, more intense... Peter still can't see its origin. By now he has all but forgotten the beam that drew his earlier attention.

Suddenly the shadows become more than just moon and wind. A screaming boy bursts into the meadow.

It's Ramie.

He's running as fast as he can with quick glances over his shoulder. A roaring black bear is barreling down on him, some ten yards behind.

Peter springs to his feet. The beam, the light and the echo are of little concern now.

Before running for his bike, Peter yells, "Run, kid! Stop looking over your damn shoulder!"

Peter spins to follow his own advice and his foot gets caught in an invisible curtain. A sliver of a door of silver light opens and he falls backwards through it.

Peter is thrown left and right, up and down, inside a transparent sphere as it zips him through the universe. The walls of the globe around him are so pliable that hitting them causes no harm. The sensory overload causes him considerably more pain than the tossing about.

Living in the northwest hills doesn't drown out the stars like city lights do, but this full kaleidoscope of the heavens, free of Earth's atmosphere, is overwhelming.

And then come the surges.

Peter's not as science-oriented as his kid brother... but common sense tells him that when the relationship between two stars shifts, he could be going thousands of miles per minute - even if he doesn't feel the speed sensation in the bubble.

The surges are mind-blowing.

They sweep him in and out of wormholes... light becomes a blur and he emerges in whole new glorious landscapes of different galaxies. All sense of time is lost.

As he's drawn into another wormhole something large, bright red and round bumps his sphere, rocketing in the other direction. Caught in the middle of the impossible, he has absolutely no idea what it was... nor does it strike him as any more unusual than anything else at the moment.

The rollercoaster ride through space rushes on.

Jerry steps out of the cave for a bit of air. Looking down the hill he sees the faint ghost beam Peter chased.

With a stoned smile, he utters, "Whoa, that's cool... "

He sits down on a boulder to watch. He lacks the sobriety to feel like chasing cool things, but it's interesting enough to look at.

With lightning speed a glowing red lump, with a black core, shoots down the beam, like a hamster engulfed by a straight, translucent snake. The lump impacts the ground.

A humongous explosion erupts!

Jerry slips off the boulder onto his butt.

The explosion sends out a ring-of-fire shock wave that plows down the surrounding forest in an ever-growing radius.

A thoroughly sobered Jerry jumps to his feet. Eyes wide, he backs up against the rock, terrified as the wave rapidly spreads out.

He holds his ears at the deafening rumble... the earth shakes under his feet... rocks start falling from the mountain that houses the cave.

Within a few seconds the impact wave hits... everything goes black!

Chapter Six

S han sits at the log with a puzzled expression. She casually swings Ramie's pack back and forth. It's almost evening and she's seen nothing of her brother all day.

She mutters, "OK, where are you, Rockhead?"

The Graveyard of Spells looms closely and she senses that it has something to do with what's in play. Ramie doesn't just leave his pack lying around. She's not the angry sister now, she's the worried one. There will be plenty of time for anger once she gets her hands on the brat.

A light slit flashes before her and Peter is spit out onto the ground. He lands face first, a foot in front of Shan. Unlike her brother, Shan is not easily startled.

She looks down at the stranger and calmly says, "Boy, you almost hit me."

Disoriented, Peter shakes his head and looks up at Shan, "Where am I? In some kind of dream... or nightmare?"

"If it's a dream, it's certainly not mine."

Lying on the ground, Peter tries to get his bearings. He reaches out and touches the log... it's real. He moves his hand over and touches Shan's leg.

She slaps him!

With a jerk back, he staggers to his feet. He looks around for the first time. He knows he's not in Oregon anymore!

Looking back at Shan, he rubs his chin, "What was that?"

"A dream." Standing up, she says, "I don't know what spell dropped you here and I don't really care. Just be on your way."

For Peter this is getting weirder by the moment, "On my way where? ... From where?"

"Why ask me? I have no idea where you came from."

Stress is slipping into Shan's voice and she doesn't like it. She gets enough of it from dealing with her brother and is not about to take it from a stranger... especially one she's already decided she doesn't particularly like.

She calms herself and says in an articulated, condescending manner, "Don't you know where you came from, boy?"

"Yeah, Goldendale, and that ain't here." He adds, "And, my name's not boy. It's Peter!"

"I could care less. Now that you've figured out your name and where you're from, please go back there."

Peter decides he dislikes this arrogant girl but he needs to make some sense of this.

"Look, whoever you are, you mentioned a spell. What does that mean? I mean, like... what gives here?"

As she tries to think of something bitingly appropriate as a response, the slit of light opens again and Ramie comes tumbling out. He jumps up, full of overflowing energy, not noticing Peter behind him.

"Whoa! ... That was strange! I went someplace that had big, scary, hairy things."

Shan lifts her hand next to her face and points a single finger to something behind him.

Ramie throws a glance back at Peter and turns back to his sister, "Who's he?"

From behind Ramie, Peter says, "It was a bear."

From in front of him, Shan, "I don't know... he doesn't either."

Ramie's confused. He turns back to Peter.

"A bear was chasing you," repeats Peter.

A light clicks on in Ramie's head.

Panic replaces puzzlement, "Jazmar! You came through the door?"

"All I know is I fell into some kind of light and landed between her legs." Peter gestures at Shan.

"You what!"

It's clear from her face that if Shan were closer she would slap him again.

Peter ignores this and grabs Ramie by the collar, "Look, runt, whatever you did to get me here... "

Shan raises her hand and an invisible force slams Peter to the ground. She steps around Ramie and takes a stance over him.

"He might be a runt, but he's my runt... whatever that is."

Hands on her hips she's clearly challenging him to just try to defy her.

Peter jumps up and holds up his hands, "All I meant was that what got me here has something to do with him."

"Maybe, maybe not, but hands off the kid. We don't hurt each other here."

As Peter rubs his shoulder, "You could have fooled me about that last part."

Shan shows a touch of embarrassment that she let her temper get the best of her.

As a background to Shan and Peter's little squabble, Ramie frantically thrashes at the air mumbling, "He has to go back now... Where's that door?"

A few minutes later, Shan and Peter sit on the log watching an exhausted Ramie still searching for the door.

Peter lets out a little laugh, "Funny, what you said."

Shan, sounding a bit more amiable, "What's funny?"

"Hands off the kid... That's why I have to go home. I got one, too... I think, maybe a little smarter than yours."

With a slight smile, "Wouldn't take much."

Peter surveys this colorful new world as if it's the first time he's noticed anything outside of his own problems.

Groping for something for small talk, he says, "Got to admit, your world is, um... bright."

Shan rolls her eyes. That didn't go over so well.

Peter goes back to the basics, "You still haven't told me where I am."

"Spirin," is all she says.

Peter shakes his head and decides to give up on attempts at small talk with a very contrary girl for the moment.

Finally Ramie surrenders and plops down, "It's gone."

Shan stands, "What's gone? And this better be good."

Ramie scoots away from her, "I sort of evoked a spell from, you know..." nodding towards the Graveyard. "I was going to return it, honest."

Sheepishly he holds the pendant up to Shan. She snatches it from him, looks at it, then up at the Graveyard. Shan rubs her hand over the pendant and there's a brief glint from the center jewel. She pulls her hand away.

"This can't be from the Graveyard."

"It is. I should know, I took it from there... and I don't con-fess that often."

Dangling the pendant out in front of Ramie, "It can't be... because spells are locked in cylinders before they're put in the Graveyard of Spells. Gran-D told me so, long ago."

Peter gets up. "Look, I don't care where it's from. If that's what the kid used, use it again to send me home."

Staring at the pendant, she's truly puzzled. She knows it should be encased. Even if it isn't, it shouldn't react when she runs her hand over it... spells are disabled before they go into the Graveyard.

Ramie's a brat, but he's not an outright liar, especially when he confesses. It doesn't make any sense. She loses herself in thought.

Trying to bring her back to the moment and what's important, Peter says, "Hey, you. Did you hear what I said?"

Shan glares at him, "Maybe it's what he used... and, no."

"No?" Peter exclaims.

Shan pays little attention to Peter's outrage. She turns to Ramie and holds out the pendant.

"You are going to put this back in the Graveyard, exactly where you found it."

Peter insists, "What the hell does 'no' mean?"

"It means welcome to your new temporary home... as I said, the Land of Spirin."

With this she tries to push Ramie towards the Graveyard, but he stands fast.

She keeps on, "The reason spells are locked is so things like this can't happen. Now, get your tail up there and put it back."

Waving back at Peter, Ramie says, "What about him? Can't we take him home with us?"

"No!" After a sight pause, "When we get home I'll tell dad and he'll tell the Council. They'll come and get it."

Peter bristles, "It? I'm not a thing! And I'm not going anywhere."

"Fine, I didn't invite you. Just stay here."

Shan conjures her hoverboard. This clearly astounds Peter, but he's got other things on his mind at the moment. She snaps her finger for Ramie to do the same but he's being stubborn. He refuses to move.

Shan lets out a sigh, and in an irritatingly polite manner to Peter, "OK, you are going to come with us while Ramie puts the spell back. Then we are going to take you home where someone will do their very best to get rid of you... You ride with the runt."

Shan turns back to Ramie, "He's yours to explain. Now move."

With a quick smile at Peter, Ramie conjures up his board and says enthusiastically, "Just hop on the back."

For now, Peter figures he's left with little choice. With some apprehension he steps up behind Ramie on the board.

As the three take off, Shan looks back at Ramie, "Dad's going to fuse your hands for this one."

After a slight panicked look, "He can't do that, can he?"

Peter stands next to Shan outside the front gate of the Graveyard of Spells. He's clearly bewildered by the ornate metal fence somehow holding in a deep layer of green fog but Shan volunteers no explanation. She'd simply prefer to ignore his presence.

Irritated by her silence, he finally says, "What gives with the spooky graveyard scene?"

She grimaces at the fact that he's not satisfied with being silent. She says, "It's where we put spells that don't work, if it's any of your business."

"You mean like the one that screwed up and got me here?"

Shan glares at him and says curtly, "That one really didn't work! Rockhead is putting it back where it belongs before anything worse... shows up."

Before he can think of a retort, Ramie emerges from the forest of tall columns. He looks a bit disappointed as he brushes his hands through seemingly inert mist. His face shows he's still hoping for some kind of interaction. At last he shrugs and heads for the exit.

As he reaches the gate and starts to make a smart-ass remark, a large paddle-sized plank of green mist forms behind him. Before Shan or Peter can say a word, the paddle slaps Ramie through the gates. He tumbles into the grass, surprised but not harmed.

He gets up and glances back at the graveyard with a big smile... at least he got some more play out of it.

Peter is at a loss to say anything.

As the three kids float home, Peter really looks at Spirin for the first time... this time, for more than small talk. He can't hide his fascination. The colors are so vivid. Is blue grass really brighter than green grass? Are the reds stronger here, or is he just seeing it differently?

Maybe it's just the newness of it all, but he can't help feeling there's something magical about this strange place. Seeing Shan's powers help support this feeling.

Peter has to hold on as Ramie banks the board up near a glowing yellow bush. The golden petals take flight, revealing an orange bush that was actually covered by yellow birds. They swirl up like a harmless tornado of vivid yellow, past two low setting suns. Peter looks back at the transformation in awe.

Shan sneaks an occasional peek at Peter riding behind Ramie. She appears satisfied by his overwhelmed expressions. Naturally, when he catches her watching she turns away, showing no interest whatsoever. And, of course, he starts glancing at her even more often.

Two small animals scurry across the meadow below as the kids fly over. It's obvious they are playing rather than running away. Other animals stand up and watch the kids pass by. The animals are alien to Peter, somewhat like light blue hairy frogs.

Ramie leans back, "They're just babies."

Peter mumbles to himself, "Baby what's?"

Peter looks up at two of the three moons that circle the Sphere, each a different size. It feels so odd to him to see multiple moons and two suns out at the same time. He doesn't know the Sphere actually only has one sun that it orbits... the other large one is much farther away in a neighboring system.

Peter thinks about it all. He's always seen himself as no more than a motorcycle mechanic in some small shop somewhere, with few prospects and a limited imagination.

These new visions surprise him. Somehow, it makes him feel more alive than he can ever remember feeling. Only problem... he doesn't belong here... wherever here is.

Atta Dee floats plates out of the kitchen for dinner as Shan comes in the front door. Kalish sits in the living room and looks up at Shan.

"Where have you been all day?"

"Ramie has a little surprise for you."

Shan turns back to the front door but no one's there. Like a female drill sergeant she snaps, "Rockhead, get in here!"

Ramie sticks his head in the door to test the waters.

Getting up, Kalish looks at Ramie, then at Shan, "Gran-D said you mentioned the Graveyard... You haven't been messing around up there, have you?"

Shan smiles, "Funny you should ask."

Ramie hasn't come all the way in and there's no sight of Peter yet.

Shan turns back to the door, "All the way inside, both of you!"

"You shouldn't yell at your brother like that," her mother admonishes.

"Just wait and see."

Ramie slowly enters, followed by Peter.

With his head tucked down and his hands hidden behind him, Ramie says in a mousy voice, "Hi, Mom. Hi, Dad." Looking up, he stretches out his words, "There's something."

He's cut off as Atta first sees Peter, "You should have said you were bringing company home. Ah, that's OK. We always have room for one more at the table."

Shan makes a little side-headed nod at Peter, trying to get her mother to take a better look. Appearing puzzled, both Kalish and Atta take another glance at Peter.

Atta exclaims, "Kalish, look, the ears."

"I see, mother," he says stepping closer to Peter. Peter feels at his ears uncomfortably.

Atta tilts to the side to get a better view, "Kalish, you know what the Prophecy says about... "

He cuts her off, "Nothing, it means nothing." Then to Peter, "Boy, where do you come from?"

"What's with the ears thing?" Peter bristles.

"Boy, I asked you a question."

Not being great with authority figures, Peter's guard rises. He didn't mind fencing with Shan, but he's not going to take it from another new face, especially an older one. His muscles tense up.

Shan intervenes, "His name is Peter and he's from somewhere called Golden Dale." She lightly slaps Ramie on the head, "Seems Rockhead here messed with a spell from the Graveyard, and... " pointing at Peter, "that's what happened."

Peter eases down, "Look, I don't want anything from you people, if you are people. All I want is to go home... or wake up, if this is a dream."

Atta, in her motherly tone, "We are real, and dinner is getting cold. When Gran-D gets home he'll straighten this out."

"Great, another alien nut!"

Kalish responds, "Look boy, you're the only alien here. Now, I'm holding my temper because you're out of your element and my idiot son may have had something to do with that... but I expect you to keep a civil tongue about you."

Peter's fists curl and his teeth grind almost enough to be heard as he glares at Kalish. Kalish matches glare for glare. The standoff is broken up when the front door bursts open and Gran-D comes dancing in - truly dancing.

Like a circus performer, he juggles a variety of colorful fruits and vegetables in the air along with a jug. They whip up and down in a full circle around the old man.

But he's not using his hands for this juggling... his hands dance with the circle. With a wand and a wandering eye he directs everything like conducting an orchestra. He spins as fast as the toys he juggles. At a brief pause in his symphony, he snatches the jug from the air and takes a swig.

From outside the house a man yells, "Nice party, old man."

Atta snaps, "Father, the sun hasn't even gone down!"

Gran-D burps and replies, "Daughter, it is Carringer's birthday... a very special occasion."

This gets a huff out of Atta and smiles from the rest of his family.

Gran-D now notices Peter, watching drop-jawed. He dances around him, still juggling the assortment.

"Hi, you must be new. Welcome to the Dees' house."

Before Peter can even think of a response, Gran-D dances away and into the kitchen. Peter stares at the closed door.

After a moment's silence, he says, "That was...?"

Atta nods with a touch of embarrassment, "Yes, Gran-D."

Peter still stares at the door, "Well... he's colorful."

"He's not always that... odd," Atta adds.

Ramie chimes in with a perky, "Sure he is."

Kalish snaps, "Ramie, mouth shut!"

Atta, with no other explanation to ease Peter's mind, says, "Anyone ready for dinner?"

Chapter Seven

After dinner Peter stands alone in the living room staring out the window at the night sky. His head is spinning from all he's had to take in. What little more he learned at dinner let loose a whole new can of worms in his mind.

He's in a world where everyone is a sorcerer of some sort. When he asked why everyone spoke English, he was told that they don't. For some magical reason, everyone understands each other in this world – no matter what language they speak.

Adding to his frustration, no one will talk to him about the spell that landed him here. It seems it's a matter that must be taken before some kind of Council... whoever that is. It's all giving him a whopping headache and an enormous feeling of loneliness.

All he can think of is that somewhere out there beyond the stars is a brother that's wondering where he is.

Atta comes in with bedding and lays them on the sofa.

"Peter, I'm sure you'll be comfortable here, Shan's being a little stubborn about the loft. Kalish will conjure up some other arrangement soon."

Peter knows she's being kind but the thought he may be here long enough to need another arrangement weighs heavier on him.

He turns to her and with the best smile he can muster, "I'll be fine, ma'am."

Atta knows when a boy, from any world, is hurting... but she has no answers. All she can offer is, "Peter, we'll do all we can to get you home... but while you're here, we are your family."

She sounds sincere, but at the moment Peter feels too lost to respond. Atta understands this as well.

She gently pats him on the back, "I hear you".

When she heads for the kitchen she nudges Gran-D, who's just outside the room, to go in with some of his magic.

Gran-D comes in and sits down by the fire. He lights a pipe and watches Peter stare out the window.

After a bit, "What do you see in those stars?"

Without turning, "A brother... very far away."

"What's the lad's name?" Gran-D asks.

"Devon," says Peter distantly.

"There's the tone of responsibility in your voice... sounds better than anger," notes Gran-D tossing a log on the fire.

Peter, not turning, "I wasn't really angry, just confused. As far as responsibility, it's never been my big thing."

Gran-D smiles, "Responsibility isn't talk. I think you're more responsible than you let on."

Peter turns from the window, "So, you're a magician?"

"Sorcerer," Gran-D proudly corrects.

"What's the difference? You believe in illusions... I believe in carburetors, nuts and bolts, things I can fix... things that make sense." Peter waves around, "This doesn't."

"You believe you're in an illusion?" Gran-D asks.

With a nervous laugh, "I'm a little shy of understanding what I believe I'm in right now."

Gran-D gets up and steps over by Peter, "Did you see anything else in those stars?"

Peter glances back out the window, "How tiny I am."

Gran-D looks out the window with Peter, "They'll do that to you." Still sharing the view, "Multiply all those stars by the largest number you can. That's how many kids are staring into the night sky wondering what's going on with their lives."

Atta stands in the kitchen with the door slightly cracked. She leans against the door jam, smiling as she listens.

Gran-D continues, "Some will change little in their lives and others will change whole worlds."

"All I want to change right now is where I am. My brother and I are blood... all we got is each other. And for now, I have to be the grownup. I can't do that very well from here."

Gran-D knows it's too early for Peter to see the big picture.

"Don't be in too much of a hurry to grow up. We live a lot longer here than you do on your Earth." In an instant Gran-D sees that remark puzzles Peter, "At least, I assume so."

"Why don't you just use that toy and send me home?"

Warm and cuddly time has its limits for Gran-D, "Using that toy is responsibility too. The spell has problems. You'll have to trust me. It will work out... but on our schedule."

Peter responds coldly, "Trust is another of my weak suits."

It's late night at the Dees' and Peter lies in the living room darkness. He stares up at the ceiling, unable to sleep. Somehow he can't shake going over what Gran-D said: 'The spell has problems'. He didn't say it was broken... maybe it's not.

After all, how well does he know these people? It doesn't always work out well, but he's never been the kind to sit around and wait for things to be worked out for him. Why should it be any different on another world? He gets up, dons his jacket and heads outside.

Peter doesn't know this house and he's not sure which is Ramie's window. The last thing he needs is to wake up the redhead shrew. He picks up a small stone and tosses it at an upper window, hoping he's chosen right. It hits with a light tap. Nothing.

It dawns on him that maybe the kid sleeps like Devon, which means it might take a brick. He crosses his fingers and tries another small stone.

Finally Ramie cracks open his window and looks out with sleep in his eyes. Peter waves for him to come down. At first Ramie waves him off but that doesn't deter Peter's insistence. After a couple more stones and waves, Ramie reluctantly nods OK.

A few minutes later he staggers out the front door, still trying to wake up.

A large yawn and then, "What?"

"Kid, I need your help."

With another smaller yawn, "The name's Ramie... Is this going to get me in trouble?"

As if that ever made a difference.

"I don't know, maybe. I still need your help... Ramie."

Ramie ponders this for a second and shrugs, "OK, I'm in."

The two boys stand just outside the Graveyard of Spells. It's a bright moonlit night. Most nights on a planet with three moons are well lit. Both boys seem hesitant to inch into the mist. The Graveyard is eerie enough in the daylight and downright spooky at night.

Ramie says, "Watch out for the green mist."

It's not what Peter wants to hear.

"OK, what's the story with the green mist?"

"I'm pretty sure it's alive."

Ramie explains how on his first trip into the Graveyard, the mist guided him to the pendant. On his second trip to return the spell, though not sure... he thinks the mist laughed at him.

This is all new territory for Peter and it's taking a bit of blind acceptance to get used to it all... but talking fog?

"We'll have to take our chances. Once in there, what are we looking for?" Peter's determined to control his own fate.

"The pillar with Sorcerer's Door carved on it."

Peter looks up at the carvings over the gate and Ramie realizes that even though the newcomer shares a common spoken language, he can't read their written language. He picks up a nearby stick and starts to draw the Spirinese words in the dirt.

Before he can finish, a finger of mist winds its way up the support truss towards the gate's arch. When the tip of the misty finger reaches the signage it spreads over the wording. It clears and the arch now reads, 'Graveyard of Spells' in English.

Ramie turns to Peter, "Told you it was alive."

Both shrug and walk forward into the graveyard. The cold mist stirs around their legs. It feels like no more than fog to Peter. He brushes his hand down through it, creating smoke like curls.

The two stop at the first red stone pillar. The mist is high enough that they have to stroke it away to see the name on the tombstone. The inscription reads 'Night's Ink'. Peter glances at Ramie, who only shakes his head at its meaning.

They proceed deeper into the forest. The stone pillars surrounding them add to the darkness of the night. It's cold and the breeze whistling through the columns makes it feel even colder. Maybe it's just their imagination.

Suddenly the mist grabs the ankles of both boys. Though they struggle, neither can move their feet.

Peter, in a loud whisper, "What's going on?"

Ramie's feet are as firmly held as Peter's, but he is twice as frightened. A cone of mist starts building up around each boy, as if each is being wrapped in a personal cocoon.

The mist builds until it covers their heads - and now two tall green cones sit in a blanket of mist, each boy wiggling in their own cone.

The grip on Peter's ankles releases him and he bursts out of the foggy cone. The mist cascades down, melding with the groundcover.

He gasps for air, reacting more to being enclosed than to the lack of breath. Shaking off the terrifying encounter, Peter looks around. There's no Ramie and no sign of the cone he was captured in.

Peter's alone. He yells out, "Hey, kid, where are you?"

Nothing comes back except a hollow echo.

The mist's ankle grip on Ramie releases in the same manner, but when he erupts out of his cocoon he finds himself back at the front gate. Refusing to be sidetracked, and against his better judgment, Ramie turns and starts back into the forest of tombstones.

The green wall of mist shoots up in front of him. He pauses a second, ducks his head down and charges through the cloudy barrier.

Emerging from the other side, he's back at the front gate again. He turns around and the wall has formed again between him and the interior of the Graveyard.

He tries again. He runs through yards of dense mist only to come out at the gate yet again. The green mist has no intention of letting him back into the forest of pillars.

Ramie yells out, "Peter, the green stuff is not playing fair! I think you're on your own."

Peter doesn't hear Ramie's yell. Since he has no idea what has happened to him, all he can do is try to find the right pillar on his own. From what he has been told, he understands that each pillar is a tombstone for an abandoned spell.

Why they were placed here is beyond him. Maybe none of them work, but then, how did Ramie use it?

Ramie explained on the way to the Graveyard that a dead spell sits atop each pillar. All he has to do is find the one named 'Sorcerer's Door'. Peter has no idea what to do with the pendant after he finds the pillar... but he figures he'll deal with one thing at a time.

Peter approaches a pillar and brushes away enough mist to read the spell's name, 'Cold Lightning'. He wonders what that might conjure up... but he realizes he doesn't want to be here long enough to worry about it so he moves on.

At the next pillar, before he leans over to clear the name, the fog separates on its own. It reveals the sign, 'Three Eyes'... another mystery.

The mist does the same at the next gravestone. This time the name is 'Cave of Darkness'. It's as though the mist is giving him a tour... or playing with him.

Peter can't tell. Fog back on Earth is just fog... it doesn't think and it doesn't play. All he can do is follow the tour until it brings him to the right gravestone.

When Peter comes to the next pillar he stops, but the mist doesn't move away on its own.

"Make up your mind!"

He can't believe he just said that... to fog. When the mist refuses to move from the pillar he reaches down to brush it away. With each swipe of his hand the mist only gets denser. It doesn't seem to want Peter to see the sign.

Before he tries again, a finger of mist rises, tilts up and points towards another column. Peter glances in that direction, but turns back to the column standing before him. The finger points away again, but Peter crosses his arms and defiantly shakes his head.

He's standing in the middle of a graveyard arguing with a puff of smoke, but he knows somehow this is the grave he's looking for. The mist finally relents.

It parts and exposes the sign, 'Sorcerer's Door'. Winning the argument, Peter smiles and feels foolish about having the argument at all.

Peter looks up at the glow atop the pillar. That's where the prize is. Though it's been frustrating, nothing has really caused him harm thus far, so he starts to climb.

Back at the entrance, Ramie tries one more time to sneak into the forest and one more time the mist deposits him back at the front gate. He gives up and plops down in the mist to wait for Peter.

Looking at the mist, "You know any other games?"

Peter climbs towards the top determined to fix his own problems in his own time. The last few feet hearten his spirits, but when he reaches the pinnacle all he finds is an empty energy field. His heart sinks.

The one thing he's seen in this world is that things aren't always as they appear to be. He reaches into the field on the off chance the pendant is invisible.

As his fingers penetrate a couple inches, a sudden bolt of energy zaps him. The charge sends Peter flying off the pillar and plunging towards the ground.

He tries to right himself to break the fall. No luck. Just as he is about to slam into the ground, the mist catches him and softly lowers him the last few feet. He's not sure, but it almost sounds like the mist is laughing.

Gran-D has a little chuckle and blows out the candle beside his bed. He rolls over and goes to sleep.

Chapter Eight

The sun drifts through the living room window onto the sofa where Peter sits. His bedding is folded and neatly stacked next to him. He appears tired. Not much sleep came from thinking all night about the Graveyard.

Why did the mist play with him so? Why did it show him the other spells? Why did it zap him off the pillar only to save him?

He realizes that in such a strange land these questions may never be answered. Neither he nor Ramie was hurt so why rack his brains over such matters? He reminds himself he's getting home... somehow.

Gran-D clears his throat, breaking Peter out of his thoughts. "You boys have fun last night?"

Peter turns to him, knowing somehow the old man already has the answer to that question.

"I told you that you would have to trust and be patient. The spell is in the right hands to resolve problems."

Peter can't hide the frustration in his voice, "What do you expect me to do while the right hands resolve my problems?"

"On such a fine day, enjoy yourself... and try to learn a few of our ways."

Peter quips, "If Ramie promises not to get lost this time."

Gran-D offers a smile that hints of a hidden surprise lurking behind it, "Just wait outside. It's a glorious day."

The old man is right about one thing. It is a fine day. Peter stands by the Dees' front fence staring out over Spirin.

It's spring and it is as pretty a view as he has ever seen in Oregon, though he is still trying to get used to the unusual colors. His gaze follows a flock of lime green birds as they pass by lavender clouds.

The front door opens behind him and Peter turns expecting to see Ramie coming out. Instead, a sour-faced Shan comes out and walks by him mumbling to herself.

She stops just on the other side of the fence. As if her mood hasn't already been established, she kicks at the dirt with a few more choice unrecognizable words. Peter wisely decides to let her open the conversation.

Without turning, Shan says, "Hear you and my idiot brother had an outing last night."

"Everyone know about everything that happens here?"

Shan snaps around, "Only when it messes with my day." She shakes her head. "Gran-D dumped showing you the ropes on me, before the Rockhead gets you in more trouble."

It seems to Peter that every time he and Shan get together there's friction.

"Look, if this is a problem..."

She cuts him off, "You don't add up to being a problem. I just don't need another little brother to watch out for."

Peter laughs, "I know the feeling. I promise not to be your little brother."

His words cause a slight smile to escape Shan - which irritates her even more. After letting out a resigned sigh, she motions for Peter to come around the fence. She waits till he's fully around to put on her figure-of-authority look.

"First thing we start with is you learning to generate a hoverboard."

She snaps her fingers and hers instantly forms.

Peter shakes his head 'no'.

"I'll just ride along with you. I'm not going to be around long enough to learn all this hocus-pocus stuff."

In truth, Peter doesn't think he's suited for magic after he let a puff of smoke fool with him last night. Down deep he's also a little frightened of getting too comfortable here. He wants to keep the mindset of getting home.

Shan has a simple answer, "Learn... or walk."

"I'll walk," Peter responds coldly. They share a common stubborn streak.

She gets on her board and points down the path, "It's that way."

With that, she takes off, leaving him in the dust. He watches for her to turn back. She doesn't.

Peter starts walking, half regretting his stubbornness.

Gran-D and Kalish peer out the kitchen window as Peter heads off down the path.

Kalish, sounding concerned, "You sure she's going to be OK with him? There's an awful lot of friction between them."

Gran-D, with his usual flair, "She'll be fine. Where there's friction, there's fire. They'll be great."

"I was afraid you'd say something like that."

Peter shuffles along the path wondering how far he'll have to go to catch up with Shan. He's thinking maybe he should have just gone back in the house.

It's a nice day for a stroll, but he has no idea where he's going or how long it will take to get there. For that matter, he doesn't know why he's even going.

As contrary as that girl is, he still finds something fascinating about her... What exactly, he's not sure of yet.

The purple-leafed trees flanking the path remind Peter of Oregon Ash, except for the colors. It's funny how memories come up. Peter remembers his father told him how the Oregon Ash was used to make his favorite baseball bats.

A brief glancing memory of childhood and he casts it off as he usually did with such thoughts.

It was long ago when his parents died and left him and Devon to the mercies of Social Services. Peter finds no comfort thinking about family. He trusts more in things he thinks he can control right in front of his face.

Some of the foster homes weren't that bad, but they weren't family. They were always temporary. He had honed himself at not trusting in many. He only felt safe dealing with what's at the next corner.

Now he's stuck in a world where what's in front of his face are illusions... and he can't even see the next corner.

Peter turns a bend in the path and sees Shan sitting on a rock in the distance. She's leaning against one of those purple trees... and not smiling. He straightens up as he walks towards her, trying not to appear even slightly tired.

As he reaches her, "Not waiting on me, are you?"

Rather curtly, "We could have been to Klavedar three times by now." By Klavedar, Shan means the largest village in the realm.

She notices Peter, despite trying to hide it, is a little short of breath, "And you'd have all your wind."

She calmly waits for Peter to wave the white flag but he remains stubborn.

Shan conjures her board, gets on and takes off. As she flies away he lets out an exhausted breath. He truly wishes she would stop but can't bring himself to say so. Taking another deep breath, he starts to walk again.

Down the path she stops, grits her teeth and turns back.

She yells, "OK. Get on."

Peter lets out a sigh of relief. As he approaches he can hear her mumbling something under her breath and knows better than to ask what. She gives nothing but a head nod for him to get on the back, figuring she's given in enough.

As he steps up behind her, he utters a soft, "Thanks."

The board is small so when he gets on they're almost spooning. It feels different than getting on behind Ramie. Shan notices it as well and snaps her fingers. The board doubles in size.

Glancing over her shoulder, "Now you have plenty of room to back up."

Her tone makes it clear this is more than a request.

Shan whips along the path with Peter riding behind her. When she banks hard at one sharp turn, Peter grabs hold of her to keep his balance. This doesn't sit well with Shan.

She yells back to Peter, "Here's another trick you should know."

She nods at her board. It splits in two like an amoeba separating, leaving Peter wobbling alone on the back half.

Dense hedges appear at the next bend and an anticipatory smile comes to Shan's face as Peter wobbles directly towards them. At the last second, he swoops up into a half-roll and avoids the collision. He comes out of the roll beside her, "Neat trick, wrong guy."

This infuriates Shan but she's not about to give him the satisfaction of responding. She speeds up. Her only consolation is she at least got him riding on a hoverboard.

As they float along Peter pulls up beside Shan, "You've slapped me, zapped me and tried to crash me... I thought you said no one hurts anyone here."

This hits home. She brings her board to a sudden halt. This is one of those rare moments that Shan doesn't have a quick comeback. She has to think about it - it couldn't be some stupid behavior masking an attraction to this alien boy. She concludes it's not - she's too sharp for adolescent games like that.

There's something else about him, as if in some way he threatens her world. It's driving her a little nuts that she can't simply put a finger on it.

Peter watches the gears turning in her head.

Finally he says, "Were you going to say something?" He adds, "You know, you don't have to."

After all her thought on the matter she turns to him with an appreciative look, "No." She forces a smile, "I'll try not to do it again... I mean doing stuff to you."

She floats away down the path. A moment later, she glances back and waves for him to follow.

Klavedar is a large medieval-style village. It could be loosely called a very spread-out city since it's the largest village in Spirin. There are no high-rises. It just covers a great deal of area. Though large, it retains an intimate feel with a good number of neighborhood town squares.

Peter floats along behind Shan, still somewhat wobbly. As they come to the edge of Klavedar, she lets her board settle to the ground and takes to foot.

He follows suit and asks, "What are we doing here?"

Shan holds out her hands and two big baskets materialize in them.

As she hands both of them to Peter, she says, "Shopping."

Getting over amazement at the magically formed baskets, it quickly dawns on Peter that he's the beast of burden.

Many of the buildings they pass are pyramid-shaped, some-what like the Dees' house. Some are large and some not so large. All are colorfully decorated in the full spectrum of colors. Peter's eyes dart all over as they walk towards a village square.

Shan catches this and snaps "Keep up."

The square is filled with vendors floating their bright wares. Peter stops at one stand that has what resembles Peking duck suspended mid-air. He reaches out to touch one, but before his finger comes near, the duck snaps at it.

Peter jerks his hand back, "Whoa, I thought it was dead!"

The vendor, a little old lady, warns, "It is, but it has excellent afterlife reflexes."

Peter doesn't know how to respond to this so he just nods in bewilderment.

Walking away he mumbles, "How do you eat it?"

He thinks he is speaking to himself but he hears the old woman laugh behind him.

"Very carefully," she cackles as he looks back.

Shan takes his arm to keep him moving forward.

One thing Peter notices, with some discomfort, is that many people they pass silently critique his ears.

He taps Shan, "Is anyone going to tell me what's with the ear thing?"

"Don't pay any attention," she continues walking.

They pass by a vendor selling beautiful scarves and Shan pause to look at one.

Peter leans over her shoulder, "Something you like?"

She breaks off her gaze and moves on.

He shrugs, "Are you ever going to warm to me?"

She glances at him, and then turns back to her business.

"I guess not."

Some time has passed and Peter sits at one of the square's fountains. Shan has deposited him there to watch the supplies she's gathered. He tries not to notice people's continued stares at his ears as they pass.

By now Shan has conjured up a few more baskets for carrying home goods. They sit before him, full of produce and supplies. She finally joins him with one more basket.

He looks at the haul, "How do you pay for all this? I didn't see any money."

"We trade." She says, as though what else could be the answer... why would it be done any other way?

Peter appears a bit puzzled.

She adds, "My father is a builder, so when I get something there's an understanding that someday he will build something for that person or for the community in trade. What's money?"

"What if you don't have anything to trade?" Peter asks.

"Everyone has something they can trade, some skill."

He's still appears a little baffled.

"It's just the way we do things here, get used to it."

It dawns on her that she something, "Wait here, I'll be right back."

Peter nods. He looks down at the pile of baskets, thinking about who's going to be carrying this stuff home.

He looks up, "Wait a minute, I need to get something."

Shan is already out of range. He glances back at their booty and assumes that in this hippy society, nobody will mess with their things. He heads off.

Peter stands at the scarf booth and picks out the one Shan admired. He's not really sure how to buy it. He reaches in his jeans to see if he has anything that might be of value in this world. The hulk of a man behind the scarves is not very good at hiding his interest in Peter's ears.

Peter pulls out a lighter, trying to ignore the ear thing. He sparks a flame and offers the lighter as payment. The man chuckles and lifts his finger. A small flame appears on its tip.

"Keep the scarf. I'll be happy to say I gave one to a round ear." He chuckles, "It's really not your color."

"I take it you won't tell me about the ears."

The man just smiles and shakes his head 'no'. Before Peter leaves the man says, "Ask your family."

"I don't have any... here." As Peter walks away he turns back, "If you ever invent a motorcycle I'll be happy to fix it, but I'm only in town for a while."

The man nods with a smile at Peter's offer, even though he has no idea what a motorcycle is.

Peter gets back before Shan. She joins him a couple minutes later and hands Peter a folded parchment.

"Thought you might need this. It's a map of Spirin."

Peter glances at the map and tries to sound like he appreciates it, "Thanks, but you shouldn't have. I'm not going to be around long enough to..."

She cuts him off with a wave of her hand and a surly response, "Oh, I forgot, you're just passing through."

Shan can't believe her words have come out that way. It sounds way too childish for her.

A little embarrassed she snaps, "Time to go."

As they swoosh out of Klavedar, Peter sees he's right about one thing - he is the mule! He has a pack on his back with stalks of produce jutting out and four baskets on his arms. Shan carries one.

She looks back at him wobbling from side to side with the load, "That will help you learn how to balance on the board."

He gives her a 'sure' nod and tries to regain his balance.

After a while Peter seems to be getting the hang of flying on the board. Maybe she was right.

He struggles to use a couple of free fingers and pulls the scarf out of his shirt. With his basket-draped arm, he holds the scarf out to her.

Shan sees the very scarf she admired dangling between Peter's fingers, "What's that for?"

"A peace offering," he says.

She cautiously accepts it. He can see she's not sure how to react. To save her discomfort he hovers on down the path.

As they float home Shan every so often sneaks a peek at her new scarf.

Chapter Nine

I t's evening at the Dees'. Kalish and Ramie help Atta in the kitchen. Peter watches the sunset outside and Gran-D sits in his favorite chair by the fire. Shan comes in and glances all around to make sure he's alone. Then she sits down by her grandfather.

She remains quiet till Gran-D tires of waiting for a question, "What's on your mind, child?"

Shan hems and haws because she's not quite sure how to put it. Gran-D gives her one of his 'out with it' looks.

She blurts out accusingly, "He learns too fast!"

Gran-D laughs. Sometimes he irritates Shan. This is one of those times.

She snaps, "No one learns that fast!"

He pats her on the knee, "Don't you mean, 'No one from our world learns that fast?'"

"You mean people from his world are smarter than we are?"

"By no means, child. Sorcery is just an interaction with nature. Maybe his mind interacts with our nature well, or..."

Gran-D's answers often end with a puzzle so Shan waits for his next shoe to drop.

"Or it could just be ignorance... Sometimes knowing your limitations are your limitations."

Shan rolls her eyes at this. Exasperated, "You mean he learns fast because he's too stupid not to?"

Gran-D gives her another irritating smile.

She's not going to play into this so she switches tactics, "Does this have anything to do with the Prophecy?"

Gran-D pauses a moment, letting her feel he is taking her question seriously. It never helps to let the young think their queries are frivolous.

Then he says, "I think not. After all, the Prophecy speaks of two round ears and they come of their own choosing." He adds, "For the present, I think we should keep this between us. OK?"

"As you wish," but she can't leave it at that. "Well, I don't think I like him anyway."

"Awful lot of thought about someone you don't like."

Shan tromps out of the room, now certain that she's sorry she brought it up in the first place.

All are gathered around the dinner table. Peter looks at what's on his plate, wondering if it has excellent afterlife reflexes.

Gran-D leans into him with, "It won't bite."

Peter now wonders how the old man knew what he was thinking.

"Shan said you took to the hoverboard pretty well today."

Shan grimaces at the comment.

Compliments have always made Peter a bit uncomfortable. He sees Shan squirm at the statement so he tries to deflect it.

"Well, she's a good teacher."

This causes her to blush in spite of her best effort not to. It doesn't help that everyone at the table notices.

Once more to the rescue, Peter changes the subject, "Those trees along the path looked a lot like ones we have at home, except for the color. We use them to make some of our best baseball bats."

Ramie chimes in, "What's baseball?"

"A game we play on Earth with a ball and bat."

"We play Orb here. It uses sort of balls, but no bats," Ramie says enthusiastically.

Kalish appreciates what Peter has tried to do. He's not oblivious to Shan's sensitivity.

"If Peter is able to ride a board, maybe the two of you should take him out and show him how to play... granted you all stay away from the Graveyard."

Ramie perks up like a puppy. He's more than happy to. Shan knows she would enjoy it too, but she's not going to be so openly enthusiastic.

"It will help him learn to use the hoverboard better."

"Settled. I've got a separate room to build for Shan tomorrow and it'll keep you all out from under foot. When you get home, Peter, you'll move up to the loft with Ramie."

A polite smile is all Peter can manage. Kalish's words cause an echo in his head, 'I'm not home... I'm not home.'

The three kids stand in a meadow. Shan and Peter are already at it. Peter explains, "I'm not a sorcerer. What makes you think I can create a board?"

"Because you rode one all day yesterday," snaps Shan.

"Devon and I were always good with skateboards and I'm not bad with a motorcycle. Just because I can ride, doesn't mean I can do magic."

Peter is not simply being stubborn. He really believes this. He also knows maybe - hidden behind his belief - is fear that he may be good at it.

Shan puts her hands on her hips, "I made the board, but you held it together in your mind. Like it or not - and I'm not sure I do - you already have the powers of sorcery."

She stands firm on the matter.

Peter caves, "OK. What do I have to do?"

"Imagine your board in this world and let it form."

Shan makes it sound so simple that Peter thinks maybe it is. Peter scrunches up his face for imagining and Shan laughs. He snaps her a glare and she uses her hand to wipe the grin off her face. Then she laughs again.

"That supposed to be motivation?"

He scrunches up his face once more, trying to ignore Shan's antics.

With all his will he thinks about a board, but perhaps a little too much Earth slips in. A board generates in front of him... a fence board!

This time it's Ramie who falls down laughing. The fence board disappears.

The one thing he realizes is that if he can create a fence board, though it is of little use, he can probably create any board. This excites and frightens him.

He knows he has a lot of mental baggage about magicians, sorcerers or witches. He tries to set this aside and makes another attempt.

This time a hoverboard appears, floating six inches off the ground.

Both Shan and Ramie clap. But when Peter steps on the board, his foot goes through it as if it were the mist in the Graveyard. He looks dumbfounded at Shan.

Peter is now her student and she lets go her reservations about him being an alien.

"Not to worry. For some reason you're having a hard time accepting that you created it." She can't help a little dig, "But trust me, it flies better with you on it then in it... sorry," she adds.

He creates another board. This time he peers at Shan's eyes to remain focused and then steps up on the board. It holds him.

Ramie, with an impatient tone, "OK, can we play orb now?"

Peter nods his 'thanks' to Shan and swooshes away to make sure the board works. As he test-flies it, his mind rushes with what all this might mean. At least here on Spirin, he is a sorcerer! He likes the thought.

Fast-paced footsteps echo down a barren cold hallway of the Dark Fortress. Witch Racinda and her new assistant, Rupert, head briskly towards the Grand Hall where she's been summoned. She walks quickly because Lord Kildemar has no tolerance for waiting. Rupert walks quickly to keep up.

Out of breath, Rupert asks, "Why are we rushing?"

"We rush to keep our heads."

"Surely Lord Kildemar would never harm you. You're far too valuable to him."

"I know that. He may not. Now hurry along."

Witch Racinda served the father of the Lord Kildemar. He did value her service - all the way up until his death at the hands of his son.

Things change with changes of regime. The present Lord is power hungry and paranoid, a dangerous mix. Racinda has no illusions about this. Behind every summons lurks the possibility of an inflamed temper, even death.

Witch Racinda enters the Grand Hall, unaware of whether this summons is a whim or serious. Lord Kildemar sits flanked by his personal guards and sons. She was able to read the room with Kildemar's father in charge, but the current court is too volatile to read. Her assumptions could prove painful.

The Dark Lord becomes aware of her presence, "It took you long enough, old woman."

Racinda simply nods, knowing an argument would be futile. "Of what service can I be, sire?"

Racinda often thinks the Lord really does know her value. After all, she's the only person in Goreipor with magical powers. His manner may just be his misguided way of keeping people in line.

Then she reminds herself, assumptions are dangerous. He has threatened to take off her head so often that she's become almost numb to it.

"Have you sensed any further activity from the door?"

The Lord thinks he's vanquished his enemies from this other distant world but, as always, he's far from content. Mistrust is engrained in him.

This feels like a 'whim' call and Witch Racinda breathes easier.

She points out to the Lord, "There is a fair chance the pendant that controls the Door was destroyed on the distant planet, my Lord."

She hopes this is enough to ease his paranoia. It's not.

"I'm aware you served my father and, with his death, I inherited you... and your history. That means I'm aware that at least two pendants exist because one was stolen from Goreipor. There are possibly even more, so don't try to appease me with your speculations."

She bows with a nod of submission.

He goes on, "Since you are responsible for the loss of our pendant, you will devise a way to find it again. Understood?"

This request is ridiculous but she is not about to say so. Trying to sound sincere, "I will do my best, sire."

She starts backing out, hoping he will not have any more to say. Only when she makes the door can she sigh a breath of relief. Maybe he will let the order slide - probably not.

With Racinda gone, Lord Kildemar turns to Janick, "Have Captain Pirus increase the patrols of our Eastern border. That nasty tale of my father's of a Prophecy may hold some truth and I will not tolerate outside threats."

"Father, there has been no activity along our..."

His father's sudden glare stops him mid-sentence. He says no more lest he face harsher wrath.

Kildemar turns to Taligarr, "Keep a watchful eye on the witch."

Taligarr is more in tune with how to react around their father. He nods with a sincere understanding though he has no idea what his father wants him to watch for.

Chapter Ten

It's been half a moon since Peter first arrived on Spirin. Though he's often asked about it, he is no closer to knowing where things stand with repairs of the Sorcerer's Door. He fears he's become complacent about pushing against a boulder that doesn't want to move, but he fears it less each day. Sometimes he realizes this, but not today.

He and Shan are heading into Klavedar on hoverboards. Just before they enter the village, Peter does a 360° loop in the air.

Shan turns back to him, "Quit showing off."

Peter lowers to the ground with a smile.

"Use it or lose it."

"No. It's called showing off."

Today is another supply run. Peter thinks he's capable of handling part of the shopping and Shan lets him get some of the items on his own.

People's silent interest in his ears still bothers him a little, but he figures why worry... no one will tell him about it anyway. It's as though the truth of his ears is something buried long ago in the Graveyard. On occasion it's an irritating secret, but most of the time he just turns a blind eye.

Peter swings by a booth displaying new Orbs, though it's not on the shopping list. He's gotten pretty good at handling an Orb and wants to test out a few.

Peter takes a bright red one, sends it out and wills it back like doing a wide arc loop-to-loop with a yo-yo... without a string.

He turns to the elderly woman in the booth, "It's got a nice balance. How much is the trade?"

With a big smile she hands the Orb to Peter, "Alien boy, you haven't got the hang of trading yet. It's not about an amount. It's just about a commitment. How do I know what I need in trade today?"

What the woman said is logical though he really doesn't understand it. It's just another thing coming up to remind him he actually doesn't belong here... no matter how well he can create or ride a hoverboard.

"I'm sorry... I..."

She cuts him off, "With time you'll learn." She hands him the red Orb, "I want the first round ear in our land to have it."

As Peter looks like he's going to ask, she holds up a finger and waggles a 'no'. Peter shakes his head, smiles and accepts the Orb graciously. Other things are on his mind now. All that echoes in his head is the 'with time' part.

Shan can tell Peter's less upbeat when he rejoins her at the village square. In addition to his lack of a smile, also missing are the goods he was supposed to get.

"What happened to you? Where are the things on your list?"

It's clear something is wrong.

Taking a seat at the fountain Peter quietly says, "Sorry, this isn't me."

He looks at the baskets she's gathered, "I can wait here while you get the rest."

The relationship between the two is usually prickly, but Shan senses that now's not the time for it to be so.

"We have enough for this trip. Let's get going."

Peter nods at this and starts to gather up the items Shan has purchased. He's being unusually quiet, not even a complaint about being the mule.

As they're about to head out, a seventeen-year old boy named Yadar approaches. Even from a distance Peter knows the type - a smart-ass bully is his bet. Seeing Yadar coming over, Shan grimaces and shakes her head.

Peter leans in, "What's his story?"

"Just leave him to me. He's..."

Before she can say any more, Yadar is in front of them.

Yadar looks at Peter's ears... first the left, then the right.

"So this is the odd one. He doesn't look like much of a Prophecy to me." Getting no reaction, he adds with a nasty tone, "Doesn't look like much at all. What spell dropped you here?"

Peter can already see the outcome of this situation and braces to get in Yadar's face. Shan steps in between them.

She says, with a biting glare, "What do you mean by 'odd one'?"

Yadar steps back a pace, "How would you like to be a Grimick for a couple dashes?"

He raises his hand as if he were going to cast a spell.

Without warning, Peter disappears and reappears in front of Shan... face to face with Yadar, puffed up and ready for action. Shan staggers back, startled by the move.

So is Yadar. He jerks back and, perhaps out of reflex, raises his other hand. Yadar's not the only one who has reflexes. Peter is running on pure instinct, with a touch of adrenaline. He swings a right hook to Yadar's nose and sends the boy flying.

Yadar lands on the ground with a thud. He feels at his nose and is stunned when he sees blood on his hand. Shocked, he stares up at Peter as though this was his first fight.

Peter shrugs with a triumphant smile. None of this surprises Peter... it's exactly what he intended. What surprises him is Shan.

She grabs his arm and pulls him back, "What did you do?"

"Struck first... before he did."

Peter looks pleased with himself since the little scuffle is resolved so quickly... and in his favor.

All the Spirinese in the village seem to be aghast at this tiny drama. They move in closer, but cautious to stay clear of Peter. All mumble in disbelief as if they had never seen such a thing. Looks range from curiosity and horror.

Peter scans the crowd, completely puzzled by all the commotion. After all it was just a squabble.

"I don't get it. What's the big deal?"

Shan looks like she could die of embarrassment on the spot. She reaches down and tries to help Yadar up. Others rush to assist.

She looks up towards Peter, "He wouldn't do that. We don't hit each other on Spirin!"

"You're joking... No one gets into fights? Ever?"

She snaps, "Never!"

She goes back to helping Yadar.

As the others stand around she turns to them, almost in tears, "I'm sorry, he doesn't know our ways."

She breaks it off because she doesn't know what else to say. Everyone continues to stare accusingly at Peter.

He feels as though he has just shot someone. He has yet to adjust to the ear thing. This new accusation in everyone's eyes is too much for him. Peter grabs some of Shan's baskets and storms away.

Once Yadar is safely on his feet, though still in too much shock to say anything, Shan grabs the remainder of the baskets and heads out after Peter.

Zipping along the path, Shan tries to figure what she's going to say to Peter once she catches him. She feels guilty because he's just a newcomer, but what he did to Yadar is so alien to Spirin. If anything could bring home the idea that Peter is truly alien, this is it.

As Shan swoops around a bend, she sees Peter sitting on a rock. The baskets he took lie on the ground nearby, half spilled. Shan comes to ground and walks the last distance. She racks her brain at how to handle this.

Even though violence is not part of this world in any sense, she realizes he was trying to defend her. How does she tell him defending her like that was wrong? Does she truly believe his attempt was wrong? Of course it was, but that answer nags at her.

When she reaches him, it's clear Peter is distraught.

He looks up before she formulates what to say.

"Is the boy OK?"

Shan takes a deep breath and nods 'yes'. Then she sits down beside him. They both remain quiet for a few moments.

Shan breaks the silence, "I'm sorry, you don't know our ways and I forgot that."

Admonishing him further would be contrary to what she just said.

"You weren't kidding. Nobody here fights?"

"We tease, we argue, but we never harm each other."

This seems so natural to her. The thought comes up that it seems natural because she knows no different. It's still beyond her why people would fight.

"On your world, do you fight a lot?"

"Me, personally? Or everyone?"

This comment distresses her even more. "Either?"

"On my world, dads... well, not mine... but most, tell their sons not to get into fights."

"What do you mean? Yours didn't?"

"I lost my parents a long time ago. Even if they had been around, boys get into fights. Nothing serious. It's just part of growing up."

"Sorry."

"As far as Earth goes, we probably fight too much."

He sees Shan is trying to understand something that clearly makes no sense to her.

"Sometimes we have to fight for good reasons. The big problem is what are actually good reasons and who gets to decide what those reasons are. Everyone thinks they're right and too often they're wrong."

"What do your people think a good reason is?"

He searches for a good answer. Though it's not something that Peter reflects on a great deal, he has little trust in the sanity of people in his own world... at least, not those in charge.

Trying to explain why mankind, as a whole, fights is much more complicated than explaining why he might fight. He also has a gut feeling that if tries to justify the amount of violence of Earth he may scare the hell out of her.

He decides to stay on the personal level. How many on Earth fight, as a whole, would scare the hell out of her if a little fist fight affected her so much.

"I can only speak for me. I defend my blood, my brother. I have to admit, sometimes it's simply because I get angry, but not that much. Don't your people ever have to defend themselves?"

"From whom?" Shan answers as if it were an odd question.

"I don't know. Other villages... other lands... whoever might threaten you... Enemies."

Peter is trying to use the right words.

For Shan this still makes little sense, "We don't have any ene-mies, never have."

In an odd way the conversation allows Peter to feel a little better about the day. Normally he and Shan are adversaries. This is a rare time that they are just talking.

With a slight chuckle, "I've landed in a world of hippies."

Shan's expression shows she has no idea what he's talking about, but she appears to be glad he's begun to lighten things up.

Peter looks up, "Wait a minute. You hit me when I got here."

She bites her lip, then, "That's different, you're not from here... and I really wasn't trying to hurt you."

Shan knows that sounds like a feeble excuse but it's all she can come up with for the moment.

"So it's not that you don't defend yourselves. It's just if you find a reason, you choose to do it?"

From his tone she can tell he's not after a gotcha moment. A sincere question deserves a sincere answer.

After thinking about it a second, "You're right, we've never had the need. I don't know what we would do if we ever had the need."

"And what about me?"

"I didn't exactly hurt you... No, you've got a point."

She's been wrestling with the friction she's had with Peter from the start. It's something more than childishness, but she can't put a finger on it. Somehow she knows that he threatens her world somehow.

She settles for, "I don't know what that was about. I'll let you know when I do."

"Good enough."

Changing the subject, "In the village, how did you do that?"

"Do what?" he responds.

"The disappearing thing? What else."

"I thought I had to move fast and so I did. How the hell do I know how I do things? They just happen."

He's not being modest. He doesn't know how he does half the things he does in this crazy land. It actually scares him that this hocus-pocus stuff comes so naturally to him.

Shan's pleased that Peter's moodiness from before seems to have lifted a bit. But his answer only further sparks her interest. It's not something she can discuss with Peter at the present. She's sure it is something she first needs to talk with Gran-D about.

Getting up, "Time we get home."

Being one of the few occasions Peter has had more of a heart-to-heart with Shan, he decides to push a little further, "I may not get an answer but I have to ask. The kid in the village brought up the ears thing again... and a Prophecy."

Shan appears uncomfortable, but he continues, "Why won't anyone tell me about anything? Now, in addition to the ears, there's some kind of Prophecy that has to do with me. What's up with it all?"

A lot has happened today and Shan figures she owes him a little, "After we get this stuff home, there's something that I want to show you."

Peter smiles at the slightest hint that he might get some answers.

"By the way, what's a Grimick anyway?"

Shan laughs slightly, "You don't want to know."

Chapter Eleven

It's late afternoon when Peter and Shan fly over a hill next to the wall between Spirin and the Land of Goreipor. As they crest the bluff, Peter comes to a sudden halt. He has heard vaguely about the Wall before, but now that it is in front of him it's way beyond his expectations.

The wall is a mirror that stretches from the ground to the clouds and as far to the North and to the South as Peter can see. The reflection in the mirror makes Spirin appear to go on forever but, like many things in Spirin, this is an illusion. Where there's a wall there must be something on the other side of it.

Peter sees his and Shan's reflections in the wall.

He turns to her, "You said there was a wall, but this is so…"

"Isn't it?" Shan says, pleased by it's effect on him.

Then she notices Gran-D sitting on a stone by the Obelisk near the wall far below. Almost to herself, "Wonder what he's doing here."

They float down to Gran-D. Peter can hardly keep track of where he's going because he can't take his eyes off the wall.

As soon as they arrive where Gran-D patiently waits, the first thing out of Peter's mouth is, "Can I go touch it?"

Gran-D smiles, "Everything that is should be touchable."

While Peter walks to the wall, Shan plops down next to her grandfather.

"What brings you here?"

"Thought there might be questions. I got wind of what happened in the village and that Peter heard of the Prophecy. I figured he would be plying you for answers."

"Does anything escape you?"

She already knows the answer to this. Shan's happy he's here because she doesn't want to even try to explain something like the Prophecy to Peter. Actually, she doesn't know enough about it to explain it with any certainty at all. All she knows are the rumors that many in the Land of Spirin only vaguely remember... ancient rumors.

Peter examines the wall. At first he just stares at his reflection. It almost has a life of its own. Then he brushes the wall with his hand. Its surface is soft and pliable, like a living membrane. He leans in and places the side of his head and both his hands against it. He tries to listen and presses in as though merging with the wall.

Suddenly he recoils!

His stares at it, less reverently now... more filled with fear. Peter's not the type to be frightened easily, especially without understanding what frightens him.

He backs away a few more feet but can't take his eyes away, trying to see into his own reflection.

After a few moments of silence from Shan, Gran-D says, "There's something new on your mind, isn't there?"

She states with concern, "He became invisible today. I'm skilled and I can't do that. Very few can."

Gran-D thinks for a second and addresses her concern, "I knew he'd have powers, but not how quickly they would grow. And, child, about being invisible, maybe you just think you know you can't."

She frowns at this, knowing nothing from Gran-D is ever a straight answer. There's always a little puzzle in there somewhere.

Gran-D cuts their conversation off as he sees Peter heading back up to join them, "If you don't mind, I think I should talk with Peter alone for a bit."

She looks a little hurt, but nods, knowing Gran-D must have his reasons. She gets on her board and to save face says, "Good. Then he won't be bugging me with more questions."

Peter arrives just as Shan is away. "Where's she off to?"

Gran-D shrugs, "She got a tug from Atta. I have something else to talk with you about. Take a seat."

Peter is filled with so many questions he's happy to sit.

The first thing he has to get out, "What's beyond that wall is scary. Beats me what it is or how I know it... but I do."

Gran-D smiles, "Then it's a good thing someone put a wall right there." After this light dismissal, "Shan says that's not the only thing you're puzzled about not knowing. Seems you have quite a knack for our sorcery."

Peter's never been big on people talking behind his back and his response comes out a bit curtly, "All I really want to know is how to go home. I mean my home... Earth. Can you tell me that?"

"Only that there is still a problem with the spell, but something I have in mind may be a solution."

Now Peter is all ears.

The old man continues, "Here in Spirin we have a group of Masters who, in special cases, teach a level of sorcery that few of us ever know. I think you might be one of those special cases, if you are interested."

Peter thought he is finally going to find out about his ears... or maybe about the Prophecy... or maybe even about the spell that landed him here. The last thing he expects to talk about is schooling. This is a subject that didn't interest him back on Earth, much less so here.

The day's experiences in the village still weigh on him, "Look, Gran-D, I think it's better for all of us if I just hang low-key till you guys find me a way home."

"Whatever that means... better for whom?"

"Why would I want to study magic anyway?" Seeing Gran-D frown, he corrects himself, "OK, sorcery. I've learned a few tricks Shan showed me to get by while I'm here, that's all. And, with what little I've learned, I still manage to offend people."

"Going to let a bruised ego send you to a dark corner? Think about it... the more you know the less you will stumble. The more you know... the more you can get done."

There's something in his tone that's trying to prod Peter.

Gran-D remains quiet as Peter connects the dots. A light clicks in Peter's head when he finishes maneuvering this maze.

"These Masters... do they know the sorcery that's needed to work with... I mean, work on spells?"

"They're the only ones who do."

"OK, I'm in."

"Question is... do they want you in?" Gran-D pauses briefly to let Peter's desire grow. Then, "I'll set up a meeting."

With this, Gran-D starts to get up.

"Someone mentioned a Prophecy in connection with my ears. What's that about?"

Peter doesn't really expect to get a straight answer... but nothing ventured, nothing gained.

Gran-D pauses and sits back down. He gestures towards the Obelisk that sits near them, "There's the Prophecy."

Bewildered, Peter looks at the large pinnacle-shaped stone. On the smooth surface of the stone are etched many symbols.

Even from Peter's limited experience in Spirin, he can tell they are not Spirinese words.

"So, what is it?"

Gran-D says, "What it is... is very old. There's one at each of our borders. What is written on it is..."

While Gran-D speaks Peter reaches toward the stone's surface. As his hand gets close, the stone starts to vibrate and the letters glow slightly. He pulls his hand back and it stops.

Gran-D suddenly stops. Now it's he that is puzzled.

"Interesting. Peter, do that again."

Peter looks at him with an 'are you sure' expression and reaches out toward the Obelisk once more. The stone vibrates and the letters glow even stronger this time.

He turns to Gran-D, "You going to explain what's going on?"

Gran-D seems a little distant in thought as he stares at the Obelisk.

After a second to refocus, "Not at the moment. Please keep this between us... including what you felt about what is beyond the wall."

"But?" says Peter.

Gran-D goes distant again. It's clear to Peter that the conversation is over. As usual with this old man, Peter ends up with more questions than answers.

Resigned to this, he finally says, "You heading home?"

"Not just yet, go on without me."

A bit frustrated, Peter conjures his board and flies away.

As soon as he's out of sight, Gran-D stands up. He raises his cane to the Obelisk. As if it were a paint sprayer, a green mist comes from the cane's tip and washes over the Obelisk.

It coats the stone with a gray layer that neutralizes it - no more vibrations, no more letters. Best to keep these secrets secret... at least until he can figure out what they might mean.

Chapter Twelve

A lone man, tall and thin, darts around the black jagged rocks of a canyon. He wears soft, off-white clothes that don't blend with these dark surroundings. His ears have the bottom curl of a Spirinese. A wound in his side stains his shirt blood red.

Around his neck hangs the pendant Ramie used to bring Peter to Spirin, but weakness owing to the wound greatly limits his powers of sorcery. This is Master Carringer.

Carringer keeps glancing over his shoulder as he staggers from rock to rock. The sounds of men pursuing him echo from the canyon walls, adding to his confusion. The moonlight plays tricks with shadows amid the jagged outcroppings.

Leather-hard, heavily armed soldiers are in chase through the canyons. They yell as if driving their prey on. There are a few soldiers in each finger of the canyon, all pushing him forward towards a clearing.

His journey is thwarted. All Carringer is trying to do is find a clear path home with his hide intact, but they're on his heels and he's had little chance to rest.

He freezes behind one rock when he sees two soldiers emerge into the clearing ahead. He realizes they've been driving him into a trap.

Panicked, he scans the terrain for another avenue of escape. Nothing! With no recourse left, Carringer starts to climb the steep canyon wall.

The rocks are slick and hard. He struggles with painful effort to work his way up. Pausing at a ledge he frantically fumbles with the pendant. An arrow strikes the rock near his head, setting off sparks.

A soldier below bellows, "Take him alive."

Another soldier starts to climb after Carringer.

Carringer scurries up to another narrow ledge and tries to use the pendant again to create the Door. Nothing happens. The jewel in the middle of the pendant shows no gleam. The climbing soldier gets closer.

Suddenly Carringer realizes he is using the wrong ring. He's been dialing the Door to open from Spirin into Goreipor, but he's in Goreipor! That's why it's not working!

'No time, must go higher,' races through his head.

As he tries to widen the gap between himself and the man that's almost upon him, he slips. Carringer slides down the wall a few feet, almost into his enemy's grasp. His foot catches a lip of stone and he scrambles back up.

All he needs is enough time to redial the spell into the pendant. Fingers shaking, he struggles to turn the two rings. Other soldiers yell from below. Just as the climbing soldier is almost upon him again, the jewel glows. A swirl of white light bursts open in mid-air in front of him.

A moment before, Carringer would have let the swirl reduce in size, but now there's no time... the soldier is inches away. He dives into the light, not knowing if it will take him home or lose him in some void forever.

In a flash, he's gone.

The soldier lets out a scream of anger, "Kaldic Sha!"

The Dees sit around the family dinner table exchanging small talk. Peter's not even aware how he's adapted, it's all happened so naturally. If he were to give it much thought, it would bother him.

"Peter, I hear you saw our wall today," says Kalish. "It's something, isn't it?"

To Kalish it's not, because it has been there all his life, like the air and the clouds. Shan's not the only one who likes seeing Peter's fascination with Spirin.

Gran-D carefully watches Peter from across the table. He suspects the boy will be good to his word about secrecy. He's been wrong before... but not often.

"Yes, sir, it's truly something," says Peter.

He leaves his observations at that, without the slightest hint of anything else that was discussed.

Gran-D is pleased. He clears his throat in his usual manner of saying 'listen up'.

"Shan said Peter's training is going so well that maybe I should introduce him to the Masters."

Shan looks both horrified and embarrassed, "I never said that. I didn't even hint at that!"

"Of course you did, child... in your own way."

Peter is not oblivious to Shan's embarrassment. He's found himself in the same kind of awkward spots in his life.

He chimes in with, "It's just that she's a good teacher... and you, Gran-D, put words in people's mouths."

From Shan's look, it's clear she appreciates his attempt to support her.

Atta is overjoyed, "Peter, you know how much of an honor this would be... for you and our whole family."

By Peter's expression he doesn't see as much importance in this as they do, "Well, I figure it's a way of helping me to get home."

From Kalish's look, Peter immediately realizes how his words must have sounded to Atta. Unfortunately he has already shoved his foot in his mouth.

"I mean... What I mean is... You've all been nice to me and I do appreciate it... honest. But, as nice as it is here, I can't forget my brother back home."

Atta is the first to want to get him off the hook, "Peter, not to worry. We understand. But when you think of the word home, please realize you can have two families."

Not wanting to dig a bigger hole, Peter just nods.

Suddenly Gran-D stiffens and glances around. He jumps up and without a word rushes out the front door, forgetting his cane and customary old man posture.

An exasperated Atta says, "Now, what was that about?"

Kalish shakes his head, "He's your father."

Carringer lies against a tree panting and staring at his own reflection in the mirror wall. His clothes are torn, smudged and bloody. A distorted circle of dark ripples radiate from a point next to his reflected image. Carringer's hand still has a white-knuckle grasp on the pendant.

A curling wisp of smoke drifts in and Gran-D appears where it alights. He rushes to Carringer's side. Carringer wants to talk but Gran-D puts a finger to his friend's lips. First things first, he must stop the blood.

Gran-D rips Carringer's shirt open. There's a fair-sized sliver of sharp black stone embedded in his side.

Gran-D places one hand on Carringer's forehead, "This will hurt, old friend."

He pulls the sliver out with a quick jerk. Carringer yelps. Gran-D causes his hand to glow a bright blue and places his glowing palm on the wound. This temporarily seals the wound till Carringer can be gotten to the Healer.

Master Carringer lets out a breath of relief and gasps, "Those men... are not men like us. They... "

Gran-D cuts him off, "You used the Door, didn't you?"

"I had to. When Ramie used the spell it brought back old questions." It's still a strain for Carringer to talk.

Gran-D interjects, "The Spell Masters, your parents, died getting that pendant from those men... or whatever they are."

Gran-D knows Carringer's motives are honest but he is the youngest of the Masters and is driven more by passion than logic.

"My father died... that doesn't mean my mother did."

Gran-D tries to speak calmly, appealing to Carringer's logic, though he knows such appeals are weak when it comes to family. No one in Spirin is accustomed to death by any violent means.

"Your father told me of what was beyond the wall before he died. Your mother was too gentle to have survived it."

"But the pain of not knowing..." Carringer pleads.

Now Gran-D speaks with a voice of authority, "Master Carringer, you're our Spell Master. You're too important - and too inexperienced - to handle Goreipor. Study the spell, but don't use the Door again." Gran-D adds, "No one can know of this."

Gran-D looks up at the distortion in the wall. He hopes Carringer didn't unwittingly weaken the wall that separates Spirin from that place of darkness.

Carringer struggles to get out, "There's something else about the Door... It has a memory."

Gran-D cleans around Carringer's wound, "Not now, you're too weak. First let us get you to the Healer."

In spite of his condition, Carringer insists, "You need to know... It's something about Peter's world."

Back in Goreipor the squad that cornered Master Carringer, but did not capture him, stands at attention in the Grand Hall of the Dark Fortress. They do their best not to show their fear.

Kildemar lets them stand before him for a while to play on that fear. He is big on psychological abuse.

Finally he walks from his throne to the line-up, "You had someone in your grasp...? Then why is he not here before me?"

After a moment Lieutenant Ricken, only thirty years old, steps forward. The men in question are his, though he did not lead the squad in the canyons.

"Sire, he was dressed much different than..."

Lord Kildemar cuts him off, "You were not there, were you? Let the men answer for their deeds!"

Lieutenant Ricken dutifully remains silent and steps back.

Kildemar walks along the line of soldiers, staring at each one for a couple of seconds, striking fear in each as he does so. He says nothing as he goes man to man, heightening their fears.

Then he turns his attention away, towards Witch Racinda, "And you had no idea of this intruder's presence? This intruder who dared to set foot in my land."

Witch Racinda takes her chances with an answer she knows will not please the Lord, but a lie would be more dangerous, "I cannot see everything at all hours of every day, my lord."

Kildemar shakes his head and turns his attention back to the squad, "Which of you got the closest to this man?"

After hesitant silence, the soldier who chased Carringer up the cliff wall steps forward, "I did, my Lord." He adds in his defense, "I almost grabbed him, but he dove into a light and disappeared in a flash."

Lord Kildemar walks back down the line.

As he moves, "And I suspect that before he disappeared he fought you all off with magical weapons."

The court lets out an uneasy laugh. The squad does not. When Kildemar reaches the soldier who stepped forward, he puts his bladed hand gently on the soldier's shoulder.

In a softer more ominous voice, "He was gone in a flash?"

The soldier nervously nods 'yes'. Lord Kildemar pulls his bladed fingers away, across the soldier's face, leaving deep gashes spurting blood.

"A flash like that?"

The soldier collapses to the hard floor in pain. Two of his fellow soldiers attempt to help him to his feet but Kildemar yells, "Leave him!"

Then he turns to the court, "They have dared to use their spell in my land."

Witch Racinda tries to interject, "My lord…"

"I care not to hear from you! You did not foresee this."

She knows she's walking a fine line, but a line she feels necessary.

"But, my lord, the intruder, though not caught, created a weak spot in the wall. With time I may be able to exploit it."

Kildemar snaps at her, "Give me results. I will determine how much time to give you." He turns to Lieutenant Ricken, "Get your men out of my sight." With a wave at the downed soldier, "And take that with you. I care not to see him again."

As Lieutenant Ricken does as told and the squad leaves carrying the hurt soldier, Janick leans into his brother, Taligarr, and whispers, "At times I think our father's temper does not serve him well."

Taligarr hushes him, "Hold your tongue. Do you think he would not strike down a son?"

"I only meant..."

"Little brother, power is kept by seeing the seeds of thoughts, not waiting for the actions of them."

The Land of Goreipor is a very dangerous world. All in it must constantly remind themselves that its ruler sees enemies in every dark corner. He may even be right.

Chapter Thirteen

Peter and Gran-D walk along a path enjoying the summer's day. Peter drags his feet because he's a bit nervous about today's audience with the Masters. What he's heard of them - and it's been quite a bit since Gran-D announced he would be introduced to them - is that they are highly respected in the Spirin community. To hear people talk, it's like going before the Supreme Court.

Peter thinks how bad could it be, 'After all, Spirin is a small land of villages... that happens to be filled with magicians... and these are the top ones.'

Now he's even more nervous.

Gran-D glances over, "Come on, the Council is waiting."

"So, are you going to introduce me?" Peter says, hoping to have an ally at his side as long as possible.

"It wouldn't be fitting."

"You're just going to throw me to the lions?"

"Whatever those are, I guess so," Gran-D responds.

There are times Peter does not appreciate Gran-D's quirky sense of humor. Now is one of those. Peter thinks about whether condemned men have flashes of thoughts rushing through their minds just before the end?

He knows it can't be that bad... but just a little over a month ago, he was a dropout mechanic with plans no more complicated than partying in a cave and taking care of a kid brother.

Now he's halfway across the Universe in a land of hocus-pocus about to meet the Supreme Court of magic nuts.

Gran-D laughs, "If you don't turn off your head, you'll go crazy before we get there."

What replaces those thoughts is how the hell did Gran-D know?

The two reach a bend in the path. Master Melick's cottage sits a hundred yards off to the side. It's larger than the Dees' home, very different but just as whimsical. It is constructed of purple wood in a somewhat Finnish style. Two totems of unusually carved animal heads flank the front door.

As they walk towards the cottage, Peter keeps asking questions about the Masters - what they might ask, what they're like, why they were made Masters... Gran-D talks of Shan's red hair, Ramie's losing another Orb... of anything except what Peter wants to hear.

Reaching the front door, Peter turns to Gran-D with his most serious question. Gran-D vanishes into smoke and whiffs away.

Peter mumbles to himself, "I wish he couldn't do that."

As he stands there, the front door creaks open on its own. Peter hesitates, peeks into the darkness and walks in.

Standing in Master Melick's receiving room, the reference to the Supreme Court crosses Peter's mind again. The room is spacious and richly darkened by that same purple wood as on the outside of the cottage.

Directly ahead of him are six Masters sitting in very formal chairs arranged in a quarter-circle. Peter fidgets as they say nothing for the longest time. Maybe it's not that long but it sure feels like it to him.

The Masters are from all over Spirin but since Klavedar is the unofficial capital they have made their homes close by. Actually there is no government per se and what authority that exists lies solely in the hands of these six Councilmen who now stare at Peter. Peter squirms a little more.

Standing in the deafening silence Peter takes the time to scan the Masters from left to right.

Master Imton, the sourest looking of all is on the far left. He's the same age as Gran-D, but looks older, more worn and much less happy. Peter can feel a dislike in his stare. What he's unsure of is which direction it's traveling.

There's something unusual - his ears have a shorter curl that spirals in the opposite direction as most ear curls in Spirin. Peter figures most likely it's due to the area of Spirin he must come from.

Next to him sits Master Sashaw, a bald, fat lawyerly-looking Spirinese. Peter doubts Spirin that has lawyers but, if they did, they would look something like Master Sashaw. His stare at Peter is hard to read. There's a slight smile with a hint of larceny in it. If Peter had to choose just from appearances, Master Sashaw would be the one to trust the least.

Then there's Master Melick who owns the dwelling they are in. Melick clearly has the most statesman-like appearance, though Peter has no idea why he would think that.

Maybe it's because he's tall with a squared jaw and seems like a straight shooter. Peter thinks that most politicians try to appear that way and he reminds himself that looks may be deceiving.

So far Peter has reached a zero for three 'like' rating. He wonders if he's being a bit hard on them.

Next comes Master Warnig, the only woman on the Council. Though a sorceress, she doesn't resemble a witch. Warnig has a motherly smile that looks like it hides the nature of someone you don't to mess with. Peter guesses she's in her mid-fifties. Master Warning nods a welcome to Peter, perhaps because he appears so uncomfortable.

The next almost draws a laugh from Peter but he knows that would be very unwise. It's Master Haring, a dwarf-like man who looks like a very mini-Viking. Haring sits on a chair that is much too high for him. When Peter glances at him, Master Haring grumbles under his breath. He's definitely the curmudgeon of the group if anyone is.

The last, but definitely not least, is too much for Peter to keep his laughter restrained. He – it - is a six-foot orange lizard sitting with legs crossed and smoking a pipe. When the slight laugh breaks from Peter, the lizard's smile broadens.

The first Master to speak is Master Imton who turns to the orange lizard, "Carringer, for Geffen's sake, stop showing off and act like a Master."

The orange lizard morphs into Master Carringer, still smiling and smoking his pipe.

Peter lets slip out, "Cool."

"Enough of this nonsense. Let's focus on the boy," says Master Melick with the voice of authority.

From the refocus of the group, Peter figures he was right about Melick being the leader.

Melick turn to Peter, "Young man, move forward so we can get a better look at you."

"The name's Peter." Remembering he is there to get something from them, he adds, "If you don't mind."

Master Haring, the short Master, scoots forward and climbs off his chair. Peter does his best to keep a straight face. Haring walks forward and circles Peter, inspecting him.

He doesn't actually say anything. It's more like grumbling un-der his breath as he looks the boy over. After two trips around, Haring goes back to his chair and starts to climb up.

Peter tries not to, but he lets slip, "Can I help you up?"

Haring, now back on his chair, turns and glares at Peter. Sud-denly the carpet under Peter's feet jerks forward and Peter falls on his rump.

Master Haring smiles, "Maybe it's you that needs help up?" Haring looks both directions at the other Masters, "I'm not im-pressed."

Peter gets to his feet and dusts himself off. He's smart enough to keep his mouth shut.

"Peter, what makes you think you deserve to be taught by us?" asks Master Melick.

"Nothing. I'm not here to learn from all of you."

Melick gestures for him to continue.

"As I see it, I ended up on your world because of a messed up spell you have. Now if one of you who's good with spells teaches me how to work on them, I'll fix it and be on my way." He adds, "Back on Earth I fixed broken things like motorcy-cles. Oh, I forgot, you don't know what they are. Whatever it is, I'm good at fixing things if I have tools."

The six masters patiently listen to Peter ramble until Master Sashaw says, "Can you believe this boy?"

It's not said as a compliment. Many nod their agreement.

In Peter's defense Carringer chimes in, "Give the boy a break. He's from another world. By the way, his misguided logic makes some sense to me."

Peter gives him a smile.

Master Haring grumbles, "It would."

Master Warnig, irritated, "Talk, talk, talk... you men. Melick, give the boy the test."

Peter sees he was right about another one. She's not one to mess with. What Peter doesn't realize is that they are all powerful... none should be messed with, not even the orange lizard.

Master Melick stands up and abruptly throws something at Peter. Nothing appears but, out of pure instinct and reflexes, Peter snaps his hands up to catch the nothing. For nothing, it has quite a wallop. Peter staggers back.

When he opens his hands there's a blue Orb.

Peter looks up at Master Melick, "That was a test? You looked like you were throwing something and all I did was react."

"What color is the Orb?" Master Melick calmly queries.

Peter holds it up so everyone can see it's blue.

Melick adds, "I threw a red one. It's you that changed it to blue. Maybe you like blue, I don't know... but you're able to tune nature. The problem is that you don't have any idea of how - or why - you do it. Not knowing means, at the moment, you really have no skills."

Peter has an automatic off-switch in his head when it comes to being schooled. It's taken years to cultivate. He is trying not to have it turn off.

"Great, does that mean I'm in?"

There's more than one sigh in the room.

Melick raises a hand, "No. It does not mean you're in. It means we'll let you know."

Peter appears a little disappointed in not having instant answers, but why should this situation be any different than all the non-answers in Spirin he's gotten so far. To perk up the mood, Master Carringer lifts his hand and a starburst erupts high in the room, sending sparks everywhere.

Master Imton turns to him and snaps, "Carringer!"

Peter starts to say something but the front door creaks open loudly behind him. He gets the message and turns to leave.

On the way out he can't resist mumbling a little too loud, "That was interesting, orange lizard and all."

As he passes out of the door, it slams on its own behind him.

Back inside the cottage the quarter-circle of Masters' chairs magically slide into a tighter grouping. Melick gets up, goes to the fireplace and tosses a log on.

After a pause he turns back to the group, "I sense he will train fast. Whether the boy knows it or not, he has powers."

In his normal curmudgeonly manner, Master Haring grumbles, "I sense he will be a pain."

For a world devoid of violence Haring oddly sounds much like a Marine drill sergeant, but along with that gruffness comes a sense of fair play. Unfortunately old drill sergeants tend to resist change.

"As Melick pointed out, the boy has powers already, even if he doesn't know it. Imagine how much he might have if we help him," Master Imton says with a clear negative tone. "He is of a world that I think is dangerous and I think the boy himself is dangerous. I was in favor of sending him home from the start, but I was outvoted."

He glances into a dark nook, exchanging a hint of secrets with the darkness.

A few nod in agreement with Imton's statement, but not all.

A puff of pipe smoke drifts from a dark corner of the room.

Master Warnig peers at the darkness and then back toward the group, "We're only considering him for one reason, regardless of where he comes from."

All now glance at the dark corner.

The familiar voice of Gran-D comes from the darkness, "And that reason has reasons."

Gran-D walks out of the corner smoking his pipe - now as Grand Master Dat.

"If he's already using powers, is it not better to guide their use?"

A seventh chair slides out of the shadows and across the room for Gran-D sit in.

"You have voted to not open the Door to send him home out of fear it would bring more from his world, so we've chosen to take responsibility for him."

Master Sashaw turns to Carringer, "Are there not ways we could just stop his powers? You're the Spell Master."

Carringer, with his usual smile and lighthearted tone, "I know of no spell that stops time or growth. Some things are beyond our control. I think Peter has natural powers and, may I add, he looks like a good kid."

This time Imton and Haring grumble together, "You would."

Master Warnig insists, "We are dancing around the Grimick in the room... the Prophecy."

"We are not because it's already been decided that Peter does not fit it," Gran-D insists. He goes on, "We did not write the Prophecy. Either it is true or it isn't, but that should not be the basis of our decision about training Peter. Remember, training is our best control."

Some show discomfort over the coldness of what Gran-D says, but all know it's the truth.

"Anyone else feel as lousy as I do? The poor kid is only asking to be trained so he can go home... and we're planning both to control and lock him here on our world", says Carringer.

The Spell Master is the voice of youth on the Council, with more life ahead than behind.

Master Melick clears his throat. All know what that means.

"It's time we vote on the matter."

He closes his eyes, as do the rest of the Masters. Votes within the Council are taken mentally.

The evening is filled with silence at the Dees'. Everyone but Peter and Gran-D seems to be on the edge of their seats awaiting the decision of the Council of Masters. Gran-D rarely shows being on the edge of his seat over anything.

As far as Peter goes, he figures that either way he will still find a way to get home. This might be faster, but he is not going to be stopped by a group of quirky old men.

A knock on the front door startles Atta.

Kalish puts his hand on her shoulder, "I'll get it." He goes to the door and lets Master Melick in.

Peter looks up, "That was quick."

Melick says coldly, "I always like to get unpleasant news out of the way as soon as possible."

Atta's heart drops, but Peter has been around cynical old men before so he waits calmly for the actual answer.

Gran-D watches Peter's coolness with some concern. He had hoped for more enthusiasm. Has he made the wrong decision about the boy? Only time will tell.

Melick finally continues, "We have decided to train you."

All seem happy, even Peter - with some reserve. He glances over at Shan. From her expression, he can tell she's battling two emotions.

She's proud for him and the honor the family gets from this and she's frustrated that someone new to Spirin is receiving such an honor. Clearly she would relish being trained as well. What must be especially taxing is that she knows he does not view the training in such high regard.

Shan struggles to set these thoughts aside and smiles.

Peter breaks off his thoughts about Shan, "So, do I have to go live with the lizard to start training?"

"That's Master Carringer and, unfortunately, no, you begin training with me." Melick has a slight grimace on his face as he says this. He knows what's going to come out of Peter's mouth next so he strikes first, "You will start when we choose for you to start and move where we say."

"But Master Carringer has the skills I need. You can save all the rest of the stuff."

"I know what you need, but I'm going to train you anyway." Before Peter can say more Master Melick holds up his hand, "Show up at my place tomorrow... and, please don't bring your bags."

Peter tries to get in the last word, "But I think..."

Melick holds up his hand again. Then he bows to Atta and Kalish, nods to Gran-D and heads for the door.

As he goes, not looking back, "I know I chance missing your wisdom, but luckily I'm running late."

Before Peter can say what he wants to say, Melick is out the door and gone.

Well after the dust settles from the evening's announcement, Peter sits alone in the living room, staring out the window at the stars. He wonders what he has gotten himself into. All he wanted was to learn the tools that might allow him to fix the spell.

One step at a time he's getting more and more entrenched in Spirin. Though he tries to ignore the thought, it nags at him... Will he ever get home?

Chapter Fourteen

Peter patiently watches Master Melick have his morning tea and Melick takes his sweet time about it. This truly irritates Peter but he's trying, with mixed success, not to show it. Melick continues enjoying his tea.

Peter, exhausted, blurts out, "So, do you fix spells?"

Master Melick calmly looks up, "Sorcery is a matter of manipulating everything in nature around you. Everything in sorcery is a spell." Adding, "If it has to be fixed, it's not a good spell," he goes back to sipping his tea.

This reminds Peter of a high school teacher telling him that what some Greek philosopher said - who knows how long ago - makes him a better motorcycle mechanic. Peter figures if it doesn't apply to the moment, it doesn't apply at all. He's young.

Just before Peter's about to make another comment, Melick says, "I heard you think you know how to practice sorcery, but don't always know how you do it. Is this accurate?"

Peter's not sure how to answer so he shrugs, "Sometimes."

The manner of Peter's utterance of 'sometimes' causes Master Melick to cringe, as if hearing the scraping of a chalkboard. Melick has promised himself to remember that while people of Spirin know the wisdom of the Masters, this boy does not. He will not lose his temper. He smiles at the thought of how Peter will be received by someone like Master Haring, who is far less even-tempered.

Calmly Melick gets up and says, "Come with me Peter." Then he heads for the front door.

Peter blindly follows.

Outside, Peter stands on the roof peak of Master Melick's cottage.

Melick yells up, "I was told you are able to float, right?"

Melick is not that far down so Peter just speaks loudly, "Yeah, most of the time."

This is just about as grating as 'sometimes' but Melick sets his emotions aside. "Then float down."

Peter estimates it's just a bit higher than the roof at home on Earth, maybe a bit higher, and he's jumped off that. Worst case, he lands in the bushes.

He thinks that most likely it will work. Peter steps off the roof and gently floats to the ground, smiling triumphantly all the way.

Master Melick simply says, "That's nice." He walks over to Peter and says, "Take hold of my arm."

Peter appears a little disappointed by Master Melick's lack of enthusiasm over his feat. He reaches out and does as he's told. Without warning the two of them turn into wisps of smoke and shoot straight up into the air.

They travel over Spirin as a winding stream of smoke streaking through the sky. Peter is fascinated by the view far below.

He's not sure he can talk in the form of smoke but he tries, "Master Melick, I assume you're here."

He hears back, "Hush Peter, I like to focus... unless?"

Peter cuts him off quickly, "No, no, that's fine. Keep focused."

He hears a faint laugh. Peter can't believe how free he feels without a body zooming in and out of the clouds. They are flying so fast that Peter only sees the Graveyard below as it rushes by. They go over hill and dale, valleys and mountains, all part of the colorful land of Spirin.

After a while they land on the summit of the highest mountain in Spirin, or at least that's what it feels like to Peter. Unlike the cliffs of Goreipor, the mountains of Spirin have a friendly feel... but they're still high! They're so high that a dusting of clouds surrounds them.

When Peter materializes it's with an astounded look on his face. The particular spot they landed is at the edge of a sheer precipice. Beautiful or not, Peter feels nervous standing near the edge.

Melick gestures out at the open air in front of them and calmly says, "Now, Peter, please float for me once more."

Peter glances over the edge. Gigantic trees below look like tiny toothpicks. Knees almost knocking, he shies back from the edge. "You're joking!"

"Your spells work sometimes... don't they?"

To entice Peter, Melick floats out from the cliff about ten feet and turns back towards him.

Bobbing in midair, "It's no different than my roof. Come out and play."

Peter can feel his reckless streak creeping up. He's not about to be laughed at by this old teacher. He forgets how many times that same reckless streak has gotten him into trouble and he steps off the edge.

To his surprise, and without much effort, he floats out to about three feet from Master Melick. He glances down at the void below, stirring few butterflies in his stomach, and smiles triumphantly at Melick.

In a rather nasty manner Master Melick says, "What's so important about going back to that odd planet, I think you call it Earth... and taking care of some brat?"

Peter glares at him and loses his focus, which abruptly causes him to plummet downwards. He's in a free-fall - a panic fall actually. He tumbles totally out of control, screaming at the top of his lungs. Terminal tumble velocity is fast approaching.

Master Melick swoops down beside him, descending vertically with total control.

At such speeds Melick has to yell, "See, Peter, sorcery is not a matter of sometimes knowing how."

Peter is not paying attention, he's screaming.

Melick continues as the ground approaches, "We are going to forget what you think you know. Is that all right with you?"

Peter screams again, not sure if it is coming out as a 'yes' or just loud gibberish.

Melick realizes he might have to repeat himself once they are on the ground, but he thinks Peter is getting the point.

As the ground rushes up towards them, Master Melick takes control of Peter's fall for the last thirty feet and gently lands both of them in the meadow below the mountain.

Peter collapses to the ground and kisses it. From the few moist blue blades of grass pressed on Peter's forehead, Melick is now pretty sure he's gotten the idea. So is Peter.

Now on the ground Master Melick says, "By the way, I didn't mean that about your brother. I'm sure he'll be all right."

Though Peter's most immediate thoughts are about being safe on the ground, the last thing Melick said about his brother strikes him as odd.

That night Peter sits on the front porch lost in thought. He feels no closer to home and wonders what he's gotten himself into? It seems that every step he makes towards that goal takes him farther away from home and closer to being more rooted in Spirin.

The front door opens behind him and Shan comes out. She takes a seat beside him.

After a couple seconds of silence, "You were pretty quiet at dinner. How did the first day go?"

Though he's physically and mentally exhausted, "OK, I guess. I have a reason to put up with the classes..."

"I know. You don't have to repeat it."

"I'm not that good with lessons, never have been. I think you'd be better at it." Peter knows Shan would love to have been chosen by the Masters. "Why do you think Gran-D hasn't taken you to the Masters? From what little I know you're far more talented than most."

She appreciates the gesture. "I don't know, but thanks. You're the first one to notice it bothers me." She scoots a little bit closer. "Peter, I hope you get what you want from them. I mean that sincerely."

With a slight laugh, "Getting out of training alive each day would suit me just fine." Looking at Shan, "You know Gran-D's pretty sharp. About the training, maybe I'm just the first one to say it. I'm sure I'm not the only one to notice."

"Maybe," says Shan and, returning Peter's look, "Don't worry about the Masters. You're better at this stuff than you know. I see it in you."

Peter glances back at her in a slightly different way. He's surprised he hasn't noticed. Shan is exceptionally cute - tomboy, contrary nature and all. He reminds himself he's gotten too lost in his own problems to notice things like a pretty girl. He needs to watch that in the future.

A military encampment is set up on Goreipor's Eastern wall. Lord Kildemar has doubled his patrols on all the borders, but he's particularly concerned with the one between Goreipor and Spirin. Witch Racinda is also interested in this area's wall because it's where Carringer's escape created a weakness.

The encampment's contingent is twenty-four soldiers and a few Goreiporians to help Racinda with her task. There are a half dozen tents and about as many fires. Patrolling the torch-lit perimeter are a few heavily armed sentinels. The rest of the men warm themselves by the fires.

A large scaffold is erected next to the wall leading up to the circle of distortion in the wall's mirror surface. Torches illuminate Witch Racinda and the few soldiers at work up on the scaffold near the weak spot.

Hoof beats echo from the canyon walls as Lord Kildemar, his two sons and their escort ride into the encampment. The Lord won't let it be openly observed, but he takes joy in leading his troops. He has conquered all the warlords in Goreipor. He misses and longs for new battles.

The soldiers in the camp snap to attention when Lord Kildemar rides in. As the party dismounts, a sergeant rushes over to show Lord Kildemar the way to the tent prepared for him.

Kildemar is an impatient man, "Take me to my witch now."

"Yes, sir."

The sergeant bows and leads the way.

The Lord, his sons and Lieutenant Ricken climb the scaffold to find Witch Racinda hard at work. She has directed lights upon circles of discolored ripples in the wall. Deeply engrossed by the circles, Racinda barely notices their arrival.

Kildemar looks over her shoulder at the dark spot with curiosity, "Witch, what have you got for me?"

She knows not to sugar coat her progress, "I'm trying to weaken the hole while the wall tries to heal it."

He snaps back, "I don't want to hear about it in terms of healing, nature consciousness or any other nonsense. I want to know if I can use it to get to my enemies. Does it work or not?"

Racinda picks up a stone. She carefully tosses it at the dead center of the discoloration on the wall. The stone goes through or, at least, disappears. She has no idea if it comes out the other side.

"The rock went somewhere... perhaps to the other land, perhaps to nowhere, perhaps it was destroyed. Manipulating, controlling nature consciousness, is what I do." She's quick to add, "It's what I do for you, my lord."

She knows this violent man could care less about the ways of sorcery, but she knows no other manner of explaining it. Lord Kildemar is simply about results.

He turns to one of the soldiers on the scaffold, "Go through that hole, then come back if you are able to."

"My lord, we need to test it further," Racinda protests.

"That is what he will do. Say no more."

The soldier unlucky enough to be chosen knows that to go through the hole means possible death... but not to go means certain death.

Racinda feels for the soldier but knows he has little choice. She just hopes she has weakened the hole enough.

Turning to the soldier, "Take off your gear and dive head first into the very center of the dark spot, understand? I think it will work."

He nods nervously at her and removes all his extra gear.

"Take a weapon," Kildemar commands. He turns to Witch Racinda, "If it does not allow a weapon, it does not serve me."

The soldier takes a sword in hand and backs up for a running start. He mumbles to whatever deity he believes in.

The Lord yells, "Go... Now!"

Taking one last deep breath, he runs and dives head first into the dark spot. The front half of him makes it through, but only to his hips. His legs freeze like a two-legged dart stuck in a dartboard.

They jut out suspended there for scant seconds before they start to glow. Everyone backs away. Then the legs explode into a cloud of gray dust. The spot seals.

"Well, that didn't work," Lieutenant Ricken cracks unwisely.

Lord Kildemar snaps a glare at him and turns to his witch, "Continue work on it."

As he starts to climb down the scaffold, Kildemar passes by the Lieutenant and quietly says, "When it is ready to try again, you will have that honor."

Chapter Fifteen

The seasons change and Peter's training continues. Now he is with the dwarf-like Master Haring. They stand in the rain... or at least Peter does. Master Haring stands under an invisible umbrella, a transparent round dome floating over his head. A fire with its own dome crackles next to him so the Master remains both dry and warm as he barks orders.

Peter is neither dry nor warm. He stands, drenched to the bone, trying to keep his focus on the task before him. The task is learning to master his control but Peter's not sure which is the harder element to deal with, control of the objects around him or control of his temper with the short taskmaster.

A half dozen tall, thin four-sided obelisks surround Peter. A glowing globe floats above each one. The light from the globes highlights the streaks of rain, giving the scene the look of a pencil sketch.

Peter has his hands stretched out, fingers on two more globes as he tries to control two floating crown stones meant to cap the obelisks. What he's supposed to do rotate these top stones within the circle of obelisks, replacing one with the other.

It takes all of his concentration to do this and the downpour makes it especially hard.

All the while Master Haring yells at him like a drill sergeant, "Lad, if you were any slower the stones would be moving backwards! Concentrate!"

The crown stone controlled by Peter's left hand makes its mark, but the one he tries to place with his right topples to the ground. Peter stomps the mud in frustration and with a swipe of his hand sends the fallen stone flying towards the nearby rocky cliff.

Haring yells, "Temper has no place in sorcery!"

The flying stone stops inches before crashing into boulders. Struggling, Peter levitates it back towards his target obelisk, all the while grumbling words under his breath - words that would probably not be wise to allow Haring to hear.

Master Haring gives a slight curmudgeon's nod of approval.

Peter stumbles into the loft he shares with Ramie. He's cold, wet, tired and, most of all, he's out of sorts. He stands there staring at his welcoming bed.

Ramie barges into the loft. Before he can unleash his youthful banter, Peter glares at him and holds up a hand. Ramie's shoulders slump.

Peter collapses on the bed, wet clothes and all.

Arriving outside Master Sashaw's home, Peter stomps the snow off his boots, then uses the doorknocker. From outside he can hear the hollow clang the knocker makes inside. The massive door squeaks open. Peter enters.

Master Sashaw's home matches the coolness of the man himself. It consists of gray slate-like walls with very little added color or decoration. Everything is appropriately in its place. It screams efficiency.

Peter thinks how much like a lawyer's home this looks. He knows no lawyers but, if he did, this is what he would imagine.

A voice echoes into the room, "Sit at the desk. I'll be with you shortly."

Peter glances around but sees no one. The desk is covered with very neat piles of papers and books. Again, it's just as Peter would have imagined for a lawyer.

His apprehension grows as he takes a seat. It dawns on him that these presumptions will have him hating the man even before he meets him, so he tries to quiet his mind.

Master Sashaw enters. He has an aloof, cold, insincere smile. Instantly Peter doesn't like him.

"Do you have any idea what I do?" says Sashaw.

Peter starts to shake his head 'no', but Master Sashaw continues, showing no actual interest in Peter's answer.

"I evaluate all spells in Spirin to determine their suitability and safety," Sashaw looks off as if making a court summation. "Any questions thus far?"

"So you're a spell censor?"

Peter figures this is a reasonable conclusion, though he doesn't see much magic in it. He thinks how inappropriate the word suitability is in relation to magic. From his experiences in Spirin so far, safety doesn't apply well either.

A little irate, Sashaw says, "I wouldn't put it that way, but I guess, stretching a bit, it could be seen so. Spells can be very dangerous and the sorcerers that create them sometimes don't see the danger in them. I do."

Seeing Peter's blank expression, Sashaw continues, "I write up a report and submit it to the council."

This lights no more spark in Peter than before. Peter's not sure what to say.

Finally, "Master Sashaw, what am I going to learn - how to read the fine print on spells?"

It's clear from Master Sashaw's expression that he sees Peter is belittling his work and is not pleased.

"I'm going to teach you the history of our spells and their hidden dangers, so when you create spells yourself, you will know what the fine print is."

Still no light comes on in Peter's eyes.

"Why don't we start with giving you a proper perspective on the matter?"

Sashaw raises his hand and flicks a finger at Peter. Little more than a slight spark comes off his fingertip.

Peter quickly begins shrinking. He gets smaller and smaller and the room gets bigger and bigger. When his transformation is complete, Peter is just two inches tall, standing near Sashaw's enormous shoe.

Master Sashaw reaches down and uses his fingertips to take Peter by the collar. He lifts him up and deposits him on an open book on the desk.

"Now you can read the fine print better."

Peter, in a squeaky voice, yells, "Give me a break!"

Master Sashaw smiles, "Very poor choice of words, all things considered."

He walks away, leaving Peter to think about insulting him again.

Before leaving the room he looks back at his student, "Read that spell and think about the inherent problems with it. I'll be back later."

Peter plops down on the book page and shakes his head in exasperation. Then he realizes that if Sashaw sees the problems in spells, he must see the problems in the Sorcerer's Door. He may even have been the one that put it in the Graveyard.

Peter starts reading, determined to try being a student, one who can get the specific information he's after from each teacher.

Shan, Peter and Ramie walk along a snow-dusted path. Ramie drops back and makes a snowball. He throws it at Peter, but it doesn't distract him from his attention to Shan.

Ramie appears saddened, forgotten and alone. What small amount of time Peter has off from training is spent with Shan. The two of them are becoming close, and Ramie is becoming distant from them, feeling totally forgotten.

Spring has sprung and Peter sits in a stand of trees watching Master Warnig's cottage in the hollow below. It's not so much of a cottage as it is a small gypsy wagon without wheels. It floats above a large patch of bright vegetables and flowers.

All Peter knows of her is that she specializes in potions. He figures she must use many of the items from her garden in her spells.

He finds the picture below somewhat odd, not because Master Warnig lives in a wagon that floats over a garden, but because every so often a young person arrives and goes in. Occasionally one leaves, but far fewer than the number of those that enter.

It's bewildering how this cozy little wagon admits so many. Considering the number of kids in there it also crosses his mind that he doesn't relish such an audience at his training. He glances up at the sun and realizes it's about time to show up - that is, if there's room.

Peter goes up the steps of the floating wagon and knocks.

The door opens and a young lady carrying a few books says, "Excuse me." She squeezes past him on her way down the steps.

From inside the wagon he hears Master Warnig beckon him. He enters, expecting to have to squeeze through to find her.

No one is inside other than Master Warnig. She sits in a spacious room, much too large to fit in the small wagon. The room is about as long as a train car, but wider. It's filled with books and elaborately shaped chemistry lab equipment.

Where is everyone? He knows he has seen at least ten more arrive than have left... but now there's only the Master and him.

A bit puzzled, he says, "A girl just passed me as I was coming in."

Master Warnig comments rather nonchalantly without even looking up, "Ah, yes, that was Kate, I think... Yes, I'm sure that was Kate. She was on her way home. Come on in and sit down so we can get started."

Just as Peter is about to ask about the others who have not left yet are clearly not, a light knock sounds at the door.

Without waiting for an invitation, a young man enters. Warnig pays him little attention as he walks to a set of cupboard doors, opens them and goes in. The doors shut.

Peter stares at the small cabinet - are a dozen people hiding in Master Warnig's cupboard? Obviously, she knows but seems to pay little regard to it.

Master Warnig notices Peter's distant gaze, "Oh, the traffic bothers you. I'll fix that."

With a wave of her hand an accordion wall divides the interior. The part of the wagon she and Peter are in expands to adjust back to its former large area. Peter is speechless.

"Now can we get started?" she says.

"Where did they go? I mean, where can they go? It's a cabinet."

"Is this going to distract you all day? They're going to the library. Satisfied?"

Of course this doesn't satisfy him, far from it. At last, she waves her hand and the accordion wall opens back up.

"Go take a look if it will settle your mind and get you back to the present so you can focus on your lessons."

He glances at the cupboard, then back at her. He can resist no more. He rushes for the cabinet. This is something he has to see, even if his desire belies the cool that most seventeen-year olds try to maintain.

He opens the cupboard doors and finds a massive, ornate staircase leading down - one suitable for any big city library. Peter starts down. Half-way to the bottom he sees about ten young people sitting at tables studying. There must be thousands of books on rows and rows of tall shelves behind them.

No one seems to pay much attention to his presence. Having sufficiently had his mind blown, he turns and heads back up the stairs.

Once back in the room with Master Warnig, he takes a seat across the desk from her. The accordion wall closes. Peter is not quite sure what to say. Master Warnig realizes nothing will be get accomplished until she gets all this out of the way.

"Did you think you were the only one that studies? That all of the Masters have been sitting on their hands for generations just waiting for you to come along?"

Still a little overwhelmed, he slowly shakes his head 'no'. She continues, "Granted, the kind of training you are getting is different than that of those you saw. They get specific lessons addressing their specific needs and skills. You're getting the full package. We haven't done that for anyone since young Carringer."

His situation is not what's boggling his mind right now, though he has no doubt it will all sink in later.

"How come I never heard anything about a library? Not from Shan or Ramie or anybody?"

"Simple. When they need to use the library they just remember where it is. Once they are done with it, they forget where it is. It's quite a chore with all the coming and going - all the re-membering and forgetting - but somehow I manage to orches-trate it all. Imagine how crowded my little home would be if everyone remembered where it was all the time. Now, can we get back to your lessons?"

Peter shakes his head at this logic. It's much too confusing to ask her to explain it any further.

But another question nags at him, "If you train so many, why hasn't Shan been trained in some way? I mean, like in my way. She is the most talented young person I know."

She sighs as if the subject is not exactly new to her, "Go ask her grandfather. Now, enough of that subject... or for that mat-ter, any subject other than brewing spells!"

Peter can tell there's little use in asking more so he settles down to see what he can learn from this new teacher.

A few hours have passed and the gypsy wagon floating over the colorful garden appears peaceful from the outside. Sud-denly an explosion inside sends purple smoke drifting out the windows. Peter and Master Warnig stagger out from the back door, both covered in purple soot. She is doing her level best to hold her temper as she points Peter towards home.

He coughs and manages to spit out, "Honest, I'm sorry!"

She points again. If she did so any more rigidly her arm would probably snap off.

"Go home!"

Peter staggers away with an overwhelming desire to laugh, but he holds it in.

Gran-D walks along a path, leisurely enjoying the afternoon. Peter swoops up to him on his hoverboard and settles on the ground. He's still somewhat purple from the day's class. It's clear he has something on his mind.

Says Gran-D, "OK, out with it... whatever's eating at you."

Before Peter speaks he wonders again how Gran-D always seems to know? He shakes off the thought for now.

"How come Shan has never been put up for training? I mean real training."

Gran-D smiles, "Ah, you've been talking with Master Warnig."

He takes a seat on a rock and gestures for Peter to do the same.

"She's not ready. Yes, she has more powers than most, but she's still living in her limitations stage."

Peter is rarely disrespectful toward Gran-D, probably because he has a feeling about who the old man truly is... but there are times his answers are frustrating.

"Come on, old man, give me a straight answer."

"She's probably the one closest to be worthy of training but it can't happen too soon."

"I've been here less than a year. Why am I different?"

Gran-D ponders this a second, then, "From conjuring a hoverboard to crossing universes you know all of this is impossible. Then again, you can't deny it's happened. Thus your emotions have come to accept that nothing is impossible regardless of your mind... That makes sense?"

Peter shakes his head with a blank expression. It seems to make sense but he can't quite grasp it.

"Let's leave it at this - if Shan is trained before she is ready it will ruin her. Someday I hope the Council will see she is ready, but we all have to wait for that day to arrive."

Peter doesn't completely get it, as with many things from Gran-D, but he sort of gets it. He knows he is completely open to what he can do because it's all too ridiculous to be aware he can't do it.

He nods his half-understanding. He can't shake the thought that Gran-D is still hiding something... like why he was put into training so quickly?

Yes, he has the goal of getting him home, but there's something else. He fears it might be something more sinister.

Gran-D adds, "To tell her of this conversation would lessen her chances. Please don't do that to her Peter."

Peter has become very close to Shan over the past year and though he doesn't like keeping things from her, the last thing he wants to do is hurt her.

Then the thought that it's already been nearly a year fogs his mind. He tries to think of the last time he has thought of home and Devon. A slight sadness washes over him.

The colors and warmth of summer overflow outside the windows of Master Imton, Peter's newest taskmaster. Imton's home is as different as each of the other Masters' dwellings.

It's rich wood interior reminds Peter of some upper-class hunting lodge he's seen in magazines back on Earth, except there are no animal heads mounted on the walls. The main room is massive with an exposed log beam ceiling.

Of all the Masters, Imton makes Peter feel the most uncomfortable. In turn, he's the one Master who seems the most uncomfortable around Peter. The two don't exchange many words, which is more than fine with both of them.

They're in the middle of a lesson. Master Imton generates a four-foot spy globe high in mid-air. Inside the globe is an image of people milling about a village square in Klavedar. It's a current live real-time image of the village folk.

Peter can't help but think that if anyone would create a way to spy on people, Master Imton would be most suited... in the same way that Master Sashaw is suited to be a magic censor. He wonders how many realize the Masters have the ability to spy on them?

Imton lets the spy globe pop and he gestures for Peter to create one of his own. Peter forms a globe in the air that contains nothing at first. He feels Imton's stare.

After a moment Peter generates within the globe an image of Shan by the log, surrounded by summer flowers. His warm choice of image causes Master Imton to shake his head.

Then he just nods - his way of saying that Peter has sufficiently done what was expected of him. Imton rarely offers much more input, as though he is only willing to do the bare minimum. Peter has no idea why he feels this is so, but somehow he knows it's true.

Master Imton says dryly, "That's enough for today. Be back tomorrow."

With that, he turns and heads for his private library.

Peter picks up his pack and starts towards the front door, but stops and turns, "Why do you dislike me so much?"

As Master Imton goes into his library he simply says, "You're dangerous for Spirin."

He closes the door before Peter can ask anything more.

Peter thinks about what Master Imton said for a moment and exits, no closer to an answer about what Imton sees wrong with him.

This coldness makes him feel that things are taking place that he is not being told of. He doesn't know enough yet to challenge Gran-D over the matter, but he's become sure Gran-D has a hand in it as well.

Chapter Sixteen

Book in hand, Shan suns herself at the log this afternoon. Peter floats up and comes to ground. He walks around in front of her but she keeps reading, ignoring him.

He clears his throat. Nothing. He begins whistling a tune, as if ignoring her in turn. This brings a crack in her façade and a slight smile leaks out.

Her smile feels like sunshine. Sometimes it reminds him he's been in Spirin a long time, but at this moment it's a pleasant feeling.

She looks up with a slight glare, "Look what the wind blew in. What are you doing here? In the daylight?"

Her words cloud the pleasant moment. Peter knows he's been preoccupied with his training and that's a lame excuse to use with Shan for a number of reasons.

After trying to think of a comeback, he simply raises his hand and spreads his fingers. A flower sprouts from each digit. He lowers his hand to the ground and each flower hops from his fingertips and takes root in the bed of blue grass.

Her leak of a smile broadens and she gestures for him to sit on the log.

She's not about to let him off the hook completely, "You come home late, leave early... lately we hardly ever get to talk."

"I can't help it if the Masters keep me busy. There's so much to learn."

Only after he lets this slip out does he realize it isn't what he meant to say. He also said it with too much enthusiasm.

He tries to go in reverse, "Can't you just be happy I found some time off?"

"You seem to have changed your tune about the Masters."

She doesn't seem as sensitive about his training as he thought.

"Aw... they aren't so bad... at least not most of them."

He scoots off the log and lowers himself to the ground beside her. She doesn't protest.

After a second Shan says, "What are they teaching you, other than making flowers? By the way, they're nice flowers."

"I don't know... all sorts of things. Do we need to talk about them right now?"

He inches over towards her.

She stiffens up, "You mean all sorts of things that I wouldn't know about?"

Apparently he is wrong about her sensitivity. Peter has had about enough of this dancing as he can handle.

"You're determined to pick a fight. I took some time off to have a chance to be with you and all you want to do is argue."

Shan is taken aback, "I'm sorry. It's just been nagging at me that while you're busy learning new things, I'm not. It's not your fault. If I had the skills needed..."

"Don't go there."

Peter so much wants to tell her what Gran-D said but he knows the old man is probably right that it would not serve her well. What can he say?

Finally, "You shortchange yourself. You don't need the Masters any more than I do. I only agreed to take the classes because it was quicker than figuring it all out by myself. If they are too stupid to offer you classes, then learn on your own."

He knows she needs some experience to get her past seeing her limitations... but he has no idea what that experience could be. If he could generate it, he would.

Peter tries to shift again, "How's the runt doing?"

It doesn't work.

"Which Master are you with now?"

"Imton, Master Imton, I don't think he likes me much. Our days are short. At least it gives me a little more free time, like now. The only problem with the Masters is that they keep shifting me all over... everywhere but to Master Carringer the Spell Master."

His thoughts drift to Earth for a brief second.

Shan snaps him out of it, "Oh, I forgot... the spell that can get you away from here!"

Seems he can't win today. When it gets to that point of absurdity all he can do is laugh out loud. It partially works because Peter can see Shan is having a hard time keeping a stern face. He thinks, what the hell, maybe a kiss will finish turning the tide. He leans into her.

She pushes him away, "No. You have places to go!"

"If you haven't noticed, I've been here a year. I haven't exactly been rushing to get away!"

"Only because you don't know how!" she snaps back.

Peter now thinks he might have been better off staying at Master Imton's. At least there he knew where he stood. Which Master is going to teach him about girls?

They both get to their feet rigidly.

Shan conjures her board.

Before taking off she turns to him, "You wanted to know what a Grimick is? Let me show you!"

She claps her hands.

Like being hit by a bolt of lightning, Peter glows blinding white. When the glow dims, he is a Grimick. He's now sort of a cross between a human-sized toad and a jackrabbit - a tall hairy frog with the face of Peter.

He glances down at his new suction paws and looks up yelling at her, "Aw, come on! This is better than punching someone?"

His tongue darts out and snatches a passing bug.

Lord Kildemar leans with both hands on his war table looking at an inlaid map of the whole Sphere flattened out. The map only shows the terrain details of Goreipor.

The other five lands are blank, save for their names - Acculas, Creatorn, Capulia, Spirin and the Portal. It's his Eastern neighbor Spirin that frets at him the most for now, but he wants his brand on all of them someday... even the tiny sliver named the Portal.

The door to his war room creaks open just enough for a guard to stick his head.

"My liege, Madame Racinda's assistant brings a message."

Lord Kildemar turns, "You mean my witch. Let him in."

Rupert, Racinda's assistant, enters. He is clearly frightened at being sent before the Dark Lord on his own.

Lord Kildemar snaps, "Out with it, boy. Why is my witch too busy to bring word herself?"

He realizes he cares not for an errand boy's opinion so he restates it, "What message do you bring from my witch?"

Rupert stutters, "She bids you to the wall. She weakened the hole enough, she thinks, for a person to go through."

The Lord dismisses Rupert and yells for the guard to find Lieutenant Ricken. He turns back to the map on the table and slowly runs his hand over the Land of Spirin... aching for what it might hold.

Peter the Grimick sits slumped on the log, occasionally glancing up at a passing bug. He hears someone approaching and attempts to turn his head. As a Grimick, his new anatomy doesn't work that way - he has to stand up and turn his whole body to look behind him.

It's Gran-D struggling up the hill with his cane. Peter knows he can speak but he's doesn't know what to say. He croaks his displeasure.

At first Gran-D laughs but muffles it on seeing Peter doesn't find the situation at all funny.

"Thought you might need some help," he says. "Actually, Shan sent me because she forgot to put a time limit on the spell."

Gran-D raises the tip of his cane above Peter's head. Peter starts to spin, faster and faster till he becomes a blur. When Gran-D lowers the cane Peter winds down.

He is once again Peter... a very dizzy boy. He staggers to the log and plops down.

Gran-D, holding back laughter, takes a seat beside him, "Aren't girls just as confusing on Earth?"

"Yeah, but on Earth they can't zap you."

Somehow, Peter thinks Gran-D already knows this. Too many words and tones slip out here and there... telling him the old man knows more about Earth than he lets on.

Gran-D can sense Peter's gears grinding.

Trying to sound exhausted, "That was quite a hill, wears on an old man."

Peter looks at him cynically, "Gran-D, if you had a mind to, you could probably lift this log and balance it on your nose. Or should that be Master Gran-D?"

After a moment, the old man lets out a laugh, "No one calls me Master outside of the Council... and, it's Grand Master Dar within it." After another moment, "Does anyone else know?"

Peter thinks on the question for a moment and glibly says, "Let's see... I think Atta may not, but I haven't canvassed the entire village yet."

Gran-D stares straight ahead a few seconds and lets out another laugh, "All are comfortable with the façade, so let it be."

Gran-D knows his disguise was an illusion long ago. He just doesn't know how many are on to it or simply don't care. Most people figure he has his reasons and are more than happy to play along.

For Gran-D, the point is simple. He hates the title Master, let alone that of Grand Master. He likes his little non-deception and illusion of freedom.

"Shan was in a huff about my training again," Peter says.

"Peter, I tell you again, there's nothing you can say that will get her over her own demons. It's going to have to be an experience - what experience, I don't know. We will just have to wait and let it play out."

Peter feels he has to push another matter, even if it doesn't meet with approval.

"When am I going to train with the Spell Master... Master Carringer?"

"You still think you belong back on Earth?"

"I still have a brother there."

In truth, Peter wonders if he's sure about that. He's a year older, so is Devon. His brother is probably permanently pissed at him for disappearing and has adjusted to him being gone.

Thinking of the training Gran-D clearly orchestrated him into, "If your training was preparing me to stay here, then it backfired. I have to go back even if I may not want to. Part of my training tells me it's the right thing to do."

Gran-D smiles, "We didn't train the sense of responsibility into you. Granted, a little discipline didn't hurt, but the rest is all on you."

He goes on, "As for the spell, you'll just have to trust me a little longer. Speaking of homes, it's about time we head there for dinner."

Seeing Peter glance at a passing bug, the old man adds, "That is, unless you are full?"

As they walk away, Peter asks, "When do I start training with you?"

"You have been since you got here," Gran-D answers.

Chapter Seventeen

In the camp at the Eastern border of Goreipor, Witch Racinda continues laboring over the weak spot in the wall. In place of torchlights flanking the discolored circle on the wall there are now a ring of lights encircling it.

A thin finger of illumination from each light leads to the edge of the dark spot, as though unstitching it. A few soldiers stand on the platform and hold a rope that disappears into the center of the circle.

Witch Racinda yells, "One more pull!"

The soldiers have already pulled many yards of rope back through the circle onto the pile of rope at their feet. They pull one last time and a grotcher pops out of the hole, very unhappy.

A grotcher is like a black boar, but with four tusks. With care not to get gouged, the soldiers untie the beast. As soon as it's freed, it scurries down the stairs of the platform.

Rupert comments, "At least it's alive."

Lord Kildemar waits for the grotcher to pass and climbs the steps to the platform. Lieutenant Ricken follows him.

The Lord looks at the darkened spot in the wall and turns to Racinda, "Did the animal visit Spirin?"

"I think so, my Liege, but the breach in the wall is not a simple Door. It will only allow one living being through... and that one must return before another may try. The wall is trying to mend itself as we speak."

She adds, "We dare not try it with a person yet. Only two of ten grotchers returned intact. Give me a little more time to wedge the opening."

Lord Kildemar snaps, "All this time you've had and you come to me with a weak half-spell?"

"I come to you with something. Do you think you can do better?"

After saying this Witch Racinda backs away. She rarely snaps back and knows instantly the chance she has taken. She has to remind herself that this monarch does not respect her in the same way his father did.

He glares at her, deciding how to react to this insolence. Taligarr places a slight hand on his father's arm, all the comment he dare make.

After a quick judgmental glare at his son, the Lord says, "Careful witch, your tongue may be your undoing!"

"All I was trying to say is that if we delay and the breach heals, we have nothing."

He grumbles under his breath and goes on, "As for testing it, we have Lieutenant Ricken here to do that. As you say, we dare not wait for it to heal."

Racinda knows this is not a matter for debate.

Kildemar turns to the Lieutenant, "All I want of you is to go through and observe. Get the lay of their land, the strength of their troops and find any weakness. Do not be discovered and return with a report. Understood?"

Lieutenant Ricken is distracted by the hole. He wonders if he will be able to come back at all? The grotcher was tied to a rope. He will not be. The grotcher wore no armor and he will.

Will the wall crush him into dust as it did the first soldier? If he does make it through, what kind of magical powers will he face? A mountain of doubts races through his mind in a few split seconds.

He suddenly feels the burn of Lord Kildemar's glare and struggles to attend to the moment.

"Yes, sire, as you order."

Racinda turns to Lieutenant Ricken, "I don't know what freedom you will have beyond the wall. Just listen to your body. The longest we have tested a grotcher beyond the wall is a day, but a leash restricted him. I would suggest that you stay no longer than that."

"He will stay as long as it takes," commands Kildemar.

Racinda tries to get back to point, "If I'm correct, there will be an identical dark circle on the other side of the wall. We will send a rope tied to a rock through to mark the spot for your return."

Lord Kildemar snaps, "We will do no such thing. It would give our hand away if it were seen. Leave a simple marker to find your way back. If you do not accomplish your tasks, you will not need a way back."

Racinda is not militarily minded, but she knows a soldier has to have some kind of hope to function effectively.

She offers a slim glimmer, "The hole will be too high for you to reach... when you return to it throw a rock through and we will send you a rope."

She glances at Lord Kildemar to see how this goes over. With a grumble he nods in agreement.

Kildemar exits the platform just in case Lieutenant Ricken blows up like the first soldier into the hole. It's not an action that encourages Ricken, but Kildemar could care less.

Lieutenant Ricken stares at his target. He knows that to delay will show him as weak. Since going is his only choice, he might as well appear strong.

Racinda breaks his concentration, "Aim for the center."

It's earnest advice, but just another thing to worry about. He takes a deep breath, plunges forward into the spot head first - and disappears.

Lieutenant Ricken tumbles out of the mirror into the Land of Spirin. There's a softness to his surroundings that he has never experienced in Goreipor, but he pays little attention to that. He's more concerned with having all his body parts intact.

Taking a quick inventory and satisfied that everything he started out with is still there, he lets out a breath of relief. He gets up and looks back at the wall.

The dark ripples of distortion in the mirror are on Spirin's side, as Witch Racinda thought - another good sign. He stacks a few stones near the wall, not obtrusive but clear enough a marker for him to know where to get home... that is, if he survives that long.

Now he turns to survey this strange new land. It's a bewildering sight. Where's the hardness of the world he has always known? He reminds himself to think like a soldier... danger can hide behind any facade.

There are no defenses to be seen anywhere. Surely there should be patrols or, at least, sentry posts near the border. None are within sight.

The moonlight gives the gentle rolling hills an electric blue glow. There are dozens of bright pink bugs floating across the landscape. Ricken has no idea that they are just large, harmless butterflies.

He makes note to be on guard against the strange creatures. They could care less about his presence.

He was hoping that his task of reconnaissance could be accomplished near the border where any normal military presence should be. Now he has to go look for something... without a horse or any idea of where to start.

It's not the path he would have chosen but, the sooner he gets to it, the sooner he can try to get home – if getting home is possible at all.

He reminds himself that to go back empty handed means going back to a death sentence. The last thing he can do is return saying he saw a pretty landscape.

As Ricken starts to walk inland, a sudden twinge reminds him of what Witch Racinda said, "Listen to your body."

It makes no sense, but what his body is telling him is that in some way he is connected to the wall. He doesn't know how or why but it's as if an invisible thread tethers him to the hole he came through.

It doesn't encumber his movement yet, but he wonders if it will get stronger the farther he gets away from his point of entry. Will it be like an elastic strap that becomes tougher to pull on? All he can do is go on and adjust accordingly.

Ricken was trained to run all day with a full pack. Though he doesn't think he will need that stamina, he is aware that time is of an essence. Not knowing where to start, he takes off straight inland from the wall at a three-quarter sprint.

Aware of Peter's experience as a Grimick, everyone around the table has an overwhelming urge to laugh at him. They do their best to hold it in.

Peter tries to ignore them. At the moment, he's dealing with another form of confusion. He is not sure what he should apologize for.

Even with his limited experience with women, he has come to believe that sometimes it's best to simply say you're sorry... whether you know what you're sorry about or not.

He braces for this ritual and turns to Shan, "Shan..."

She cuts him off, knowing he has no idea why he's apologizing, "That's OK, I'm over it." As a little dig, she adds, "Nice to see you back on a normal diet."

All break out laughing. It's so contagious even Peter joins in.

Kalish leans over and quietly says, "Not to worry, lad, her mother has done worse to me. Don't give up."

Lieutenant Ricken has jogged steadily through the evening. Following a faint glow of light in the night sky, he has found the village of Klavedar. Again, Ricken is surprised at what he does not see.

There are no defensive walls or towers, no moat - for that matter, nothing that remotely looks threatening. It's beyond his understanding. Perhaps their defenses are camouflaged, but they must be very well hidden.

Ricken sneaks into the village with little difficulty. Once there he steals a cloak hanging on a line to wear over his battle gear. Its hood easily masks his leathery face and lack of curly ears.

So far, there's no sign of any military - not even a hint of what he would consider civil authority. Wearing the cloak, he's able to move easily without being challenged. Such behavior by civilians of Goreipor would naturally be challenged at checkpoints.

There must be a stronghold somewhere else. A society cannot exist without a military or some form of authority.

From watching the people of the village, it's apparent to Ricken that many of them can do small feats of magic. Trivial things like floating items... but, by Goreipor's standards, magic nonetheless.

At one point, he stands in the shadows and eavesdrops on a few men speaking of some kind of a council making decisions. This must be the authority that the lieutenant seeks.

He drifts in and out of the village shadows, trying to gain more information. He's aware he could probably walk around more freely, but that would feel totally unnatural to him as a soldier.

Ricken reasons that those in the village are the mere sheep. He may need to explore farther away to find the wolves.

Just as he's about to give up on the village and expand his search, he happens upon four men gossiping about a Council of Masters training some boy that's not from Spirin.

This seems worth knowing about. Apparently this boy has stronger powers than many and he lives with a family named Dee. Ricken inches his way closer, hoping to pick up some more information about the outsider.

They switch their topic to Jeemer races, not because a stranger is close by, but because they simply feel like talking about Jeemers. Ricken is a touch curious about what Jeemers are... but that's not important now.

Half hiding his face, Lieutenant Ricken dares ask the men directly about this Council. One of the men gladly states he thinks they meet at the Dees'.

He's corrected by another who thinks they meet at Master Melick's, quickly adding that they are probably not meeting tonight because he saw one of the Masters in the local pub.

Lieutenant Ricken can barely hide his dismay at their looseness. Before he can even try to wheedle out a hint to where this Dee cottage might be, a man volunteers the information. He and another man actually argue about how far it is.

Ricken thanks them and backs away into the shadows... as if anyone cares. He thinks, 'What kind of absurd security is this?'

Such laxness in Goreipor would surely cost heads.

Peter sits in the living room, his brow scrunched up as he studies the chessboard lying between him and Shan. Chess is alien to Spirin but since it is Devon's favorite game, Peter has carved a crude set.

Exhausted, Shan snaps, "Come on, your move."

Peter looks up with one of those 'don't rush me' looks. At last, he cautiously moves a piece.

Shan smiles and, without hesitation, reaches out and moves her white knight.

"Checkmate, I think."

Peter stares at the board in disbelief and collapses back in his chair.

Adding insult to injury, she says, "What's the big deal? It's just a matter of strategy."

"Devon used to say strategy and war." And in an exhausted voice, "Isn't there anyone I can beat with this stupid game?"

Just then, Ramie comes out of the kitchen.

"Hey, Rockhead, how about a game?"

Ramie pretends not to hear as he walks on by and tromps up the stairs without a look back.

Peter turns to Atta, "What's up with him?"

"I think he's jealous. You don't have much free time and what you do have you spend with Shan."

Peter looks at the empty staircase and realizes she's right.

"I know what to do. Tomorrow I'll take him out for a game of Orb. Master Imton will probably be happy not to have me around for a day."

Peter looks to Gran-D with an unsaid 'can you fix it'. Gran-D nods back that he can.

The brief image of a man's shadow crosses the Dees' window.

Gran-D glances up, seeming to sense something unusual. Something is amiss in the Land of Spirin, but his puzzled look says he doesn't quite know what.

Chapter Eighteen

Peter and Ramie swoosh across a meadow towards the base of a cliff playing their long overdue game of Orb. Near the cliffs the game turns north. Ramie loves playing along the cliff face because he can bounce his Orb off the walls for tricky shots.

He whips an Orb shot at the rocks and it redirects itself at Peter. It doesn't actually bounce because there's an energy field around the Orb.

Peter has to strain to control that one and Ramie's pleased to have caught him off guard. This is just what Ramie needs, a little one-on-one attention.

Peter is enjoying their play as well. The afternoon reminds him of getting away with Devon for a little sibling skateboard competition.

Atop the cliff, a dark figure watches the boys play far below. He hears Ramie yell Peter's name. From the village gossip, he knows this boy is the outsider being trained by Masters.

Lieutenant Ricken calculates that maybe he can score points to get himself back in Lord Kildemar's good graces... if he takes a little initiative and rids this strange land of a potential threat to Goreipor.

Ricken grasps a hefty stiff branch and wedges it into a pyramid of rocks resting precariously near the cliff's edge. He watches... waiting for the right moment to strike.

All he can do is estimate the boys' movements since their game is so fast-paced. If things go as he expects, the few rocks will become many, increasing the chance of crushing his target.

Ramie spins and rockets an Orb back at Peter. It flies well over Peter's head, making him reverse direction and lengthen his distance from Ramie. Snagging the shot, Peter triumphantly does a 360 loop. As a touch of gloating rises, he sees a rock tumble down the face of the cliff.

"Ramie, heads up!"

Far away and too busy whipping around on his board, Ramie does not hear Peter's warning. The rock slams into the ground a few feet behind him. Ramie doesn't even notice.

He turns back towards Peter. A few more rocks fall. Peter yells again, waving his arms. Ramie looks up to see what Peter is being so insistent about.

A fist-sized stone glances off the back of his head!

He tumbles into the grass, stunned. More substantial boulders follow the smaller rocks.

Peter races towards Ramie who struggles up off the ground, trying to get his bearings. Rocks start slamming down all around. The few large rocks Ricken has released act as expected and compound into a thundering cascade spreading along the cliff wall.

Peter zigzags boulders crashing all around as he attempts to get to Ramie. He concentrates as he races for the fallen Ramie, causing a flicker of a globe to start generating around him.

The flicker grows into a clear bubble enclosing him. A large rock bounces off the bubble, only slightly jarring Peter. He maneuvers fewer zigzags, shooting straight towards Ramie. As the avalanche intensifies, more rocks bounce off his protective shield.

Getting to Ramie, Peter sweeps him into the globe just as the heaviest downpour of rocks falls. The boulders jar the boys this way and that. None breach the shield and Peter whisks himself and Ramie out of harm's way.

As soon as the two are well away from the cliffs Peter settles his board by a tree. Ramie is a bit disoriented and a trickle of blood runs from a lump on his forehead. He appears all right to Peter who tugs for the family.

A little while later, Ramie lies under the tree milking all the attention he can get from his family. Peter looks up at the crest of the cliff and sees Gran-D walking there.

Gran-D picks up a stout branch and notices deep scratch marks on one end, as though it has been used as a pry bar.

Scanning the area all around he sees no one - but there is a boot print near what appears to be freshly exposed rocks. It strikes him as an odd print for someone to make in Spirin.

He drops the branch and turns into a wisp of swirling smoke curling its way down towards the other Dees. Gran-D materializes near them and glances back up at the ridge with a concerned expression.

Atta and Kalish are busy babying Ramie who continues to soak it up. Shan knows her brother is sucking in all the attention he can. She figures why not - he was almost seriously harmed.

With a subtle signal, Gran-D beckons Peter off to the side with him.

Once out of earshot he asks Peter, "Did you see anyone up on the cliff before the rock slide?"

Peter hasn't thought of the rockslide as being anything more than an accident. Back home rockslides didn't happen all the time, but they weren't unusual. They were just a side effect of living in the mountains.

He glances up to the ridge and shrugs, "We were busy playing till the slide, and I was a little busy once it started. You should know better than I... people don't hurt each other here. It was just a rock slide, that's all."

"You're probably right, but keep an eye out for anything unusual," says Gran-D, gazing up at the ridge and scanning the surroundings.

Peter can tell there's something behind the old man's concerns, but he's not sure what.

"Sure, I'll keep an eye out."

"Remember, anything odd or out of place. I want you to tug me first, understand?" Gran-D insists.

Peter thinks Gran-D's cautious behavior is the only odd thing at present, but he nods his agreement anyway.

As Peter turns back toward the family, Gran-D asks, "Who taught you to create that protective shield?"

"No one, it just seemed like a good idea at the time. Something wrong with that?"

Up till then Peter has dismissed generating the protective sphere as something other Spirinese must be able to do. He has stumbled on it just like he has so many other spells.

Lost in thought, Gran-D says, "No. It's just interesting, that's all... but it saved both of you."

With this he turns and walks off thinking about this new turn of events.

Peter watches him walk away. Once again he has the feeling of things playing out that are being kept from him. He's trying his best not to distrust the old man.

Word of the rock slide spreads quickly throughout Spirin, though the stated facts are far from the truth.

Two days later, Masters Sashaw, Warnig and Imton walk through the village. Their ears burn from all the gossip floating about.

As they pass by a small group of men they hear one say, "The rocks just bounced off the round ear."

Another says, "I heard they wouldn't come near him."

A third man says, "He's that powerful?"

A more ominous comment, "Remember what he did to Yadar."

The Masters continue their walk. Sashaw turns to the other two, "Dar has us playing with fire."

Master Warnig nods, but Imton looks off in the distance as though privy to more. Master Sashaw notices this.

"Imton, what do you think?"

Without looking at them, "It's difficult to say at present."

He has no interest in discussing Gran-D's plans for the fate of Spirin. He just continues walking as if none of this gossip is of interest to him. Master Imton would make a great poker player, if poker existed on the Sphere.

The Grand Hall of the Dark Fortress is abuzz with talk that someone crossed the wall into a world that no one knows about. Everyone wants to know what's out there.

Lord Kildemar could care less what everyone wants, though he is a little curious about how word spread so quickly. The leak is something he'll have to deal with later.

His standing orders are that as soon as Lieutenant Ricken arrives from the Eastern border, he is to be brought before him. Then all but the chosen few are to clear out of the Grand Hall.

Kildemar knows the value of information and controlling it. With information as his primary weapon to get the upper hand, he staged his coup d'état against his father.

The tower bell rings, indicating soldiers are approaching. Without a word his court clears. Lord Kildemar relishes that power over people and their fear... they're one and the same.

Lieutenant Ricken and Witch Racinda arrive together. She goes up and takes her place by the Lord while Lieutenant Ricken bends a knee in front of Kildemar.

Lord Kildemar waves for him to rise.

"Good to see you yet alive. What do you have for me? Mind you, Lieutenant, keep your report to the point."

Lord Kildemar has little patience for talkative people. He deems that rambling gives away too much information - both about the rambler and whom he represents.

Unfortunately, Lieutenant Ricken is a rambler. He rambles on about the village... the kind of people there, how they don't know how to be on guard and how they stupidly even gave him directions. He spews all this before taking five breaths.

Janick elbows Taligarr, knowing their father will soon explode. Taligarr's look warns Janick not to see this as funny.

Lieutenant Ricken is about to prate on when Lord Kildemar slams the end of his staff on the rock floor. It echoes throughout the hall.

"I am going to ask you questions and I expect simple answers... not what you think of everything!"

The Lieutenant nods.

"Military! Did you see any?" the lord demands.

Lieutenant Ricken says, "No. I think they have some kind of Council that..."

Kildemar cuts him off, "Do not think! Just supply answers. Did you see this Council?"

The Lieutenant tries to rein himself in, "Only a few of them. They are training some boy from somewhere else that all the people in... "

"The boy? Everything!" Lord Kildemar demands.

"He is just a kid named Peter... but he did seem to have defensive powers," Lieutenant Ricken says.

"How would you know that?"

Thinking to score a point now, Lieutenant Ricken smiles, "I felt he was a threat so I attempted to kill him."

Lord Kildemar screams, "You what? I did not send you there to make decisions. You were there to observe, no more."

The Lieutenant says quickly, "He wasn't hurt. He created some kind of shield and escaped."

Lord Kildemar knows that Lieutenant Ricken may have aroused suspicions that someone has visited the land and pinpointed a target of interest... both serious errors.

If looks could kill, the young officer is half way to his grave.

"I'm sorry, my lord. Next time I will do no more than watch... unless you have other orders for me."

The Lord quietly says, "I will not."

He turns and looks at Witch Racinda. She knows the look and what it demands of her.

Racinda lowers her staff towards Lieutenant Ricken. A ball of light shoots slowly from its end and engulfs Ricken. The lieutenant grabs his chest in pain and collapses to the rug.

Within a few seconds his body stops twitching. He lies there, motionless. Without needing to be told, two guards take the edges of the rug and drag Lieutenant Ricken's body from the hall.

After the body has been removed, Lord Kildemar waves for Captain Pirus to approach.

"Captain, I want that boy, Peter, dead. Can you do that for me?"

Captain Pirus simply nods his understanding of the orders with no need of words.

Chapter Nineteen

A thin trail of smoke comes in through Master Imton's window and materializes into Imton himself. A second stream follows and Peter appears.

Master Imton, in his less than friendly tone, "It all comes rather easily to you boy, doesn't it?"

Peter would view this as a simple question, but with Master Imton he's not sure. He does not enjoy training under this master who won't let up on his dislike. In return, Peter doesn't particularly like Master Imton either. It continues to bother him that Imton has yet to offer any further explanation for the remark that Peter is dangerous.

"I guess so. Did it come easy for you?"

Imton takes umbrage, "What do you mean by that?"

"All I meant was, back when you were first learning... nothing more."

As usual, Peter's at a loss as to what sets Imton off so. Actually he's getting a little tired of it.

"What is your problem with me?"

Peter's not talking like a student right now - he's a pissed off kid.

"I can't get on the right side of you and I want to know why!"

He figures he's started down the path so he might as well push as far as he can. Surprisingly Imton has not interrupted him yet.

"When I asked you why you disliked me so, you said I was dangerous. Why do you feel that way? All I'm looking for is a straight answer."

Imton responds with more emotion than Peter has ever seen in the man, "I don't dislike you, Peter. You're just a dangerous gamble, from a dangerous world... and I know of what I speak."

"What do you mean by gamble?"

Imton catches himself, "I've said more than I should."

"But you haven't said anything."

Master Imton is back in control.

He coldly states, "That's enough of lessons for the day. I'll see you back here tomorrow... and I don't want to discuss this matter again."

Before Peter can protest, Imton waves his finger at the door. It opens on its own. The master turns and walks towards another room, making it clear that he is through talking.

Peter can't leave at that, "Does Gran-D have anything to do with this gamble?"

Master Imton freezes a second, then continues walking without answering. Peter senses he hit a nerve. In spite of a slight tinge of guilt, it pleases him.

Once outside Master Imton's cottage Peter realizes he forgot his pack. He doesn't relish the idea of going back in, but he wants it.

He knocks. No answer. He knocks again. After no answer again, he opens the door and sticks his head in.

"Master Imton."

Nothing.

Peter slips in. All he has to do is grab the pack and be gone. He reaches his pack and sees the door to Master Imton's private library open a crack. Not wanting to appear that he's sneaking about, he goes to the door.

He sticks his head in, "Master Imton, it's Peter. I forgot my pack."

There's no one in the library. This is the first time he's seen inside the library and, though he knows better, he can't help wanting to at least get a good look from the doorway.

It's a very scholastic-looking library, its walls lined with book-cases. A massive desk, covered with books and scrolls, sits by a large standing globe of the Sphere. From the door he can see the globe only shows details of Spirin, with simple outlines of the other lands on the planet.

Shan has told him the planet is made up of five other lands, but to see the blankness of most of the globe registers what she said about their isolation. It's strange for someone from Earth to live on a planet where you know nothing, absolutely nothing, about the others who inhabit the same world.

Near the globe sits a side table with an intricately carved chess set on it.

Peter hears a sound behind him and jerks his head out of the room. When he turns, no one is there.

The door to Master Impton's library creaks closed on its own. Peter figures he's pressed his luck as far as he should. Pack in hand, he quietly heads out the front door.

It slams behind him!

Shan and Peter visit the village on what has become a regular supply run. Peter is now thoroughly accustomed to the magical nature of the vendors and their floating wares. In fact, now he can make their wares disappear if he has a mind to - of course, he would never have a mind to.

Over time Peter has become less of an oddity. Few villagers give attention to his round ears. Of course, incidents like the rock slide flare interest, but every new story tends to linger less.

Like any community, gossip about one thing gets old. Still, Peter is aware that in some ways he'll always feel like an outsider, and he tries not to stir up unneeded controversy.

Shan glances at her basket.

"I forgot something, I'll be right back."

Peter nods and plops down on the edge of the square's fountain. He can't remember a time that Shan hasn't discovered she's forgotten something when they're shopping.

No big deal, it's a pretty day out and lots of people to watch. Though he has learned many of their ways, there are still times when he finds the differences from Earth fascinating.

The boy Peter hit some time ago, Yadar, enters the far end of the square. He doesn't notice Peter at first, but Peter is quick to notice him. This is because Peter has wanted to catch up with him eventually.

To Peter it's a matter that needs to get squared. He's not sure the boy will have the same sentiments.

Peter gets up and heads for Yadar. When Yadar sees him, it's clear from his body language that his first inclination is to run... but he nervously stands his ground.

To ease the situation Peter puts on his best smile for the last few yards of his approach.

Unsure if the alien has changed his ways, a number of people in the square stop to watch. Shan arrives back at the square from a side street and also watches from afar. Her interest is more curiosity than lack of trust.

As Peter nears the other boy, he reaches out a hand, "Hey man, I've been hoping we'd run into each other. I wanted to say I'm sorry for hitting you."

Peter knows a true apology isn't based on someone accepting it, but he hopes for the best.

Hesitantly, a smile comes to Yadar's face. Shaking hands is not a Spirinese custom, but after a moment of puzzlement Yadar figures what Peter's outstretched hand might mean.

He shakes it.

The boy is not sure how long he is supposed to shake hands so Peter releases his grip to help make it clear.

Before Yadar lets go, he leans into Peter and whispers, "Can you teach me how?"

Peter is now the puzzled one, "Teach you how to what?"

"How to defend myself... what else?"

From the way Yadar asks, it's clear he's sincere about this odd request.

"Defend yourself against who?" Peter says in bewilderment.

"Maybe you", Yadar responds with a smile.

Both break out laughing.

"You don't know how lucky you are you don't need to know that stuff... and you won't need it with me."

Having squared things, Peter starts to turn.

Yadar taps him on the shoulder, "You know, I know someone who can fix those ears for you... on the sly."

Peter puts his hand to his ear. He hasn't thought about them, at least not for some time. He finds it an odd suggestion.

"Why, they're just ears and they work fine. Thanks for the offer anyway."

Yadar reaches out to shake hands again, maybe because it's a pleasant novelty. Peter obliges and they separate.

As Peter walks away, he thinks about his ears and why anyone would want to change something like that? And why would there be someone who could do it on the sly? Then he thinks of Earth and how many people change their features for who knows what reasons. Finally he shakes his head and dismisses the matter. He likes his ears just the way they are.

When Peter gets back across the square, Shan comes up and playfully nudges him, "What was that about?"

"Nothing. Just setting some things straight."

He nudges her back and adds, "You like my ears, don't you?"

Her smile answers the question.

The shadow of a man watches from a bluff high above a wooded grove. Down below, Yadar and a few of his friends whip around and among the trees on their hoverboards.

They're like kids on Earth at a skate park, trying all kinds of daring maneuvers and occasionally whipping out. Just having fun.

The kids whoop it up at every more absurd hoverboard move each one of them makes. Yadar is one of the most daring. He races towards a tree, goes vertical to hover up the trunk till his board loses its grip and he loops back to the ground. He taunts another boy to try to get as high.

The hand of the watcher is old. It lifts the tip of a cane and aims it towards the unsuspecting kids.

Suddenly Yadar's board takes off into the woods with him on it, but the expression on his face makes clear that he's not controlling it. It jerks this way and that, barely missing one tree trunk after another. Faster and faster it goes.

Yadar yells his fear. He's used to doing stunts, but not used to stunts doing him. He falls forward to lie on his board and holds on for dear life.

The hoverboard glances off a tree, sending bark flying. It shows no sign of slowing. Everything passes Yadar in a blur. He holds his board so tight he is almost melting into it.

Straight as an arrow, they race at one very massive tree. The board shows no sign of swerving. A split second before crashing into the trunk, Yadar's board pulls up and to the right and upside down.

Yadar drops from the board into a thicket of bushes.

His friends catch up and help him out of the bushes. Yadar is scratched and well frightened, but not seriously hurt.

Up on the bluff the point of the cane pivots down, exposing an intricately carved headpiece that resembles a black knight. Shrouded by a black cloak, the person turns away.

After a side trip to the log where they have lazed around for the afternoon, Peter and Shan arrive home. As they walk in, there's heaviness in the air.

Peter picks up on it immediately, maybe because he's been there before. His defensive instincts come to the ready before a word is said.

Kalish, who has been sitting at the table, stands up, "Peter, the boy Yadar got into an accident today. You know anything about it?"

Atta is quick to get up and urges Kalish to sit back down.

In Peter's life he's been accused of many things - some he did and some he didn't do. Long ago he's learned how it feels to have fingers pointed at him... and he doesn't like it.

He's also learned to take pause - often to formulate his story for when he is actually guilty. With all his experience of being in trouble, what puzzles him this time is how much it hurts.

More in a numb than angry tone, he replies, "Looks like you've already decided."

"Of course not. It's just that it's so unusual to hear of someone getting hurt by someone else... at least, here in Spirin," Atta says, thinking she's helping... but this cuts even deeper.

Shan is the first to jump to Peter's defense, and rather aggressively, "Whoever said he had anything to do with this is lying!"

Atta's shocked by her daughter's harshness.

Shan starts to go on, but Peter places a hand on her arm. "It's OK" is all he says and he heads up the stairs. Shan doesn't know whom she's more pissed at - her parents for the accusation or Peter for walking away from it.

Gran-D comes in from the kitchen to see what the ruckus is about, as if he didn't know. Kalish explains they were just asking Peter about Yadar.

Gran-D laughs. "Let the villagers wag their tongues. They have nothing else to do with them. The boy's fine. Peter had nothing to do with it."

Kalish turns to Atta, "That's good enough for me."

Atta nods in agreement and starts for the stairs. Kalish reaches out and stops her.

"As head of this house, it's my job to do the apologizing," and he heads up the stairs to talk with Peter.

Gran-D turns to Atta, "Always liked that man of yours."

The next morning Peter reluctantly shows up for his lessons with Master Imton. Though Kalish took it back, after being accused of the Yadar incident, Peter's not in the greatest of moods. When Imton enters, Peter instantly senses another blow is coming.

Master Imton, with almost a hint of sadness in his eyes, says, "I'm afraid we have to stop classes for a while."

"Rumors travel fast, don't they? Does it matter that I didn't do it?"

Master Imton shakes his head 'no'.

Peter figures that there's no use discussing it with the one Master that dislikes him the most. He turns to leave.

Imton adds, "I'm sorry. Even though I know you didn't do it, it still doesn't mean you're not dangerous."

It's early evening. The mirror wall of Spirin looms in front of Peter. He's been sitting in front of it all afternoon, trying to sort things out. Maybe the turn of events happened for a reason... to remind him that he still has a brother to get home to. Sure, there are many things he loves about Spirin, but no matter what he does, many will still see him as an outsider. Back home he was an outsider by choice. Somehow that made being on the outside more bearable.

Finally he stands up and stares straight at his reflection.

"Blood's the only thing that counts."

He turns and leaves with a determined gait.

With Master Carringer out, his cottage is dark. Dark... – save for the floating light dot moving just above Peter's head. He figures that Carringer as Spell Master must have the pendant that controls the Sorcerer's Door stashed somewhere in his home. Peter expects to have to dig to find its hiding place and hopes Carringer will be out long enough for an extensive search.

Finding nothing in the living room, Peter moves on into Carringer's workroom. He's prepared to look in and around everything, crossing his fingers that it will not be well- hidden.

To Peter's surprise two clear, softball-sized globes float in plain sight over the mantelpiece. Each contains a pendant. Peter's only aware of one pendant existing.

He looks closely into each globe without touching either. The pendants seem identical.

An image of Peter in Carringer's workroom floats in a spy globe hovering high in the middle of Imton's living room. Master Imton, Gran-D and Master Carringer silently watch Peter.

"Where's your floating menagerie of tokens?" says Imton.

Master Carringer doesn't appreciate this comment about his valued possessions.

Without taking his eyes off Peter he says, "I want him to find the pendant... if it's any of your business."

Peter reaches out to one of the pendant bubbles. He stops just shy of touching it, shakes his head, turns and leaves.

Carringer proudly remarks, "Told you the boy has character."

"Sometimes too much," says Gran-D.

Master Imton shakes his head in doubt, "Dar, you're playing a dangerous game - both with him and with Spirin."

Chapter Twenty

S han floats over a ridge near the log to find Peter exactly where she expects to find him... there, sulking on a perfectly fine day. Gliding down, she gets off her board and steps directly in front of him.

With hands on her hips she barks, "What gave you the right to not defend yourself the other day?"

"What's the point?"

"The point is you don't have the right to allow a lie."

"You know they cut off my training."

"I heard, but that's only temporary. The Peter I saw apologizing to Yadar the other day isn't the same Peter that came here. Give the others time."

Peter thinks on it a bit and squints up at Shan, "I almost stole the Door's pendant from Carringer's last night."

Shocked by this, "You broke into Master Carringer's?"

"It's not exactly breaking in if nobody locks their doors... but, yes. I didn't take it... but I almost did."

She's not interested in fine lines, "You wanted to take it, that's all the matters."

Shan is now steaming. She came to the log mad over one thing and Peter has added fuel to the fire.

"My kid brother and I have been in a bunch of foster homes, some good, some bad, but all temporary. I'm as close to your family as I've ever been to any, but Devon's my blood... the only thing I've known that lasts."

Shan starts to leave, but stops and turns, "With all you've learned, you don't belong back in your world anymore."

She shakes her head and conjures her board, but before leaving, "If you can't see who cares for you, then everything will be temporary. Family is not always what you so distastefully call blood. You want to go home... then, go home!"

Dinner is unusually cold and quiet, especially between Peter and Shan - to the point of avoiding looking at each other. Peter wonders if Shan has told Gran-D about his attempting to take the spell. Little does he know that the old man is well aware of it.

Gran-D watches the chill treatment between the two long enough.

Breaking the ice, "Now's a good time for one of my dancing potions."

Atta knows what her father is doing.

"Those are always fun. It's the only time I can get Kalish to dance anymore."

Kalish isn't quite as enthusiastic.

"You don't have to go to work the next day with an overwhelming urge to tap dance."

Ramie laughs, but seeing he's the only one, cuts it off.

Shan excuses herself, gets up and heads for her room. Before Atta can react, Peter does the same and heads up to the loft. Kalish and Atta turn to Gran-D.

He just shrugs, "Kids - and universal hormones."

It's early morning. A light mist hangs in the air.

Peter races along a country trail on his hoverboard. He's not really going anywhere, just letting off steam - same as he used to do on his motorcycle back on Earth.

He thinks of what Shan said about what he has learned and about belonging on Earth... and wonders if he would still have powers if he went back. When he first saw Ramie on Earth he was running from the bear and not using any sorcery, so it may be a moot point.

They used to burn people at the stake for revealing even a hint of unusual powers. Nowadays the government would probably lock someone up in a research lab if they displayed any of what Peter has learned to do here on Spirin.

Being on Earth feels so long ago.

He tries to shake off all the incessant noise in his head by doing a 360° barrel roll.

At the top of the roll a black arrow zooms past Peter's head, close enough to feel its breath. The arrow embeds in a tree trunk nearby.

Peter doesn't have time to think about who or why... all he can think of is survival. He starts to generate the protective globe he used with Ramie.

As the shield flickers into existence, another arrow flies at him. The uncompleted shield slows the arrow but its point pierces deep into Peter's chest. The globe and his board vanish and Peter falls hard on the ground.

He lies motionless!

Fifty yards north of the trail, Captain Pirus stands by a tree. He slings another arrow in case it's needed.

Pirus glances up at the sky to estimate the time he has remaining. Witch Racinda has told him that the wall has strengthened and he should keep the visit to half the time Lieutenant Ricken took. Most of that time has been used locating the boy.

He takes one last look, from afar, at the dead boy's body.

Then he comments to himself, "Spirited kid ... What a shame."

Pirus turns and heads west for the wall.

Master Carringer is the only Master suited for or willing to use a hoverboard. He floats along the trail on his way home.

He sees Peter lying beside the trail and rushes to him. The first thing he does is close his eyes and tug for Gran-D. Then he turns his attention to Peter.

In short time, a thread of smoke shoots down beside Carringer and Gran-D appears.

He asks urgently, "Is he dead?"

Carringer cradles Peter's head, "He has a faint pulse. I called the healer. I wasn't sure where you want to take him."

"Home," Gran-D says.

Before helping Carringer lift Peter's body, he goes to the arrow stuck in the tree. With some effort, he manages to pull it out.

Captain Pirus stands before Lord Kildemar in the Grand Hall. He glances down at the stone floor below his feet and back up at Lord Kildemar.

Knowing the Lord's desire for reports that are to the point, he says, "The boy is dead."

Lord Kildemar leans forward on his throne, "Are you sure?"

"I do not miss."

Captain Pirus is no Lieutenant Ricken. He follows orders but does not fear his master. He's been a professional soldier too long to waste time showing fear.

He knows fear is part of the life of being a soldier and he's used to living with it. You live, you die - the quality of each is what counts. Lord Kildemar knows and respects this in him.

"Anything else to report, Captain?"

"Yes... if you want my opinion," responds Pirus.

"I do", says Kildemar.

He respects that the Captain knows the difference between rambling and a thought-out opinion.

"From what I observed, if they had a leader they could become a formidable enemy. All the people have powers that they put to menial tasks, but if they re-task them it would be a problem for any invading force. As Ricken described, they have no concept of defense at present. Somehow that boy was different. I almost regretted having to kill him."

Captain Pirus glances down at the floor again, then back up. Standing behind the Lord, Witch Racinda clears her throat to get attention.

Irritated, Kildemar turns to her, "What is it now, woman?"

She answers with caution, "The wall has healed itself. There can be no more trips through it."

"I've done what was needed for now, but find me another way to pass through walls if you relish life... I will have that land."

He turns back to Captain Pirus, who is caught again glancing at the floor.

"Captain, why do you keep doing that?"

"Just wishing for a rug to break my fall," he says glibly.

Lord Kildemar breaks out in a rare booming laugh.

Shan paces back and forth in the living room, every so often stopping for a worried glance up the stairs leading to the boys' loft. She goes back to pacing and stops again.

"What are they doing to him up there?"

Atta smiles at her, "What they have to, child. Now, would you quit wearing a path in my floor." She can't resist a little dig, "I thought you were mad at him."

"Mom!"

Shan leaves it at this and goes back to pacing.

Atta shakes her head with a smile, "To be that young again."

Up in the loft, Gran-D fiddles with the arrow from the tree while the Healer works on Peter. As he rubs his hand along its shaft, long barbs spring out sharply.

The Healer yells at him, "Old man, one patient at a time is enough! Those barbs are coated with poison."

Gran-D carefully places the arrow back on the table.

"How could he survive something as dark as this?"

"Normally he couldn't. Even without the poison, the spin of the barbs should have torn him up beyond repair."

She picks up the arrow she took out of Peter and hands it to Gran-D. A peculiar substance coats the front end. Fingering the coating, Gran-D finds it flexible like a clear membrane. As he pulls at the edge of the membrane, a barb springs out just like the other arrow.

She snaps at him again, "Do I have to send you downstairs like some twelve-year old? I told you to be careful!" Snatching the arrow from him, she holds it up, "You said the boy was able to create some kind of protective shield?"

"Yes, something of his own invention."

"What I assume is that after the first arrow passed by, he tried to create that shield. It wasn't fully formed enough to stop the second one, but I suspect that it was sufficient to coat the end."

She sets the arrow down - out of reach of Gran-D.

"So, he'll survive?" Gran-D says with hopeful relief.

Daubing some icky looking goop on Peter's chest, "It made a nasty hole in him, but it was a clean hole and I can patch him up." She turns to Gran-D in a bossy manner, "Now get out of here so I can do my work."

Gran-D starts to snap back, but he's known the Healer too long and it would do no good.

Before he leaves he says, "I have to ask a favor... His death. His life depends on no one knowing he lives - at least for the time being,"

Though intrigue is not the norm on Spirin, the Healer knows Gran-D must have a good reason.

She nods her agreement.

Then, pointedly, "Now get out of here."

Gran-D stands at the top of the stairs and announces, "Thanks to our Healer, Peter will survive. He'll be good as new in half a moon."

Shan appears as if a ton of weight has been lifted from her shoulders.

Gran-D adds, "It is very important that it appear that he did not survive - at least until the Council works things out."

Shan could care less about that at the moment. She starts to rush up the stairs, but stubbornness strikes. She knows Peter will live, so it's OK to be angry with him again.

Shan turns to her mother, "Could you go up there and hold his hand?"

To her irritation, all but Atta laugh. Atta squeezes Shan's hand to let her know she understands before heading upstairs to be her daughter's surrogate.

Chapter Twenty-One

A half moon has passed and Peter is going stir crazy cooped up at home.

He sits on one end of his bed, Ramie on the other. They play a game using a single mini-Orb. The object is to wrest control of the Orb from the other and get it through a small plane of light. Peter's letting Ramie win just enough to not let him know he's doing so. Apart from a bandage across his chest, he appears healthy.

Gran-D comes in but, before he has a chance to say anything, Peter says in a half-joking, half-pleading tone, "Please, say you're up here to set me free."

The old man lacks his normal jovial nature.

"Not exactly, but we do need to talk." Giving Ramie a look that produces no effect, he adds, "Alone."

Ramie jumps off Peter's bed, goes over and plops on his own. Gran-D glares at him. The youngster finally shrugs and sulks out the door.

Gran-D sits down on the end of Peter's bed but, before starting, he turns to the door, "Ramie, downstairs!"

The crack in the door closes and the sound of footsteps tromps down the stairs. Gran-D turns back to Peter and takes a moment to decide how to start.

Peter senses this, "Don't tell me. After all, I'm dying."

"Good, a sense of humor will serve you well. I hope you keep it," says Gran-D. "Peter, what I have to say must remain a secret, even from Shan."

Peter leans in, sensing this is serious.

With sadness in his voice, the old man continues, "I have to ask you to go home... or, more accurately, the Council is asking you to go home."

Of all the things Peter might have guessed, this would have been on the bottom of the list. He stares at Gran-D as if the words have become a physical presence - something to look at, to examine, to doubt.

All he can think of saying after it sinks in is a puzzled, "Over the boy?"

Gran-D quickly shakes his head, "No, Yadar was never in harm's way... that was a move to discredit you. Well, it did add to the Council's fears. But, no, the attempts on your life have the Council frightened of you."

"Attempts?"

"The rockslide was not an accident, any more than the arrow. The Council is afraid that you might bring even more violence to our land if you remain here."

He says this in a tone that hints he doesn't agree, but then Gran-D is an excellent actor when it serves him.

"The Prophecy?" Peter asks.

"Yes. They don't understand that the Prophecy is probably inevitable."

Since that day at the wall, Gran-D has never made mention of the Prophecy again. He doesn't know what Peter may have heard about it from others, but he assumes not much since it's a taboo subject for most Spirinese.

"Why haven't you ever asked about it again?"

"I got caught up in life here... and training. After a while, I just didn't want to know."

Peter realizes that a year has passed so easily because he has chosen to let it do so.

"I guess it's time you tell me what I'm supposed to be part of."

He tries to remember that going home has been his goal from the start... so why is this upsetting him?

Gran-D carefully sculpts in his mind the little he wants to tell Peter of the Prophecy.

"To start, the Prophecy doesn't fit you. It talks of two round ears from the stars who come to the Sphere by choice."

As Peter listens, his eyes ask, 'Then what's supposed to happen?'

"The round ears are supposed to bring about the downfall of the walls that separate the lands."

"Is that good or bad?" Peter asks out loud.

"That's the problem with these ancient prophecies... they don't always say. When the outcome is unknown, people fall back on their fears. That's the Prophecy in a nutshell. Like I said, it doesn't fit you because you didn't choose to come here."

The old man takes a breath to observe Peter's reaction, but sees none.

"Some of their fears have a foundation in that the attacks against you come from someone beyond the wall."

"I thought that was impossible."

"It was till Master Carringer experimented with the spell and caused a breach in the wall. It's now healed so I'm sure no one else can come through. Unfortunately, not all agree and they're frightened... and whoever came through might still be here. I don't know."

Peter watches carefully, "He was trying to fix it for me?"

"Something like that."

Peter sees what he is looking for in the old man's face.

"The spell was never broken, was it?"

Gran-D is not surprised by Peter's sharpness.

"I said there were problems with it." Then, seeing that Peter doesn't want euphemisms, "No, it never was broken. We thought it better to just not open it again. I'm sorry."

Peter sits back, "I guess I should be mad, but I don't think I am. I've found things here... and I have a brother there. I don't really know where I belong anymore... or how I feel."

"There's more," says Gran-D.

Down in the kitchen Ramie pouts, Shan paces and Atta deals with preparing dinner. Shan knows that something beyond what has been said is going on.

"What are they talking about up there that requires all of us to stay away?"

Atta turns to Shan, takes her by the shoulders and sets her down into a chair.

"OK... Peter is going home to check on his brother."

"What!"

Shan starts to bolt up, but Atta holds her in the chair.

"It has already been decided... Shan, he has a right to check on his family back there."

Atta turns, not wanting to give away the whole truth.

In the loft, Gran-D continues, "When Carringer was working with the Door, he discovered that the spell has a memory and that memory revealed that when Ramie opened the Door to your world something else went to through... and whatever it was didn't come back. Do you remember anything strange about the trip here?"

With a 'duh' look on his face, Peter cries, "Outside of everything? I was caught in a bubble in the middle of the impossible! But, for a split second, I think a larger bubble hit mine."

Gran-D's interest peaks, "You remember what was in it?"

"A purple elephant," says Peter glibly. Seeing Gran-D's puzzled expression, Peter speaks directly, "I have no idea what was in it."

Then Peter poses a question that surprises even himself, "What if I refuse to go?"

Peter has no idea how well this question plays into Gran-D's plans.

The old man puts on his best concerned face.

"It will be rough for the Dees to go against the Council. I head the Council, but even I can be outvoted... as I have been this time."

While Peter ponders this - and why Gran-D even brought it up — the old master deftly offers an 'out' clause, "The Council thinks Carringer is taking you home and leaving you. If what I think may have happened in your world actually has happened, I'm sending you home alone... with the pendant. That way you can come back if you need to."

Peter is confused about his emotions. He finds himself in conflict between getting home to his brother and fighting to stay in a world he's become close to... a world in which he may never truly belong.

Peter goes with one of his gut feelings, "I don't think that will happen. I have a brother to see to." He adds, "But you should know one thing... whatever's beyond those walls will eventually get in here. No one will fight your battles for you... and for the Council to avoid that is not the solution."

"You may be right. What's beyond the walls is dark. Their land is made of this."

Gran-D pulls out the stone he took from Master Carringer's side and hands it to Peter.

Peter holds the shiny black sliver up to the light. There's a hint of purple glistening in it. He starts to hand it back but Gran-D gestures for him to keep it.

"May I ask one other thing of you?"

"As if I could stop you."

The old man is happy Peter's holding on to his sense of humor.

"Make the trip appear to be a visit. It will be easier on everyone. I've already told Kalish and Atta the truth, but not Shan and Ramie."

Gran-D gets up to leave and turns back to Peter, "If you do choose to come back, I'll stand with you against the Council."

"Like I said, not much chance of that. I'm going to miss all of you - even the hocus-pocus stuff - but it's time to go home." Peter turns to look out the window... wondering if he's trying to convince himself or Gran-D.

Now thinking as a Grand Master Dar, Gran-D heads for the. He softly says, "Maybe... maybe not."

Lights are dim and a small fire crackles in the fireplace of Master Imton's home. The dark nooks and low lighting heighten the cloak-and-dagger feel. Gran-D tosses a log on the fire.

"So what did you tell the boy?" asks Master Imton.

Gran-D turns to him, "Why do you have such a hard time using Peter's name?"

"Because I know of the world he comes from. I asked you, 'What did you tell the boy?'" repeats Imton.

"I told him what was needed, no more. He leaves tomorrow."

"If you're so sure of things, why not be honest with Peter?" Master Imton letting slip a slight hint that he might even like the kid.

"It's a fine line we walk. He has to choose to come back entirely on his own."

Gran-D knows the jeopardy of this all too well. Nudging the future is always a fine line to walk.

"And if he doesn't come back?"

The Grand Master sighs and places a friendly hand on Imton's shoulder.

"Then he's not meant to do so and I will have been wrong. It won't be the first time – and it won't be the last."

Peter sits on the log near the Graveyard dangling the pendant between his fingers. He looks up at the Graveyard of Spells, knowing here is where the adventure started.

He thinks of how - way back when he arrived - the green mist of the Graveyard had its own way of talking to him. He wonders why it showed him different spells... why it played with him, why it protected him?

He suspects Gran-D's conclusion that he is not part of the Prophecy is not the whole story, but just a façade. He longs for when things were less complicated... almost.

Peter takes a deep breath and reminds himself that he is being sent away. He has a brother who's been alone for over a year. He remembers that he is not a changer of worlds. He's just a lost eighteen-year old kid with a chance to go home. Last, but not least, he reminds himself that he thinks too much.

Shan floats up behind Peter but he's so lost in thought that he doesn't notice. She steps around in front of him and places her hands on her hips.

"So you're going to leave by yourself just because I'm pissed?"

She has a knack of bringing him back into the moment.

"Thought it would be better if I just shoved off. We can talk when I get back."

Peter hates to lie to her, but the truth would hurt even more.

She snaps back, "Boys! Young and old, you're all the same."

Just then the other one shows up... Ramie. He's in a huff.

"You're letting her see you off, and not me? I brought you here!"

Peter smiles, "I was waiting for both of you."

"Liar," says Shan with a warm smile and she takes his hand. "I don't agree with your going, but I'll try to understand... as long as you come back. We still have an argument to finish."

"That's supposed to motivate me?"

She wraps her arms around him and gives him the kiss he has been waiting on for some time. It was worth the wait.

Ramie grumbles, "This is getting icky. Go already... and don't forget your way home."

Peter nods and steps back from Shan. He puts the pendant around his neck and dials it as Master Carringer has taught him.

The swirling pool of light appears mid-air in front of him. It reduces itself down in diameter, getting brighter as it diminishes... all the way down to a dot that winks out.

The invisible curtain distorts the air as it has before. Peter brushes his hand against it and a slit of light flashes for a second. Everything is ready.

He takes a last look back at Shan and a single tear runs down his cheek.

Seeing the tear, Shan dives forward and grabs hold of Peter...

They both tumble through the Door.

Chapter Twenty-Two

Shan and Peter tumble out of the slit of light onto ash-covered ground. A plume of gray dust drifts up around them.

Both are disoriented from their lightning trip through the Universe... especially Shan, since it is her first time.

Peter shakes the buzz from his head and turns to her, "What the hell did you do?" This is not playful banter - he's mad.

She just smiles, infuriating him even more. He jumps up, still oblivious to their surroundings, and grabs her arm.

Before he can do or say anything else, the slit of light opens again... Ramie spits out onto the ground.

In Spirinese he says, *"Oh, Jazmar, what a ride!"*

Shan pulls her arm away from Peter and snaps at Ramie, also in Spirinese, *"Who invited you!"*

Peter yells, "Who invited either of you?"

He grabs her arm again, along with Ramie's, and pushes them towards where the Door should be.

"You have to leave before..." - the slit of light appears, condenses and blinks out - "... the door closes," Peter's voice drops off as he ends his now-pointless order.

Ramie glibly says in Spirinese, *"Oops, it's not very predictable, is it?"*

Peter lets go of the kids and collapses to the ground. The same plume of gray ashes rises around him.

Noticing it for the first time, he reaches down and grabs a hand full of gray groundcover. It's so fine it sifts down through his fingers. He lifts his head and looks all around at their surroundings.

Everything is gray, like a post-apocalyptic landscape. He slowly stands up and looks to the valley far below in the distance... the grayness extends as far as he can see.

Shan steps up to Peter's side and takes his hand, *"Your world isn't very colorful."*

Stunned at the bewildering desolation, Peter asks almost absent-mindedly, "Why are you speaking Spirinese?"

Realizing they are not in Spirin, Peter turns to her... their words are not being translated automatically.

Not only has he dragged them into who knows what, but he's going to have a hard time communicating with them. He knows some Spirinese from his studies but - due to the nature of Spirin - he's rarely had to use it.

After a moment, Shan says, "Is this better?"

To Peter's surprise, the words have come out in English.

"How did you do that?"

Shan, smiling with satisfaction, "Sorcery. You know I'm talented... Didn't the Masters teach you that one yet?"

Peter doesn't have time to think about it right now. He faces bigger problems, like what happened to his world? And, what is he going to do with Shan and Ramie, who don't belong here?

His mind overflows with confusion at all the what's. He reaches for the pendant around his neck, knowing he should send them back before they try to talk him out of it.

Then, he lets go of it.

Shan sees he's going a little crazy at the moment. "Look, Ramie and I have been in trouble before, and it's just a visit, isn't it?"

He takes her shoulders, turns her towards him and locks eyes with her, "No, it's not a visit. The Council sent me away... for good."

"I knew it. I could tell at that last moment."

Moot point at present.

His eyes dart to her, to Ramie and to the post-apocalyptic surroundings they're in.

He takes a deep breath and says, "If things were normal, I'd throw the two of you through the door right now."

She defiantly puts her hands on her hips, "I'd like to see you try."

Ramie doesn't say anything, but mimics her stance.

Peter thinks out loud, "As it is, maybe that can wait a bit. You might need to take back word to Gran-D."

He doesn't bother mentioning any of the other things that Gran-D talked of. He turns and just stares out at the unknown.

Witch Racinda stands at her arched window in the fortress, peering out at a landscape that's never felt like hers. Her hands white-knuckle the stone as if she were in pain.

Rupert, rushes to her side, "What is it, mistress?"

Racinda staggers back and collapses in a chair.

After a second she looks up at him, "The Door has been opened again."

"Through the wall?"

"No... Bigger."

Rupert starts to gather up Racinda's cloak, assuming she needs it to go to the Grand Hall.

She sees what he does and says, "Leave it."

"Aren't we going to tell Lord Kildemar?"

"Not if we wish to keep our heads. You have to trust me on this. Now is not the time to bring up outsiders again."

Racinda is taking a chance on Rupert. For the little time he's been with her, he has not betrayed her trust. If he had magic abilities of his own, she would not take such a chance.

Peter stands quietly struggling with thoughts of what to do with his two unwanted passengers. They stand off a ways watching him. Shan's never seen Peter so freaked. She knows it's a time to best keep quiet and Ramie follows her lead.

Peter finally points off in the distance, "Somewhere down there is where my brother should be. In some small town that I can't even make out now. I need to see what happened."

He thinks.

"I can give you the pendant and create shelter here for you, then..."

Shan stops him, not interested in hearing where this is going, "We are together on this. Either we all go home right now or we all go find out what happened... and find your brother."

She stares at him and adds, "We can help." After a quick glance at Ramie, "At least I can."

Peter has been around Shan long enough to know when she is immovable.

He takes a breath to say, "And if things get hairy, you have to agree to go home." Hearing no objection, he adds, "OK, no magic... you understand?"

Ramie is not keen on this.

"Why not?"

"People here see us practice sorcery and we will be locked away faster than your head can spin. We don't want to attract attention. You got it?" Peter mainly addresses Ramie.

Without the slightest desire to have his head spin, Ramie feels at his neck and glances around at the bare wilderness.

"What people?" he asks.

Peter is already rethinking his decision.

Shan slaps Ramie on the shoulder and he bursts out, "OK, OK! No spells!"

Both Shan and Peter shake their heads at him.

Taking a breath and hoping he has not made a bad decision, Peter leads the way down the hill.

Shan follows.

Kicking the ground in frustration over not being able to conjure a hoverboard, Ramie tromps after them.

The three walk along a road. It's so blanketed with ash that it's hard to tell where its shoulders are. Peter walks silently. Shan and Ramie follow and stay quiet, perhaps to allow Peter to adjust to his decision to let them stay.

Shan finally says, "What did you mean... for good?"

As he walks, "It's not complicated. They're frightened of me and they invited me to leave... one-way."

"Including Gran-D?"

"Including Gran-D... You mind if we don't talk about this right now?" With no more comment he continues walking.

Their surroundings remain as desolate as on the hill. Most of the trees lie on the ground, just logs ripped out by their roots and all stretched out in the same direction. Peter suspects it must have been caused by some kind of powerful blast. This fits Gran-D's warning all too much.

They walk around a bend and Peter sees a partially knocked down road sign. He walks to it and bangs off the thick coating of ash.

It reads, 'Welcome To Goldendale, Oregon – Pop. 1014'.

At first, the gray-on-grayness of everything disoriented Peter. Now he has a sense of where he is... about a mile outside of Goldendale.

In a deadpan voice, "It's just up ahead."

"What's just up ahead?" Ramie grumbles with resentment over having to walk so far. "I haven't seen…"

Peter and Shan cut him off simultaneously, "No magic!"

Around the next bend they see the rubble of Goldendale's outskirts in the distance - gray, like everything else.

The silhouette lines have some straight edges, meaning that at least parts of buildings are still there. They move forward with caution.

Farther into town, they find many block structures have been reduced to rubble and the wooden ones are burned almost to the ground. Silently they walk on.

One building is semi-intact. Peter recognizes it as the town's courthouse. He wonders if he might be able to find some information in it.

He might also find a bear in there, but the thought of finding a bear isn't so bad. At least it would mean some things are still alive. So far there's been no sign of life, not even birds.

Starting up the steps, Peter says, "You two stay in the street."

Ramie whispers loudly, "What about those big hairy things?"

Peter turns, smiles to ease Ramie's concern and continues up the steps.

Suddenly, coming out of what's left of the courthouse, appears a woman… unaware of their presence. Dressed in tattered rags, she carries a blanket-wrapped bundle in her arms.

She looks up, sees the kids and freezes. Panic washes over her face. It's hard to tell who's more surprised - the kids or the woman.

With some difficulty, Peter thinks he recognizes her.

"Mrs. Reese, is that you?"

The woman swivels around, looking for an avenue of escape.

Peter steps a little closer, "It's me, Peter Capwell. Don't you remember me?"

She inches back. A dented tin can of food falls from her bundle. She scrambles to pick it up and shove it back in, as if it were rare treasure.

Mrs. Reese rambles not quite intelligibly, "I don't have any-thing for you... please leave me be!"

Peter speaks as calmly as he can, "I'm not going to hurt you. It's just me, Peter Capwell... from the high school."

She stammers, "Peter Capwell... he's dead."

Determined to learn something from her, Peter ramps up his tone, "Where is everyone?"

"All dead! Leave me be, I have nothing for you!"

Though it's hard to imagine it possible, her panic grows.

Shan steps up behind Peter and places a hand on his arm, "Can't you see you're not going to get anything. She's hurt and you're scaring her."

He realizes she's right. Maybe if he backs up a step the woman will settle down. As soon as he does, Mrs. Reese bolts to the right and, like a jackrabbit, disappears into the rubble of another half-demolished structure.

Peter starts to chase after her, but Shan yells, "Peter, leave her alone, she has nothing for you."

He stops.

Ramie says, "I've never seen anyone that scared."

Peter's face says he hasn't either.

"I don't know what happened here, but she's proof that there are survivors."

Gran-D's warning that things might have changed rushes through Peter's mind. This is far from what he could have pos-sibly expected... How widespread is this hell? Is it like this everywhere on Earth? Is there even a slight chance of finding Devon?

Shan has a knack for sensing when Peter gets stuck in a loop and steps up beside him.

"Where was your home? We can start looking there."

Peter takes a breath, now grateful for Shan's company. He calmly nods to her.

Chapter Twenty-Three

R amie trudges along after Shan and Peter.

"Peter, can't we use our boards?" he whines.

Without looking back, Peter says, "For the last time, no magic! You don't even know if it works here. You'll probably blow up trying it."

He's joking, but after Mrs. Reese, maybe a little joking is called for.

"I used it before," Ramie proclaims, figuring he might win.

"All I saw before was a boy pissing his pants and running from a big black bear. Again... no magic."

Ramie grumbles something under his breath as he tromps along. Non-magically tossing his Orb up and down like a simple ball, he thinks, 'What a boring way to use an Orb.'

Shan squeezes Peter's hand, happy that he's lightening up a bit. She has a ton of questions, both about Earth and about Peter being sent away... but she knows it's best to hold them for now.

They pass house after house or, more accurately, pile after pile of rubble that might have been houses. Between the level of destruction and the thick coating of ash, the houses blend with the landscape.

Occasionally the remains of a brick chimney stick out of what appears to be a foundation. The only thing that is clear is that they walk on something hard that appears to be a flat path. A year ago it was a street.

Peter is hard-pressed to make out which pile of rubble is the one he once lived in. He sees the bottom of a mighty oak still rooted. The upper part is shattered off as if it has exploded.

Pointing at some rubble, "I think that was our house. The tree's in the right place."

He rushes to the remains of a house that's almost completely flattened and starts pulling away some shattered pieces of lumber.

Shan isn't sure what he's looking for, but she and Ramie are quick to join in to help pull boards away. He directs them toward a particular board that has some flooring attached and the three pull together. It topples to the side and a dark basement is exposed below.

Peter tells them, "Look, this is all loose rubble. Stay here while I climb down to check on something." Seeing Shan's puzzled expression he adds, "This could be where Devon might hide if he survived."

It's clear that Ramie wants to go with Peter but Shan takes his sleeve and motions 'no'. He dons his 'no one will let me do anything' look and settles back to watch.

Carefully, Peter climbs down amid the loose debris, making an effort not to bring down more rubble as he goes. There's just enough light from the cloudy sky to be able to make his way around. Considering the condition of the house above, things in the basement are relatively intact.

It was set up as a game room. A broken TV monitor is near the wall where it once hung. There are a sofa, a few chairs, a card table and a fridge. On the table near the sofa are four X-Box controllers.

Peter has expected to find these things since Devon used to hang out here, playing video games with his friends. He looks for signs of post-disaster activity. Much of the stuff in the basement is half-buried with ash that he has to brush off.

Trying to see what he's missing out on, Ramie accidently loosens a board at the edge of the hole. It tumbles down, giving Peter a start. He glares up at Ramie.

Ramie quickly backs up with a 'sorry' look. He nervously whistles to himself, starts tossing his Orb and saunters away from the hole. Shan keeps watching Peter, but shakes her head at Ramie's antics.

Peter goes back to scouring the basement. He finds a couple emptied store-sized boxes of candy and Red Bull. Then he sees a few boxes that once contained Buck knives and an emptied box of 30-30 shells. He even finds one loose Buck knife that someone overlooked. It's brand new. Peter slips it into his belt fearing he may have need of it. All this is enough to convince him that Devon at least survived the initial impact. The big question is, where is he now?

Shan, in a loud whisper, "Peter, I heard something!"

Peter quickly to climbs out of the hole.

He stands by Shan, listening, "What was it?"

She points off towards a shattered stand of woods near the ridge, "I don't know. It sounded like breaking limbs."

Joining them, Ramie shakes his head. "Oh, no. Not another bear."

There's nothing but silence for a few seconds. Then a raggedy, dirty looking man runs over the ridge, panicked by something that must be after him. He's far enough away to not notice the kids unless he's looking for them. From his frantic running, they see they are the least of his concerns.

Shan and Ramie start to move in his direction, as if they hope to help him.

Peter grabs both of them, "Get down in the basement! Now!"

They appear puzzled by this callousness towards another being, but Peter ignores this and pulls them towards the basement.

Without knowing what has happened here, he's not about to take a chance on a stranger. They'll just have to accept that for the moment.

Once all three are down in the hole, Peter slides a loose floor section over to conceal them. He waves for the two to be quiet as they try to peek out and watch the man run.

Shan and Ramie don't understand that on Earth, especially the way it appears now, there's a good chance someone is running because something is chasing.

Peter's proven right.

Suddenly a pickup flies over the ridge, motocross-style. It carries two armed men holding on to the truck bed as it lands hard. As far as Peter can tell, the pickup has been outfitted for guerilla warfare, with a caged cab and a gun mount above it.

It heads straight for the running man. The men whoop and holler, taunting their prey. The man changes his direction. Now he runs directly towards where the kids are hiding, not knowing they're there.

Ramie starts to scramble on his belly out of the hole but Peter pulls him back in.

"What the hell are you trying to do? Get caught?"

Ramie points at his Orb lying in the rubble about fifteen feet from the hole. Peter shakes his head with an emphatic 'no'. Reluctantly Ramie ducks back down.

Shan and Ramie can't believe the scene that's unfolding above ground. The men in the truck are herding the running man and taunting him as if it were a fun pastime. Adding to the horror of it all are their yells and the truck's sporadic backfires.

As they rumble by the running man, one of the men in the truck bed hits him with the butt of a rifle. Sadistically, he hits him just hard enough to make him stumble, get up and try to run again.

They're toying with him. The truck kicks up so much ash the man can't even get his bearings. The kids can barely see what's going on.

The man driving the truck yells out his window, "Don't bruise him too much. We want to keep him fresh!"

They all laugh.

Shan can't comprehend the meaning of this... and it's good she doesn't. Such behavior is totally unthinkable to Shan and Ramie. They look at Peter and, thankfully, they see it's just as alien to him.

The men in the truck stop playing with their prey. As they pass one more time, one of the men in the back hits the running man hard enough to knock him out.

The truck slams on the brakes. Both men in the back jump out and put a wrist tie on the unconscious man. They pick him up like a sack of potatoes and throw his body in the bed of the truck. The driver gets out, glances in the back and lights a cigarette.

Relaxing after the hunt, he shakes his head, "Game's getting scarce."

The truck is too close for the kids to dare try and peek. One of the men walks towards the hole where they're hiding.

Another says, "Where you going?"

"To take a piss, if it's any of your business."

He walks right up to the edge of the hole leading down to the basement, undoes his fly and urinates in the hole. The three kids have their backs pressed tight against the wall, no more than four feet below him.

The stream of urine barely misses them. Ramie tries to move a bit so as to not get hit, but Peter's hand puts pressure on his chest to stay still.

As the man finishes his business, another saunters around kicking at this and that, looking for anything worth salvaging. From his casual manner he doesn't expect to find much. Everything has been picked clean and hoarded over the past year.

He stops and stares into the rubble about fifteen feet from the hole. He picks up Ramie's yellow Orb. Puzzled, he peers at it. The shiny hard ball is not coated with ash. The man scans all around. Where could it have come from?

Ramie tries to press himself tighter against the wall and loosens a small stone. It doesn't make a loud sound, just enough to get the attention of the closest man. He pulls a handgun from his belt and starts to walk slowly towards the hole.

The driver yells out, "Enough messing around. We need to get back before dark. Load up!"

The man with the handgun stops and glances back at the truck, then continues towards the basement.

The driver yells again, "Baker, that means you!"

Baker stops about two feet shy of the hole, gives it a cursory glance and holsters his weapon. He turns and heads for the truck.

Peter, Ramie and Shan still hold their breath. After they hear the truck's engine turn over, they let it out... but don't move. Only after they hear the truck rumble away do they allow their muscles to relax. Peter silently gestures for the two to stay down while he inches up for a peek.

Sure that the scene is clear, he signals the kids to climb out of the basement. Once out neither of them know what to say about what they have witnessed. Maybe it just hasn't fully sunk in yet.

Shan's the first to quietly say, "Are those your people?"

Almost sounding like an apology, Peter says, "Not my people, but they're humans. I don't know what's happening here."

Clearly upset, Ramie picks up a stick and throws it. Peter and Shan turn to him.

He looks at them, "They took my Orb!"

Shan glares at her kid brother in disbelief, "They took a man. Who cares about your toy?"

"I do," Peter snaps. "If they figure out the Orb doesn't belong here, they'll know something else doesn't... Us!"

Shan turns to Peter, "What do you think we should do?"

Ramie is quick, "We use the pendant and go home."

Peter nods agreement, "For once the Rockhead is right. The two of you have to go home."

Ramie snaps, "That's not what I said. I said 'we' go home."

"We've already been through that - whatever we do, we do it together." Shan says this without a trace of fear in her voice.

Peter is not about to waste time arguing.

He thinks for a second, "What I found down in the basement tells me someone took time to stock up after whatever happened. By the looks of things, they were kids - maybe Devon."

He glances up towards the hills.

"If he survived, I think I know where he would be."

Shan, with determination, "Then let's go there."

Peter nods 'yes'.

As they start off, Shan asks, "What do you think those men are going to do with the one they caught?"

"I don't know."

He's not being quite honest with her because the thought of what might happen to him is too horrific to tell her. She would never look on him - as a human being - the same again. Peter's not willing to jeopardize this, even if he could comprehend the horror of what he's thinking.

Ramie asks, "Can't we use our boards now?"

Peter realizes it won't make a difference now and time is now an issue. "OK... to the boards, if they work."

At last something makes Ramie smile. Then he wonders if Peter might have been right about blowing up.

"Where we going?" asks Shan.

Peter generates a hoverboard. Apparently they do have powers on Earth. They may need them.

He turns to Shan, "To the caves."

Chapter Twenty-Four

Pacing back and forth in the dining room, Atta mumbles, "I've tugged and tugged. Nothing, absolutely nothing."

Kalish is a bit calmer, but not much. He tries to get Atta to settle down.

When Gran-D comes in the front door with his usual smile, Kalish, with Atta behind him, storms up to the old man, "I hope you have an idea why my children are not around."

Gran-D scratches at his beard, meaning he does, but he is trying to figure out how to exactly put it. Kalish's glare tells him that he better put it some way - and quickly.

Gran-D finally says, "I have a hunch, but you probably won't like it."

The kids hedge-hop, flying low over the ground to avoid attracting attention, though they don't know who or what - if anyone or anything might be watching.

As they head towards the cave Peter guesses, by the way the trees have fallen, that the blast came from somewhere around Gypsy Meadow... that is, if a blast caused all this. The meadow is where he departed from Earth.

The farther out from the blast's origin, the more trees remain standing, though not many. Within sight of the cave, Peter sees concertina wire strung between a few of these trees. The spiraling line of wire is about a hundred feet from the cave entrance.

He waves at Shan and Ramie to land their boards along with him. They do so just outside the wire. The wire is strung with tin cans containing stones to serve as a sound alarm.

Peter points to it, "Someone has been here to set this up. I want you two to get down behind this log while I check what we're walking into."

Before he moves, Ramie - ever the curious one - touches the concertina wire.

He jerks his hand back with a loud "Ouch!" The tin cans rattle. Peter flashes an irritated glare at him.

Ramie shrugs, "What? It hurt."

Shan shakes her head at the Rockhead's foolishness, even if she's not quite sure why all the caution. Thinking from a position of fear is new to her.

Peter advances toward the cave before Ramie finds a trumpet to announce their presence. He steps carefully over the wire and stays low as he approaches, seeking what little cover there is.

He stops by a half-tree trunk. The front entrance of the cave, once completely open, now has a heavy makeshift door constructed of wood planks. There's a gun port in the door.

As Peter steps out from behind the tree, the barrel of a rifle emerges from the port. Before he can say anything a shot rings out. It hits the tree just above his head, sending splinters of the dead wood flying.

It was too accurate to be a miss, he thinks, but he could be wrong so he steps back behind the tree. This is not so much to take cover as to acknowledge that he knows he's been warned.

He waits.

From inside the cave a voice yells, "Clear off or the next round will mean business."

Peter responds with only one word, "Devon?"

Bang! Another shot hits the tree, this one closer to Peter's head. He drops to the ground in case he's judged wrong.

"Devon, you ass-hole, that one almost hit me. It's me, Peter!"

The voice comes back, "Peter's dead!"

"You used to be smarter. How do I know your voice?"

There's silence from the cave for the longest couple of seconds. Then a latch is heard unbolting. After another long second the door creaks open.

The barrel of the rifle comes out first, slowly followed by Devon Capwell - now sixteen years old. It's a Devon who Peter barely recognizes.

He's gaunt and dirty with a pronounced scar on his left cheek over youthfully soft stubble of a beard. His M16 is held on target with experienced steadiness. Though his dead combat eyes are hard, his lips quiver... as if slightly in shock.

Ramie nudges Shan, "Why doesn't Peter use his shield?"

She waves him to hush and keeps her eyes on the activity near the cave.

Peter realizes this is testing all of Devon's senses so he speaks slow, "Devon, lower the weapon... please."

Ever so gradually, almost despondently, Devon starts lowering the end of the rifle. Suddenly he collapses to the ground. Peter rushes forward to try and catch his long lost brother.

Nestled in a rock canyon split by a river, the once- peaceful Beaker's Wood Mill has been turned into a fortress for the Rovers. The men in the truck were Rovers - armed survivors within the now-quarantined zone of Oregon.

The Zone is the direct result of the black crystal ball Lord Kildemar sent to Earth through the Door a little over a year ago. It's roughly three thousand square miles - a circle of land stretching out forty miles in all directions from the point of im-pact... a whole lot of no man's land.

The Rovers are the vicious self-proclaimed warlords of the Zone. Their leader is Peter's old friend, Deputy Tom Clancy. Deputy Clancy no longer upholds the law, he is the law - and law in the Zone is life or death... sometimes worse.

The front access to the mill is closed off by two rows of metal perimeter fencing topped by concertina wire. Inside the fences are about a half-dozen war wagons, trucks with a post-apocalyptic look like the one the kids saw. Some are armed with mounted machineguns... all look like they're ready for war.

Perched on the perimeter fences are manned guard towers, each armed with a 30MM cannon. About twenty survivors - some women, but mostly men - make up the Rovers. Even that small of a contingent is difficult to maintain. Newcomers are not welcome, at least not to join.

Built upward in tiers going into the canyon, a compound of wooden buildings forms the Rovers' fortress. The top tier is a shack serving as Deputy Clancy's headquarters, a position that allows him to keep an eye on those he lords over.

Deputy Clancy still wears his old uniform, soiled and tattered with age... as is the deputy himself. Clancy stands at a window staring down on the compound and his meager domain.

Zachary, Deputy Clancy's second in command, comes in where few are allowed. He carries the Orb the so-called troops have found earlier in the day.

"Patrol came back... they found one stray. I had him thrown in the pens."

"They were out all day and that's all they bagged?" Deputy Clancy asks in a commander's growl.

"Slim pickin's. They also found this."

Holding up the Orb, Zachary walks over to Clancy, "You see anything like it before?"

The deputy glances at it. As far as he knows it's just a ball of some sort, nothing to be that concerned about. It's neither eatable nor a weapon. In the Zone, that means it's of little use.

Clancy off-handedly dismisses it.

Zachary adds, "It isn't affected by heat. Baker tried it."

Now he has Deputy Clancy's attention. Clancy takes the Orb and now gives it a closer inspection. He holds it up to his ear. There's a very slight hum. Deputy Clancy looks for a seam to see if it can be opened, but there is none.

"Where did they find it?"

"Eastern edge of Goldendale," Zachary replies. "You think it might be of any value to the military?"

"I don't know. It might raise some interest... worth a try." Placing the Orb on a table, he says, "See if you can raise someone on the box... though I doubt it."

All modern forms of communication out of the Zone have been blocked long ago. Once they established control, the government military had confiscated all functional radios that could make contact with the outside world. If you're going to take the rights away from Americans, it doesn't sit well to have them talking with each other.

Stationed around the perimeter of the Zone, the military has one purpose - make sure nothing gets out... alive.

The 'box' is a patched back together military radio Clancy salvaged from a wrecked Humvee during the few early days of resistance. It was a short fight. The box survived.

Shan wrings water out of a rag and goes over to a bunk where Devon lies unconscious. She puts the damp rag on his head.

To Peter, "What's wrong with him?"

Peter appears concerned. "I don't know... shock, I think."

He stares at Devon, still trying to adjust to this brother, so radically different from the one he once knew. The boy lying before him is not the innocent student who likes skateboards, school and chess sets. A pang of guilt rushes through Peter.

Shan, as usual, can read Peter's mind. She looks up, "You got back when you could. He is who he is."

He appreciates it but it still doesn't settle his mind. Funny... when Shan reads his mind, Peter feels their closeness - when Gran-D does it, he feels suspicious. Peter thinks that's an odd thought to have right now, maybe it's to justify having Shan by his side.

Devon's eyes open. The first thing he sees is a stranger – Shan - leaning over him. He bolts up and pushes her away hard enough to send her sprawling on the cave's dirt floor.

She leaps up and grabs the closest thing available - an ax. She holds it up defensively.

Peter grabs Devon, forcing him back down on the bunk, "Take it easy. You passed out."

Devon stares in disbelief.

Peter glances over his shoulder at Shan holding the ax. It's such a contradictory image of her that he has to say, "Contagious, isn't it?"

She looks at the ax clasped in her white knuckles. She throws it to the ground. Shan turns away, confused.

"Peter... you're supposed to be dead," says Devon, a trace of clarity returning to his voice.

Peter smiles, "Sorry. The rumors were exaggerated. I sort of accidentally got lost. But I'm here now."

Peter's not sure what to expect - a brother throwing his arms around him or one striking out at him. He gets neither.

Devon sits up on the edge of the bunk, showing little emotion either way. Maybe it's all just taking a little this all to register. Peter needs to give him a little time. He owes him that - and more.

Coldly, with no anger or joy, Devon says, "You accidentally got lost for quite a while. Where did you go?"

Peter knows this will take a while to explain. He pulls up an old chair by the bunk, almost ready to tell him.

Bang! A rifle goes off farther back in the cave. Both Shan and Peter hit the ground. Devon doesn't even flinch.

Ramie throws a rifle he has been examining to the ground and backs away. Looking up, he meekly says, "Sorry."

All the survival stuff around the cave was too tempting for Ramie not to explore. After all, he doesn't even know what a rifle is. The only one he's seen was the one the Rovers used earlier to hit someone - and they didn't shoot it.

"Careful with the guns, kid. Ammunition is too valuable to go wasting it," is all Devon says.

Shan is not so casual. She goes and grabs the curl of Ramie's ear and walks him over to a boulder. She uses ear leverage to make sure he sits on it.

"Stay there and keep your hands off things!"

He frowns, but is smart enough not to open his mouth.

Peter stares at Devon, "Ammunition is valuable? How about someone getting hurt?"

There's a coldness to Devon's reaction that Peter can't quite fathom — words coming from a sixteen-year old that simply don't fit. Until he gets to know his brother a bit more, he decides to delay explaining too many details of where he's been.

"Devon, we've been on foot for a while. Do you have anything here in this fort to eat? We can talk after."

Devon eyes him suspiciously, but gets up for some stores.

"Who are those two... and what's with their ears?"

"Shan... and the clumsy one is Ramie. How about I explain after we eat."

The cave is a survivalist lair. Barrels of water, small stacks of canned goods - and weapons, lots of weapons - lie around everywhere. Off in one corner is a tarp that partially covers a couple of dirt bikes. Peter can't tell from where he sits, but one of them looks like it might be his old one.

On one section of the rock walls is a map with the Zone outlined by hand. Crudely marked on the map are military checkpoints along its perimeter. As well as Peter can tell from a distance, it seems that the military is pretty serious about the Zone... they have units stationed about every ten miles.

None of this makes any sense to Peter until he sees some front pages of newspapers taped to another wall. He walks over to take a closer look. Shan follows him to the rock wall.

As Devon makes his way back with a couple cans of food, Ramie starts to say something to him.

He cuts him off as he passes, "Not now, kid."

He's too busy watching Peter and Shan head to the wall, as if he's sizing up the situation.

Peter reads the first headline out loud for Shan's sake, "UNDETECTED METEOR STRIKES NORTHWEST." He moves on to the next front page, "DOUBLE WHAMMY! METEOR CARRIES VIRUS."

Shan gives him a puzzled glance, "What's a double whammy?"

He silently scans the article a couple seconds, and then, "It means they were hit with two blows. First, the meteor - a large rock hit the Earth - and then they discovered it must have carried some kind of sickness with it."

She nods, without really understanding what he's talking about. Watching, Devon sits at a table made out of a wooden door.

Peter moves on to the last headline. "3,000 SQUARE MILE QUARANTINE ZONE DECLARED BY MILITARY," he reads the text to himself.

Shan pulls on his sleeve and speaks softly, "Don't get mad, but your brother scares me."

Peter glances at Devon and then back to Shan, "I always thought there was some bully back here that I couldn't protect him from... nothing like this. To tell you the truth, I'm not sure why yet, but he scares me a little too."

Having softly said it, he goes on, "According to these papers, it took a lot for him to survive this long. I need to give him a chance. I need to find out what really happened."

Devon has had enough of the two whispering, "Thought you were hungry?"

He takes a hunting knife from the back of his belt and, not delicately, impales the top of a can.

"And, girl, scaring others keeps people alive in the Zone."

This actually pisses her off.

She turns and puts her hands on her hips, "You don't scare me that much."

"I like her. She's got guts."

Deputy Tom Clancy slings a knife across the room. It impales the center of a crudely drawn wall target... closer than where Zachary's blade struck.

Zachary grumbles, "Lucky throw, chief."

There's a squeak from the ham radio set. Surprised, both men turn. They have often attempted to entice the guarding military outposts to open communications, mostly to no avail.

The few times they've gotten a response there has been little interest in what was going on inside the Zone.

Regarding the Orb, Clancy has simply broadcast what has been found to dead air... with little hope of getting a call back. They rush to the box, hoping it isn't just static.

It squawks again, "Rover One, this is Lockdown, Post Ten. Over."

Clancy grabs the handset, "Lockdown, this is Rover One. Over."

He releases the button, not wanting to sound pushy - yet.

"About object found, interested. Any other unusual activity in area. Over."

After all this time, Deputy Tom Clancy reckons he maybe has something to bargain with, so he's not in a rush. Zachary nudges him to answer.

He smiles at Zachary, "Give them a moment to think. This is a poker game."

Finally he keys back in, "All kinds of strange stuff happens in here. It depends on what you're willing to trade. Over."

What Clancy may be forgetting is that he's dealing with a military just waiting for them all to simply die off. He's been a big fish in a small pond for too long.

America is not interested in what happens in the Zone. They just want it to fade away. That doesn't leave the deputy a lot of leverage... no matter what he has.

Chapter Twenty-Five

Peter, Shan and Ramie sit around a small crackling fire listening to what Devon wants to tell them about the Zone. Peter senses Devon's being selective with what he says, but he pushes for as much information about what happened... before deciding how much to tell in return.

After a sparse general description of the year's events on Earth - no more than Peter would have gleaned from the news articles on the wall - Devon says, "OK, that's my story... What's yours?"

Even with only Devon's superficial overview, Shan is flabbergasted by what could - and did - take place in this alien realm. She stealthily tries to pinch Peter's leg, hoping he will take at least a short break to discuss how much he should say.

The maneuver doesn't escape Devon's notice.

"Missy, if you want a time out to talk with my brother, just say so."

Alert to Shan's look of embarrassment at being caught, Devon gets up first.

"I gotta check on something. Go ahead and get your fears out of the way."

As he walks towards the far end of the cave, Shan tries to say, "I'm not..." but Devon's not listening.

She turns to Peter, "I know he's your brother, but how much should you tell him about our world?"

"Your world... Remember, I was sent away." He's quick to add, "Sorry. The thought is crossing my mind as well. He's not the brother I left behind, but I probably wouldn't be either if I had to survive what he described."

"It may not matter."

Looking worried, she points to the back of the cave. Devon stands chatting with Ramie. There's not much Grimick to keep in the bag after Ramie opens his mouth.

Devon sees his parley with Ramie has been noticed. He breaks it off and heads back towards Peter and Shan. Ramie follows him.

As he approaches, Peter starts to say something but Devon is quicker, "From talking to Curly Ears, it seems you've got a more interesting story to tell."

"My name's Ramie."

"Whatever, kid."

Devon's focus remains on Peter.

"Yeah, we do have an interesting - almost unbelievable - story. But there's a couple things I still want to hear about."

Peter watches Devon run his tongue under his lip trying to figure out how to play this. He used to do the same thing when they played chess so long ago. After a moment, he sits down and motions Peter to continue.

"I got the part about you, Jack and Robbie being saved from the meteor by being in the basement playing games. You didn't mention what happened to them?"

Rather nonchalantly, "They're dead. Jack couldn't take it and tried to get out. Robbie was taken by Rovers a couple months ago... two months, I think. How long has it been since you left?"

"A little over a year," Peter answers.

Devon appears a bit distant, "That's all, only a year?"

Shan just stares at Devon, her face filled with horror mixed with disbelief. Disregarding Devon sitting right in front of them, she turns to Peter, "Peter, this is no place for us."

Devon lets out a laugh. "Girly, you'll get used to it."

Peter glares at Devon, "What happened to you?"

"Had to grow up... real fast."

Before anything else can be said he raises his hand, as though in a class, "My turn! I've showed you mine, now you show me some of yours. Though a bit unbelievable, the kid says you got whisked across the universe to some planet of pixies... magicians... whatever. Like I said, that's a lot more interesting than my story."

"They're sorcerers," says Peter ignoring Shan's squeeze on his leg. "I accidently got caught in a spell that took me away."

Devon is quick to interject, "You mean the same accident that caused this hell that I live in? You don't want to leave that part out. Hardly a fair trade."

"I didn't have any idea about what happened here till I came back. If I had..."

Devon cuts him off with another wave of his hand... this time gesturing to be quiet. He listens intently. The kids hear nothing at first, but clearly Devon does.

After a couple seconds, they all hear the faint whop-whop of chopper blades approaching. It gets closer. The sound of the blades echo throughout the cave as the chopper passes over. By this time Shan and Ramie cower down to the floor.

Devon laughs at the newcomers' fears. Then he casually says, "A Blackhawk... probably doing a grid. "

Peter looks like he would like to slap Devon along the side of his head, but that kind of Peter is long gone... he thinks.

Peter says, "Do they ever land?"

"Nah, they do infrared runs to see if we've died off yet. Some of us are the stubborn type," Devon says with a sly smile.

Peter remembers that when he fell out of the Door into this very bleak, drastically changed version of his old world he had to find Devon and rescue him from it. Now, he's not sure when he decided that he could not take Devon away. Maybe it was when he first saw him. He knows now Shan is right - they do not belong on Earth and Devon does not belong on Spirin.

"So, you gonna take me to this magic planet of yours?" Devon says glibly.

Shan flashes another look at Peter. Again, it's something that does not escape Devon's notice.

He smiles at her, "Don't worry. I grow on ya."

Peter doesn't want to answer his brother yet, maybe because he wonders how Devon will take his answer. No, he knows how Devon will take it, and he knows he prefers not doing it with Shan and Ramie around.

"All I want to do right now is get a night's sleep. It's been a long day. Let's talk plans tomorrow." He doesn't know why, but he adds, "Are we good for the night?"

Devon says, in a slightly creepy manner, "In the Zone, nothing is guaranteed... but I guess you're safe for the night." Pointing over to a corner, "You guys can bunk over there."

He tosses a stone that hits a large wooden box.

"There are some blankets in that crate... By the way, nice seeing you, brother."

Then Devon goes to his bunk at the other end of the cave.

Peter knows no one but his brother will sleep well tonight.

Peter, Shan and Ramie sleep fairly close to each other, though Peter is not sure any of them sleep soundly. When Peter opens his eyes in the morning, he sees Devon crouched like an animal perched on a boulder above, just staring down at him. Peter sits up and looks around to make sure Shan and Ramie are OK. They're still asleep... or, rather, finally got to sleep.

He gets up and quietly goes over to the fire Devon has already started. He warms his hands as he glances back towards his brother.

Devon jumps off the boulder and lands as quietly as a leopard. He joins Peter. There's silence between them.

Handing Peter a cup of coffee, Devon finally says, "So, what are you planning?" After a calculated pause, "For today?"

"Can you show me where this meteor hit?"

Peter thinks there may be something there that Gran-D might need to know, though he's not interested in explaining that to Devon at the moment.

"There's nothing much there. The army came in and took most of the fragments just before they locked the door on us."

"I'd still like to take a look... and it will give us a chance to talk."

Peter needs to get Devon alone before letting him know his decision. He's not even positive about his decision, but whatever it is he wants Shan and Ramie out of earshot when he makes it.

Shan has awakened and comes up to them, "Where are we going this morning?"

It's clear she heard them making plans. Peter gives her a look he hopes she understands to mean stay out of this.

Devon solves it for them, "You're not going anywhere. It's bad enough having one rookie to look after out there."

Peter nods, "He's right. I want you two to stay here."

Shan realizes this isn't a request. Maybe he's even right, so she nods OK.

Peter glances over at the covered dirt bikes, "Those still working?" He thinks a ride with Devon would be a good thing and, in fact, he would love to take his old bike out again.

"They purr like kittens... that is, if you haven't forgotten how to ride."

It's good to hear a touch of Devon's lighter side.

As Devon heads over to uncover the bikes, Peter takes Shan aside. He pulls the pendant from his neck and pushes it into her hands.

"If anything happens to me, go home and tell Gran-D what you've seen. Ramie knows how to work the pendant."

She tries to give it back but he grabs her hand and squeezes it around the pendant.

"Whatever happens, don't take Devon with you," Peter orders.

This last remark brings real concern to her face. "Understand?"

Reluctantly she does. Quietly, but strongly, she says, "I do... but I am going to take you!"

Before any more can be said, Devon walks up on them. He shoves an extra rifle between them, slapping it against Peter's chest.

Peter pushes it back, "I don't need that."

"If you're going with me, you do."

Peter remembers that if Devon's not the kid brother he has hoped to find, he is the kid brother who has survived in this hard land. He takes the weapon.

A thought crosses his mind, 'Is it loaded?'

Two loud dirt bikes whip along a hillside road. It's not like when Peter used to open it wide up. They have to be more cautious with all the ash and the downed tree limbs. It's actually fun for Peter to be back on a bike, but it's more jarring than the softer hoverboard ride he's gotten used to.

Devon pulls up next to him and yells over the sound of the bikes, "I would have thought you had a magic carpet by now."

Peter yells back, "Not as fun. I love my old bike. Thanks for keeping it up."

Though he's having fun, he tends to glance all around a lot more than Devon. His brother seems totally at ease in this dangerous world.

The road disappears entirely long before they get to Gypsy Meadow - or at least where Peter remembers it to be. They go to riding cross-country.

All of a sudden they're at the edge of a deep crater. Knowing it was coming Devon abruptly pulls his bike up short. Peter's more surprised by it and almost goes over the edge. There is no Gypsy Meadow... just a hole where it once was.

Devon looks over at Peter, "Don't chicken out on me now."

With this, he guns his bike over the edge of the crater.

The back tire Devon's bike rips this way and that as he races down the thirty-degree slope into the crater, kicking up a dense cloud of dust as he goes.

Peter laughs, lets out a rebel yell and goes over the edge to try and catch up with Devon. He hopes he's as good as he once was. Halfway down he's holding his own. He hasn't forgot how to rip with the best of them.

What surprises him is how good Devon has become. Regardless of what he's been thinking about his brother, a touch of pride seeps in.

The crater bottoms out a hundred feet down. They stop the bikes and get off. Both are covered head to toe with ash. Peter shakes off the ash like a dog shedding water and scans all around. The meteor must have made an awesome blast to create the bowl he stands in.

Devon is right, there isn't much here beside dirt. It's not exactly dirt, more like fused ground... an almost glass-like skin created by blast fire. It crunches beneath Peter's feet.

From all the fractures, it's clear that they are not the only ones to have been here. He walks around toeing up spots here and there.

"Like I said, there's not much to find," says Devon. "The military picked it pretty clean. I guess they knew about the virus because they were in all kinds of protective gear."

He kicks at the dirt, "One thing for certain, they didn't care about people. No one that knows about this site has gotten out alive."

"How long did the virus last?"

"Not long. You either caught it right off, or you didn't. If you caught it, you got lucky and died. If you didn't, you had to learn how to survive."

Sadness creeps into Devon's voice that says he is not joking about the lucky part.

Peter stops and kneels down. Digging in the broken shell of the dirt, he uncovers a shiny black shard of stone. He holds it up to the light. There's a purple glint to it.

He reaches into his pocket and pulls out the fragment of stone Gran-D gave him. Peter holds it up to the other stone. They glint together.

There has already been little doubt in his mind, but now he's positive that this destruction was delivered to Earth by whoever lies beyond the wall - in the Land of Goreipor.

Still kneeling, Peter hears the bolt of Devon's rifle. He remains still, waiting to hear what comes next.

Behind him Devon says, "You're planning on leaving me again, aren't you?"

Peter speaks as he rises slowly, "No, we're both staying."

"Why?"

Peter turns to him, "Because you don't belong in their world and I've left you alone long enough in this one."

That's the conclusion from a sleepless night's worth of agonizing over what's right to do.

"I can get us both out of this hell. Anywhere you want to go... here on Earth."

After the longest uncomfortable pause, he adds, "I've got what I needed here. Are we going back to the cave?" Having played his cards, Peter waits. The next move is up to Devon.

It takes a couple seconds before Devon lowers his weapon.

Peter will never know if his brother was actually prepared to use it... he doesn't want to know.

Heading back, the two ride along a ridge road. Suddenly Devon pulls his bike to a stop. Peter figures there's a good reason and does the same. Devon is quiet as he pulls binoculars out of his satchel and looks off in the distance.

Peter, in a loud whisper, "What's going on?"

Devon shuts down his bike and lowers it to the ground.

"We go in from here on foot. Follow me."

Devon's in his element now. He clicks the rifle safety off and moves out... and not interested in explaining why.

Peter never was around guns that much, but he knows the basics and he chambers a round before following his brother. It crosses his mind that Devon actually did give him a loaded weapon.

They stay along the hillside as they move towards the cave. About a hundred yards from the entrance, Devon climbs up near the dirt road. He points to fresh tire tracks marring the dirt. Peter starts to move ahead of Devon, fearful of what might have happened to Shan and Ramie.

Devon pulls him down.

"Someone's been here. Don't know if they still are. You can play big brother some other time. You're in my territory now."

Pointing off to the south, he says, "You work your way up that side. I'll take the other. Go slow and low. Those look like Rover tracks... they don't play nice."

Peter knows Devon is right. It's not a matter of who's older - it's about experience. He nods that he understands and slowly moves out.

A ways from the cave's entrance, Devon finds boot tracks around the concertina wire. He waves at Peter to stand down. At a quick pace, Devon storms the cave entrance.

Peter waits. Nothing. After a few seconds, Peter can wait no longer. He readies his rifle and charges forward.

Devon comes out, waving his hands to avoid getting shot.

"They're gone. Tracks near the wire show the same number that entered left - plus your friends."

He laughs at Peter's tight grip on the M16.

"You look like you're about to piss your pants. You think I'd charge a cave if I thought men were still in there?" Losing his smile, he adds, "The assholes took my stuff!"

Chapter Twenty-Six

Devon storms around kicking over empty boxes in the cave.

Peter yells, "Forget your stuff. They have my friends!"

"Stuff is how you stay alive here!" Devon snaps back.

Seeing Peter could care less, Devon finally sits down across from him.

"Look, your friends are OK... trust me."

"How do you know?"

"These were Rovers. They wouldn't take on my cave just to steal stuff. They had to have a damn good reason to go up against me."

Peter senses this is not an idle brag.

Devon continues, "Are you sure you and those kids didn't come in some kind of spaceship? That is, if all this about a magic planet isn't a bunch of bull."

It's a fair call - Peter hasn't shown any magic abilities since being back.

Peter thinks a moment.

"No ship, but we might have been detected if the military was monitoring energy spikes."

"If the Rovers made some kind of deal with the outside, it will be a first and they'll move on it quickly." A smile comes to Devon's face, "You're gonna love this."

"What?" Peter says, not seeing much funny about any of it.

"The head Rover is an old pal of yours... Deputy Clancy."

"You've gotta be freakin' kidding!" To Peter's surprise, he does find it a bit ironically funny.

"Yeah, he liked you so much that he even sent some of his men after me. The only mistake he made was not moving on me before I learned a key trick of the Zone."

"What's that?"

Deadpan, "Not caring."

Peter doesn't know how to respond to this, but he does know his decision about Devon and Spirin is right. The only rub is that he has to trust Devon to have any chance of rescuing Shan and Ramie.

He sets the dilemma aside.

"You know where these Rovers are?"

While he talks, Devon rummages around the mess the Rovers left, looking for any ammunition they might have over-looked.

"Yeah, they have a compound in a canyon about twenty miles the other side of where Goldendale used to be... the old Beaker's Mill."

He finds one box of shells - in the Zone, a Christmas gift.

"I'll give your friends one thing - they must have kept their mouths shut."

"Why would you say that?"

"If Clancy knew you were here, he would have left a squad in the cave... just for you."

He hands Peter some of the shells he recovered.

"If you weren't bullshitting about magic, now's a good time to put it to use."

With no more time to be timid, Peter simply says, "Gather your gear... we're going for a ride."

A swirling stream of smoke descends on to a ledge of the canyon looking down on Beaker's Mill. When the smoke clears, Peter and Devon stand there.

Peter smiles, "How's that for magic?"

Devon is speechless for the first time.

Devon pats his body to make sure he's all there.

"Neat way to travel. We could get out of the Zone with it."

Glancing down at the heavily fortified old mill compound, Devon adds, "You sure your friends are worth it?"

Peter's look is his answer.

"Just checking before we wake the giant. Those are real bullets down there." He points to the uppermost shack, "That's where they would be, if they're already here."

Answering Peter's puzzled look, he adds, "I've been here before and I'm probably the only guest of the Rovers that managed to escape. That's how I got the scar."

He gestures to his cheek.

A truck pulls into the compound and stops. The boys see Shan and Ramie in the back, guarded by three Rovers.

Devon leans to Peter, "Thought your smoke thing got us here ahead of them."

The compound yard is a poor place to stage a rescue. There are a number of armed men milling around, not to mention the guard towers.

Devon says, "We need to let them get up to Clancy, if that's where they're being taken. If they take them to the pens, it's a whole different ballgame."

That alternative doesn't sound good to Peter.

"I'm not gonna ask what that means."

Even from this distance he can see how frightened the two kids look. All Peter and Devon can do is wait to see what the Rovers' move is... and in turn, see what their own will be.

The two kids are manhandled out of the truck. Zachary comes down the stairs from Clancy's roost and approaches the guards. From this distance it's impossible to hear what's being said.

Watching, Devon leans over to Peter, "If they do magic, why don't they just do that smoke thing and escape?"

Not taking his eyes off the kids either, Peter says, "For some reason, I have more powers here than they do."

Devon takes note of that comment.

The boys catch a break, Zachary starts back up the stairs and two guards push Shan and Ramie after him.

Peter is itching to do something, but Devon calmly says, "Patience... we need the kids in the shack and as many guards out before we make a move. You can smoke us into the shack, can't you?"

Peter nods 'yes'.

All of a sudden the two hear bolts of multiple rifles behind them.

A man's coarse voice says, "I was told one of you might be tricky. If anything happens I'll shoot you both, no questions asked." He adds, "That would be a shame because Commander Clancy is anxious to meet you... again."

The man speaks into a walkie talkie, "Got strays, two of them. Over."

The response, "Bring them to the tower. Over and out."

Devon smiles, "Well, that's another way to get in there."

Clancy sets down his walkie-talkie and turns to a new military communications unit sitting on the table, no doubt delivered by the chopper the kids heard pass over the cave. It was probably dropped in because the chopper wouldn't chance landing till there was something tangible to get.

The deputy picks up the handset, "Rover One here. I have the two birds you were looking for, possibly more. Over."

The comeback, "Rover one, have chopper on pad. Advise when you acquire full number. Over."

"Will do, but remember our deal. Over and out."

Zachary comes into the shack, followed by Shan and Ramie and their guards. Deputy Clancy walks up in front of the kids. Before saying anything he dismisses the two guards. As they leave, one glances suspiciously at the new radio.

Clancy looks the two kids up and down, "Why, you're just pups. My men say you have powers. Don't try using them here." He turns to walk away, but stops, "By the way, we have two others about to join you."

Shan and Ramie share a panicked glance.

Clancy addresses Zachary, "Put them in the corner."

Zachary warns, "The men are getting suspicious. They think you made some kind of deal that leaves them out."

Clancy responds without much concern, "They're not as stupid as I thought." He thinks for a second, "Gag the kids. After the other two are delivered and the chopper is inbound, pull that cord."

He points at a cord by the door with a ring on it, "They're only offering two passes out. One for you and one for me."

Puzzled, Zachary looks at the cord.

Clancy says, "It blows the last two flights of stairs. I always have a back-up."

Shan and Ramie sit on the floor, tucked away in a corner. They have their hands bound to each other, back to back. Gagged, they quietly watch the activity in the room.

Ramie nudges her, as if to say, 'let's do something'. She shakes her head 'no'. Shan knows she can break the bindings and do a few other moves, but she senses that it's a matter of timing... like in a chess game.

She also fears that what little she knows won't be enough. One thing she is sure of is that she has no idea how to stop a bullet.

Of all things to notice right now, Ramie sees his Orb lying on a table. He smiles.

The door swings open and Peter and Devon are shoved into the room, hands bound. They both topple to the floor.

Deputy Tom Clancy smiles broadly and walks over to Peter, "Peter Capwell, it's taken a long time. Told you there would come a day."

As one of the guards pulls Peter up to his feet, Peter responds, "Why, Deputy Tom Clancy... No beer can?"

Clancy backslaps Peter. He falters but does not fall.

The deputy tells the two guards, "I don't want to take any chances. You two take positions two tiers down and keep guard."

They hesitate.

One of them says, "You wouldn't be pulling a fast one, would you, boss? It wouldn't be wise."

Clancy answers by putting his hand on the 9MM pistol in his belt. Not prepared to challenge his leadership, the guards turn and exit.

"Told you," comments Zachary.

Clancy disregards the warning. He intends to complete this transaction before any uprising.

He goes to the radio and keys the handset, "Rover One here. Have two birds, and two friendly passengers. Over."

The comeback is, "Other acquisitions? Over."

Clancy keys again, "Burned. Over."

"Chopper on route. Will home on your signal. Over and out."

While this goes on, Devon manages to stand up by Peter. Both can see Shan and Ramie nearby, unharmed.

Clancy finishes with the radio and steps back over to the two boys. He glares at Devon, "The steadfast baby brother." He moves the back of his hand over Devon's scarred left cheek, "I see you still wear my mark."

Clancy turns his gaze to Peter, "I gave him that because he wouldn't tell me where you were." With a laugh, "Come to find he didn't know where big brother ran off to either. It's nice of you to come back. Too bad it's going to be such a short visit."

Peter, with guilt in his eyes, glances over at Devon.

Clancy turns to Zachary and nods towards the door. Zachary understands and he goes over and yanks on the cord.

Seconds later there's a loud explosion outside the shack. They're now isolated. Clancy reckons that by the time the others figure things out, they should be on their way.

In the corner, Shan breaks her bonds and pulls away her gag, "Peter, someone's coming to take us away."

"Only some of us." Clancy pulls the 9MM from his belt.

Peter mumbles something under his breath and thrusts a hand forward, breaking his bonds like paper. Instantaneously, the shack explodes in a dense cloud of purple smoke. Gunshots ring out in the blinding cloud. Footsteps shuffle all over.

The smoke clears almost as fast as it formed. One last round ricochets off a protective globe Peter has generated around the three kids and himself. It hits Deputy Clancy in the shoulder. As he falls his gun skitters across the floor.

Zachary grabs for a rifle. Ramie waves his hand at the Orb on the table. It shoots across the room and knocks Zachary against the wall. Ramie's pleased with himself.

Shan slaps his head and turns to Peter, "What kind of spell was that?"

"Ask Master Warnig - her trailer is still purple."

The globe flickers away and Devon scrambles for Clancy's 9MM. Once he has it, he jumps up and levels it at Clancy's head.

Peter yells, "No, Devon, don't... Wait!"

"We don't leave enemies... and I owe this one!"

As he cocks the hammer, Shan jumps, grabs a piece of wood and knocks the gun from Devon's hand. It fires when it hits the floor and the shot ricochets off the iron stove.

Peter gives her an odd look, "All your powers and you use a stick?"

She holds her stick up like a bat, "It worked, didn't it?"

Devon collapses to the floor, wounded by the shot. The smile Peter and Shan share is short-lived. They rush to him - only to see he's bleeding badly.

While they are focused on Devon, Deputy Clancy reaches for a hide-away revolver strapped to his ankle. He manages to get it out.

He struggles with his wound to take aim, making the mistake of opening his mouth, "I'll have the last word."

Peter dives for him though he's too far away. With lightning speed Shan waves at Clancy - in a blinding flash of light the Deputy is a Grimick!

Grimicks don't have normal hands and the revolver falls to the floor. Deputy 'Grimick' Clancy falls back in total confusion.

Peter turns back to Shan, "Nice."

She winks, "Thought you'd appreciate that one."

They refocus on Devon. Somehow they have to stop the bleeding.

Barely conscious, Devon struggles to say, "Burn the wound."

Shan looks around for something to do this with. She sees the potbelly stove and rushes for it.

In the meantime, with trusty Orb in hand, Ramie goes to the front of the shack and looks out the window. A couple of shots from the men below strike the wall near him.

"They're shooting at us. Does everyone here have one of those things?"

Peter yells for him to get back.

Ramie does, all the while mumbling, "Everybody shoots everybody in this world!"

Shan comes back with a frying pan from the potbelly stove.

It's hot, but Devon grabs her gasps, "Not hot enough."

Peter takes the pan from her and points a finger at its edge. It slowly begins to glow red-hot. He slaps the hot edge against Devon's belly wound. Devon screams out... and then passes out.

More shots from below hit the shack. Mumbling about having to hear all of this, Ramie covers his ears.

Shan grabs Peter, "Your brother needs the Healer!"

"He... this... none of this belongs in Spirin."

He had wanted to get Devon out of the zone and was even willing to stay with him. But he knows Shan's right about one thing - if they don't do something, Devon will die.

Rovers are below trying to kill them and a military unit is flying in to lock them away. From the smell and the smoke drifting in the door, Peter can tell that the blown up stairs are on fire. All things considered, it's not looking too good for them at the moment.

The radio squawks. "Chopper inbound. Over."

Above all the noise from the radio, the crackling fire and the popping gunfire, Ramie yells, "Can we go home and talk about this later?"

Shan shoves the pendant into Peter's hands.

"Rockhead's right. You can't leave your brother to die and I'm not leaving you in this insane world!"

Reluctantly, Peter nods his head in agreement. He turns to Zachary, who has come to... and sits staring at Clancy the Grimick.

Peter yells over, "Take your so-and-so rabbit and run."

Zachary nods yes with vigor and helps Clancy to his feet... now hind paws. He heads to the back of the shack. Shoving a stack of crates out of the way, he exposes a rear door.

Peter's ploy has worked. Now he knows a way out.

Devon has slightly regained consciousness. Ramie and Shan help him to his feet while Peter starts dialing in the first symbol on the pendant. Shan doesn't notice that Devon has slipped the loose 9MM into his belt.

"We have to be outside!" cries Peter.

They head out the rear door to a small dirt area backed by the canyon wall. Zachary and Clancy can be seen scaling their way down an embankment alongside the shack.

All the while the gunfire continues from below and a cloud of smoke grows from the fire.

Peter dials in the second symbol and presses the center jewel on the pendant. The pool of liquid light forms against the canyon wall and reduces down to the Door.

Before telling the kids to go through, Peter notices the gun in Devon's belt. He snatches it out and tosses it to the ground.

Devon weakly protests, "I need my gun."

"Not where you're going!" Peter looks at Shan, "Get him through ... I'll follow."

Shan makes Peter promise with his eyes. Then, supporting Devon, she and Ramie dive through the door.

The pilot inside the military chopper sees a second bright flash of light from the canyon.

He speaks into a com-unit, "Second flash of light, sir. All hell's breaking loose. Your orders? Over?"

The radio squawks, "If subjects can't be acquired, sanitize. Over."

The pilot flips up the trigger guard, "Roger. Engaging. Over and out."

He fires. A sidewinder streaks from under the chopper towards the compound.

The moment before Peter is about to jump through the door, he glances down at the 9MM in the dirt. He's not sure why but, for some reason, he reaches down and grabs it.

Peter stuffs the gun in his belt and dives into the light.

The compound explodes in a massive fireball!

Chapter Twenty-Seven

The kids tumble out of the Door into the deep blue grass of Spirin. By accident or by design, they land near the familiar log that welcomes them back... with the newcomer. As if rejoicing, the green mist in the Graveyard of Spells swirls up like whitecaps on a storm-tossed ocean.

Shan sits up and smiles... she's home. Ramie wastes no time smiling... he just kisses the ground.

With a glance over at Peter, Shan quips, "You're getting pretty accurate."

Peter sits up and looks slowly around. He has always felt Spirin is beautiful, but it has never shined brighter than now. This feels more like coming home than when he tumbled out on Earth.

He does not fear the Council... nor does he fear what might be beyond the wall. He knows his family is truly here... and there's not as much fear when fighting for family.

Devon lies groaning in the grass nearby. He tries to lift his head but can't manage it. Peter rushes to him. Though very weak, Devon gestures to lift him up just a little so he can get a better look.

Peter does and Devon's eyes widen at the rolling hills spotted with purple trees... at the two moons that share the sky with the warm suns... at a flock of birds dancing in and out of the soft clouds. Devon reaches up, grabs Peter's collar and pulls his face close to his own.

In a strained voice, "Thank you, brother, for coming back." His strength gone, he passes out.

Peter can't find words for the warmth that sentence makes him feel. In Spirin, his kid brother can let go of the darkness and reclaim his lost youth... at least, Peter hopes so.

He glances over at Shan, knowing her gentleness is the reason they escaped that nightmare. He knows that even if he and Devon managed to escape the Zone, Earth held nothing more for them.

In her usual direct way, Shan halts his musing.

"I've tugged for the Healer. Your brother's lost a lot of blood. We have to get him home."

Peter stands up, and Shan and Ramie help Devon into his arms. They all conjure up their hoverboards.

As they float away from the log, Shan nudges Peter, "We don't have that argument to finish anymore."

Peter glances at her, "I'm sure you'll find another one."

They both laugh.

Ramie, flying nearby, just shakes his head at the ickyness of their courting rituals.

Witch Racinda holds a faded drawing clearly made by a child. She appears to agonize over it as if it were both a fond remembrance and a painful reminder. Racinda knows she's beyond redemption.

Rupert's entrance breaks her moody train of thought. He has seen her wrapped in this moroseness before. Of late, the depth of her despair seems to reach new lows.

She has never been much at confiding in anyone. He is still surprised that not more than two days ago she told him of the Door being used again... and that she would not tell Lord Kildemar of it.

Rupert knows she has placed her head in his hands by doing so. He's not sure if she has done so out of trust - or out of desire for the betrayal that would end her servitude.

If it were the latter, she has judged wrong, for Rupert has no great love for the Dark Lord. Kildemar took him from his home and enslaved him in this fortress. The witch has been the only one to treat him well.

Rupert fetches some water for her.

"Madame Racinda, is there anything I can do?"

She doesn't respond.

He glances at the drawing she holds, "Is that from someone you know?"

Without looking away from the drawing, "It's no longer important." Looking up at him, "The Door was used again."

"Madame, you mustn't say that, even to me... if you do not plan to tell Lord Kildemar."

"You have just showed me how far you may be trusted. It serves no purpose to tell the Lord anyway. This activity is beyond our reach."

Rupert nods and prepares to leave.

Before he can, she says, "My son drew this long ago. Thank you for being someone I can tell."

He's not sure if the telling she thanks him for is about the drawing or detecting the spell. It doesn't matter. Having someone take him into their confidence makes him feel less like a slave... especially in this realm filled with shadows of intrigue.

As he leaves, "Anytime, Lady Racinda."

She smiles at being called Lady Racinda so many years past her youth... and almost as many past her innocence.

Kalish takes a peek out the front window at Atta sitting on the porch. He turns to Gran-D, "She's still mumbling to herself. I haven't seen her this upset since... you know... "

Gran-D laughs, "You mean when you got drunk and forgot to show up at... "

Kalish cuts him off, "'You know' was sufficient!"

Atta sits on the front porch chair where she has been all night. She mumbles incoherently to herself as if carrying on an angry conversation. Suddenly she stops and looks up.

Shan, Ramie and Peter float over the ridge sloping down towards the house. She jumps up and rushes towards them.

Seeing Atta, Ramie says, "We're in for it now. Think I'd rather have dad mad at us."

"Don't worry. We'll get both of them," Shan assures him.

Atta continues to mumble as she rushes towards them, but stops abruptly upon seeing Peter carrying a hurt boy. She kicks into 'mother' mode, with only a slight growl at the kids as she passes. She rushes to Peter's side to check Devon's wound.

"Get this boy inside and upstairs now. I'll tug the Healer."

Shan is quick to say, "I already have, mom."

Atta snaps her a glare. Shan realizes that it's best to keep quiet and simply do as she's told.

Shan holds the door open for Peter to carry Devon inside. Seeing the hurt boy, Kalish sets conversation aside and helps get him upstairs.

With the kids safe inside, Atta goes back to pacing and mumbling outside. It's more intense than before the kids' appearance... with a tinge of anger to it. After a few seconds she comes in, but remains in the entry, mumbling and pacing back and forth like a caged animal.

Gran-D watches this, struggling not to laugh.

Shan starts towards her, but Gran-D grabs her, "Not now."

Kalish comes back down the stairs, sees Atta pacing and cuts a wide berth around her.

Shan starts to approach him but he snaps at her while keeping an eye on Atta, "Not now!"

The Healer comes in, takes one look at Atta and also knows to steer clear. Without a word Kalish points her up the stairs. Atta, still mumbling, storms out the front door.

There's the feel of an absurd comedy about it all, but no one dares laugh. Gran-D goes to the window and peeks out at Atta.

He turns back to everyone, "At least she's sitting."

Kalish lets out a breath of relief, "Good, she's starting to wind down." Turning to Shan, "Now, who is the boy upstairs?"

Shan says meekly, "Your second new son, Devon."

All sit quietly around the living room. Every time one of the kids starts to open their mouth, Kalish's glare closes it. Kalish watches Gran-D, who in turn watches Atta outside the window. Suddenly Gran-D moves away from the window and takes his seat by the fire, as though he has been sitting there all along.

The front door opens and Atta comes in, completely composed and with a motherly smile.

"Now... time for some answers."

They all stare at her, not sure how to react.

She looks at them as if they're the ones who have been acting crazy and innocently says, "What?"

Later, with everyone at the dinner table, Peter finishes his tale of their trip, "... and through the last light of the Door, we could hear a loud explosion. That's about it."

Kalish starts to say something but the Healer appears at the top of the stairs.

"He's asleep now. He'll be up and about in a half moon. Should I take a place closer by to keep fixing these round ears?"

Atta snaps, "They're not called round ears in this house."

The Healer shrugs at this, "Whatever. At least both have luck."

She places a spent bullet on the stair rail, swirls into a spinning light and pops away.

Gran-D laughs, "She does like her flair."

"She's a nut," says Kalish, turning back to Peter. "I can't believe you took Shan and Ramie with you."

"Come on, dad, you think he could have stopped me?" Shan puts in. "And, as for Ramie, he's always on auto-trouble mode."

Peter appreciates the help but he really doesn't have a valid argument. He knows he should have sent the kids back right off. He only gained a little more information by stalling.

In truth, he was probably looking for an excuse to come back. His desire to get home has now brought the second round ear to Spirin.

"He's right," Peter says.

That admission is adult enough for Kalish and he backs off.

But no conversation is complete without Ramie's two-cents, "I'm just glad to be back where there's no guns."

Kalish says, "I would say, 'Keep that in mind next time...' though I think I'd be talking to a rock."

Ramie takes this as his father's way of saying, 'I'm glad you're home...' and smiles.

Gran-D gives Peter an understanding nod and Peter excuses himself, "It's been a long couple days. If you all don't mind, I need to go for a walk to clear my head."

He gets up to go and so does Shan. Gran-D clears his throat in a way that Shan understands and she sits back down. Gran-D likes to think he gets by with all this silent language.

Kalish simply says, "If you two have something to talk about, then just go do it."

The old man shrugs like he doesn't know what Kalish is talking about. He still lets Peter leave on his own, figuring the boy does need a few minutes away from everyone to get his thoughts together.

Sitting near the Obelisk in front of the wall, Peter stares at his own reflection. He appreciates the quiet time, even if it's painful to look at his own motives.

Though he doesn't always see the point to it, he never has been good at lying to himself. It's even harder to deceive himself in front of a thousand-foot mirror.

The wisp of smoke carrying Gran-D touches down about fifty feet away so he can walk the last distance. Peter's glad to have that time to bring his thoughts back to the moment.

Gran-D has that style of doing things - good or bad - that makes Peter think the old man's often played him. It's as though the old man always seems to know what he's thinking. Perhaps he's being paranoid - then again, perhaps it's true.

Gran-D sits down next to Peter on the boulder. He remains quiet, giving Peter the chance to begin.

Hearing nothing, he finally says, "Now it's time for the be-tween-the-lines part of your story."

Peter figures its best to say what's nagging at him, "I wasn't planning to return, but you knew I would, didn't you? You've been playing me from the start."

"First, I'm thankful that you got my grandchildren back safely. Second, you've played yourself from the start... I only helped out."

Peter looks puzzled.

Gran-D continues, "Haven't you had the feeling for some time that you were meant to be here? You remember the day you touched the Obelisk?"

Peter nods.

"It never glowed like that before. It was a sign that the time has come... as well as the person. Your level of training would have made a stone suspicious. I think you've known all that for some time, even if you didn't want to see it. I only told you things that allowed you to continue denying your suspicions."

Setting aside the unbelievable thought of being some kind of prophetic fulfillment, Peter says, "Then why the game with sending me back to Earth? Don't tell me it was the Council's decision. We both know you could have swayed them."

With a sly shrug, "Formalities... You had to be the one to choose to be here. Whether I nudged things along or not, you made that choice."

"Devon didn't," Peter responds.

"He would have died where he was... so, in a way, he did as well."

Gran-D speaks logically, without a hint of doubt. He only wishes he could be as convinced in the depths of his mind.

"You're right, he would have died there. But... I still don't like being used. I'm not your Prophecy."

"Of course you aren't. No one is the Prophecy. For that matter, no one even knows what the Prophecy will bring. I think you are an element in beginning it... and I think you know this." Gran-D then remains quiet to let this sink in, allowing Peter to be completely honest with himself.

There are too many things that Peter can't explain since his arrival in Spirin... and, to be completely honest, are hard for him to dismiss. From the beginning this land has reacted to his presence in ways beyond explanation... from his ease in picking up sorcery to elements like the green mist seeming to communicate with him.

He also can't deny that the attacks on his life are so alien to Spirin that they must be somehow directly about him.

Could Gran-D be right? Could he have known this is all meant to be... No, Peter can't go so far as accepting this. But, he can't pretend he's been oblivious to all the signs.

If nothing else, he has to accept his coming back was out of choice, even if it was a necessary decision... a necessary reaction to the immediate circumstances.

Gran-D can see this spinning Peter's brain like a whirlpool. Attempting to bring it into focus, "Leave that be for now. What did you find on Earth that you didn't tell at home?"

Relieved at not having to answer definitively, Peter reaches into his pocket and pulls out the black fragment of stone he picked up in the crater. He hands it to the old man.

"That's a piece of the purple elephant that passed me on my way here the first time."

Gran-D peers at it closely. "So the devastated Zone on your world did come from beyond the wall."

Peter nods 'yes'.

"That must mean two things. One is that whoever is beyond that wall wants the Door."

"And the other?"

Peter points at the stone Gran-D holds. "If they get it... rather than take the chance of having more round ears come from my world, they would send more of that through the Door to try and destroy Earth."

The weight of what he has said lands on his shoulders even harder than on Gran-D's. He's answered his own question! In some way he knows he is part of this Prophecy that he knows so little about. For a fraction of a second he hates Gran-D.

Holding up the stone, the old man says, "Thank you for bringing this back. It will help with the Council."

He figures enough has been dumped on Peter for one day and stands up.

Before leaving, "If the Prophecy is meant to be, I don't fear it... as long as it starts with us. You shouldn't either. You coming home?"

"Not right now. I need a little more time," says Peter.

With an understanding nod, Gran-D disappears.

It's late and all three moons wash the hills. Colors are darkly vivid. Peter floats over the crest of a hill and sees the Graveyard of Spells upon another. He takes the long way, pausing by the log, a landmark that has become special to him and Shan.

He proceeds up towards the Graveyard. Once he gets near he settles to the ground and walks the last few feet to the front gate. Peter has no idea what the green mist within the gates is or - for that matter - what it thinks of him.

If it does think, does it think on its own or does someone manipulate it? All he knows is that it feels alive as it swirls more each step closer he gets. He stops just outside the gate and watches the mist for a few seconds.

Peter pulls the 9mm pistol he brought from Earth out from under his shirt. This is one thing he didn't want to mention to Gran-D because he isn't sure why he took it in the first place. He has decided to set that straight.

Peter disassembles the 9mm, ejecting the clip and pulling the slide from the grip. He stares at the parts, wondering if there is a reason he needed to grab the gun at that last moment?

Finally, he cocks his arm and throws each part of it as far into the graveyard as he can... one part at a time... each in a different direction. It would not do to have someone like Ramie fooling with it. Satisfied with his decision, Peter turns and begins walking away.

A 'burp' sound comes from behind him and he turns. The gun flies out of the Graveyard and lands at Peter's feet... fully assembled. He picks it up and turns to the Graveyard.

"As you wish."

Of course there's no reply.

He adds, "Someday, if it's needed, I hope you tell me what other weapons you have hidden in there."

The green mist swirls silently... almost like saying it hears his request.

Chapter Twenty-Eight

Now healed, Devon has quickly mastered conjuring and flying the hoverboard. He is still new enough to Spirin to find many things fascinating, but the glow in his eyes is wearing thin faster than it did for Peter.

He leans towards seeing the darker side of this colorful world. Peter understands, considering what Devon has gone through, but hopes his view will soften soon.

He and the other three kids are out for a friendly game of Orb, but Devon plays to win... so how friendly is up in the air. He's teamed with Ramie who has taken quite a liking to him. This isn't surprising... what free time Peter has is often spent with Shan.

To pull off a surprise shot at Peter, Devon fires an Orb that barely misses Shan's head and whips around at Peter. It almost works.

Peter's thrown off balance because his focus is on how close it comes to Shan and if she's OK. He ignores the Orb, letting it fly on by.

Not about to just let it pass, Shan cries, "You almost took my head off!"

Devon swooshes by her, "It almost worked."

In response she sends an Orb right at Devon's back, stopping it in mid-air a foot before it connects with his head. Peter sees this, though Devon doesn't, and waves for a break in the game.

Pretending he doesn't see the time out signal, Devon fires another Orb at Peter, which just about hits him. Even Ramie can see the game is going over the top.

As Devon's Orb boomerangs back to him, Peter raises his hand. Devon's Orb explodes in the air, far enough away not to harm anyone... but Peter gets the point across. He goes to ground for the break, whether Devon likes it or not.

Shan's pleased Peter is trying to draw the line.

Devon storms up, "What the hell was that?"

"Defective Orb. Bring your play down. It's just a game," Peter tells Devon.

His brother shoots back, "Nothing is just a game. You either win or you lose. There's no in between. That's the point! When are you going to learn that?"

Shan says, "I thought the point was to have fun."

Peter smiles at Devon, "Since you don't have an Orb, I guess the game is over anyway."

Considering all that's taken place, Peter knows a bit of his mind understands what Devon is saying.

Devon snatches Ramie's Orb, "Let me borrow this, kid." Then to Peter, "Hey, one on one. Full contact! You got the balls?"

Peter looks like he's about to take him up on it as they eyeball each other.

Shan flies over and places herself between them, "Both of you dump the attitude... and I mean now!"

Peter breaks first.

He cracks up laughing at Shan's stone face, "You win." Then to Devon, "I'm not the one you need to worry about. You need to learn not to get her pissed off." Peter figures tempers just got a little hot - no harm, no foul.

Devon doesn't wind down as easily. It takes a couple seconds for him to break his glare. He floats Ramie's Orb back to him and silently flies away. Ramie shrugs at Peter and Shan, and, like a puppy, tails after Devon.

Shan looks at Peter, "You said he saw chess as a game of strategy and war. I think he only sees war. I'm through playing with him."

"He'll be OK. Just give him a little more time to ease up," says Peter with a hint of doubt.

"I'm not worried about him easing up. I'm worried he will start hardening you."

With this she floats away.

Peter is left there alone to wonder if Shan has a point. He knows she usually does, even when he doesn't like it.

Seeing Devon's powers growing faster than Peter's have, the Council of Masters decides to resume Peter's training and to start training Devon. The decision is for the same reason as before... training means control. At least they hope so.

Not all the Masters support this decision so they also decide to train Shan, one of the strongest young candidates... and one of their own. Never has the Council had three young people in advanced training at the same time.

It's a sign they feel change may be coming. Not all welcome change, but most fear to think they cannot control it. None realize that absolute control is beyond anyone.

Gran-D knows how to work their fears when he feels it's for the greater good of Spirin. The greater battle he has to wage is that inside his own head - does he know what's good for Spirin?

Shan and Peter fly along the path early in the morning, each heading for a different Master and a different lesson.

Reaching a fork in the path Shan says, "This is my turn off. I'm with Master Imton today. Who are you with?"

"Master Carringer... now that I don't need the Sorcerer's Door. I like him. I think I've liked him ever since I met him as an orange lizard... he's fun."

Shan waves goodbye as she veers off.

Peter yells, "Imton's loads of fun, too."

Master Carringer is brilliant at what he does - spell making - but he does tend to get a little lost in things. Some days Carringer ebbs and flows with how present he is. Peter has learned to roll with the tide of the day.

Today Carringer is preoccupied with digging through scrolls and stacks of books. He goes from one pile to another, seemingly unaware that Peter is sitting in the room.

Peter finally says, "Master Carringer, can I help you find something?"

Somewhat startled, "Like what?"

Peter shrugs, "Whatever you're looking for."

"What am I looking for? Oh, of course, you wouldn't know because I'm the one doing the looking... would you?"

Today is not one of Carringer's best days.

Peter shakes his head 'no' and goes back to reading a large parchment in front of him. Master Carringer goes back to looking for who knows what.

Abruptly, Master Carringer stops looking and holds his head high in the air. He turns different directions, as if trying to tune his head into a frequency or use it as radar.

Peter thinks he misses the orange lizard. Sometimes Master Carringer, in his natural form, is much weirder.

"Master Carringer, is there something wrong?"

At first Carringer appears not to hear him, and then he comes back to the present.

"Peter, I said the use of Master is so formal. Can't you just call me Carringer... at least while you're here?"

Peter just nods, without any idea what that has to do with what he asked.

Then Carringer asks, "You know where Devon might be?"

"I assume at Master Haring's for lessons."

"So did Haring... that was a tug from him," says Carringer.

Master Carringer generates a spy globe in the air and tries to focus it. A dense, dark gray cloud appears inside. Carringer tries harder which only increases the denseness of the clouds.

He says, "That's odd. I'm totally lost."

Peter struggles to refrain from laughing, considering how often Master Carringer seems totally lost. Peter looks up into the spy globe and the clouds thin to reveal Devon at a rock formation near the western wall.

"There he is... by the wall."

Master Carringer stares at the globe, still seeing nothing but gray clouds.

"Where do you see that?"

"In the spy globe. Can't you see him?" Peter asks.

Glancing at Carringer's face peering hard into the globe, Peter realizes that the master can't see Devon.

Has Devon come up with a way to hide himself? If so, why doesn't it work on him? He decides to let it go until he can figure it out.

"Master Carringer, I thought I saw him in the smoke. Guess I was wrong."

Carringer looks at Peter suspiciously, "Very well... and once again, it's Carringer here. When you say Master I feel as old as

Gran-D. By the way, when you find your brother, ask him how he blinded the globe to me and not to you?"

Peter nods, aware that Carringer is not always as scattered as he lets on.

Two ribbon streams of smoke drift through the air, one red and the other purple. They curl all over, in and around the clouds... but the red one doesn't flow as smoothly as the purple one does. It makes a sharp turn, stalls and then speeds up.

Suddenly the red stream turns into Shan. She plummets out of control towards the ground far below. The purple stream darts down after her. Just as Shan is about to slam down into a field, the purple smoke turns into Master Imton and he catches her.

Shan sits on the ground with her knees tight to her chest, heart beating a mile a minute, out of breath from her near- accident.

Almost in tears, "I can't do this. I told Gran-D so. I can't get it right!"

"Get what?" Imton sternly says.

"This being invisible, what else?" she snaps back.

Master Imton has a reputation for being enormously grumpy at stake, but he chances messing that up by sitting down next to her.

He almost sounds sympathetic when he places a hand on her shoulder and says, "Lass, you're fighting your mind, not your abilities. I've rarely seen anyone that picks up on the craft as quickly as you, even Peter."

Shan calms down as he continues.

"You have set up an expectation in your head of what you can do and what you can't. You have such a strong mind that it comes true. Expectations can be good, but they can also work against you."

Shan looks up at him with a puzzled expression.

He goes on, "Since you don't know which expectations work and which don't, it's better to let go of them altogether. Hone your skills and set your expectations aside. That's the best way to stay in the moment."

It dawns on Imton that he's truly ruining his reputation.

He stands up with a sharp, "Now get on your feet and try again."

Shan's not sure it's as simple as that, but she appreciates his effort.

"You're not as mean as people say."

"If you repeat that, I'll deny it", he says with a slight smile. "Now, let's get back to the moment and fly."

Master Carringer lets Peter out of lessons a little early so he can try to track down his hooky-playing brother. Peter floats up to the wall where the Obelisk sits and he scans along the wall, first north and then south - no Devon.

He realizes that using his eyes is not the way to find Devon - he must see through his mind. In his head, he sees an outcropping of rocks and a hole near its base. A cloud of dirt explodes out of the hole.

Peter opens his eyes and turns north. That's where he will find Devon. Maybe because they're brothers - or maybe it's the nature of Spirin - either way, Peter now knows Devon cannot be far from him.

As Peter approaches the hole in the rocks, another blast of dirt explodes out. Devon emerges, covered head to toe with gray dust. He looks like a moving granite statue - or as if he were back in the grayness of Earth. Devon doesn't seem that surprised to see Peter.

"Keeping an eye on me, big brother?"

"Nah. You think you're all grown up now, so if you want to skip classes that's your business. What are you up to way out here anyway?"

Despite his casualness, Peter still wants to guide his brother, but he knows from experience that confronting Devon is not the best way to get through to him.

Devon relaxes a bit. "Sometimes I just feel a little cramped in that loft with you and Ramie always around. Thought I'd use some of my learned skills to create a sort of home away from home. You know, for when I need to get out and think."

Peter nods as if this makes sense. What he sees is that for some reason Devon is building himself a cave like the one he had on Earth. Peter doesn't let on how much this concerns him.

"Which class taught you demolition?"

Devon laughs, "Just a matter of adapting the skills."

"You gonna show me inside?" Peter says.

Devon comes off defensively, "No, not yet. Wait till I get it done." He adds, "Remember when we were kids and your cave was always off limits to me? For now, this one's mine, OK?"

Peter knows it will do no good to push it. Devon's right - Peter rarely allowed him up to the cave, but what Devon doesn't get is that it was to protect him. For now, it's best to give him some space.

"You coming home for dinner?"

"Sure, a little later. I'm not going to move in here and become some kind of crazy hermit."

Peter hopes not, but can't deny his fears.

Chapter Twenty-Nine

All the Masters except Grand Master Dar are gathered at Melick's house - some are there to discuss how things are going, others just to worry. They stand around a spy globe floating in the middle of the room.

Devon and Peter walk along a path within the globe. The colors of Spirin's early fall surround them - blues, deep purples and reds. The Masters watch without speaking. Everyone knows the subject at hand, but no one wants to be the first to admit they may have made a mistake.

Gran-D enters, looks at all the concerned faces and lets out a sigh, "What's got you old women, no offense meant Warnig, all hot and bothered this time?"

Master Sashaw is the first to open his mouth, "You know as well the rest of us? We're creating a powerful sorcerer, maybe too powerful."

He waves at the image in the globe.

Gran-D doesn't seem concerned, "No, we're dealing with a talented sixteen-year old who's only been here four moons. He's a boy who came from a place where people hunted each other and somehow he survived. That means he is drawn towards defensive skills - which we may eventually need. We all knew it was going to be tough training him but, contrary to my advice to wait, you wanted control. Maybe we should have let him heal first."

Warnig states, "He would have advanced without our guidance."

"Then, for the same reason we started training him, we now have to stand by him," Gran-D responds.

Master Imton, well aware he's been part of Gran-D's scheming from the start, speaks, "I'm not concerned about his power. I am concerned about the way he views sorcery. He finds every dark facet of a spell... in ways even I don't understand."

"His brother can steer him," Melick says, without conviction.

Sashaw, in his usual worried tone, "And the Prophecy?"

"The Prophecy! The Prophecy!" Is that all you old fools can fret about?" cries Gran-D. "It's going to happen or it isn't. We have to understand that burying our heads in the sand is not going change that. You all have to realize that Spirin is not our whole world. Someone from our world – our world, despite being from the other side of that wall - laid waste to those boys' home. That makes us responsible."

They all glance back up at the two boys in the globe. Suddenly Devon turns and looks out from the center of the spy globe... as if staring directly at the Masters themselves. He raises his hand and the globe pops into nothingness.

A glint of a smile comes to Carringer's face.

He wipes it off, saying, "It seems that Devon can sense when he's being watched and he doesn't like it."

All look concerned.

Master Warnig says, "I'm glad we have Shan, one of our own, also studying."

"She has talent, but her head gets in her way," notes Imton.

Gran-D shifts the subject, "Peter's right about one thing."

"What?" asks Master Melick.

"If darkness comes, no one will fight our battles for us."

Master Imton stares at where the globe was, "The question is - who will be on our side?"

Peter turns to Devon, "What was that about?"
"They were watching us."
Devon turns and goes on walking.
"You're just being paranoid," says Peter lightly.
Devon stops, deadly serious, "You know, they don't trust either of us. We're being trained so they can control us... And, no, I'm not paranoid. The Zone gave me a sixth sense for these things."
"Our actions will win them over. We're a team," Peter says.
"Are we? I made it so they can't detect me. Your mind is still open, so they can find you... and, in turn, me."
He turns and continues to walk.
Peter stands there a moment, thinking of what his kid brother said. He has a point.
Peter realizes that all the Masters don't trust them and that he and his brother have been manipulated by Gran-D. The old man has good motives, but Peter can't blame Devon for resenting being used.
Trying to salvage things a little, he says, "We're part of a larger family now. Can't you just enjoy that?"
Devon doesn't respond. He just keeps walking.
Peter wonders whom he's trying to convince.

That night at the Dees' everyone gathers around the dining table about to sit down for dinner. Kalish is a bit puzzled because Atta is the first to take her seat.
Kalish leans into her, "Your dad's not cooking, is he?"
His answer comes as Gran-D dances out of the kitchen floating a large bowl precariously in front of him. He spins as

does the bowl which bounces down in the center of the table, splashing a bit of stew out.

Atta whispers to Kalish, "He likes fixing things up and I sometimes like a break from the kitchen."

Kalish whispers back, "Yeah, usually trouble."

For a bear of a man like Kalish, a whisper isn't that quiet.

Gran-D sits down.

With a smile to the kids, "Listen to them. They talk like I'm not here."

Peter, Shan and Ramie are amused, but Devon tries to keep his look of indifference.

Kalish eyes his bowl suspiciously, "What's in it?"

Gran-D smiles mischievously, "Ah, that's ancient history."

Peter and Devon have no idea what they're talking about and the rest struggle to hold back their laughter. Kalish cautiously ladles some stew into his bowl. He sniffs it and takes a timid taste.

Atta grins, "Kal, I liked dancing the night away."

Ramie adds, "Me too."

After a glare at both of them, Kalish takes a deep breath and tastes a bit more of the stew. No apparent effect... so far. He relaxes a bit, still not completely convinced.

Shan, seeing an opportunity for some fun, eats a spoonful of stew and taps her feet under the table, as if dancing.

Ramie giggles.

Kalish snaps at her, "That's not funny, young lady."

Ramie giggles again and joins her in tap dancing under the table. Kalish glares at his stew, then up at Gran-D. Gran-D shrugs.

Peter catches on and taps under the table, too. He nudges Devon to get in on it but gets no response from his killjoy brother.

Gran—D waves at a piano and it starts playing on its own. With this accompaniment, Shan gets up and offers her hand to Peter. He takes it and they start dancing.

Kalish gets more steamed by the second. Atta gives him a judgmental frown, gets up and offers her hand to him. Relenting with a laugh of surrender, Kalish gets up and dances with his wife. Gran-D and Ramie get up and do solo jigs.

Gran-D nudges Devon's chair as he spins, hinting that he join in. After all, this was the intended purpose.

Devon can't help but smile at all the activity... almost appearing guilty for tapping his own feet to the music under the table. He finally gets up but, instead of joining in, he heads up the stairs to the loft.

While the rest are having fun, Peter and Gran-D can't help but pay attention to Devon's exit.

Kalish breaks off dancing to finish his dinner, but not before Atta jabs him and winks, "Nice to see it doesn't take one of Dad's potions to get you to dance with me."

It's a perfect sunny day near the cliffs where Master Haring trains Devon. At least it's sunny for all but Devon. He trains under an isolated cloud floating directly above, pouring pounding rain over him.

Master Haring sits just out of range of the cloud in a lounge chair - dry, warm and basking under the marvelously clear sky, sipping a drink.

Master Haring shakes his head as he watches Devon haplessly float another triangular headpiece towards an obelisk column, just as Peter once did.

Haring barks, "You've got more rock between your ears than that floating stone!"

Devon snaps a glare at him. The stone wavers in the air. With the hand that does not control the stone, he wipes rain from his face.

"Why am I training in this ridiculous way?"

The stumpy drill sergeant snaps back, "To focus. It didn't bother your brother. Do you have less strength?"

Looking snappish, Devon clearly resents being compared to his brother.

"What the hell has this got to do with anything? These damn stones... I'm not planning on building stupid poles with cute cap stones!"

Haring yells back at Devon, "It's about control... and you have none. We are going to stay here till you get it right... or till you drown!"

Devon shakes the rain away like a wet shaggy dog and tries to steady the stone.

Master Haring gives another drill sergeant yell, "I called your brother a rockhead. You give the word new meaning."

Devon's eyes flare up at being compared to his brother again. The open outstretched hand he's using squeezes into a fist. The stone explodes in mid-air.

He spins and, with an angry swipe of his other hand, a wooden post near the rock wall goes flying - point first - at Master Haring. Six inches from Haring's head the post freezes in the air and drops to the ground.

"How's that for accuracy? Remember that next time you yell at me, you little troll!"

Peter comes in the front door at home to a dark and heavy silence.

Kalish steps up and says, "Do you know where your brother is?" In case Peter is unaware of the day's events, he adds, "He threatened a Master... almost harmed him."

"I know about it. You don't know Devon... if had really wanted to harm Master Haring, he would have."

Seeing Kalish's stern expression unchanged, "He's in a cave near the wall. Leave him be overnight to let off some steam and then I'll bring him in."

Peter's not been to the cave lately but he has honed his senses to locate Devon... just in case the skill would be needed.

He says, "How's Master Haring?"

Gran-D steps out of the living room, "To use one of your Earth phrases, he's a little pissed... but he's all right. Devon can't continue doing things this way. I understand the dark influences from his past, but the people in Spirin don't."

Peter realizes it has come to the breaking point that he hoped would not come.

"I'll go talk with him tonight." He adds in dead seriousness, "But nobody is sending him away."

Gran-D sounds sincere, "No one said anything about sending him away, but he has to find a way to embrace change before someone gets hurt."

As Peter turns to leave, "I warned you that Devon didn't come from a peaceful place. You manipulated us both back here and you have tried to use him... both of us. He knows that and he resents it. I don't know if I blame him."

Gran-D has no answer to this.

Peter arrives outside Devon's self-made cave. It's a sanctuary where Devon feels safe, created from memories of a world with very few safe places. Since Peter discovered his cave, Devon has never invited Peter into his creation.

Just like back on Earth, Peter feels he has to coax him out. He knows Devon can sense his presence so he waits.

After a reasonable time, Peter finally yells in, "You going to let me just stand out here?"

Devon comes to the opening and nods for Peter to come in. At least this time he has not come out with a weapon in hand... but he appears no more welcoming.

As Peter passes, he says calmly, "Come on easy, big brother."

Inside Peter can see that Devon has been busy. It is very reminiscent of Devon's survivor's lair back on Earth. There are stacks of supplies and barrels of water, as well as Spirinese hunting weapons, bows and spears taking the place of the numerous guns Devon once had. Peter knows Devon is aware that his mind is a stronger weapon, but he figures having a few physical weapons makes him feel more at home.

On the cave wall hangs a crudely drawn map of the Sphere, just as the map of the Zone once did. He must have copied it from the one in Master Carringer's cottage.

Along one wall is a mini-workshop, consisting of a small forge and bench tools that look like they belong in a blacksmith's workshop. Peter's not sure what it's for, but he suspects it may be for making weapons... but to use on whom?

There's a cot and a roughly made worktable. Peter finds it odd that these are hand-fashioned... Devon could have easily bartered for better-made ones in the village. They're probably here as his brother made them for his familiar comfort.

Peter eyes some project Devon has covered up on the worktable. Without Devon's permission, it would not be a good idea to uncover it... things are heated enough for the moment.

Turning to Devon, "This a shrine to the old cave?"

At ease in his own setting, Devon laughs... something Peter hasn't heard him do in a while.

Peter gestures at a bench, "Mind if I sit?"

"Sure, take a load off."

With Peter on the bench, Devon plops down on the edge of his cot. "What did your Masters send you here to tell me?"

"I came here from the family, not the Masters," Peter says.

Devon quickly responds, "Your family, Peter. Not mine. To me they're just another foster home." After a moment, he goes on, "What happened to us as a family? You know, brains and brawn? Can't you see that between you and me, we could have more power than anyone on this planet?"

"You happened. You grew up too fast... and too hard."

"I didn't have a choice, but I'm giving you one now. I'm your brother. Are you going to side with me?"

"What? Choose to be an outcast... not to care about anyone except us? Can't you see they care about you?"

Peter truly wishes he knew the words that would get through to him, but he doesn't.

"You gonna stay out here in your hole, like a survivalist gopher... or are you coming home with me?"

"Of course, I'm coming back. I don't like my cooking that much. I'm just gonna stay out here a couple days till things cool down."

Devon picks up a book and starts writing in it, as if Peter were already gone. Peter takes this to mean the conversation is over.

He gets up, starts to leave and pauses, "You know, while I've been here you haven't even asked how Master Haring is doing."

Devon looks up, "I'm sure he's fine. If I had wanted to hurt him, you know I could have."

He goes back to his journal.

Peter shakes his head and leaves.

Devon glances at the empty door way, actually sorry it's come to this. He figures Peter will eventually come around when he realizes the strength they could have together... or when the others turn on him.

Even this Prophecy that most won't talk about tells of how powerful the two of them will become.

He figures that their best foster homes were only temporary. It's just a matter of time till they are forced to have each other's back once more.

Devon goes to his worktable and pulls the cover off his new project. On the table lie a number of roughly shaped round metal disks, each about ten inches in diameter. The inner ring of each disk has five finger holes.

He takes one over to a pedal-driven sharpening wheel. Once he has the stone wheel up to speed, Devon starts grinding the edge of a disk. Sparks fly everywhere.

Chapter Thirty

A couple days have passed and Devon hasn't shown his face at the Dees' home yet, making things a little more uncomfortable for Peter. Not so much because Devon has stayed away... but Kalish has found out Ramie has been skipping school, most likely to hang with Devon at his cave. He also has found out Peter knows of it.

Peter comes downstairs, relieved not to find anyone around. The problem with living in a land of sorcerers is that when you think there's no one around, you're never quite sure.

Peter's startled when he gets a sudden invisible tug from Gran-D to meet him at Melick's cottage. There are many things he loves about Spirin... but having an iPhone wired in his head is not one of them.

Peter's not in the mood for more Devon antics, but he knows it's bound to be exactly that. He longs for the days when being fascinated by the wonders of Spirin was his only concern. Now worries over Devon overshadow everything.

Peter floats towards Master Melick's cottage, not in any rush to get there. In his head, he's busy going over the past four moons... actually, for that matter, the year and half since this whole adventure began - it seems much longer.

Shan floats up behind him, but he's so lost in thought he doesn't notice. Finally she clears her throat to get his attention.

Peter, a bit surprised, looks over his shoulder, "How long have you been there?"

"Long enough to know you need an ally. I got a tug that the Council wants to see you," she says.

"From Gran-D?"

Peter's surprised they would want her along if they were going to ream him again over Devon.

Shan smiles, "No, Master Carringer. He thinks they might gang up on you and doesn't think it would be fair."

This makes sense to Peter. Master Carringer is the only Master closer to being in his spring than his winter.

"I'm learning that they're being Masters doesn't always mean they're fair... or wise. Happy to have you at my side."

Shan likes this answer.

Master Melick's living room is filled with old sour-faced Masters... all but Carringer, who appears glad that Shan came along.

Gran-D appears neutral. For a man that smiles most of the time, Peter figures that is equivalent to a sour face.

In a condescending manner, Master Sashaw says, "Shan, darling, this is a meeting with Peter, if you don't mind."

Shan's answer is not what he expects, "I do mind... and don't call me 'darling'."

Peter holds back his urge to laugh at her candor. He takes a step closer to her.

"She stood beside me on Earth, beside me all the time I've been here and I'm glad to have her beside me now. We have no secrets."

Shan puffs up a little bit with pride.

Peter goes on, "Now, what's this witch hunt about?"

The Masters are not used to Peter's confrontational style.

Sashaw says, "Remember, Peter, you're the student."

"The student you chose to train, just as you chose Devon. I assume that's what this is about, so let's get on with it."

It's clear Peter is not there to be lectured at. He wants to discuss a problem and a possible solution without the trappings of hierarchy or pretense. This is what he has decided on his way there and he intends to stand his ground.

Master Haring stands up, putting him about chest high to Peter, "OK, lad, you want us to speak clearly. That's fair. Your brother has become a problem and we want him to return to your Earth."

"That's not going to happen," Peter says definitively.

Taken a little aback, "And why not?"

"For a couple reasons. The most important one is that you don't have the right to push us wherever you choose. You almost manipulated us into returning. Then out of your own fears of some Prophecy, you shoved him into training without caring what was best for him. You should have let him heal. Now that he didn't turn out exactly as you hoped, you want to abandon him and send him home."

Master Warnig asks, "What's the other reason?"

"You don't have the power to send him back... and I won't. When I was on Earth I had the powers I learned here. You helped create Devon's strength and you have no right to unleash that now on a planet you know nothing about. You created a monster - he's your monster."

But, not to sound like a defeatist, Peter states firmly, "It's time to slow down and win his trust."

Shan squeezes Peter's hand in support and joins in, "In their world no one has powers like ours. I have seen this with my own eyes. I've also seen how violent the people on Earth can be. Even with Peter this had to be un-learned."

Gran-D finally speaks, "I'm most at fault here because I sensed our fate was inevitable and wanted to guide it safely. That said... what do you suggest for Devon?"

"He's already strong enough to not need your training. Leave him be. In time, I hope to win him over - not to a cause, but to a conscience. Stop trying to make us into your saviors. The fate of your land lies in your hands, not ours."

Peter has struck a few nerves - maybe it'll cause them to think. He figures that's about the best he can do.

"With your permission, we would now like to go try and find my brother."

"Thank you for your candor. We have much to think about," says Master Melick. He turns to the other Masters, "If there's no objection, I suggest we let young Peter carry on."

The room is silent.

Master Carringer sneaks Peter a thumbs up.

On their way away outside, Shan gives Peter a hug. He appears a little distraught.

Quietly he says to her, "Truth is... I don't know if I can influence Devon any longer."

Shan says supportively, "We can try."

They fly away in search of a possible lost cause.

"What do you think they'll do?" asks Shan.

"Who knows? I wasn't thinking that far ahead."

Back inside Melick's cottage the mood is somber. They had not summonsed Peter to be lectured to, but none can deny what he said.

Some try... like Master Sashaw, "Are we going to be told by a boy how to proceed?"

Master Melick appears irritated by this, "Get off your pedestal, Sashaw. The boy has some valid points. He is right that we cannot unleash a sorcerer created by our land on his Earth... even if he did come from there."

This remark spurs an uneasy look from Master Imton.

Gran-D speaks up, "The bottom line is that we've never had adversaries, so we're not prepared to defend ourselves. If the Prophecy is true, three young people will not determine our fate. We are going to have to learn to stand on our own feet. About Devon, I suggest, as Melick, that we give Peter and Shan a chance... and, that we be grateful we have the two of them solidly on our side."

Imton quietly says, "Do we?"

A few days after the Council meeting the sun shines down on the kids' favorite log.

Wham! A razor sharp, glistening disk with finger holes slams itself into the log. The deep cut sends red wood chips flying in all directions.

Devon stands there pleased with his aim. He wears a leather belt - much like a gunslinger's - with hooks on both sides in place of holsters. Razor disks hang from each hook, three deep.

Devon gets in a wild west stance, glances over at Ramie, and says, "Call it."

Ramie is fascinated. He crouches down beside Devon, watching and learning every move this new-fangled gunfighter makes. He bites his lip... and then, "Go!"

Devon whips off another disk and slings it at the innocent log. The disk hits home hard and more wood chips fly high in the air. Ramie jumps up and lets out a shout of joy.

He pleads impatiently, "Let me try it, will ya?"

"A couple more, kid. I want to get as good with my left hand as I am with my right."

He starts to get into his stance again, determined to perfect this new skill.

Shan and Peter come floating over the hill and see what's taking place. Without a word Peter speeds towards the log below. He doesn't make it before Devon strikes another blow to the log.

Peter swoops up next to the log and glares down at the damage the three razor disks already embedded there have caused. Fresh wood chips lay all around, strewed out over the soft grass he and Shan often lie peacefully in. It's as if the log were bleeding on sacred ground.

He turns his glare at a stone-faced Devon. Peter's posture says he's not about to move.

"That log belongs to all of us. Haven't you done enough damage already?"

Devon smiles, "We talking about the log now?"

"You know damn well we're not," Peter snaps back at him.

Devon gets into his stance to quick draw another disk, but Peter holds his position between him and the log. Devon's muscles tense up as he glares at his brother.

"You think I won't do it?"

Shan flies down near Devon and Ramie. A look from Peter tells her that this moment is between him and his brother. Shan gets it and glares at Ramie to back up. He starts to say something but Shan takes his ear and pulls him away from the stand-off.

It is a stand-off. Peter won't move and Devon doesn't appear to be backing down. Instead of a quick draw, Devon slowly pulls another disk from his belt in a very deliberate manner. His and Peter's eyes are locked.

The disk in Devon's hand shakes with tension. Peter locks his knees. Devon swings, releasing the disk full force. It flies within inches of Peter's head and imbeds in the tree that shades the log.

Having gotten his point across, Devon turns away.

Shan rushes to Peter and throws her arms around him, relieved to know no harm was done. Peter knows the opposite.

He tells her, "Take Ramie and leave us alone."

She understands and waves for Ramie. For a moment he seems torn but, after another look at the red in Devon's eyes, Ramie figures Shan is right.

The two create their boards and, before leaving, Shan leans into Peter, "Take it easy on him."

She turns to Ramie, "Come on, Rockhead."

Grumbling under his breath, Ramie follows her away.

With the two gone, Devon turns to Peter, "You gonna to try and play big brother again?"

Peter doesn't know what to say that might temper Devon anymore... especially now, feeling that his brother shows he's almost ready to cause harm. Devon has blinked but Peter's not sure he will next time.

"No, I think it's gone beyond that. They chose me to tell you you're suspended from training. They're afraid of you... and maybe they should be."

Devon doesn't appear bothered by the news.

"As if I care. I don't need their training. Move this rock, turn that a different color, make something jump... what uselessness. They have the power to move mountains... and they tickle stones."

"Move mountains - or destroy them?" Peter dryly responds.

Devon's emotions start to boil.

"What would you know of having to destroy, having to survive, having to kill?"

"That argument is getting old. I wasn't there because of an accident. I got back to you as soon as I could. I'm tired of you playing the guilt card. Grow up!"

With this Peter turns to walk away.

Devon almost stammers like the boy he is, "I didn't need you then. I don't need you now... and don't think you or those Masters are sending me away."

Peter turns back to him, "I wouldn't let them... and I'm sure as hell not going to try. You want to know why?"

After Devon doesn't respond, "You're too dangerous of a boy to put back on Earth. Go hide in your cave till you really grow up and decide you care about someone beside yourself. If that time comes, you are welcome home... but not till then."

Without waiting for a response, Peter flies away.

Devon glares at Peter's exit, snaps a razor disk from his belt and throws it with all his might at the log.

The disk's violent impact cuts the log in half.

Chapter Thirty-One

Witch Racinda senses something she has never felt before, an unexplained feeling of conflict from beyond the wall... from a land that knows only peace. She can't put her finger on it because it shouldn't be possible, but she can't deny it.

It's something so strong that it breaches walls that have never fallen. Could it be that someone is about to collapse a wall?

She has no idea, but she is aware that if she doesn't report this it will cost her dearly. Witch Racinda has spent too long keeping her head - though there are times she doesn't think she deserves to - to keep this from the Lord. But how does she tell Lord Kildemar of fluctuations in nature when he only understands hard military facts?

It dawns on her that Rupert has been talking.

His voice fades into her consciousness, "... and General Corning had to admit... "

As if coming out of a fog, Witch Racinda says "What?"

Rupert realizes he's been talking to the walls.

"Milady, have you heard a word I've said?"

Still distant, Racinda mutters urgently, "Rupert, go to the Grand Hall and tell Lord Kildemar that I request an audience in private with him. Return with the answer." She adds, "Make no mention of any of the things we have discussed."

"As you wish, Milady."

Rupert leaves, hurt that she feels need of telling him to keep quiet about privileged communication. Another emotion suddenly washes over him - fear of having to approach Lord Kildemar. Very few in Goreipor dare approach Lord Kildemar with a request - much less anything hinting of a demand.

Peter gets back to the Dees' to find Shan and Ramie waiting on the front porch. He comes up and settles near them.

Knowing this has been hard on Peter, Shan waits a moment and asks, "How did you leave it with him?"

Peter is exhausted. "It's in his court now. He'll be staying out at the cave till he figures things out."

"What do you mean, he's not coming home? That's not fair." Only seeing the loss of a friend, Ramie says defiantly, "I'm going out to the cave and stay with him. He showed me where it is."

Kalish, who has been standing behind the screen door listening, abruptly opens it.

"No you won't, young man! Till Devon works out his problems, he's off limits... understood?"

Busted, Ramie bites his lip, but doesn't look back.

Kalish repeats, "Do you understand?"

Finally Ramie grumbles, "Yes, sir."

Witch Racinda, upset over something she can't explain, comes into the Grand Hall. The message Lord Kildemar has sent back was clear. With bruised face, Rupert has brought back word that the Lord does not give private audiences upon requests delivered by a messenger.

Lord Kildemar pays no heed to her arrival. Observing the focus of his attention, Racinda keeps her distance for the moment. The lord's focus is on Taligarr and Janick.

They wield swords in a heated practice match in the center of the hall. The court stands cheering them on. Lord Kildemar walks the perimeter monitoring the bout, but not cheering it on.

Taligarr is more the aggressor, initiating attack after attack. Janick defends himself well but shows less commitment to the fight.

After another fierce attack by Taligarr, Janick raises a hand. He allows the point of his sword to kiss the stone floor, a sign that he wishes to call a halt to the match.

Taligarr looks over at his father. Lord Kildemar storms into the circle and grabs Taligarr's broadsword.

Without warning, he attacks Janick with full-force swings of the blade. Janick does his best but every swing of his father's blade beats him down more. Another massive clash of the blades and Janick's sword clangs out of his hands and across the floor.

Lord Kildemar doesn't break off the attack. He advances and arcs his blade at Janick, veering off only at the last second. It takes a nick out of his son's ear. Janick cowers on the floor.

Kildemar steps back and yells, "Next time I will take that ear! You never ease up in a match!"

He turns away, still holding the sword.

Janick stands and gasps, "Father, we train and we train, but we have no enemies."

Lord Kildemar spins with amazing speed for a man of his size. Swinging the heavy broadsword in only one hand, he brings its tip within a fraction of an inch from Janick's throat. He holds the blade steady.

"War waits in every shadow for any sign of weakness. Never forget that!"

He throws the sword down. It echoes throughout the hall.

Racinda stands in the background watching this display, re-minded again that Lord Kildemar only understands the lan-guage of steel.

Making his way back to his throne, Kildemar snaps at Witch Racinda, "What is it you wish to talk of that you would send a lackey to arrange a private audience? More of your vague senses that tell me little?"

On her trip to the Grand Hall, Racinda has begun to have second thoughts. The farther things go, the more she rues her involvement. She has helped to exploit the weak spot in the wall, but has convinced herself she did so to stop the wall from falling... in some distorted way, protecting those beyond the wall.

This fight confirms her doubts. In truth, she has no illusions about the dark world she's part of.

Racinda knows she's opened the Door and now has no choice but to disclose that she doesn't understand the immen-sity of what she's done. How to temper this disclosure is the trick.

Deciding to play off the great Lord's nature, she starts, "My vague senses serve you best if you are the only one that is privy to them. Do you not fear information that falls on all ears?"

"I've said your tongue and tone may be your undoing, but you have a point, witch." Lord Kildemar yells to the hall, "All but my sons clear the hall!"

Lord Kildemar never has to command anything twice - all rush to obey. Within a minute, only he, Taligarr, Janick and Witch Racinda remain. With the Grand Hall almost empty, their voices echo hollowly off the walls.

Satisfied they are alone, the Dark Lord turns to Racinda, "Now, out with it, woman."

"I have sensed a feeling of turmoil beyond our eastern wall that I should not be able to sense. This alone tells me something is coming to pass," she says, knowing this vagueness will incense Kildemar.

Kildemar lets out a booming laugh, "A feeling of turmoil? This is your matter of great importance... this feeling?"

His laughter stops, "Tell me details of the people beyond that wall. That would be information of some use to me."

Lord Kildemar is well known for his use of his enemy's kin as a formidable weapon - learned from his father. Witch Racinda is very aware of this. For many years, she has assumed that the wall could not be brought down... at least not by the Land of Goreipor. Recent events bring this into doubt.

The one condition for her services set forth with Lord Kildemar's father was that Racinda would never be forced to harm her own people. Now she inches towards doing exactly that... one slight measure at a time. She can tell that Lord Kildemar sees the conflict going through her mind.

He makes this clear, "I know the promise my father made. Why should I keep a promise made by a dead man?"

This brings it out in the open.

Though she fears Lord Kildemar, there is no compromise in her tone as she says, "If you demand I break that agreement, you can have my head... and lose my powers. I will inform you of what I sense beyond that wall... or inside your land... and no more."

Kildemar often finds Racinda infuriating. He has wanted to strike her down more than once... but he knows how well her powers served his father in taking over Goreipor.

The use of her powers are self-restricted from direct dealings beyond the eastern wall only. If the day comes when the other walls may fall, her powers may be useful against whatever is beyond those walls.

He restrains his urges.

"Be away with you. I'll tell my generals to watch out for 'feelings' along the eastern border."

Having said all she's willing to, Racinda leaves.

After Racinda is gone, Janick asks his father, "Why do you put up with that woman who comes so close to defying you?"

Kildemar responds, "When I go into battle I use my sword, not my knife... but I do not throw my knife away."

"Your orders, father?" asks Taligarr.

After a moment of thought about the witch's advice, "Increase the patrols along the eastern wall."

Ramie shows up at Devon's cave, as he does more often than his father would care to know. Per Devon's orders, Ramie yells in... he never enters without an invite.

To Ramie this is like a couple of kids having a fort with a secret code, even if he has to play the role of underling. To Devon it's not about play, but he might as well humor the kid... he may come in useful someday.

Announcing himself Ramie hears nothing back. He has an urge to break the rules and go in on his own, but admits to himself that he fears Devon... a little. Maybe that's why he finds it so enticing to hang around with him.

He overcomes his urge and turns to leave. Then he sees Devon down next to the wall. Devon is doing exactly what Peter had done so long ago.

He holds his head and hands against the wall, almost caressing the mirror membrane. He does not recoil from it, as Peter did.

Ramie runs down to him.

"What are you up to?"

Devon pats the wall and slowly turns around. He's not startled because he heard Ramie up at the cave.

"You're a good kid, not going in the cave when you're not supposed to. I'll remember that."

Beaming that he's scored a point, Ramie repeats his question, "What were you doing with the wall?"

"Listening to our neighbors," Devon says, aware that Ramie won't understand.

He knows too many others who would look for a darker meaning in it. Ramie doesn't and that's why he prefers his company. Devon likes being in the unquestioned lead.

Ramie shrugs, "I never heard anything through it."

Devon takes a last glance at the wall and quietly says, "That's because you don't have the hunger."

He turns and heads for the cave. Ramie dutifully follows... with no idea what Devon is talking about.

Once inside the cave Ramie sees Devon has fashioned yet another new weapon. It's a lance with a sweeping blade at one end and a metal ball at the other.

Devon's new toys always fascinate Ramie. Outside of a brief glimpse of violence on Earth, though, he has no real concept of their deadly gravity. But, on his visit to Earth no one was actually killed... at least, not that he saw.

Trying to sound casual, Devon asks, "Ramie, you know that Sorcerer's Door spell that we traveled in... you used it the first time when Peter came here, didn't you?"

Playing with the newly created lance, Ramie says over his shoulder, "Yeah, I used it, but pretty much by accident."

"It required that pendant, right?" Devon leads on.

"Yeah, why you asking?"

Ramie sets the lance down. His curiosity has been tickled.

"You have any idea where they keep the pendant?"

"I put it back in the Graveyard of Spells, but when Peter and I tried to get it back from there he said it was gone. It's probably at Master Carringer's because he's the Spell Master."

Now his interest is really peaked.

"What are you thinking about doing?" Then more panicked, "You're not thinking of going home?"

Devon smile, "No, I have no interest in going back to Earth... but it might be fun to have a little adventure here."

Ramie catches on and nods his head in the direction of the wall, "You don't mean?"

With the best innocent glint Devon can manage, "Aren't you just a little curious about what's on the other side of that?" Easing into the idea, "I was just thinking of a quick peek. What harm would that be?"

He sees alarms going off in Ramie's head, but he also sees his mischievous curiosity taking hold.

Ramie fights his urges. "I think there's a reason for the wall being there and for no one crossing over."

"Ah, it was just a thought. You're probably right." Devon figures he's pushed as far as he should for the moment, "It's getting late, you better be heading home."

Devon steps over and picks up one of his throwing disks. He spins the disk like twirling a six-gun. It fascinates Ramie... and Devon knows it. "If you can get away, meet me here tomorrow night after dinner and I'll show you how to use this."

Ramie nods with a more than willing smile.

Devon says, "Don't mention anything I said about the pendant. It was just a crazy thought and they think I'm nuts already."

He adds a laugh as convincing spice.

Any suspicion Ramie might have is overshadowed by a gleam

in his eyes at Devon's numerous toys. What Ramie doesn't know is that the new toys are part of a scheme Devon is carefully planning.

Ramie will take part in it - like it or not.

In their loft late that night, when Ramie starts to put out the lights, Peter asks, "How's he doing?"

Peter's sticking to his guns about Devon staying away till he changes, but that doesn't mean he doesn't care.

"How is who doing?" Ramie says innocently.

"Remember who you're talking to, the guy you helped break into the Graveyard my first night here... Like I said, how's he doing?"

"He's doing OK, but he likes when I visit. I think he's getting lonely out there. I don't know why everyone is so down on him. He's just a kid."

"He's a kid that can get you in trouble," Peter warns.

Then he thinks that's absolutely the most useless warning to say to Ramie. It's like putting out a fire with gasoline.

"He wouldn't do that."

Ramie puts out the candles.

He appears like he's itching to tell Peter more but all that comes out is, "You're not going to tell dad, are you?"

Peter lays his head on the pillow, "It's our secret... but promise not to let him talk you into anything too stupid without running it by me. OK?"

Ramie rolls over, torn a bit by guilt, "OK."

Peter looks up at the moons glowing through the ceiling, warmed by Ramie's words, 'Don't tell dad'. For once in his life he really feels the words fit.

Now if only he could get his brother to understand that feeling.

Chapter Thirty-Two

It's dusk. The Dees and Peter are just finishing dinner. It's been another day without Devon. Though he's chosen to stay away, everyone misses him to one degree or another. The Dees are not the kind of family that takes adopting lightly, nor do they like living in anger.

Ramie scarfs down his dinner before everyone else and impatiently waits for the first reasonable opportunity to excuse himself. They're a family that tends to finish dinner together.

His impatience gets the better of him, "Can I be excused early?"

With a suspicious tone Kalish says, "What's the hurry?"

As usual Ramie hasn't thought things out and he scrambles for an excuse, "Um, Peter told me about, um, jogging on Earth... and I wanted to go out and try jogging this evening. Um, can I be excused?"

Shan rolls her eyes, "Jogging?"

Peter does as well, but Kalish smiles and says, "Say 'hi' to Devon for us all. Tell him he's welcome back when he wants to come home."

As the last sun goes down, Devon crouches in some bushes overlooking Master Carringer's cottage. He wears his throwing disk belt hung with new sharp disks. He's not dressed for a friendly visit.

Soft lights glow from the cottage below. He slips a disk off his belt and holds it, debating how ready he is for such a commitment... or perhaps trying to find his nerve. There's a difference between dealing with Rovers and harming someone who has never been a threat.

The bushes directly behind Devon rustle. He spins around, holding the disk concealed to his side.

It's Ramie.

Devon snaps, "I thought I told you to meet me at the cave."

Stealthily he places the razor disk back on his belt, hoping Ramie didn't notice. It would not do to have Ramie aware of what lengths he's willing to go.

If he did notice the blade, he doesn't let on.

"Knew you were going for the pendant. I figured I could help."

Devon says doubtfully, "OK. What can you do to help?"

Ramie scoots up beside Devon and peers down at the cottage. Master Carringer's shadow crosses one of the windows. A glint of an idea flashes across Ramie's face. He turns to Devon.

"I can imitate tugs. I learned to do it to get out of trouble. I can do dad. When I'm hot, I can pull off Gran-D."

He waits for a reaction from Devon... a sign of approval.

Devon glances back at the cottage, "You could call him away?"

Ramie nods vigorously.

"Pretty good, kid. Great idea."

Truth be told, Devon's grateful not to have to test his resolve on someone he doesn't dislike. Master Carringer was probably the least condescending of the Masters.

He smiles at Ramie, "Go ahead. Give it your best shot."

Ramie scrunches up his nose and concentrates on the cottage. Nothing at first - then lights start going out. A few seconds later, Carringer comes out the front door. Glancing around, he generates a hoverboard and heads off.

It dawns on Devon that, as dense as Ramie is, he's not a total fool. He might even know he just saved someone from getting hurt.

Rising to go down to the cottage, Devon tells Ramie, "Nice job, kid. You stay out here and keep an eye out while I get the pendant."

Ramie nods OK with a look of satisfaction.

A tiny glow globe floats over Devon's head as he works his way through Master Carringer's cottage. Though he has trained in the cottage, there are many rooms he hasn't been privy to. As far as he knows, he's never seen the pendant.

Considering the clutter Carringer leaves around, this doesn't surprise him. There are piles of books and scrolls everywhere... on desks, on bookcases and on the floor. It's like maneuvering through canyons of words and that's just in the living room.

Devon comes to the sliding double doors that lead into Carringer's library. He slides them open to a menagerie of spell tokens floating all over.

Devon doesn't know that every spell has a token like the pendant. But while the pendant is required for the Sorcerer's Door, not all the other tokens are needed to work their spells. They are just physical signatures for each one.

Master Carringer, being the Spell Master, is the keeper of all the tokens. Like Master Warnig's gypsy wagon, the exterior is an illusion masking the size of its interior. The library is massive.

When Peter had come to steal the pendant, Carringer had thinned the room out to make the pendant easy to find. Now tokens are everywhere. They range from being simply tiny bright colored stones to ornately decorated medium-sized statues. Only Master Carringer knows which token represents what spell... and Spirin has a lot of spells.

Even the hard-nosed Devon finds the library fascinating, but he reminds himself that he's there on a mission... and on the clock. He needs to get the key to the Sorcerer's Door before Carringer returns - or see how far he's willing to go to attain his prize.

Refocused, he weaves his way through all the tokens. The single glow globe that moves with him causes them to cast bizarre shadows on the walls and bookcases.

At the far end of the room is a large desk, backed by an enormous fireplace. On the wall above the fireplace is a map of the Sphere.

Though Devon has seen a smaller version of it in the living room, this is a larger, more ancient looking version. He figures this must be the original map.

The desk is like the rest of Carringer's home - cluttered. He moves scrolls around on the desk, looking for anything that might give him a clue to the location of the pendant. He picks up a framed picture of a man and woman standing with a teenage boy.

As he peers more closely, he realizes the teenager is Master Carringer and the two adults must be his parents. He sets it down and re-focuses on his search.

He stops. Devon figures he's thinking like an Earther. He needs to think more like a sorcerer. If there's anything to the Prophecy, the token will find him... if he allows it to. He concentrates on the spell and, immediately, a red glow seeps through the cracks of a cabinet door.

Devon opens the door and two softball-sized globes float out towards him, as though answering his call. To Devon's surprise there's an identical pendant suspended in each. He had no idea there were two - of course he decides to take both.

He reaches out for one globe, but when his fingers get close, a bolt, like a tiny lightning strike, zaps him back a few feet.

Not about to let a little energy charge effect his plans, Devon pulls a razor disk from his belt and takes a piece of cloth from the desk. He wraps his hand for insulation and swings the disk with all his might.

The edge strikes one globe and it explodes into bright red dust. The pendant falls to the floor.

Satisfied, Devon does the same to the other globe.

He has lost track of time and wonders if Ramie is still on watch. Of course he would be - the boy's an obedient puppy.

Devon gathers the two pendants but, before leaving, he sticks one down into the top of his boot. The other he places in his pocket.

Not bothering to tidy up much, he closes the cabinet door and uses the cloth to brush the red dust closer to the wall so it doesn't stand out. He figures his deeds will not remain a secret long... just long enough.

On his way back through living room, he stops and cuts the smaller map from its frame, then folds it and stuffs it in his shirt.

Master Carringer knocks on the Dees' door. Atta lets him in with her usual gracious manner. Gran-D is in the living room beating Peter at chess... as usual.

He looks up, "What brings you around, Carringer?"

"You did," says a puzzled Carringer.

Devon and Ramie stand in front of the wall near the cave. He peers at the wall with excitement. Ramie doesn't have as much enthusiasm as he faces their reflections.

Devon is geared up to go, with his razor disks, two new deadly lances and a satchel. Ramie has a coat.

Suddenly Ramie grabs his head in pain. He whines out, "Everyone is tugging at me!"

Devon knows his theft has been discovered sooner than he has expected. He takes the pendant from around his neck and hands it to Ramie. Then he unfolds the map on the ground. Ramie still winces at the strength of the tugs.

Devon yells at him, "Ignore them. I need you to show me how to use that to get me there," pointing to Goreipor on the map.

There's no façade of this being just a request.

It's clear that Ramie can't focus from all the tugs... so Devon uses a little trick he developed for himself. He raises his hand over Ramie and a clear shell, somewhat like an umbrella, forms. It's meant to block the Masters from locating him, but he thinks it may filter tugs as well.

"That better?" he asks Ramie.

Ramie nods that it is, but still appears confused.

Devon's voice becomes more demanding as he points again to the map, "Now, show me how to dial to get there."

Ramie starts to back away, but Devon grabs him by the collar. Devon has decided that Ramie, outside of knowing how to use the pendant, could be useful down the road. Not that he'd be that much good at fighting, but in a land filled with strangers he would be loyal... and obedient.

Devon's cold chess-playing side also knows Ramie could come in handy for leverage, though he chooses to deny that thought... until needed.

"You wanted an adventure. Now you're in it. Do what I say."

Ramie fumbles with the pendant, lining up the symbol for Spirin on the inner ring and the symbol for Goreipor on the outer one. The pendant goes through its glowing sequence. A beam jumps out of the jewel and creates the swirl of liquid light that reduces down to the Door.

Ramie points at the spot ahead of them, "There's your Door. I don't want to go..."

Devon cuts him off, "Too late. I need a sidekick."

With this he shoves Ramie forward into the door. A slit of light appears and Ramie's gone. Devon takes a deep breath and a last glance back at Spirin...

He jumps through.

A panicked look washes over Atta, "At first I could feel him but he wasn't answering. Now I can't even feel him."

Kalish nods in agreement and glares at Gran-D.

Gran-D sees no point in mincing words.

As calmly as he can, he says, "He's gone. So is Devon."

"Why would Devon take Ramie back to Earth?" Kalish asks.

Peter stares off in the distance, pretty sure he knows what's going on. He doesn't relish what he's about to tell the family, but it's his responsibility, not Gran-D's. He offers,

"I don't think he did. I think he took him through the wall."

Atta grabs Kalish's arm for support. She knows the old story of the only Spirinese who ventured beyond the wall - and how they died for doing so.

Placing his hands on Kalish and Atta's shoulders, Gran-D says, "We'll get him back."

He turns to Peter and Master Carringer, "We need to get to your place, right now."

Shan steps up to say something. Before she does, Atta grabs hold of her.

"Don't even think about it."

Gran-D waves for Shan to stand down, at least for now - until a plan can be devised. Shan reluctantly nods her temporary agreement. She knows that pushing the point right after her mother has found out about Ramie would be too much for her to bear.

By no means does Shan settle on what might happen tomorrow.

Chapter Thirty-Three

Ramie tumbles out of the light onto a plateau of shiny black rock that scrapes his knees and elbows. He yells with a mixture of pain and fear, confused about what Devon's gotten him into.

Devon tumbles out next, landing near Ramie. Having experienced much worse, he pays little attention to the hard landing.

Ramie jumps up and runs to the edge of the plateau. Its face plunges almost straight down into a canyon. The boy staggers back and topples over. He jumps up again and runs to the other side - here the drop is no friendlier.

Beyond the gullies that surround the plateau are cliffs of the same cold black stone. He runs back to Devon, who patiently observes his fit of panic.

"What have you done to me?" Ramie screams.

Devon gathers up the razor disks that have fallen during his landing and replaces them on his belt.

He turns to Ramie, "It's done, get used to it. I'll protect you, but only if you stop thrashing around like a stupid kid."

"I am a stupid kid! I trusted you!"

Out of frustration, Ramie picks up a few loose stones and throws them at the distant cliffs beyond the plateau. None of them reach those black walls.

Throwing something calms Ramie slightly... but only slightly. He plops down on the stony ground, drops his head on curled-up knees and bangs the stone with his fists.

Devon waits for this ridiculous behavior to stop. After a few more seconds, he slaps Ramie. Then says, "You want me to start doing that to you? If not, settle down. I'm trying to get the lay of the land."

Ramie can only think, 'What land? This is just scary blackness. Land is rolling hills of blue grass and purple trees. That's not here!'

Witch Racinda approaches Lord Kildemar's quarters. A guard blocks her way. She doesn't have time for proper protocol. With a wave of her hand the guard slams back into a wall.

She barges through the massive double doors into Lord Kildemar's private quarters. Racinda knows she'll face his wrath... but if she doesn't bring this news to him immediately, she will face much worse.

Lord Kildemar pushes aside the two concubines who share his oversized tub and yells, "How dare you, woman? You take your freedom too far this time!"

She can't back down and is too old to be shocked.

"Hear me out, my lord. It's a matter of more importance than your play. It's not about abstract feelings this time."

She knows he doesn't understand the true value of her connection with nature, but these are words he can understand. She wants his attention first.

Grabbing a broadsword, he bolts out of the tub.

"It better be or I'll have your head! On my father's grave, I will!"

If the matter were not so urgent she would laugh - Kildemar himself put his father in his grave... and he threatens to take her head almost daily.

She knows better than to laugh at the Dark Lord... who flaunts a sword and his scared, fat, naked body in front of her.

Best to get the news out before this image draws even the slightest giggle.

"The Door has been opened... into your land."

Lord Kildemar grabs a robe and yells for his guard. The guard, still shaky from Witch Racinda's assault, enters.

Kildemar commands, "Get me Commander Zeron! Immediately!"

Master Carringer kneels down to clean up the red dust from the globes Devon destroyed.

He mumbles, "This containment material is hard to create. I can't believe he'd destroy it."

Peter likes Master Carringer, but sometimes he can be so naïve. If Devon merely destroyed an object and its precious dust, it would be a blessing. He knows his brother is capable of far more carnage.

Peter wonders who came up with the idea of sending Carringer a false tug - Devon or Ramie? He would like to think that under all his macho bravado Devon still has a grounded conscience... but he doesn't know.

Yes, the Council and Gran-D have pushed Devon too fast, but Peter knows his brother is still his responsibility. He says,

"I have to go after him, even if I can only get Ramie back."

Carringer glances up, "I don't see how you can. He took both pendants. The door is closed from this side."

The Spell Master glances over at Gran-D.

Peter's not sure how he knows, but he does. Maybe from Gran-D's calmness or the slight smile hidden under his concerned look... but Peter's sure the old man has a hidden card up his sleeve. He's positive.

Gran-D clears his throat and asks Master Carringer, "Could you give me a few moments alone with Peter?"

Carringer appears miffed but must understand, because he nods and goes to the other room, muttering to himself, "I have another smaller map upstairs... hope that's far enough away."

With Master Carringer gone, Peter turns to Gran-D.

"OK, how many pendants are there?"

A smile crosses the old man's face, clearly pleased that Peter is a step ahead of him.

"Only three that I know of... but I suspect that there are eight in total... to match the eight symbols on each ring of the pendants."

Peter tries to sift it out as he looks up at the large map on the wall above the fireplace.

"Let me see, one for each land, even that small one called the Portal," pointing up at the small sliver of land where all five other lands meet. "There's obviously one for Earth - or I wouldn't be here. What's the eighth one for?"

"It might be for another world like yours... or possibly it could be for where the Ancients come from. I don't know," says Gran-D, trying to be as earnest with Peter as possible.

The truth is he doesn't know... any more than he knows all the aspects of the Prophecy.

"We think that one pendant was hidden long ago in each of the worlds indicated on the rings. Master Carringer's grandfather found the one meant for Spirin. At that time, he kept it a secret from most... somehow aware that its powers were not to be toyed with."

Peter nods for Gran-D to go on... he's with him so far.

"Carringer's parents were of a different mind, like Carringer himself... always inquisitive. They decided on their own that if Spirin possessed all the pendants, any threat from the Prophecy might be avoided."

"Or controlled?" Peter interjects, knowing of Gran-D's tendency to try to manipulate circumstances... and history.

The old man nods, "Yes... or controlled. They discovered that like magnets, the pendants could attract and locate one another. Unfortunately they were as naive as we are about how dangerous other beings could be. They took it upon themselves to go to Goreipor and retrieve the second pendant."

Peter knows what's coming and he senses the pain it is causing Gran-D.

"It must have been a great loss for you."

"It was... I was a young sorcerer and Kirin, Carringer's father, was my mentor. He made it back with the second pendant, the one that belonged to Goreipor... but he was fatally wounded and his wife, Racinda, died there. Before he passed on, he told me of the darkness beyond the wall."

"Is that why you've been trying to control the Prophecy?" Peter asks.

He feels Gran-D is wrong in trying to control fate, but this explains his motivations.

"The door was outlawed. No one knows what lies beyond the other walls. Kirin and Racinda were maybe right to try... but were wrong about when. It wasn't the time to mess with the Prophecy," says Gran-D with a burning stare at Peter. "All is about timing."

This makes Peter uncomfortable. He doesn't see himself as the world changer that Gran-D does. He figures the old man is just as wrong as Carringer's parents to try to control fate.

But that's past now - Peter wants to move on. He says, "You said there are three that you know of?"

Gran-D nods.

Before he says anything more, Peter says, "Let me guess... the third pendant is at Master Imton's?"

Gran-D is not easy to surprise, but his eyes widen at Peter's guess. How could this boy possibly know?

Feeling the wheels grinding in the old man's head, Peter says, "The chess set."

Gran-D shakes his head, still puzzled.

Peter goes on, "The third pendant is the Earth pendant. You said one was hidden for each symbol, so one is from Earth. Master Imton has a beautifully carved chess set in his library. Something nagged at me about it, but I let it go. He brought the third pendant from Earth, didn't he?"

"Right, but that's another story," Gran-D responds, still taken aback by Peter's logic.

It's clear Gran-D doesn't want to get into the details about Imton at the moment - and rightly so. Now is the time for solutions... later may come the time for stories.

"OK. Can we get the third pendant?" Peter asks.

Gran-D grimaces a bit.

"Yes, I can get it, but it's best I go get it alone."

Peter can sense a half-committed tone. There is no time for maybes now.

"Is there a problem?"

"He's a little touchy about the Earth connection... it was a very long time ago. I'll get it. Anyway, you shouldn't go through the wall tonight. It's better to wait till dawn. You wait here at Carringer's and I'll bring the pendant."

Before Peter can protest Gran-D turns into a wisp of smoke... which hangs in the air a second.

The old man's voice echoes from the smoke, "By the way, don't tell Carringer where I'm getting the pendant from... not quite yet."

The wisp shoots away and, a moment later, Master Carringer walks back in.

Seeing Gran-D gone, he says, "So... did Dar head off to get the third pendant from Imton?"

Peter gives him a puzzled look.

Carringer sighs, "Dar thinks everything's a secret. He even still pretends not to be on the Council."

Peter chuckles, "Yeah, I know."

The Spell Master shakes his head.

"Everyone knows... except maybe Atta."

Chapter Thirty-Four

After what Devon considers way too long, Ramie finally settles down a bit. Devon figures he has come about a hair's breadth away from throwing the kid off the plateau... not really though. He recognizes the value of having his young Spirinese with him - but Ramie can be exasperating.

From his last year on Earth, Devon has learned to tune his defensive hearing to focus automatically on anything that might be a threat. He holds up his hand for Ramie to be quiet. There's a distant sound bouncing off the canyon walls... but he can't quite make it out.

Ramie comes up to his side and tries to hear what Devon is focused on. Nothing.

He nudges him and whispers, "What's out there?"

Devon laughs, "Whatever it is, it's far enough away that you can save the whispers."

Suddenly, whatever it is has shifted in the terrain. Now both boys hear echoes from the rock walls. Spirin has no horses and Ramie appears puzzled, but Devon knows exactly what the sound is. It's the distant thunder of hooves.

Ramie darts around looking for a non-existent place to hide.

Devon waves at him and calmly says, "It's a long ways off. The canyons are making it sound closer."

Ramie blurts out, "What is it?"

Devon looks off in the general direction of the sound, though echoes can be deceiving.

"A welcoming committee, I suspect."

Four horses and a war wagon gallop through the canyon gorges. Cliff walls hug both sides of the narrow trail. In the lead is Commander Zeron. He's as hard and scared as Lord Kildemar himself... and almost as old.

Behind him gallop three soldiers on horseback and, behind them, a team of horses pulls a caged wagon. All are heavily armed and in full battle gear. The sound is almost deafening.

Devon stands on the edge of the plateau trying to judge how far away his welcoming committee is. He knows from experiences on Earth that the first one to step forward sets the tone of an encounter and may take the advantage in a conflict.

How can he strike enough fear - or respect - in his enemy to be allowed to state his case?

He hears Ramie's knees knocking behind him. Maybe they aren't actually knocking, but he hears - or smells - the boy's fear.

He turns to Ramie, "When our friends arrive I'm going to go down and have a talk with them alone. I'm sure you don't mind waiting up here."

"Sounds like a lot of them."

"Don't worry. They don't have my powers," says Devon, trying to settle the youngster... though he doubts it will work.

It doesn't.

More worried about how to get home than Devon's safety, he says, "How do you know that? If they hurt you, I'm stuck!"

Devon smiles like he has inside information. Normally he would keep things to himself, but calming Ramie will give him less to worry about.

"You're here with me and I know what I'm doing. Our friend, Master Carringer, has been here and made it home in fine shape. He likes to talk. Don't worry... I know how to handle this."

Devon turns back to the edge of the plateau to set his mind on the upcoming task and how to handle it. He figures the echoes are misleading and the enemy is still some distance away.

Peter runs his hand over the map of the Sphere mounted on Master Carringer's wall. Carringer comes into the library and watches him for a few seconds.

"It must seem strange to you, from another world, that we know so little about those who live around us."

Without looking back at the Spell Master, Peter says, "Some people on Earth are the same way. They just don't have physical walls."

Carringer is not sure how much Gran-D has told Peter.

"Not everyone lacks the curiosity."

Peter turns around to Carringer, "Gran-D told me about your parents. I'm sorry."

Carringer knows that memories of things long past sometimes get distorted. What he remembers of his parents is slightly different than what history paints.

"Yes, I thought he might have. That my parents went on the noble cause of gathering the pendants to protect Spirin is all he remembers. The truth is my dad was a little scattered... like I can be sometimes."

His curiosity tweaked, Peter takes a seat.

"That's not the whole story. They might have been trying to gather all the pendants, but wanting to know what was over there also tempted them. My dad had a reckless side and mom followed him into every adventure. It cost him his life."

Carringer sits down across the table from Peter.

"Did he tell you I went there?"

"He said you were experimenting with the Door some time ago," says Peter. "He didn't go into a lot of details."

"Then he didn't tell you why?"

Peter shakes his head no.

"None of the Masters believe my mother could be alive, but I don't know for sure. You know how nagging that can be?"

Carringer thinks of Peter's obsession to get back to his brother.

"Maybe you do. Anyway, I went partly to try and find out. That's not true... I went mostly to find out. I have to warn you that I've never seen people as scary as those I saw beyond that wall."

Trying to find the right words, "If I knew what death smelled like, I would say they smelled of death."

Peter says, "That's all the more reason I have to try and get Ramie back... and, if possible, my brother." After a moment, "Did you find out anything about your mother?"

"No."

Carringer thinks for a few seconds now because what he's about to ask may put Peter's life in greater jeopardy.

Unable to hold it back, he says, "Peter, I know you will have your hands full trying to find your brother, but if you see any sign that my mother survived... "

Carringer stops. He's not comfortable about what he's asking of the boy.

"I understand," says Peter.

Master Carringer is aware that is all Peter can say without knowing anything of where he's going. He figures that's enough of an answer.

There's a knock on the front door. Whoever it is, Carringer is grateful for their timing. He excuses himself to go answer.

Seconds later, Shan walks in and straight to Peter.

"Gran-D said Ramie went with Devon... and you're going after him."

Feeling like a spare tire, Master Carringer clears his throat, "I was just on my way out for a walk."

Neither of them pays him much attention and he quietly exits.

The echoes of the horses are much closer. Devon knows in the confusion of echoes that the best way to determine where they are coming from is to hear the last echo. He focuses on an isolated sound and tries to block out the all the others. His mind stays on the repetition of that sound till its last bounce.

He walks to the northwestern edge of the plateau and looks over. Perfect... there's a wider clearing about seventy-five feet below. Fingers of canyon empty into the clearing.

He glances back at Ramie, "I'll be right back."

Ramie doesn't offer an argument.

Armed with his disks and one of his lances, Devon jumps off the edge. He floats effortlessly down to the clearing. He realizes the best strategy is surprise, but he wants to make a point with this first encounter.

He figures his second best strategy is to confuse – and then let their imaginations work against them. Only for the briefest of moments does it cross his mind that he's a sixteen-year old taking on what he assumes are battle-hardened soldiers. He reminds himself he is the only boy who ever escaped the Rovers... twice. He braces himself, hoping he's prepared for what needs to be done.

Dual moons bathe the clearing as the echoes are almost upon him. Devon shakes his arms and hands to loosen up in these last peaceful moments.

All of a sudden, the four soldiers and the war wagon storm around a bend into the clearing. Commander Zeron is in the lead.

Seeing Devon standing before them, they strain to pull their horses up. The horses whinny and bolt a bit. Devon remains motionless, allowing them to be caught up in their own confusion... allowing them to have doubts - while he displays none of his own... at least, not outwardly.

One soldier howls, "Look! It's just a boy."

Once he has his horse controlled, Commander Zeron snaps back, "Quiet!" Then he stares at Devon, "Boy, you made a mistake coming here."

With a slight smile, Devon remains quiet. He has created a variation of Peter's protective globe, in the form of a half-globe – a shield he holds because it's easier to control and it allows for more effective offensive actions. The edges of his new shield flicker a bit, but not enough for the soldiers to notice.

To throw them off guard, Devon says, "If you wish to live, I will accept your surrender."

The soldiers - and their commander - break into laughter.

Slowly and deliberately, Devon lifts his staff straight up, the ball end on the bottom. He slams it straight down and the ball hits the rocky ground with a thunderous bang!

The canyon walls tremble as if hit by an explosion. Broken chunks of black rock fall from above. Two of the soldiers are knocked from their horses. The others struggle to keep their mounts under control.

Devon's shield harmlessly deflects the stones that fall near him. One soldier manages to launch an arrow at Devon, but it ricochets off his shield. Devon sets his lance to the side and takes a razor disk from his belt.

Ramie inches near the northwest edge of the plateau, but he's too frightened by the commotion below to peer over. He covers his ears as men scream. It seems like the longest time... then there's silence.

Ramie scurries back from the edge. Back-peddling like a frightened crab, he picks up a sliver of rock. His back comes up against an outcropping. He braces himself, holding the shard of stone out in front like a shaky Excalibur.

He waits in the lonely, deafening silence.

Chapter Thirty-Five

"Now you want to send our last pendant over the wall?" An agitated Master Imton paces impatiently in his home.

"I was against the boy from the first, but when you told me of the Obelisk, I tried to see it your way. Old man, I'm starting to think that was a serious mistake."

Gran-D asks, "Why do you doubt Peter so much?"

Imton knows it's not the boy. His doubts come from ancient baggage he carries from Earth.

"You don't know these Earthers like I do. They can be cruel and power hungry... and they can be turned on a dime."

Imton can almost quote what he anticipates Gran-D will answer so he adds, "Before you say it, I know where I came from... I'm different. Your father trained that in me."

"I wasn't going to say that, old friend. And I, as well as all the Masters, have trained Peter. I trust him the same as I would trust you." Gran-D says this with conviction... and hopes he really means it.

"I left Earth long ago to avoid using powers," Imton replies. "You've brought this boy here to give him powers and to tell him how much those powers will be needed. There's a difference."

Gran-D is now the one losing patience.

"If I am wrong I will have to deal with that, but right now my grandson is lost beyond that wall. Are you going to help... or not?"

Imton understands Master Dar's frustration. He even realizes his part in this game so far, but he's torn about playing into it any farther.

If Peter fails - or turns - the fate of Spirin is in the hands of those beyond the wall. He's aware that Gran-D will not care for his answer. Although they're practically brothers, he refuses to decide this based on emotions.

"I have to think on it."

Gran-D starts to say, "But... "

Imton cuts him off, "I said, I will think on it. You said Peter won't leave till dawn - and dawn is when I will give you my answer. You'll have to settle for that, old man. That's my final word... until the morning."

A scratching sound rises up the wall of the plateau. Ramie squeezes up as tight as he can to the rocks behind him, trying to summon the courage to face whatever comes over the edge.

Back on Earth it felt like an adventure... and he had the trusted company of Shan and Peter. This is different... maybe because here, he did not get himself into this adventure. Here he feels totally without control over events.

Maybe, it's simply because he's plain old scared.

Devon lifts himself over the plateau wall. His clothes are spattered with blood. He walks towards Ramie and glances at the stone Ramie holds.

"Good, at least you're thinking of defending yourself, but you'd make a more impressive adversary if you stand up."

Ramie can't take his eyes off the blood on Devon's shirt.

"What... whose blood is that?" he stammers.

Casually Devon says, "Oh, it's not mine."

He picks up his satchel and gestures to Ramie to get up.

"I sent word ahead, but we should not follow far behind. It will lessen the impact."

Ramie thinks, 'Word? Impact? What is this nutcase rambling on about?'

All Ramie wants to do is go home, but Devon's arrogant, egotistical manner tells him there's not much chance of that. Somehow he's going to have to deal with it... at least till Peter, or someone, comes to his rescue.

Then the horrible thought crosses his mind - how? Devon has the only pendant.

As he gets up, he notices Devon building a pile of rocks in the shape of an inverted pyramid... like he saw outside the cave back on Earth. If he weren't expecting someone to come after them, why would he leave a marker?

A very slight glimmer of hope crosses Ramie's mind.

Shan and Peter lie on Master Carringer's roof watching shooting stars zipping across the sky. Neither of them has said anything for some time.

Peter finally speaks, "Won't they miss you at home?"

"They know where I am and that I'm not coming home tonight," Shan says without taking her eyes off the sky. "Just hold me through the night and we'll face tomorrow when it comes."

She knows all the turmoil that must be going through Peter's mind and she's there to silence it... at least till morning. Before silencing it though, she's afraid she has to get one last argument out of the way.

"In the morning we'll face whatever comes together."

"I don't know if it's a good idea to see me off," says Peter, trying to ease things for her... half hoping she doesn't mean something else.

She slides closer towards him and takes his hand. He puts his arm around her. Shan feels safe.

"I agree with you. I'm not going to see you off. I'm going with you."

There. She's said it and now she waits for the storm.

Just as she expected, Peter bolts up. She's resolved on the matter and figures she has a few hours for her decision to sink into his head. As he's about to protest, she puts a finger to his lips.

"A long time ago a boy dropped from the stars and almost hit me. Then he tried to take his anger out on my brother. Do you remember what I said to that boy?"

"I remember a non-violent girl who sent me flying to the ground. That's what I remember," Peter replies.

She smiles, "After that. What I said was that Rockhead may be a runt, but he's my runt. That hasn't changed. What has changed is that boy has become a young man whom I love... a young man whom I trust and a young man who needs me by his side."

The first thing that strikes him is how women seem to have such photographic memories. Then he comes back to the moment.

"Look, I don't know what kind of dangers I'll face over there. The last thing I need to worry about is you. You're not going," he says definitively, as if the matter were settled.

She laughs at his foolishness, "That's why I'm telling you I'm going tonight, so you can get used to the idea by the morning."

Shan would rather be kissing, but first things first.

"Do you know anyone in Spirin who has any idea of how to defend themselves... that is, other than me? Do you know anyone who does not need a cane who's stronger than I am?"

"Last time I saw you defend yourself it was with a stick!"

"It worked, didn't it?" she snaps back.

She sees Peter struggling for more of an argument. She gestures for him to bring it on... though she doesn't think it will make any difference.

He speaks up, "That's all the more reason for you to stay here. If I don't get back, someone has to train the young of Spirin to defend themselves."

Shan thinks it a nice comeback.

"If you can't make it back with all your powers, anything I train them to do will be useless. You're going to a land where, if what Gran-D says is true, only one person has the powers of sorcery... your brother. You're going to need someone to have your back. Devon is as strong as you, but he's not as strong as the two of us."

She lets this sink in a second and then goes on, "The same way the Rockhead's my runt, Spirin is my home. I'm not going for sentimental reasons or foolishness. I'm going to protect my home... same as you."

Shan can see she's starting to wear him down.

Now for a final punch, "We can either argue about this all night and you'll still lose... or you can give in and we can hold each other all night. Either way, I'm going. How do you want to spend the night... stupidly or comfortably?"

Lord Kildemar waits in his war room for word from Commander Zeron. A few generals, his sons and the witch wait with him. Though the gall of an intruder infuriates him, he has to admit the whole situation makes him feel more alive.

He has conquered all that opposed him and life is a bit boring. This is a trifling adversary, but at least it's something.

The war room doors swing open and Captain Pirus enters.

Lord Kildemar says, "Where is Commander Zeron? He should be back from his simple task by now."

"My lord, I think there is something you want to see."

Sounding exasperated Lord Kildemar demands, "What is it?"

"If you could join me on the battlement over the gate, I think you'll see. I believe our intruder has sent a message," suggests Captain Pirus, knowing it is something that should be seen - not told.

Captain Pirus is one of Kildemar's respected soldiers. The Dark Lord deems there's ample reason for the request.

Pirus leads the way. Lord Kildemar and his entourage follow.

Out on the battlement, Kildemar says, "Now, Captain, what is of such importance?"

Captain Pirus points to the road leading up to the raised drawbridge.

The war wagon that went out with Commander Zeron rocks back and forth as the skittish horses stand anxious to get back to their stables. No one is at the reins. Two rider-less horses mill about the wagon. Four soldiers, three bloodied, are in the caged wagon.

Attracting Lord Kildemar's attention most is Commander Zeron's head wobbling around on the bloody driver's seat.

Lord Kildemar glances at Captain Pirus, "You are correct, Captain. This is a calling card I can understand."

Captain Pirus points at new figures coming over the horizon - Devon and Ramie. Slowly they ride the welcoming party's other two horses down the road from the ridge.

The horse Ramie rides is clearly not happy with a boy who pulls the reins every which way. Neither is Ramie since it's the first time he's ever tried to ride a horse. He's more than apprehensive as he glances over at Devon.

"We're going to go in there?"

"If you manage to stay on that horse."

"If I fall off, we can leave?"

Devon smiles over at Ramie. At least he's adding a touch of humor to the situation - whether he knows it or not.

Devon snaps at him, "Try to man up. These are people I understand. They can smell fear."

Ramie's horse rears again.

"And try to keep that damn horse steady!"

"That's what you call this stupid thing?"

Ramie awkwardly pulls the reins to the left, trying not to go off the road. "I'm sure they, and this thing can... smell fear, I mean... it's coming from me!"

As the two boys come within range of the archers on the wall, one pulls an arrow back on its bowstring.

Lord Kildemar snaps, "Stand down. These brash young men have my attention. Lower the bridge."

Witch Racinda leans up behind Kildemar and whispers, "My lord, I sense these boys have powers."

Without turning to her, "And you don't?"

Turning to go to the Grand Hall, the lord puts a hand on Captain Pirus' shoulder.

"Captain, bring them to my court when I summon them... unarmed please. If they disagree, kill them."

The drawbridge creaks as it starts to lower.

Devon looks over at Ramie.

"My message was received well. We're invited into the lion's den."

Ramie glances at the drawbridge lowering and says, with little enthusiasm, "It looks like a giant mouth opening."

Chapter Thirty-Six

Footsteps echo along a massive corridor as Devon is escorted towards the Dark Lord's court. He has been stripped of all his outward weapons, but that doesn't mean he's unarmed.

Devon is accompanied by Captain Pirus, followed by contingent of four guards. Ramie is nowhere to be seen.

The Captain can sense that Devon, even without his toys, is far from unarmed and Pirus is on guard without appearing to be so.

As they walk along, Devon views the trappings of a true fortress, not that of an over-inflated deputy's compound. He knows the stakes have changed. Armor lines the walls, where in a castle he would expect paintings to be hanging.

The most ominous aspect of the decor is that a number of these weapons and much of the armor are worn and scarred with dings, cracks and notches. Devon figures these are the trophies of slain enemies.

Captain Pirus observes Devon's fascination with the weapons as they march forward. He leans into the boy to make the point that he sees the thoughts of his enemies.

"Yes, all of them have seen battle."

Captain Pirus is a professional soldier who is ruffled neither by friend nor foe. Killing is a job and alliances are subject to history and timing - both are fluid.

He has no more animosity towards this brash young boy than he had for the kid he killed in Spirin. He's not even averse to small talk dealing with matters he understands.

"My compliments on your meeting with Commander Zeron. He finally served some purpose."

He makes no comment about why Devon spared the rest - he understands it is good strategy. To kill the leader serves well as a statement - to kill all would appear too much like a challenge to the Dark Lord's authority.

Devon says, "Was that his name? It was nothing personal. I needed to deliver a message as quickly as possible."

Captain Pirus knows that, for the moment, this boy is an enemy. He also knows he already likes him.

"My young friend... is he going to remain safe?" asks Devon, simply as a question without a note of concern.

Pirus with the same lack of emotion, "He's safe for now. It's clear he's not a combatant. My guess is you have some use for him. Am I correct?"

Devon is not about to give strategy away - yet.

"He's no threat... and, yes, he could be useful."

Arriving outside the Grand Hall, Pirus turns to his guards.

"Keep the boy here while I see if the Dark Lord is ready for him. If he causes any difficulty, kill him."

Giving Devon a smile before proceeding through the massive doors, he says, "Don't test them. It would be a shame not to see how this game plays out."

Little does Pirus know that that would be the last thing on Devon's mind. He's exactly where he wants to be. Maybe Pirus does know.

He disappears into the Grand Hall and the doors slam behind him. The guards are not as confident as Pirus. They circle Devon and bring their weapons to semi-relaxed readiness.

Devon just smirks, knowing he could easily overpower them with sorcery.

After a few minutes, the hall's double doors swing open and Captain Pirus gestures for the guards to bring Devon forward.

In preparation for this new young visitor, Lord Kildemar has packed the Grand Hall with a show of might. Guards line the walls and his Generals are all present. The courtiers and their hanger-on's representing Goreipor's social elite are absent. This meeting is all about power and establishing who runs this world. Unseen are the lord's personal guard archers manning the 'murder holes' - slots looking down upon the hall.

Lord Kildemar sits on his throne with Witch Racinda standing directly behind him and to his right - in the event her powers are needed. Displaying his obedient descendants, his sons stand behind him to his left.

The only men in front of Kildemar are two soldiers flanking the throne's platform, no doubt to shield the monarch, if necessary.

Captain Pirus enters with Devon in front of him. He pushes him to a spot a reasonable distance from Kildemar. Devon looks around and sees it's all set up to make it clear who is in charge.

Little does this arrogant leader know who has true power, the boy muses, but for now Devon has to play a role. He takes note of Witch Racinda, realizing she's the older version of the woman in the picture he saw in Master Carringer's house. She's Spirinese! He may soon have use of her, but he doesn't let on he recognizes her.

Lord Kildemar addresses the Captain, "You had to kill the other one already?"

Devon starts to say, "He... "

Lord Kildemar cuts him off, "Silence! I was not speaking to you."

He may not be speaking to him, but Devon can tell Lord Kildemar is sizing him up.

Captain Pirus says, "The other one is inconsequential. He truly is a boy. This one is something else."

Showing no fear, Devon speaks up, "If you will allow me."

Lord Kildemar peers at him. After a pause, he casually waves a hand for him to speak.

"The boy, Ramie, did not send you the message... I did."

Kildemar speaks coarsely, "It was a message that cost me. Commander Zeron was a good soldier. Why should I not kill you for my loss?"

"Because I killed your good soldier. That either tells you something of my value or of the quality of your soldiers," Devon says without flinching.

"Perhaps he wasn't that good, but insulting my forces is not a way to impress me. I think I might take your head just as an example. What do you have to say to that?"

"Example to whom? By the look of things, you're master here. It's not as though others will be coming through the wall. Judging from the shields of the defeated enemies lining your halls, I suspect you're wise enough not to waste an asset."

Lord Kildemar is not used to a debate, especially from a youngster, but he knows that he has little use for the timid. This youngster has managed to do what very few have done. Perhaps it's worth hearing him out.

"So you consider yourself an asset. To me?"

Devon knows the leader is more interested in dealing with a threat than in revenge for a soldier that failed.

He decides it's time to cut to the chase, "I think you know I am to be part of your destiny."

This will bring either wrath or salvation. He suspects that Lord Kildemar plays his cards close to his vest. The people of Goreipor are not privileged with such information... like knowledge of a Prophecy.

The look on the Lord's face tells him he's right.

Lord Kildemar counters by dangling the Door's pendant that has been taken from Devon.

"This serves me better than an arrogant round ear boy. Why do I need you?"

Devon starts to say, "The Prophecy... "

Kildemar cuts him off, "Discussion of that will wait till a later time. Do you understand me?"

Devon nods, knowing he has gotten his message across.

Kildemar adds, "You do not fear me. I should kill you for that alone."

He takes a breath, watching how Devon might react. Nothing.

"I'm in no rush. For now you shall keep your head. Captain, find him guarded quarters." Then back to Devon, "I will find a way to test you soon enough."

Captain Pirus asks, "The other one, Sire?"

After a moment of thought, "He has powers that were not brought to serve me. I don't need problems."

Devon is quick to speak, "The boy can be won over... and used."

He knows he is pushing it, but he might as well find out how far he can do so. Besides, this shows he's a player.

Witch Racinda leans in to the Lord, "The small one's powers are weak. Put him in my charge and he will not hinder you."

Lord Kildemar ponders it a moment, and then, "Very well, but he's your responsibility."

Captain Pirus puts a hand on Devon's shoulder to lead him away... and silently to say he's gone far enough. Devon accepts the unspoken advice and allows himself to be led out.

As the Captain does so, he quietly says, "Nicely played."

Witch Racinda follows them at some distance.

Taligarr leans in to his father, "Father, why did you choose to give the other one to the Witch?"

Lord Kildemar is more lenient with his older son, "On occasion, you have to throw those that serve you a crumb. Keep an eye on his progress. He may be as the other said... useful."

The door to Witch Racinda's quarters opens and two guards push Ramie in. They exit, slamming the door behind them. Ramie hears the loud bolt of the door. Except for himself, the room is empty.

Frightened, not knowing what's going on, he starts to look all around, as if trying to find a way to escape... as ridiculous as that might be. He rushes to an open window in the wall and peers out.

Ramie has never seen a fortress so he doesn't know he's in an upper part of the keep, the highest tower in the middle of the fortress. There's sheer drop of at least a hundred feet outside the window.

Settling down, Ramie can't help but think there's something familiar about the room. All the scrolls and books remind him of Gran-D's room. There are beakers and other items that look like they could be used for preparing spells.

There's a painting on the wall covered by a cloth... at least he thinks it's a painting. Ramie walks to it and pulls the cloth back. He's not surprised to see it truly is a painting.

What does surprise him is the subject matter - a hill covered with blue grass and a single purple tree... Spirin!

Ramie is suddenly startled by the door's bolt unlatching behind him. He's quick to scurry into a dark corner. He waits for what might come. Rupert, Witch Racinda's assistant, comes in with a tray of food and sets it down on a table.

"Boy, this is for you."

Ramie inches out of the darkness.

Finding his voice, "Where am I? Where is Devon? Oh... and my name's Ramie."

"Where your friend is, I don't know. You are in the chambers of Madame Racinda. Consider yourself lucky."

Rupert starts to leave.

Ramie blurts out, "Why am I here?"

As Rupert goes through the door he says, "I suppose to keep you alive."

He closes the door and the bolt is latched again.

More frustrated than frightened, Ramie plops on the edge of a bench. He glances back up at the painting in puzzlement.

Chapter Thirty-Seven

Peter and Master Carringer stand by the mirror wall as the sun lightens the horizon behind them. Gran-D and Shan are off to the side, clearly arguing.

Peter watches them, knowing exactly what must be going on. He has a sly smile on his face, wanting to yell out to Gran-D that it's a waste of his time. He figures Shan will eventually convince him of that fact. When she sets her heels in, little can move that girl.

Carringer leans into Peter, "What's that all about?"

Peter shrugs, "Wasted words."

Shan and Gran-D separate. He storms towards Peter as if he's about to say something but Peter just holds up his hands in surrender... an answer Gran-D gets without bothering to ask.

Frustrated he turns back towards Shan and says, "This doesn't mean anyone is going anyway."

Peter knows what he means.

Master Imton has yet to show - and without his pendant, Gran-D's right. What he doesn't let on is that if Master Imton doesn't bring the pendant, he will go take it from him.

Imton is right about one thing. As an Earther, Peter is not about to be denied so easily. If that means he's dangerous, so be it.

At last, a wisp of smoke curls down and deposits Master Imton at the wall. He has his usual sour appearance.

He steps up to Peter and hands him the pendant.

"I'm putting a lot of blind faith in you because that old man over there says you can be trusted," he gestures at Gran-D. "Don't prove him wrong."

Shan comes up.

"You're putting your faith in both of us."

Imton doesn't immediately react.

Carringer, overhearing this, gasps at Shan, "You're not going. If anyone should go with Peter, it should me."

Peter knows the decision has already been made so there's little use being anything other than supportive.

"Master Carringer, you're the Spell Master. If anything should happen to us, Spirin is going to need you." Nudged by Shan, Peter goes further, "And Shan has already saved my life in rough going."

"Twice," chirps Shan.

After an irritated glance at her, Peter finishes, "I trust her to have my back... and it was only once."

Master Imton, who tends to think before reacting, gestures Shan off to the side. Peter thinks it's another useless attempt to dissuade her and knows how it's destined to end.

When Shan joins Imton, he speaks quietly, "I'm not against you going. You truly represent Spirin. But I have to tell you that if you're going to be of any help to Peter you will have to let go of your limitations. You can't tell when they will crop up, so you have to let go of them entirely."

Shan nods, hoping she can do so.

He adds, "I know you can."

Actually, his pep talk fuels her doubts... but she's not going to say so.

They rejoin the others. Gran-D is still grumbling over losing his argument with Shan.

He turns to her with one last feeble approach, "What am I supposed to tell Atta and Kalish?"

Shan grins and pats him on the chest, "Just start scratching your chin and they'll know something else beyond your control happened."

Standing at the wall, Peter watches the reflections of all those whom he has come to care for. He tries not to get caught up in speculation about what's to come.

Such thoughts, weighed against the odds of succeeding, can serve no purpose. Sometimes it's better to just step off the end of the pier. Peter just offers, "The sun's up and we need to go, if we're going."

"You sound like the Rockhead", Shan says with a nervous laugh.

As Peter dials in the Door, Gran-D says, "Try to bring Ramie back, but if you can't locate him this time, just make sure you both get back. As long as we have the pendant we can try again."

"I'll bring both Shan and the pendant back. Don't worry. This is what Devon would call a recon trip. I know how important the pendant is and it won't get lost," Peter reassures him.

He knows that when Devon learns there's a third pendant, he will probably stop at nothing to get it. He'll have to cross that bridge when he comes to it.

Peter also knows that when all the implications settle in, Gran-D will realize that protecting the pendant is the important thing. He's glad they're going before the old man accepts it.

"Not as important as you two are," says Gran-D, as if reading Peter's mind... he honestly tries to believe it.

Shan snaps, "Enough already! Let's get going!"

Peter smirks about who's in charge and conjures up the Door.

Lord Kildemar's fortress is not a festive castle, but it is a hard-drinking one and - as it is with warriors - even harder drinking when there is no war to fight.

Kildemar is slumped at the grand table, mixing his breakfast with a touch of grog to ward off his hangover. His sons, as well as some of his generals, are at different stages of unhappily coming to.

Racinda enters the hall.

Unaccustomed to seeing his witch in the morning, the Dark Lord yells, "Be gone with you, old woman. I care not for your kind of news this early!"

He grasps his head at the pain his echoing voice sets off.

Witch Racinda begins to turn away.

He yells, "Stop!"

As the haze of his hangover lifts, he realizes that he expects her visit... just not this early. He takes another drink to clear his throat.

"The Door has been used again. Is this not so?"

"It is," she responds with some puzzlement over how he could possibly be aware of it.

Kildemar can see her bewilderment but doesn't care. He knows there are two pendants. After one is taken without leave - as his new guest has done – surely someone will soon follow with the other to retrieve the first.

As a warrior, that's what he would do. Judging from Captain Pirus' assessment of the Spirinese, he is surprised that they have found someone brave enough to follow so quickly. This is exactly what Lord Kildemar has been hoping for since telling Devon he would find a way to test him.

He throws his goblet at a guard leaning, half asleep, against a column.

"Bring me Captain Pirus and that boy!"

Shan and Peter sit on the same stone plateau where Devon and Ramie arrived. Having just tumbled out of the Door, they are trying to get their bearings. Both are a bit bruised and smudged from a hard landing, but that's the least of their concerns.

In the morning light, Shan looks out at the dark, unfriendly terrain.

She says, "I don't understand it. As soon as Ramie saw this he would have screamed to go home. He's an idiot, but not a total fool."

Peter realizes she doesn't know the changed Devon as well as he has come to know him.

"There's a good chance he would not have had a choice."

Peter figures Devon is playing a game of power. Having a child of Spirin - even with Ramie's limited powers - may serve him. He hopes it is not by using him as a hostage... but he wouldn't put it past his brother.

Naturally, he's not going to tell Shan that. From the look on her face, perhaps he doesn't have to.

All he says is, "We'll get him back."

She waves at the endless black cliffs and canyons, "From where? We don't know where they are. We don't even know if we landed in the same place they did!"

Peter gets up and walks across the plateau towards something that catches his interest. He points at the upside down pyramid of rocks Devon stacked.

"My brother left a calling card. Why, I don't know."

The doors to the Grand Hall open and Captain Pirus, accompanied by Devon, enters. At Lord Kildemar's orders, his key military players are all awake and putting on a sober front. The rest of the court has been cleared.

Sitting on his throne, Lord Kildemar appears pleased with himself.

"Boy, I told you I would find a way to test you. Now I have one. Someone has dared to use a second pendant to cross the wall... to come after the first one, I presume."

He pauses to observe Devon's reaction. Reactions are very revealing... but he sees none in the boy.

He continues, "One was stolen a long time ago from my land and now it's returned. You shall make sure both remain here. Retrieve for me the second pendant and the head of the one using it. This will prove your worth... that is, if you're worth anything."

At hearing of another pendant, Devon hides his surprise well. He knows his position in this new land will depend on how well he plays the early game.

Where the third pendant has come from is a mystery to him and not important at the moment - who is using it is important. He wishes it to be Master Carringer, but he knows in his heart its Peter.

Hiding his train of thought, he casually asks, "My weapons?"

"Of course."

Kildemar gestures to a guard who brings Devon's lance and razor belt. The guard drops the weapons on the floor, a few feet away from Devon.

As Devon reaches for them, other guards take defensive stances close by. Aware of their concern, Devon picks up his tools slowly.

As he straps on the belt, his says, "I can take care of this by myself, and then I'll return with the pendant."

Kildemar smiles, "No, boy, you will not. When you serve me you shall do it as I command."

He turns to Captain Pirus, "Captain, take twelve men and this boy with you."

"My name is Devon."

"I may choose to use your name when you bring me the pendant... or I'll use your head as a footstool if you fail," Lord Kildemar warns.

Devon makes a slight bow to Kildemar's wishes, then turns and exits.

Captain Pirus follows him closely.

Chapter Thirty-Eight

S han stands on the northwest edge of the plateau peering down at Peter. He's in the clearing far below, where Devon met the Goreiporian soldiers. She sees him walk from spot to spot around the clearing, bending down every so often to examine something.

After a few minutes, he glances up towards her. Once finished he whiffs his way back to her side.

"What did you find down there?" she asks.

He'd prefer not saying but he knows if she's to have his back, she deserves to know everything.

"There was blood all over the ground. From the arrows I found, I think it came from a fight between Devon and whoever, or whatever, lives here. I don't think the blood is from Ramie or my brother."

"You don't think?" Shan says in a worried tone.

"The arrows I found are clean... no blood. I think it came from those they encountered."

Peter knows Devon is after power but he's not someone that would harm needlessly... at least he doesn't think so.

Trying to ease Shan's concerns, he adds, "Ramie is of some use to my brother, but if he got hurt this close to where they arrived, Devon would have sent him home. He's hungry... he's not a monster."

"OK. Where to now? We can't just stay here and hope... "

Peter cuts her off with a wave of his hand, sensing something in the air. He doesn't know what lets him sense Devon when most can't, but whatever it is works in Goreipor as well as it did in Spirin.

After a moment, he says, "Were you going to say you hope he comes to us? Well, he is on his way now."

Shan glances all around and sees nothing.

"He's a ways away, but he's coming." Peter points to the northwest, "Coming from that direction."

"He is? Is Ramie with him?" Shan quickly asks.

Peter focuses harder, but finally gives up.

"I can't tell. I know he's not alone, but I only have a clear sense of him."

Peter knows that just as he can sense Devon, his brother can sense him in return. That means there's no disadvantage in generating a spy globe because it will change nothing. It may not hold long because Devon hates - and pulverizes - spy globes... but it may at least give him a glimpse of what he's up against.

He forms one and hopes for the best. An image of Devon and a squad of soldiers riding through canyons slowly comes into focus inside the globe. They ride at a determined pace, but slower than a gallop. The view lingers only a few seconds before Devon abruptly looks up directly at the globe and smiles.

The globe pops.

He's getting stronger... at least against globes. Peter can still feel his presence. He's not into the game, but he can't help but smile at his brother's predictability.

Shan, who saw the brief image as well, is speechless for a moment.

"That's an army!"

Peter doesn't react. He scans the environment, trying to think like Devon... trying to see the game like his brother does when looking at a chessboard.

"We have the high ground here. It's our best bet to meet them here." Battle strategy is new to Peter. All he can do is give it his best shot.

She sees he's struggling to handle the situation and chooses to be part of the solution. Shan points at the higher cliffs beyond the ravines.

"If they get up there, won't we have a serious problem?"

Peter's relieved that she's thinking defensively.

"No. Maybe Devon can get up there, but I don't think those riding with him can. Master Carringer told me a little about the people here. As far as he could tell, they don't have powers."

Peter glances around at the sparse cover, "But they do have weapons. I need to show you how to create a shield."

The small column of soldiers gallops slowly east through the narrow canyons. Devon and Captain Pirus ride abreast at the head of the column of twelve. Devon looks all around, seeming preoccupied since the globe incident.

Captain Pirus takes a couple looks in his direction, then says, "What was that look about?"

"What look?" Devon responds.

He sees Pirus' eyes grilling him. It's clear to him that Pirus misses little, but Devon sticks to keeping his secrets.

"Nothing. Just thought I sensed something."

Pirus' face says he's certain Devon's lying, but all he says is, "You ride well. I didn't see any horses beyond the wall."

Fairly observant himself, Devon now knows who made the attempt on Peter's life. Judging him over past deeds won't help at the moment... after all, Pirus was just doing as he was ordered.

He's aware that, as they ride, they're both sizing each other up. Captain Pirus could be a valuable ally in the future... one who appears to be able to separate emotion from decisions.

Now is as good a time as any to test the waters.

"I don't come from beyond the wall. Where I come from had many horses."

He watches the Captain for his reaction and is pleased to see none. This could be a sign that he's open to play. Then again, Pirus could be evaluating him for Lord Kildemar.

That doesn't concern Devon. Just as the Dark Lord is testing him, he must find a way to test the Captain.

Devon raises his lance. He notices the Captain's muscles tense immediately, but without showing outwardly... the sign of an alert and subtle warrior coming to the ready.

Devon doesn't notice that a bowman riding behind him has discreetly readied an arrow. Equally discreetly, Pirus motions the guard to hold for the moment.

With his lance outstretched, Devon says, "See that cliff up ahead?"

The Captain nods.

A ball of energy shoots from the tip of Devon's lance and the rock formation he aims at explodes. The horses rear back as rocks cascade down, blocking one of the gullies. The rock fall is far enough away that no one is in direct danger.

Pleased with himself, Devon says, "I don't know if they told you, but I do have real powers."

Unruffled by Devon's display, Captain Pirus responds, "I've been told. Perhaps the next time you wish to exercise them, it should be on the rocks behind us."

He points to the blocked channel and casually waves to change course down another gully.

Embarrassed, Devon wonders, 'Who showed whom what?'

The last loud echo of Devon's display bounces off the canyon walls.

Shan appears worried, "Did you hear that?"

Peter glances at her with a 'duh' look.

"What do you think it was?" she says nervously.

"Don't know, but it came from where Devon is approaching."

Shan thinks he's trying to spare her from worry, which won't do at all. "Give me the truth of your thoughts, or don't give me anything!"

She knows she appears nervous, but that can't be helped. That doesn't mean she's not up to the task ahead of them. Unfortunately, another thought quickly follows... how far can she go?

Her mouth is dry and she needs to talk.

"Peter, I'm sorry. I know you were just trying to spare me because you think I'm afraid... and I am. I don't know if I can actually harm someone, you know, in that real way."

Peter sees she's dealing with her fears in her own way and lets her talk.

"On Earth I didn't really hurt anyone... and I'm the one who talked you into bringing Devon here. Maybe that's why I felt I had to come with you."

Peter stops her, "Neither one of us has actually had to hurt anyone in that way. You're no more scared than I am, but I wouldn't have you with me if I didn't trust you would be able to do what's needed... no matter how much you talked last night. Hopefully we won't have to go that far... but if we do, it will be for good reasons."

He gives her a wink. "Now, if talking helps you get through all this, I'm all ears."

This settles her some. She winks back.

The company of soldiers has been riding quietly for some time.

Captain Pirus finally turns to Devon, "What were you trying to say with that display back there?"

Devon's pleased that the Captain recognized it for more than just a child's antics... though it was a foolish choice on his part. Before responding to the Captain, Devon glances over his shoulder at the soldiers close behind.

The Captain says, "The four directly behind us are my men. They hear what I choose. I can't account for the other eight."

This tells Devon he has not chosen badly... then again, maybe he's being set up. But he has gone down the road too far to back up. Devon's pretty sure he can take these dozen soldiers if it absolutely comes to that... hopefully it won't.

"I came to Goreipor to flex my power, but not like that feeble witch of his."

That's putting it pretty bluntly and Captain Pirus has not drawn his sword yet. He might as well push farther.

"Someday the walls between all the lands will fall."

"Lord Kildemar is counting on that. It's probably the reason you're still alive," Captain Pirus injects, no doubt covering his ass.

In the meantime, without Devon noticing, the two have distanced themselves from the troops behind them. They're just far enough ahead to be well out of earshot... orchestrated, no doubt, by subtle signals from Captain Pirus.

It's time to roll the dice.

Devon says bluntly, "I saw all the destroyed armor on your walls. I assume it was from your enemies. Don't get me wrong, but your lord seems like an angry old man who would not see the potential in alliances when the walls do fall. I have the power to help him rule worlds... if he lets me. What I need is your support."

Devon is prepared for anything at this point. He's put his head on the chopping block. If what he expects to happen does, he needs to know where he stands with this escort - now.

Captain Pirus pulls his horse to a halt. He waves for his men to stay back. He stares at Devon a few seconds before deciding how to respond.

"I wouldn't underestimate that angry old man. He's defeated many. I should take your head for even suggesting such a thing."

He still has not drawn his sword... nor has he indicated anything out of the ordinary to the soldiers.

"You're a smart man who hedges his bets," says Devon.

"And you're a boy who lays too much on the line without fully scouting his terrain. I should kill you more for stupidity than treason."

"Time requires my recklessness, but don't mistake that for not thinking out my game... I play fast."

A few tense moments later Captain Pirus waves the troops to come on. He points forward and eases his muscles.

"Shall we continue?" says Pirus.

He resumes riding. Taking a breath, Devon starts to follow.

Pirus adds, "I like your brashness, but we shall see how things play out today before thinking of tomorrow. Naturally, none of this has taken place... And trust me, young lad, I may still take your head before the day is done."

Chapter Thirty-Nine

Peter and Shan hear the sound of soldiers approaching below. Although they are not visible, the sound makes it clear they're heading for the clearing where Peter found the traces of blood. Seeing them in the spy globe pales compared to hearing the hooves of their horses so close. It's amazing how sound of the unseen is so much more intimidating.

Peter knows Devon is among them. What he's not sure of is if Devon will meet with them alone. He has the ability to do so - and the arrogance. The question is, will he?

He turns to Shan with a hint of second thoughts, "Maybe we should... "

She cuts him off, "Don't say it. The only way we will find Ramie is to start somewhere... and that's here."

He takes a deep breath and nods. As a precaution, Peter takes off the pendant and puts it in a crevice in the rocks... making sure Shan sees where it is.

"If things don't go well and we are captured, there's still a way home."

They both know it's also better than Devon getting his hands on the third pendant... if anything more than getting captured happens.

Neither knows how, but someone other than Devon - or those in Goreipor - might someday find a way here to use it.

As the column of soldiers rounds the bend into the clearing, Devon leans over towards Pirus, "Here's where I must leave you for a while. Send the other eight men up to the plateau."

Before the Captain can respond Devon turns to smoke and disappears. A horse stirring about without a rider is all that's left.

Captain Pirus knows that by 'the other eight men', Devon means not the four Pirus trusts. What Devon plans beyond that is a mystery to the Captain, but it arouses his curiosity.

Shan and Peter kneel by the edge of the plateau, trying to get a glimpse of what's coming. From their vantage point, all they can see is the dust kicked up by all the horses.

With a bit of anxiety, Shan nudges Peter, "Where are they?" He can see no more than she can.

Directly behind them, Devon appears out of a wisp of smoke.

He says as he materializes, "I'm surprised there was an extra pendant. Where did it come from?"

Peter spins around. He pauses a second before reacting. Shan isn't as calm. Forgetting about being a young lady, she jumps up, charges at Devon and slaps him across the face.

"Where is my brother, you... you creep?"

Even though they are in a seriously dangerous situation, Peter can't help but snicker at the raw Shan.

Devon rubs his cheek, "So much for the hocus-pocus stuff. That hurt."

As Shan raises her hand, ready to slap him again, he backs away and holds up his hands.

"He's safe. That's all I can say."

Turning his attention to Peter, "I didn't expect someone to come after me. I'm sorry it's you. I would have preferred Carringer."

"You're my responsibility, not his," Peter says coldly.

Captain Pirus brings the soldiers to a halt in the clearing. He looks back.

"Lead four establish a perimeter. Rear eight scale the plateau. Everyone stay sharp. You saw what that boy can do. If he turns on you, don't take a chance."

Pirus reckons that Devon knows who is atop the plateau. Asking to have the other eight soldiers sent there could mean he may turn on them.

He's not eager to see any soldiers sacrificed but - since they aren't his personal guard - they may be the cost of determining his position on Devon. If the lad can't handle eight soldiers, his decision will be made easy.

Shan is not through with Devon.

"Did my brother come on his own, or did you force him?"

"Let's say I had to do a little more persuading than I expected. Does that make you feel better?"

She starts towards him again.

Devon snaps at Peter, "Call her off, Peter. I'm going to lose my temper."

Shan stops without needing Peter to say anything. She realizes that letting her emotions rule her actions is a poor defensive strategy... especially under these circumstances.

Peter notes Shan's reserve and tries to remain calm as he addresses Devon. "I'm asking you to help us get him back so we can all go home."

Peter pretty much knows this is not going to fly... but he has to put it out there.

Devon smirks at Peter's simplemindedness.

"Not a chance. I didn't go over the wall by accident. Why don't you just join me? I'll even extend the invite to your girl friend."

Shan bristles at this, but keeps her tongue in check.

With his mind now resolved, Peter says, "Then I guess I'll just have to take you back."

Devon ignores this.

"You two have presented me with a problem. I need to get that pendant... hopefully without killing you."

He backs up as if to make room if a fight is necessary.

"Peter, you don't want to do this with me."

Shan backs up beside Peter and then steps off a few paces, positioning herself for a fight. If she shows any sign of fear, Peter can't see it.

Gripping his lance with two hands, Devon raises it and slams the ball end on the ground like a pile driver. The stone under-foot fractures with a crack of thunder.

The opened crevice races towards Peter and Shan, fingering along the plateau directly between them.

"Like I said, brother, I'm serious."

"No, you're just a kid still playing chess... but you're right, it's not a game. Not when people's lives are at stake."

Peter's doing his best not to be provoked into fighting De-von. He truly has no desire to test how far he's willing to go against his brother.

With a booming laugh, Devon yells, "Of course it's a game. Join me. We'll be the brains and brawn again... as we started out to be. Blood stands together... don't you remember?"

"I was wrong. Family stands together and that comes from more than just blood. You're still family. End this now and come home," Peter pleads.

"I am home!" Devon bellows, tossing his lance to Peter. "At least have a weapon."

He looks at Shan, takes one of his razor disks off his belt and tosses it to her feet, "You, too."

Peter can't believe his brother is prepared to fight them with weapons. He has to do something more than plead. Reaching down, he picks up the lance.

He stares at Devon and raises it in the same manner he did. With a sharp motion he slams the ball end down on the plateau. There's a deafening crack equal to the one Devon created.

A fracture shoots along the ground between Devon's legs this time.

Devon jumps to the side and then makes a small bow.

"I see you've also been studying more than what was being taught."

Peter is tired of this childish toying. If he has to, he will fight to wound. He looks over at Shan.

"Try not to kill him," he says and generates a protective globe.

Devon smirks, "You can't fight worth a damn inside of one of those."

Showing Peter the better way, Devon generates a partial globe that he holds like a shield. He pulls a disk. Instead of throwing it, he demonstrates his ease of movement inside his modified shield.

"See... you protect yourself while being able to attack."

All of a sudden Peter realizes it's all a big bluff on Devon's part. He has no intention of killing them, no matter what he says - Peter hopes he's right.

To humor his brother, Peter re-generates his globe as Devon has demonstrated. He nods to Shan to do the same. With a puzzled look, she does.

Peter says lightly, "OK, much better. Now what do we do with it?"

He waits for Devon to break out laughing and make this whole situation become nothing more than a bad dream.

Suddenly, Devon throws a razor disk with full force in Peter's direction. It misses. Peter's reflexes bring him to the ready... he can't believe he was so wrong.

Shan yells, "Peter, behind you!"

Peter spins to see Devon's disk impaling a Goreiporian soldier who has come over the edge of the plateau. Another rises up near him and Shan spins with her shield, knocking him backwards off the plateau.

They are in a fight... but not against Devon.

Devon screams, "Back to back."

The three kids move into the center of the rock mesa and take up a triangle position with their backs to each other.

The first two soldiers were caught off guard - the remaining ones do not plan to give their lives so easily.

One, still out of sight, yells, "Hold till my mark!"

There's no time to debate who's on whose side. Peter's more than grateful he doesn't have to fight his brother... especially to the death. Now they are fighting together to survive.

They can hear - but not see - the soldiers repositioning themselves around the plateau. Waiting for the attack, the kids rotate in their small defensive triangle.

Devon says, "This was easier the first time... Watch the edge!"

Keeping close watch on the edge, Peter says over his shoulder, "You've done this before?"

"Yeah, but that was before they knew I had powers. They're being more difficult this time. Keep watching the edge!"

Shan yells, "We are! Stop saying that!"

Devon nudges Peter, "By the way, the lance shoots Orbs."

Peter lifts the weapon and examines the blade's end. He holds it out... an Orb fires from its tip. Flying across the ravine, it explodes on the cliff wall across the canyon.

"Cool," he murmurs as the implications of this dawn on him.

A sudden yell sounds from an unseen soldier and six men jump up around the plateau... two with spears, two with swords, and two with crossbows.

An arrow flies at Devon. Deflecting it with his shield, he downs the man with a flung disk.

With sword drawn, a soldier charges Shan. As he swings, she disappears and reappears behind him. He turns and she swings the disk Devon has given her. It cuts deep into the soldier's chest. He staggers back and tumbles off the edge.

Seeing what she's done to this man, Shan backs away, bends over and throws up. This momentary distraction gives time for another Goreiporian to bear down on her.

Devon dives between the charging man and Shan. With a thrust of his hand, a power bolt sends the man flying away. He lands unconscious near the edge.

Devon yells to Shan, "There's no time for that now!"

Shan straightens up, gives him a glare and shakes off her nausea.

A soldier rushes Peter. Peter fires an Orb from the lance that explodes in front of his chest, sending him flying far off the mesa.

Captain Pirus is halfway up the plateau's outer wall. He wants to see for himself what's taking place... with no intention of interfering. His own, more valued men are safe below.

The soldier Peter took out screams as he plummets down past Pirus. To himself, the captain notes, "At least the boy's holding his own."

Peter spins with the hard thrust of a soldier's spear against his shield. He deflects the hit but the shield flies from his grasp. Peter resorts to the lance to defend himself,

Their spears clash, making a thunderous clang.

Sparks fly as he and the soldier hack at each other. Peter puts up a good fight, but the more experienced soldier keeps charging... overpowering Peter.

Seeing this, Shan charges the man with her shield. She hits him hard enough to drive him back, away from Peter. Regaining his footing, the soldier swings his spear at her. She ducks it.

As the man readies himself to swing again, Peter thrusts his spear into his side. The soldier staggers back and topples over the edge.

This killing sickens Peter almost as much as it had sickened Shan moments earlier.

He loses his focus enough for another soldier to charge him from behind. Devon throws his last razor disk deep into the soldier's chest, stopping his charge.

The single remaining soldier looses a bolt from his crossbow at Devon. It zooms straight towards his back. With blinding speed, Shan deflects it with her razor disk but the arrow knocks it from her grasp.

Before the soldier can rig another bolt, Devon dives for her disk and flings it. It strikes home in the soldier's throat. Grabbing at his wound, he stumbles off the edge of the mesa.

Shan and Devon nod at each other. Maybe they don't like one another but - for the moment - they're comrades.

Shan freezes abruptly. The arrow she deflected from Devon has found another mark - Peter!

He lies on the ground, the bolt embedded between his shoulder blades. Devon and Shan rush to him.

Although gravely wounded, Peter's still conscious.

Trying to make light of it, he gasps, "What's it with me and arrows?"

Shan jumps up and runs to the crevice where Peter hid the pendant. She pulls it out and rushes back.

Devon's holding Peter, trying to keep him quiet.

Peter looks up at him, "At least, you didn't kill me."

Shan kneels down with the pendant.

Devon looks at it, at her and back at Peter. He closes his eyes. Under his breath, a curse escapes his lips.

Devon looks back at Peter, "You're not dead yet."

He takes the pendant from Shan and dials in the Door.

With all his strength, Peter grabs Devon by the collar.

"I'm not going through without Shan and that," he utters, nodding at the pendant.

Devon realizes he's dead serious... and almost dead. Shan looks just as stern about not leaving without the pendant. Besides getting Peter home, it's the only chance she will have of getting back to her brother.

The last thing Devon needs is this shrew to take care of. Reluctantly, he hands the pendant to Shan.

Gesturing at the pendant Shan holds now, Devon addresses Peter, "That squares it between us. It's only a loan. You know I'll have to come after it eventually... and then the fight will be between you and me."

Behind them, Captain Pirus has crept onto the plateau. None of the kids notice as he bows an arrow and draws it. He remains quiet, watching... unsure of what's playing out.

With Shan's help, Devon lifts Peter up. Readying himself to push Peter and Shan through the Door - with the pendant - he sees Captain Pirus with his drawn arrow. Defiantly, Devon shoves Peter and Shan through the light... and home.

The soldier Devon had knocked out earlier in the fight has come to and reaches for a crossbow. Captain Pirus releases his arrow. It flies past Devon and strikes the soldier, who staggers off the plateau.

Captain Pirus quickly strings another arrow and takes aim at Devon... but he doesn't fire.

"That was your brother, the other round ear, wasn't it?"

Devon just nods, waiting to see what happens next.

The Captain says, "I regretted having to kill him, so I guess I owe him a life. Unfortunately - even though I like your spirit, kid - losing the pendant just sealed your fate. I can't go back to the castle without it."

Devon, being careful to move slowly and deliberately, backs up to the pile of black stones he made earlier. He knows he could take Pirus out with some twist of magic, but he wants to play it out to see if there are better options.

"One moment, Captain."

Pirus follows Devon's movements with the arrow's aim.

Pulling a stone away from the base of the pile, Devon reaches in and withdraws the second pendant.

"Luckily, I have another pendant. Change is coming Captain. Like I told you, you may want to hedge your bets."

Captain Pirus relaxes the tension of his bow... but, not completely.

"Come peacefully and I'll think on it."

Confident that he knows Pirus' leanings now, Devon tosses the pendant to him. Keeping hold of the bow and arrow with one hand, the captain catches the pendant with the other.

Devon knows he could still be wrong about his man. Only time will tell. Since the game is in motion, he has to appear to take the risk.

If absolutely necessary, he's prepared to eventually destroy Captain Pirus.

Chapter Forty

With Devon close by, Captain Pirus steps forward to hand the second Sorcerer's Door pendant to Lord Kildemar. Kildemar peers at it carefully and sits back on his throne.

He stares at Devon, "And the head of the intruder?"

Captain Pirus glances at Devon. After a moment, he turns back to Lord Kildemar. "The intruder created the Door and tried to escape. The boy struck a fatal blow and grabbed the pendant. I'm afraid the body fell through."

"Your losses?" Lord Kildemar asks.

"Eight. As I reported before, those beyond the wall have powers... particularly the one that came through. I needed Devon to neutralize him. Otherwise our losses would have been higher."

Lord Kildemar looks back and forth between the two, trying to decide what to do with this gifted intruder.

He addresses Devon. "Very well, young Devon... "

"Master Devon," Devon interjects.

Kildemar glares at his impudence, then, "I call no one Master. I will call you Lieutenant Devon for the time being."

Devon nods his approval. He glances up at Witch Racinda. She watches him with distrust in her eyes. He knows he's going to have to be careful around her.

He also knows that Ramie is in her charge... so she will eventually come into play, as well.

With a groan, Peter awakens and sees Shan sitting on the bed beside him.

He's weak but he manages to speak, "You OK?"

She nods.

"I thought he might have sent us back to Earth."

Shan puts a hand on his chest, "You would have died. The Healer said you're going to run out of luck eventually. He gave me the pendant before we went through... I don't know why."

Peter coughs from the effort, but needs to talk, "Because he's still a boy playing a game, whether he knows it or not. Even in that dark land, he sees the game as having to be with me. Maybe he's trying to get even and teach me about war, since he feels that him learning was my fault... or maybe it's just that he's my damn brother."

"Do you think he's going to try and bring the walls down?"

"According to Gran-D, no one knows how to do that."

He knows that doesn't truly answer her real question... Will the people of Spirin ever have to do what she had to on the plateau?

If the walls do fall, Devon will not teach him of war - he will teach everyone.

Peter's grateful to be weak at the moment and not to have to tell her these things. Then again, he probably doesn't have to. He's certain Shan will play a big part in preparing the people of her... their land... if that day comes.

Peter is fairly convinced that Gran-D was right about the Prophecy coming...

And, unfortunately, he's certain that he and Devon may indeed be the ones to bring it about.

The door to Witch Racinda's chambers unbolts, startling Ramie. He backs into the shadows. Racinda comes in and walks to the window portal, hardly paying attention to Ramie.

"Come out of the dark, boy. You're going to be here for a long time."

This is the first Ramie has seen his new protector. It takes a couple seconds for him to respond.

When he does, it comes out quietly, "Why... because you never escaped?"

Without turning, Racinda says, "I've been here too long and done too many things to go home. No... because that boy, Devon, values you."

"If he liked me, he wouldn't have made me come with him," Ramie says as he loosens up and walks closer to her.

He glances at her curly earlobes to verify what he thinks he knows about this mysterious old woman.

"How long have you been here?"

Racinda now turns towards him.

With more of a motherly smile than that of a witch, she says, "A long time... You have to learn what words mean. I didn't say he liked you. I said you are of value to him. There's a difference."

Ramie is not sure why, but he senses this woman will protect him. It's the first feeling of calm he's had since landing in this cursed land. Maybe it's because she was part of his world long ago. Then again, perhaps she's using him too.

"Yes, I may use you, too. I need an assistant with skills and you need to learn how to stay alive. Those are enough answers for now. I suggest you don't go wandering around just yet," she says.

As she leaves the room, Ramie doesn't hear the door being bolted. Maybe she's just testing to see if he listens. It doesn't matter - he has no desire to explore quite yet.

He suspects that feeling will pass.

It's a fine, peaceful night well lit by all three of the Sphere's moons.

Gran-D stands at the gate of the Graveyard of Spells. He's a foot away from the edge of the Graveyard.

Peering in, he casually strokes a finger of green mist that extends out to where it can be stroked. He stares into the Graveyard, lost in thought.

The intricately carved head of a cane resembling a black knight taps him on the shoulder. Master Imton steps up beside him and says, "What are you thinking about, old man?"

"About what defenses might be buried in there... and if we are going to need them," Gran-D muses.

Staring as straight ahead as Gran-D, Imton says, "Tell me, when we were playing out this manipulative game of yours, did one of the brothers go over to the side of force and violence?"

"All became possible once the Door was opened."

"You know, once Peter was here, you could have kept the Door closed," Imton counters.

"That's not what was needed," Gran-D says as he turns away.

He starts to walk from the Graveyard. The finger of mist, having had a friendly scratch blends back into the body of green mist. Master Imton turns and walks beside the old man.

"Dar, are you absolutely sure you know what's needed?"

"Absolutely is a big word when it comes to the future. I'm only trying to nudge the outcome," he says pensively.

Imton stops and looks at Gran-D, "Old man, for a man of peace, you have a cold side to you."

Gran-D turns and looks him square in the eyes, "I'm afraid that's the part that is needed now, as much as I wish it weren't. We are getting old, aren't we?"

A full moon has passed.

Once again Peter is well. He stands by the wall between Spirin and Goreipor staring at his reflection, thinking.

Speaking in part to himself, "What have we brought into this world, little brother?"

Shan floats up on her hoverboard and settles next to Peter.

"Quit racking you brain... what's done is done. What we have to prepare for is what comes next."

"And Ramie?"

This is another cross Peter carries... the loss of his adopted brother, the boy who brought him to this fascinating land.

Shan takes his arm, "Once the Rockhead gets over being frightened, he'll find a way to survive till we can get him. He couldn't get into so much trouble in his short life without hav-ing an uncanny dose of blind luck that tends to get him out of it. Who knows... maybe Devon is even keeping him safe."

"Let's hope Ramie continues to be of some use to him," says Peter... afraid that might be the sole reason Devon would look out for him.

He has no idea that Ramie's under the protective wing of an-other child of Spirin.

At that very moment, Devon stands alone on a jagged ledge on the opposite side of the wall, looking towards Spirin.

He's sure he's doing what he thinks is his calling, but there's a sad loneliness in his eyes. He's aware that if he is going to rule a world, he has to make that loneliness his closest ally.

Devon senses Peter somewhere beyond that wall, somehow listening to him.

He shouts out, "Game on, big brother!"

His voice echoes loudly off the canyon walls and causes a slight waver in the mirror's surface.

Chapter Forty-One

Epilogue

Somewhere in the Land of Spirin, the one pendant left in the realm that can open the Sorcerer's Door floats in a glowing globe, hidden in a large box.

It has been placed there – till needed - by Gran-D.

No one is privy to its whereabouts except him. No one is even aware he has hidden it. Gran-D continues to be Gran-D... trying to control the uncontrollable.

Outside the glow of the globe, the interior of the box is pitch black. The jewel in the center of the pendant ignites its own glow, as if trying to see where it is. Maybe it's trying to see its sister pendants scattered around the Sphere.

As if following the pendant's vision, an image swoops up out of the globe... out of the box... and out of the dark room holding the box.

It flies over the beautiful landscape of Spirin.

Faster and faster the vision goes. It travels through the western mirror wall of Spirin... into Goreipor.

It swoops along, high above the black rock canyons... towards the dark fortress of Lord Kildemar. Invisible to all but itself, it flies through the walls of the fortress... past soldiers... past lords... into Lord Kildemar's war room where two other pendants sit.

The jewels in each of these pendants blink a bright glow as the vision rushes past... as if they're saying 'hi'.

It continues through the castle... exiting near a turret where Ramie stands with Witch Racinda... neither aware of the traveling eye.

It rushes over mountains and gullies of black rock... on through the western mirror wall of Goreipor... into the Land of Capulia.

The vision flies over a land made up of massive expanses of water dotted with many large islands of lush tropical forests and high cliffs.

It races across the open water. All of a sudden the vision dives below the waves... down to the depths of the sea. It zips through a submerged, long-forgotten temple... kicking up sand from the sea floor.

A lost pendant, among old broken pots and seashells, winks a glint of light from its jewel.

The vision zooms upwards and breaks the water's surface. It passes over alien-looking ships that slightly resemble oversized Viking vessels with bright red sails. They're in a harbor of large coastal town.

The vision speeds on... across more islands and oceans... till it flies though another mirror wall.

Now it flies over the Land of Acculas... made up of open plains broken by forests of massive trees the size of small cities. As it flies through one of the large trees, a gigantic colorful bird lands... and transforms into a beautiful woman.

The vision rushes past her... on towards the mountains in the distance. It travels through the mountain rocks... and into a hidden cave filled with intricate carvings... and another pendant.

As with the others, this hidden pendant blinks brightly as the vision passes by... and out the other side of the mountain.

The vision passes snow-capped ridges and desert plains on its lightning approach to another mirror wall...

It swoops through this wall... and the world changes to blood-red jungles... Pockets of steam rise here and there from the dense foliage... It races down to fly at treetop height... The unseen evil of the jungles below has almost a smell of its own... This is the Land of Creatorn.

The bird's eye view zooms towards a high cliff of red rocks... At the base of the cliff is a colossal tiered pyramid... Piles of stripped, bleached bones litter the pyramid's footing...

The vision shoots vertically up the cliff face, high above the sacrificial altar stone atop the pyramid... to find another pendant embedded in the rock... Like a ritual eye watching over all that takes place below, it winks as the vision passes...

At the top of the cliff are more red jungles... The flight exploring the Sphere levels off and rockets through the last mirror... bordering the tiny sliver of land called the Portal...

Surrounding the Portal, like the interior of a carnival house of mirrors, are the reflective border walls of all the lands of the Sphere... At dead center of the Portal is a gigantic altar stone that looks like a dramatically larger version of the pendant.

The vision flies down to a boulder-sized jewel in the middle of the altar stone... The massive jewel begins to glow with a bright white light... Suddenly a beam of light shoots straight up into the Universe...

The vision attaches itself to the beam and heads out into the stars.

Game On.

THE END